W9-CPQ-161

"An incredibly powerful, soul-searing YA. Important and necessary . . . I could not put this book down."
—PADMA VENKATRAMAN, award-winning author of *The Bridge Home*

"*We Are Not from Here* is absolutely stunning. A story that's painfully relevant today, and told with such precision and beauty, you can feel it. It's breathtaking."
—LAUREN GIBALDI, author of *This Tiny Perfect World*

"*We Are Not from Here* is a book that will mark your heart. Jenny Torres Sanchez challenges us to feel, empathize, and understand. A searing, necessary, and ultimately beautiful book."
—ALEXANDRA VILLASANTE, critically acclaimed author of *The Grief Keeper*

★ "A brutally honest, not-to-be-missed narrative."
—*KIRKUS REVIEWS*, starred review

★ "A candid, realistic story that will leave readers thinking about the characters—and about our own world—long after the last page."
—*SLJ*, starred review

★ "Gripping, poignant . . . This soul-shaking narrative [recalls] the works of Gabriel García Márquez."
—*BOOKLIST*, starred review

★ "A devastating read that is difficult to put down, this unforgettable book unflinchingly illuminates the experiences of those leaving their homes to seek safety in the United States."
—*PUBLISHERS WEEKLY*, starred review

★ "A stunning, visceral, and deeply moving read."
—*BOOKPAGE*, starred review

Also by
JENNY TORRES SANCHEZ

The Fall of Innocence

Because of the Sun

Death, Dickinson, and the Demented Life of Frenchie Garcia

The Downside of Being Charlie

WE ARE NOT FROM HERE

JENNY TORRES SANCHEZ

PENGUIN BOOKS

PENGUIN BOOKS
An imprint of Penguin Random House LLC, New York

First published in the United States of America by Philomel Books,
an imprint of Penguin Random House LLC, 2020
Published by Penguin Books, an imprint of Penguin Random House LLC, 2021

Text copyright © 2020 by Jenny Torres Sanchez
Map copyright © 2020 by Katrina Damkoehler
Discussion Questions copyright © 2020 by Penguin Random House

Penguin supports copyright. Copyright fuels creativity, encourages diverse voices, promotes free speech, and creates a vibrant culture. Thank you for buying an authorized edition of this book and for complying with copyright laws by not reproducing, scanning, or distributing any part of it in any form without permission. You are supporting writers and allowing Penguin to continue to publish books for every reader.

Penguin Books & colophon are registered trademarks of Penguin Books Limited.

Visit us online at penguinrandomhouse.com.

LIBRARY OF CONGRESS CATALOGING-IN-PUBLICATION DATA IS AVAILABLE.

Printed in the United States of America

Penguin Books ISBN 9781984812285

10th Printing

Edited by Liza Kaplan
Design by Rebecca Aidlin
Text set in Alegreya

This book is a work of fiction. Any references to historical events, real people, or real places are used fictitiously. Other names, characters, places, and events are products of the author's imagination, and any resemblance to actual events or places or persons, living or dead, is entirely coincidental.

The publisher does not have any control over and does not assume any responsibility for author or third-party websites or their content.

For

Mariee Juarez

Jakelin Caal Maquin

Felipe Gómez Alonzo

Juan de León Gutiérrez

Wilmer Josué Ramirez Vásquez

Carlos Gregorio Hernández Vásquez

Darlyn Cristabel Cordova-Valle

And all the children whose names we do not know, whose existence and demise have been hidden. And the children whose names will come after the publication of this book, who also suffered and died in United States custody while seeking refuge. For the children lost along the journey, the ones caught in between, guided only by their fragile hope, whose ghosts roam the borders and deserts of countries that failed them.

You deserved so much more. You deserved help.
You deserved to dream. You deserved to *live*.

Y para *toda* mi gente; que luchan tanto,
que son pura vida, esperanza, y belleza.

Mexicalli

Nogales Arizona

Nogales Sonora

Altar

MEXICO

Guadalajara

Pacific Ocean

UNITED STATES OF AMERICA
Gulf of Mexico
Lecheria
Apizaco
Córdoba
Orizaba
Tierra Blanca
Medias Aguas
Matías Romero
Ixtepec
Río Suchiate
Arriaga
Tapachula
Ciudad Hidalgo
Tecún Umán
BELIZE
Puerto Barrios
GUATEMALA
Izabal
Guatemala City
HONDURAS
EL SALVADOR

¿Si no peleamos por los niños, que será de nosotros?

If we don't fight for the children, what will become of us?

—Lila Downs

From “Exiles” by Juan Felipe Herrera

and I heard an unending scream piercing nature.
—from the diary of Edvard Munch, 1892

At the greyhound bus stations, at airports, at silent wharfs
the bodies exit the crafts. Women, men, children; cast out
from the new paradise.

They are not there in the homeland, in Argentina, not there
in Santiago, Chile; never there in Montevideo, Uruguay,
and they are not here

in *America*

They are in exile: a slow scream across a yellow bridge
the jaws stretched, widening, the eyes multiplied into blood
orbits, torn, whirling, spilling between two slopes; the sea, black,
swallowing all prayers, shadeless. Only tall faceless figures
of pain flutter across the bridge. They pace in charred suits,
the hands lift, point and ache and fly at sunset as cold dark
birds. They will hover over the dead ones: a family shattered
by military, buried by hunger, asleep now with the eyes burning
echoes calling *Joaquín, María, Andrea, Joaquín, Joaquín, Andrea*

en exilio

WE ARE NOT FROM HERE

PROLOGUE

When you live in a place like this, you're always planning your escape. Even if you don't know when you'll go. Even if you stare out your kitchen window, looking for reasons to stay—you stare at the red Coca-Cola sign on the faded turquoise wall of Don Felicio's store that serves the coldest Coca-Colas you've ever tasted. The gauzy orange of the earth—both on the ground and swirling in the air—that has seeped into every one of your happiest memories. The green palms of the tree you climbed one time to pick and crack the ripest coconut that held the sweetest water you gave your mother. And the deep blue of the sky you tell yourself is only this blue here.

You can look at all this and still be planning your escape.

Because you've also seen how blood turns brown as it seeps into concrete. As it mixes with dirt and the excrements and innards of leaking dead bodies. You've stared at those dark places with your friends on the way to school, the places people have died. The places they disappeared from. The places they reappeared one morning months later, sometimes alive, sometimes dead, but mostly in fragments. You've watched dogs piss in those places. On those bodies that once cried with life.

You plan your escape because no matter how much color there is or how much color you make yourself see, you've watched every beautiful thing disappear from here. Made murky by night and darkness and shadow.

You plan your escape because you've seen your world turn black.

You plan your escape.

But you're never really ready to go.

PART ONE

Mi Tierra

My Land

Pulga

Mamá tells me I have an artist's heart. She's told me this ever since I can remember, usually out of nowhere. I'll feel her gaze on me and I'll look over at her and she'll say, *You have an artist's heart, Pulga.* I didn't know what she meant when I was younger, but I didn't care because she always smiled with this kind of smile that was happy and proud and sad all at the same time, and it made me feel like this thing, this artist's heart she was talking about, was something big.

When she first said this, I pictured myself with a little mustache and beret like Tom and Jerry wear in the cartoons when they whip up a masterpiece in, no kidding, five seconds flat before they're chased by each other or that bulldog or a broom. Five seconds— that kind of illusion probably isn't good for little kids. But then again, getting chased is life, right? So maybe those cartoons did teach me something.

Anyway, the truth is that's not the kind of artist I want to be. I want to be the kind of artist my father was—a musician who made cool-ass music and dreamed big dreams.

Maybe that's what having an artist's heart means. Dreaming.

Or maybe it means seeing color in the world, noticing and searching for it everywhere, in everything, because the world can be such a dark place.

Or maybe it means you feel things you wish you didn't. Maybe it means that when you see blood on concrete, you can't stop wondering who it belonged to. Maybe it means a part of you wants to cry and run.

All I know is an artist's heart is the worst kind of thing to have around here. An artist's heart doesn't help you survive. It makes you soft, breaks you from the inside out. Little by little.

I don't want to be broken. I don't want to be in pieces. There's too much of that around us already.

What I need is a heart of steel, a heart that is cold and hard and numb to the thorny pricks of pain, the slashes of tragedy.

Chico flicks something at my face, and I shoot a tiny piece of tortilla back at him, straight into his eye. He rubs at it and laughs. He's sitting across the table from me, wearing his stupid powder-blue shirt again, when we hear Mamá's cell phone ring.

"Man, don't you have any other shirts? That tiny thing barely fits you. You look like a damn belly dancer or something." I laugh, pointing at the visible fleshy rolls around his middle.

"Shut the hell up, man. It's my favorite one, okay?" he says. "You see what it says here? *American Eagle,* okay. I'm an *American Eagle* . . . so . . . go fuck yourself," he adds quietly.

He looks over at me, waiting to see my reaction.

"No, not like that, man. Remember what I told you, you gotta put some force behind your words. Stick out your chin. Lunge forward a little, like a dog being held back by a chain."

I demonstrate, but Chico shrugs and pulls at his shirt. I've tried to teach Chico how to curse and insult properly, especially since he has the size to pull off the whole threatening thing. But Chico is too timid when he curses. Chico is too timid with everything. He broadcasts his weaknesses to the world without meaning to. Like even now, he pulls at his shirt self-consciously across his round belly so I know my comment cut right to his insecurities. If I were the kind of guy who wanted to break him, I'd just keep bothering him about it. But I love Chico, so I don't. And I remind myself to lay off him a little.

He launches a fat tortilla crumb back my way and it lands in my hair. I shake it loose as Mamá's cell phone rings again in the next room. We hear her answer, and then her voice goes from calm to frantic.

"Lucia, cálmate! I'll call Doña Agostina but you just stay calm . . . you need to stay calm. I'll be there in a few minutes. It'll be okay. I promise."

Chico looks at me, his left eye still red and teary, his finger mid-flick as worry creeps onto his face. "What happened?" he whispers.

I go to the open arch that separates our small kitchen from our only slightly larger living room, crowded with the oversized red velvet couches Mamá got for a good price before I was born. Mamá was proud she'd haggled the guy for an hour, asking him, "Who wants to sit on velvet in one-hundred-degree humid weather?" Turns out, Mamá did. Because she thought those couches looked like they belonged to royalty. And she prized them, even if it meant we had to get up every five minutes to cool off.

Mamá is pacing by our older-than-dirt television, cell phone pressed to her ear.

"What's going on? Everything okay?" I ask. I brace myself for the news that someone has died. Or been killed. Or kidnapped.

"El bebé, Pulga! El bebé is coming!" she says. A big smile spreads across her face and her eyes go wide with happiness, erasing the worry for a moment. Before I can ask any more questions, she's on another call, explaining to Doña Agostina that my cousin Pequeña has gone into labor at home, and that Tía Lucia can't move her or get her to the hospital and to please, *please* hurry over there.

Pequeña is seventeen, two years older than me, and she's my cousin, but not by blood. Just like Tía Lucia is my aunt, but not by blood. And Chico is my brother, but not by blood. Blood doesn't matter to us unless it's spilling. We're family—there for each other no matter what. And so a moment later, Mamá is shouting at us to lock up the house, over the sound of her motor scooter starting up and zooming out of our front patio as she rushes to Tía Lucia and Pequeña.

"Come on!" Chico yells as he pushes past me in the kitchen. Chico's been dying to meet Pequeña's baby, constantly staring at her belly and asking her how she feels whenever we're all together. At first I thought this was just Chico being his usual self, someone who worries about others, who thinks babies and puppies and kittens are cute. But then, one night in our room not too long after we found out Pequeña was pregnant, he told me about how he believes we come back to Earth after we die. That we're reborn and find our way back to those we left behind.

And I realized then that Chico believes a part of his mamita is coming back to him. Maybe he thinks that when he finally sees Pequeña's baby, he will recognize in it some bit of his mother and see her once more.

Mamá and I don't really believe in that stuff. But who knows. Maybe Chico's right.

I grab my key and lock up. I run in the direction of Tía Lucia's house, following the dust of Mamá's scooter through the streets of our barrio, and catch up with Chico easily because I'm small and a fast runner—a good thing around here. We're about halfway there when Chico remembers he's no Olympian and slows down to a jog, then to a walk.

"Damn," he says, leaning over and holding his stomach. "I can't breathe. Let's just walk. These things take time anyway, right?"

I figure he has a point and we slow down. He takes huffs of the thick, humid air and his face is flushed a deep burnt orange.

"Man, why'd Pequeña wait so long anyway?" he says. "I mean, shouldn't she be having the baby in a *hospital*? You think this is safe?

Her having the baby at home like this, like we're in the dark ages or something? You think she'll be okay?" He wipes tiny drops and streaks of sweat from his hairline and squints against the bright white of the burning sun.

"Yeah, of course she'll be all right. Women have babies every day, right? And you know Pequeña, man. No little baby is going to take her out." I laugh, hoping to convince Chico, but he just shrugs.

I can tell his worry is starting to eat away at him. He's getting nervous like he always does, especially when it has to do with Pequeña or me or our mothers. Like, he worries if Mamá is late coming home from work, even if it's just a few minutes, because she might get caught in the dark. No one wants to get caught in the dark around here. And then there was the time Tía Lucia was getting threatening phone calls for a week straight demanding money. Chico's gut gushed and creaked and moaned with worry like it was eating him up inside until the calls suddenly stopped, even though Mamá and Tía said they'd heard of those kinds of calls happening to others, too. Just small-time criminals pretending to be the *really* bad guys to see if they could extort some easy money. If someone doesn't take the bait, they just move on. I gotta admit—even I was a little freaked out by it. And I could tell it made Tía Lucia a little on edge, too. That's another thing about life around here—you can never be completely sure what's a real threat and what's fake.

"It's wild, you know?" Chico says next to me now. "Pequeña having a *baby*."

I pick up a rock from the road and pitch it as far as I can, watching it land and send up a little puff of dust. Yeah, it's wild. And of course Pequeña should be having her baby in a hospital. Of course she shouldn't have waited so long, so that she got to the point where she couldn't walk or move and Tía Lucia was in a panic, calling on Jesus, Mary, Joseph, and Mamá to help her.

Up ahead I see Doña Agostina hurrying to Tía's house and I feel a little better since the old woman was a midwife when she was younger. Maybe everything will be okay. And Pequeña will be okay. Even if Pequeña hasn't seemed okay for months.

The truth is, Pequeña probably waited too long because she didn't want anything to do with this baby. She refused to acknowledge its existence. She didn't talk about it. Or prepare for it. And I think a part of Pequeña probably thought she could make it go away if she ignored it. It made me feel sorrier for her than ever before, more than when her father left.

More than when he never came back.

I don't think she was ever going to tell Tía Lucia or Mamá or Chico or me about the pregnancy. And I wonder if we hadn't accidentally found out, what Pequeña would have done when this day finally came. Would she have had the baby secretly in her room one night? Emerged with it the next morning, carrying it in one arm, still refusing to acknowledge it? Ignoring all the questions that would be asked?

The only reason we found out she was pregnant was because months ago, Pequeña fell from the white bus that takes us back and forth from the open market in the center of town and ended up bruised, bloodied, and broken at the town clinic. Mamá and I got there just in time to hear Pequeña trying to explain to the doctor what had happened. She mumbled that it'd been too hot and crowded. That she'd gotten dizzy and lost her grip as someone shoved into her. *That's all,* she insisted. That's how she slipped out of the open bus and onto all those rocks just as the bus had begun to descend from the highest hill in our barrio.

The doctor explained to Tía and us that sometimes these things happened, that pregnant women had dizzy spells like that all the time, especially in crowded spaces, but not to worry because the baby was fine. He said this casually as he was setting Pequeña's broken arm and tending to her wounds.

Tía and Mamá gasped and Pequeña stared at the ceiling.

"¿Un bebé?" Tía whispered.

And then the room was silent, except for the gasping of an old man in the next room and a woman moaning somewhere out in the hall, where more patients were lined up waiting to see the doctor.

"Five months?" Tía kept saying later that day, as she and Mamá sat drinking coffee in our kitchen together. "¿Pero, cómo? Under the same roof. I don't understand. And who's the father?" Mamá patted Tía's hand and reassured her. Reminded her they were not old-fashioned viejas and who cared who the father was. *It must have been un amor que le fue mal, Lucia.* A love that went so bad it just made her want to forget about the guy. *Don't ask her about it, let her come to you when she's ready. Ay, pobrecita,* Mamá said. *Poor Pequeña. Let's focus on the baby instead. We'll raise it together.* Mamá added that Chico and I would be proper tíos. And she and Tía Lucia would *both* be this baby's abuelas. And the baby would want for nothing. On and on she went, until what at first had seemed like a disaster to Tía Lucia finally gave way to joy.

Through it all, Pequeña never said a word.

Before long, Mamá and Tía Lucia, best friends since they were niñitas, smiled over the tiny baby clothes they bought. They refurbished an old bassinet. They couldn't stop talking about how this baby was nothing but a blessing.

But their joy was not contagious. It did not spread to Pequeña, who refused to join Tía Lucia and Mamá's discussions or contribute even a single name to the long list of possibilities Mamá and Tía Lucia came up with. As the months passed, if it weren't for Pequeña's huge belly that made her nickname laughable, you would swear there was no baby on the way. She did not acknowledge the existence of the cravings or the heartburn or the sickness that Mamá and Tía Lucia insisted she must be feeling. Pequeña did not once wince at the weight she carried or her thickened feet.

It was only as another baby conversation between Tía and Mamá trickled out of the kitchen window one day, to the patio where Pequeña and I sat, that I finally saw in her something like acknowledgment.

"We are so small, Pulga," she said to me. "This world wants us to be small. Forever. We don't matter to this world." She hunched forward, and for a moment I thought she was going to fall.

"Nah, we're okay, Pequeña. And everything will be okay, you'll see," I told her, nudging her shoulder and offering her a drink of my Coca-Cola.

She sat with the arm she'd broken, now skinny and pale, propped on her belly, and stared toward the street. Her eyes were dull and far away, and a sense of resigned doom settled around her. All the assurances I'd just given her seemed like empty lies.

"What does your name mean?" she asked me suddenly.

I stared down at the soda in my hand, the red-and-white logo of the bottle. She knew it meant *flea*. Everyone did. And Pequeña knew the story behind it just as I knew the story behind hers.

"We are small people," Pequeña said again. "With small names, meant to live small lives." She looked like she was in a trance. "That's all we're allowed to live, that's all the world wants us to live. But sometimes even *that*, even that it won't give us. Instead the world wants to crush us."

I wanted to tell her she was wrong. I wanted to tell her of course we mattered. But the thing is, the way Pequeña was talking, I don't even think she would have heard me.

"I can't believe I have to bring a kid into this," she whispered. It was the only time I'd heard her acknowledge the baby. And it struck me then how tragic this baby was for Pequeña. How much she didn't want it because of what it would be born into.

"It'll be okay," I mumbled.

She laughed. "What do you know?" she said. And looking at her with her bloated belly, I felt embarrassed and stupid. She looked at me. Her gaze softened. "Ay, Pulga, you have to get out of here one day. You know that, right?"

I shrugged. We all need to get out of here. But actually leaving, that's hard.

She looked down at her belly. "I waited too long," she whispered. "Now it's too late. For this baby. And for me."

And for the first time, I wondered if she really fell out of that bus.

Chico and I sit outside on Tía's patio and I think about that conversation as Pequeña's labor screams travel through the house and out the door, cutting through the stagnant air to reach us.

A motor rumbles in the distance.

"Pulga," Chico says, "you ever think about how weird it must be to, like, have a human being inside you? And for it to have to come out of, like, you know . . . *there*?" Chico gestures between his legs, a terrified look on his face. "Man, I think I'd die. I really do."

"I don't really think about stuff like that," I tell him, staring at the dust settling back to the ground.

"It must be so weird, right? I mean, how's it even possible?" He looks down at his own stomach, blows it up so it protrudes even more from his shirt. "I mean, can you imagine? Holy hell, I'm so glad I'm not a girl. Right, Pulga? It must be so terrible to be a girl."

"Yeah," I say.

He stares into the house as Pequeña yells that she's going to die. That she can't do this. That this can't be happening. I hear her sobbing and Mamá and Tía telling her she has to calm down. I've never heard Pequeña cry like this before. The way she sounds scares me and makes me nervous and makes me think again of the women who die and leave tiny pieces of themselves behind. Chico chips away at the already peeling yellow paint on Tía's doorframe. He sucks his teeth. "Let's go get a soda, man. I can't listen to this anymore," he says, wiping at his eyes.

"You got money?"

He digs a hand into his pocket, counts what he has. "Enough to share something."

I get up and he follows.

Pequeña's grunting fades with each step we take. We kick pebbles and rocks around us as we go, feeling bad for her pain. Feeling guilty because we are boys and will never have to know it. Feeling like we're leaving her behind.

But relieved—for the distance between us and that misery.

Pequeña

The thing inside me, the thing I've been ignoring and denying and wishing gone, wants to kill me. It's terrible and vengeful. I've surrounded it in a sac of resentment all these months and now it's going to make me pay.

Another wave of pain floods my body.

"I can't," I tell Mami and Tía Consuelo. "I can't do it."

I close my eyes and try to escape, try to ride that pain into another world, let it lead me to a door where I can slip into another existence. I'm aware of this now—the way I can change reality, create new ones, pass through imaginary doors into new worlds—even though I always had it in me.

Where are you? I try to conjure up La Bruja, my angel, who showed me those doors exist. Who takes me through them.

I think back to the first time she appeared to me—when Papi was still around and we'd gone to Río Dulce together as a family for my sixth birthday. Mami and Papi were fighting because Papi was looking at every woman in a swimsuit who passed by. They didn't notice when I went to the cliff, climbed up those rocks, and walked to the edge. Nobody was around, and I looked up at the sun, closed my eyes, and leaned forward.

I let myself fall, a long fall that made my stomach flutter. I waited for the feel of water, and it came, cold and fast and crushing. Then the world went dim and silent as my head hit something sharp and hard.

I was underwater forever, watching the surface and light slip farther and farther away. And that's when I saw her coming up from the depths of the water. Her dazzling eyes. Her rippling hair. Her skeleton-like hands. She stared at me, and I could not look away from those eyes. I felt us rising together, her stare lifting me, lifting me, up from the depths of that water, from that darkness. Higher. Faster. Bubbles rushing past us, between us.

I can almost see those bubbles now. I can hear the gurgle of them. In a moment, the darkness will turn blurry and blue and *she* will be there, rising up to whisk me away from this, too.

"Pequeña," Mami says. That's it, just my name. But it cuts through the darkness and I'm back in the small cramped bedroom she and I share: The wardrobe in the corner that held my father's clothes once—until Mami sold them. The dresser in front of me so I can see Doña Agostina's hunched back in the mirror on top. Tía Consuelo standing next to her. Mami on the other side of Tía, saying my name.

My body seizes and is gripped by pain. The baby demands to be recognized.

"Push now, Pequeña, a little push, not too hard," Doña Agostina tells me.

I do what she says. And then again. And again. And again. I push, and push, and push.

Hours pass. The baby doesn't want to come out. I imagine it holding on to my ribs, refusing to be born. Refusing to dislodge from me. I imagine myself an old woman, my belly large, the child inside swirling around forever, reminding me of its presence. Refusing to let me go.

"Almost," Doña Agostina says. "Almost."

I hear Mami's voice, choked with emotion, saying she sees the baby's head. And I cry harder because her voice sounds like betrayal to me. I don't want her to want this child. I want her to not want it as much as I do. Would she love it so much if she knew?

I long for her to ask me where it came from. But I can't bear for her to ask me. She's come close a few times. I've seen the question in her eyes, I've seen it on the tip of her tongue, but I always look away. The words never come.

It's not that she wouldn't understand. That's not it. Mami thinks of herself as una mujer moderna. And she *is* a modern woman, especially compared to the grandmother who raised her. Mami's abuela had been so old-fashioned, she lashed her back when she found dried bloodstains on her underwear at age thirteen, assuming it was the loss of her virginity, not her first period. *Como sufrí, Pequeña,* she'd told me so many times. *I never want you to suffer the way I did.*

Mami had suffered as a little girl, then as a wife, and then as a mother when I tore her body and was delivered into this world. And now, if the truth were to escape my lips, I would make her suffer more. My words would be like those lashings on her back. My words like my father's betrayal.

If she knew, Mami would load the gun Papi left us in that wardrobe.

If she knew, she would kill. And that kind of killing only brings more.

We would all be dead. Though maybe that would be better.

"Now, Pequeña! Push with all your strength! Toda tu fuerza," Doña Agostina tells me. "Keep pushing, keep pushing!"

"Push, Pequeña!" Mami repeats. She's kneeling next to me, her arms wrapped around my shoulders. She's smoothing my hair and kissing my forehead. "Eres fuerte, Pequeña. So very strong, hija. And I'm here with you, we'll do this together. Like everything. Don't lose your strength now." She's holding me tight, as if she's trying to transfer her own strength to me.

But all I want is to melt into Mami's arms, all I want is for us to melt into one being and escape out of here, slip from this reality to one where magical witches and angels exist. I want to take her with me. The two of us, together, to where we emerge from water and descend from sky.

"Here it comes!" Doña Agostina's old voice calls out. "Here it comes!"

I shake my head and sob harder. No! I don't want it! I don't want it to almost be here.

But I hear Mami's voice, her crying voice, as something emerges from between my legs, slippery and warm and wet. And I feel a coldness around me as Mami lets go, as she rushes to that baby.

The baby cries, loud and angry, and Mami and Tía Consuelo hug and laugh, their joy too loud in that small room.

Look at your niño, Doña Agostina tells me. I shake my head and close my eyes as she holds the small red baby to my chest. She puts the wriggling thing there, and his small body feels so warm against mine, but I can't look at him. I shut my eyes tighter, cry harder. I won't look at him. I won't hold him. No matter how much he cries.

Doña Agostina lifts him off my chest.

A boy. I don't know what's worse. A boy or a girl.

A name, Pequeña, Mami says. *What will we call him?* Mami's voice is higher than usual. The boy lets out more cries, so loud, it drowns out Mami's voice and she laughs, saying something about how strong he is.

Tía Consuelo comes to my side, squeezes my hand and kisses it. *Pequeña, mi amor, you did it! And he's beautiful. Look, look at him. Your son*, she says. *What will we call him? Look at him!*

Their voices are full, swelling, uncontainable.

I listen to my own thoughts instead as they whisper, *We will call him nothing. He is not real.*

Mami's and Tía Consuelo's voices get louder, trying to keep me in that room, but I am looking for an escape. I look out the window, at the brightness of the sun. I stare into it until my head feels full of light. I close my eyes, and there I find it, the imaginary door, the one that leads me somewhere else, to another world.

I can hear the water—rushing, cascading all around me as I stand on rocks and fling my body into the air, leaping toward beautiful water.

My body is free, and light, and mine. Just mine.

I plunge into that water, clear and cold. Washing away everything—all memory, all blame. All pain.

The child cries. My eyes flutter open, against my will, as if his cries demand I stay *here,* in this reality.

No, I answer, and I picture the water again, see myself submerged in it, the sun cutting through it, the world a beautiful bright blur.

He cries.

I focus on the water. Only the water.

When I open my eyes again, the water has followed me here. It floods the floor and trickles like sweat from the walls. And I take a breath, sweet and full of relief.

Mami has the child and Tía stands next to her looking down at him in Mami's arms. They are both oblivious to the water lapping at their ankles. When they open their mouths to speak, to coo at the baby, to laugh, water trickles from their mouths, too, like faucets. In moments, the water reaches their knees. Then their waists. Their skirts billowed out around them like fancy muñequitas.

I feel my bed become dislodged from the floor. I feel it lift and float as the water continues filling the room.

You see, this, too, is a dream. This child. You. Everything. It's not real, my mind whispers.

How precious, Tía Consuelo says.

Beautiful, says Mami.

A wave comes crashing in through the doorway of the bedroom, and hits the bureau where Mami keeps her belongings. Perfume bottles and talcum powder, needles and thread, a thimble, shiny hair clips and brooches she wears on very special occasions. I watch them as they're carried away in the water, floating and circling around us.

The water circles around Mami and Tía and the baby, like a gentle whirlpool. It lifts them and swirls them all out of the room.

Someone is gently patting my head, a faraway voice is getting louder in my ears. "Don't worry, Pequeña," I hear. And I think maybe it is her, my angel, but then I recognize Doña Agostina's voice. When I look her way, she is unfazed by the water, unfazed by the sudden disappearance of Mami, Tía, and that baby. She smiles before another wave comes in and pulls her out the door, too.

I float on the bed, like someone lost at sea. The sound of water becomes louder as it rushes faster out of the walls, drips from the ceiling as though from the skies. My mind begins to swirl, fast, like the water, like the bed, and I become dizzy and nauseated by a smell in that room—the smell of birth, of warm blood, of my body and my insides.

I'm caught in between and I have to get out.

I focus on a crack on the ceiling and concentrate. I watch as it splits open, filling the room with sunlight like the bright yolk of an egg.

The water rushes me upward then, and through the open roof. And then I, too, am carried away on a wave as the water gushes out of the house and onto the dirt road. I'm rushed away, on my floating bed.

I'm laughing as the streets fill with water. I turn back and see

Mami on our front patio, waving at me, anxiously calling me back, that baby in her arms.

¡Pequeña! ¡Pequeña!

Something startles me back into the bedroom.

When my eyes flutter open this time, Doña Agostina is standing next to me, holding smelling salts under my nose. "You fainted, my love. Drink some water," she says. She holds a cup to my lips and I take a small sip. The wetness is shockingly cold and I feel myself tethered back to reality as she puts the cup in my hand and begins to massage my stomach, all the while telling me I will be all right, everything will be all right.

Her large hands grind my stomach like she is mixing masa. It hurts, but I don't care. I just want to feel normal again, not empty and hollowed out. I want to forget that my body ever housed anything.

I concentrate on the cracks in the ceiling, imagine myself being lifted and carried away again. The images of water and sun and rushing through the streets flicker in my mind.

But I stay where I am.

Trapped.

Pulga

We head in the direction of the store closest to Pequeña's house. But there are several cars parked in front and some yelling. Chico and I look at each other and turn in the other direction. Even though it means a twenty-minute walk, we head to Don Felicio's store instead, where Chico and I usually sit on the sidewalk outside, drinking Cokes and Gatorade, sometimes even setting off small firecrackers for fun. And I wonder if I can talk Don Felicio into giving us a few firecrackers to celebrate the birth of Pequeña's baby.

Maybe because I'm thinking of this, and because Chico keeps talking about how awful it must be for Pequeña, and because my thoughts keep wandering to that day out on the patio, neither of us notices or hears the car coming up behind until it's practically threatening to run us over. I glance at the driver. Nestor Villa. In the passenger seat is his older brother, Rey.

"Shit," I whisper to Chico.

Nestor Villa is how Chico and I met three years ago. That kid was almost as small as I was until one day, he seemed to grow overnight and started picking fights with everyone. The day he came to school wearing brand-new gleaming white shoes, he said I kicked up dust and got them dirty when I walked by. The jerk forced me down, telling me to lick his shoes clean.

My heart was racing, but I knew I had to be tough. So I told Nestor his mother could lick them and he pushed me down to the ground.

That day, when I saw Chico out of the corner of my eye, a big guy I figured was probably pretty tough, I called out to him for help.

I looked up from Nestor's pretty shoes, his hand tight around the back of my neck pushing me harder and harder into them, and locked eyes with Chico. "Punch him, kid!" I said. "Slam him to the ground!"

I spit on Nestor's shoes, refusing to lick them, and he ground my face into the dirt.

"Eat shit!" Nestor yelled at me as grit and dust made its way into my mouth, became muddy with my saliva. I spit it out onto his shoes.

"Mess him up!" I yelled to Chico, pleading with him. But Chico looked scared. His voice trembled when he told Nestor to stop and all my hopes died. Nestor was going to kill me and then kill the kid I'd brought into this.

Except that's not how it happened. Just as Nestor jammed one of his new sneaker–clad feet onto my head and started stepping on it, crushing my head into the ground, out of nowhere I heard a *thwack!* And suddenly I was free. I scrambled away from him fast enough to see him hit the ground and saw Chico standing over him, almost looking sorry, like he didn't mean to do it. He'd smacked the hell out of Nestor. And Nestor, tall but still slight, had toppled over like a makeshift bowling pin. I swear I heard his teeth clack together as he fell, like those little wind-up toy teeth and it made me laugh like crazy from relief.

Chico and I ran away, me hooting and hollering and slapping him on the back. That's the moment we became best friends.

"You just knocked out Nestor Villa!" I held up his arm like he was legendary boxer Julio César Chávez. "You did it! You fucking saved me!" I felt tough, like we were both champions. I felt stronger with Chico around. And when he smiled, I could tell he felt it, too.

Neither of us, it turned out, had siblings or many friends, and that day it felt like we were two missing puzzle pieces that had finally found each other and locked into place. So when his mamita died the following year, he came to live with us. The day we took down Nestor was the best thing that ever happened to Chico and me.

It was also one of the biggest mistakes we ever made.

See, the person who gave Nestor those brand-new shoes I spit all over was his big brother, Rey. Rey, who had done a few years in a United States prison for some kind of robbery. Rey, who had fallen in with some gang members in that prison. Rey, who, upon his release, was deported back to Guatemala, where he stayed true to his new gang family and ran with them in Guatemala City. Rey, who Nestor had called that night, giving him the rundown on me and Chico. Rey, who took the bus from Guatemala City to Puerto Barrios, ready to fight.

The sound of a horn, long and loud, brings me out of my head and back to the present. Chico and I hurry over to the side of the road so the car can pass us by.

Nestor's hair is longer than it used to be, and he looks older. I haven't seen him in a while, ever since he stopped coming to school just a few months after we heard Rey had moved back here.

"Look down, pretend you don't realize it's them," I tell Chico, and he does what I tell him. But I can feel Nestor's gaze, and I'm the one who looks up at the last moment as we lock eyes. A slight smile creeps across his face like he knew I'd look up, like he knows everything. He and Rey laugh and the next thing I know, the car speeds off out of sight, leaving us in a cloud of dust.

Chico turns to me and says, "Let's just go back. I'm not even thirsty anymore."

I'm about to agree with him, but I stop myself. One, because we're almost at Don Felicio's store. I can see the rusty tin roof from here. Two, because Nestor and Rey are gone. Three, because Chico's a bad liar. His lips are cracked and little beads of sweat cling to the dark peach fuzz that has just started to come in on his upper lip. There's nothing he'd like more right now than the coldest Coca-Colas on earth from Don Felicio's store or the banana topoyiyo his wife makes, those little frozen plastic bags of icy sweetness. And four, because I feel like an asshole for cracking on Chico's shirt this morning and teasing him just last week about looking like Cantinflas with his baby mustache. The least he deserves is a fucking soda when he is thirsty. Besides, I refuse to let a look from Nestor and Rey force us into changing our plans.

"We're almost there," I tell him. But Chico has stopped in the middle of the road and he is looking back and forth from Don Felicio's store to the direction of Tía Lucia's house. "Come on," I plead. "You saw how he took off. Besides, I'm gonna get a couple firecrackers, too. For when the baby is born."

He smiles at this, then begrudgingly starts walking in the direction of the store. "Fine, but let's hurry."

I feel a little guilty. I hate to make Chico do what he doesn't want to do. I mean, I'm the one always telling him to stand up for himself, but then when he does, I still convince him to do what I want.

"Diablo, man, what's up with this heat," I tell Chico as we walk. I don't know if it's running into Rey or the sun overhead, but it feels like the hottest day of the year suddenly. I try to take a deep breath, but the air feels thick and wet and suffocating. I take small shallow breaths instead and pull my shirt away from my sticky body, keeping in mind the taste and feel of an ice-cold soda.

"Why do you think he came back to Barrios anyway?" Chico asks as the sun beats down on us.

"Who? Rey?" I shrug. We'd all heard the rumors of how Rey missed being a big fish in a small pond so he left Guatemala City.

But really, who knew. "Forget it," I tell Chico, not wanting to think or talk about Rey anymore.

But I can't forget what happened.

Rey waited for Chico and me outside school the day after our fight with Nestor. He walked toward us, and my heart, with each thump, felt like it could take no more. Each of Rey's slow steps in our direction felt like my last breath.

But I didn't show my fear.

When he finally stood in front of us, what he did was stare at us for a very long time. Enough time for me to notice how his eyes were so black you couldn't even see the pupil. Enough for me to notice the scar that ran from his cheekbone to his chin on the right side of his face. And the way his two front teeth overlapped slightly.

The intensity of that stare, the way he held my gaze, reminded me of a snake charmer. He circled us, his eyes never leaving ours, stalking, like an animal does its prey.

And then I felt an explosion in my head, a simultaneous darkening and brightening in my mind. A flashing, pulsing light against a dark, dark night.

I thought he'd shot me in the head, that's how hard he slapped me. I staggered backward, fell hard on the concrete. And then I heard Chico, yelping like a wounded animal.

"You get slapped, because you two are little bitches," he said, towering over us. "This is a warning, because I'm a good person. And because *this bitch*"—he gestured toward Nestor—"should've done this to you instead of calling *me*." Nestor and his friends, who had witnessed the whole thing and had been hooting and hollering the whole time, suddenly stopped. I'll never forget the cold, meaningful look Rey gave Nestor. Or the look of shame that passed over Nestor's face before he looked down.

I almost felt bad for Nestor then. But it was hard with my face burning and throbbing the way it was. Either way, I think that was the exact moment Nestor decided he would sell his soul and do anything to impress Rey, to prove himself to his brother from that day forward.

Chico and I went home wearing our pain. Our faces were bruised. Mamá noticed and questioned us relentlessly, our story constantly changing until finally, we admitted we'd been in a fight. A stupid fight in the school courtyard because someone made fun of Chico's mother, we said.

We didn't tell her about Rey. And Chico and I steered clear of Nestor after that. When Rey suddenly moved back to Puerto Barrios last year, we steered clear of him, too. Because I never forgot that slap. Or the nights afterward that I spent pressing into my bruised cheek, staring at the darkness of my room, mad at myself and wondering what kind of guy takes a six-hour bus trip to Puerto Barrios and a six-hour bus trip back to Guatemala City just to issue a slap to a twelve-year-old and a ten-year-old boy.

A wolf—that's who.

Don Felicio smiles and calls out to us as soon he sees us coming up the road. He's always standing at the counter, waiting for someone who wants a soda, or ice, or batteries, or gum. The old man barely inflates his prices, even though he could. A lot of the neighborhood store owners do since it saves people a trip on the bus all the way to the market. Don Felicio, though, he's too nice. He doesn't have the heart of a businessman.

"¡Patojos!" he says, calling out to us affectionately and flashing his yellow-toothed smile. "Come, come, keep an old man company! Business is slow."

I look around, realizing there aren't as many men around here as there used to be—the ones I would listen to carefully as they talked about how they were planning to leave for the States. Or how they had already made the trip once and were headed back there again. How they crossed a river. How they rode La Bestia or paid a pollero. How they followed a coyote through the desert. Sometimes I'd even get to ask a few questions before Don Feli would look at me with a sad smile and say, "Don't even think about breaking your mamá's heart like that, Pulga."

I look at the old man now. "Bueno," he says. "¿Cómo están?"

"We're good, Don Feli, but poor," Chico answers as we step up to the counter. He takes out his money and asks for a Coke.

"Just one?" Don Felicio asks, looking at me. I shrug.

"I tell you what, I got a big shipment of drinks after Semana Santa last week—the celebrations around here wiped me out—so there are some sodas in the back I need put in the big cooler. You guys stock all those pallets I got back there, and I'll give you two sodas for the price of one."

Chico grins.

"Or . . . a pack of fireworks instead?" I ask. I feel guilty taking advantage of the old man's good-heartedness, but I also want Pequeña to someday tell her child, *Tío Pulga and Tío Chico set off fireworks the day you were born.* I want the kid to know we celebrated, and I can tell him or her about that. By then, maybe my memory of how much Pequeña didn't want this baby will have faded. "Pequeña is having her baby," I explain to Don Felicio.

"She is? How wonderful!" His eyes light up. "Well, of course, of course," he says, grabbing several packs of fireworks and pushing them across the counter toward me. "These and two Cokes for the price of one for a little muscle seems fair to me." He winks.

"Gracias, Don Feli," I say.

"You two remind me so much of Gallo," he says as if explaining.

He's not just one of the nicest old guys in the neighborhood. He's also one of these guys who says the same thing every time he sees you. Gallo was Don Felicio's son who left Puerto Barrios ten years ago when he was eighteen and hasn't been back since because he doesn't have papers. The old man talks about Gallo every time we come by. Shows us pictures of a grandson he has in Colorado or someplace, too.

"I just got a new picture of my grandson. I'll show you when you're done." He smiles a melancholy smile.

"Sure, Don Feli," I tell him, even though I don't want to see pictures for the millionth time of the little kid whose hair is as unruly as Gallo's. Even though it's boring, and heartbreaking to see Don Feli's face go from glowing to crushed when he finally puts away his phone and takes out his handkerchief to wipe his eyes, it's the least I can do for the old man. "And don't worry. You'll see them again."

He dismisses me with his hand but nods, like a part of him knows it's not true but another part of him has to believe it is.

We hop the counter and go through the door to the cramped back room, where we're greeted by the smells of sour milk and overripe produce. Chico starts singing a stupid song we made up when we saw a dog in the street with a bum leg that made him look like he was dancing. We're always making up songs, for the day I'll finally buy a guitar and put music to lyrics. For the day I'll get a band together and be a musician. Just like my father—the cool bass player from California. The Chicano who drove a slick black El Camino with red leather interior. The guy who was gonna make it big, who promised Mamá the world but didn't deliver because some drunk crashed into him one night, and crushed him, that car, and all their dreams before either of them knew about me tucked away in Mamá's belly.

Chico hands me the last two grape Fantas. We're almost done when we hear the sound of a car pulling up to the store. Voices grow louder just beyond the stockroom. We both freeze as Don Felicio's voice calls, "Give me more time! You have to understand, I—" His voice is cut off so abruptly, so suddenly, it sends a chill through my body. Even before the sound of the loud thump that follows.

Chico looks at me, his eyes as wide as I've ever seen them. His chest already rising and falling faster as his breath quickens. I shake my head.

What I mean is, *don't move.*

What I mean is, *don't make a sound.*

We stand there for who knows how long, Chico kneeling on the floor where he was handing me the sodas, me with those two grape Fantas still in my hands. I hear the rush of my own blood, and the thump of my own heart, and Chico's breathing. I hear the sound of the register opening, two car doors slamming, car tires rolling.

And then an eerie silence, and the phantom echo of Don Felicio's voice before it abruptly stopped.

"Pulga . . . what . . . what just happened?" Chico says, his voice trembling.

"I don't know." Whatever happened, we know it's bad. Really, really bad.

We need to get out of here. But first, I have to check on Don Felicio.

I hand the two bottles to Chico and hurry to the door, open it just enough to see if anyone is there, then push it open when I'm certain no one is. "Be careful," Chico whispers.

I nod.

"Don Feli?" I call. But I don't see him. I look all around, my brain trying to make sense of what happened, when I hear a gurgle.

And that's when I see him on the floor. His feet come into view first, his old but freshly polished shoes, his dark socks and frail old-man legs between the top of his socks and the cuff of his pants. My body goes weak as the strange gurgling continues and fills the air. I move closer, taking in the blood on the counter, on the floor. The blood pooling around his torso.

And then I see Don Felicio's face.

His hands are clasped around his throat, trying to stop the gush of blood that is seeping from it as it pours through his fingers. He looks at me with eyes bulging, so terrified, they seem like they might pop out of his face.

My mouth goes dry and I hurry to him, calling his name, slipping on his blood.

"You're okay," I manage to choke out, even as my voice cracks and something inside me feels loose and wild. A scream gets caught up somewhere in the back of my throat. "We'll get someone!" I tell him as he gurgles and wheezes and keeps holding his throat.

I hear Chico crying and saying something and I know I have to run and get help. *Run*, I tell myself, but I can't move. I can't leave the old man here like this, not when the blood is rushing out that way, oh my god, it's rushing out so quickly, pouring out of him like water, encircling us both.

I've never seen so much blood.

His lips come together, like he's trying to say something, like he's trying so hard to say something.

Kkkk kkk . . . His body jerks forward, like he's trying to get up. Each effort makes more blood gush forth.

"No," I tell him as he struggles. My mind races with what to do. "Don't worry, help is already on the way, Don Feli! I promise!" I tell him he is going to be okay, as his eyes go from my face to the ceiling. I tell him that his son will be here soon, too, that he figured out a way to come from the States and that he is bringing his grandson this time.

Do you see them, Don Feli! Do you see them! I cry.

He nods.

I tell him his wife is on her way, too. And that soon he will see all their faces. That soon they will all be together.

It's all lies.

The old man's eyes are full of tears. They slide out of the corners as more blood gushes from his neck, as life drains from him. His eyes roll back so only the whites are visible and then roll forward again, trying to focus on me. I want to look away but I don't, and then suddenly, the strange wheezing and gurgling stops. His head relaxes so that it's turned toward me. So that his eyes meet mine. And I see it, the very moment he dies. I see it, right there as his eyes go vacant.

Chico's words come in from somewhere far away. He is calling my name, I think, but I still can't move. I'm crying. And even though I know what happened, I keep hearing my voice like it's coming from someplace else, like it's not even my own, asking Chico, *What happened? What happened?* Over and over.

Chico keeps saying, *We have to get someone! We have to get someone!* as he grabs my shirt and pulls me up to standing.

Time doesn't make sense. We are stuck in that moment forever, even as it feels like we are in a movie on fast-forward.

We stumble out into the street. And it looks so strange and empty. The world is blurred streaks of orange-brown and blue and white that make my eyes pulse.

I'm dreaming, I think. Even as I catch a glimpse of my hands and shoes covered in blood. Even as I hear Chico's strange whimpering next to me and his incomprehensible jumble of words.

I think he is asking me where we should go. I see his face and I try to make out his words, but I can hardly make sense of anything.

All I know is we have to run—hard and fast and without looking back. Away as quickly as possible. Away so you're not a witness. So you're not a part of any of it. So no one can ask you questions. So no one knows you were there.

We run.

It's the way you learn to live around here.

Pequeña

"Doña Agostina!" A man's voice calls anxiously from the street, someone looking for the old woman.

"¡Aquí!" I hear Tía Consuelo answer. "Se encuentra aquí. Espere," she says, telling the man he can find Doña Agostina here and to wait. But he doesn't wait, and I hear Tía Consuelo's and Mami's voices coming closer, calling to the man, when he suddenly appears at the bedroom door. Doña Agostina's hands are still grinding my stomach. The man stares at us, Tía Consuelo and Mami behind him, demanding to know what he is doing when—

"Doña Agostina," the man says, out of breath. His face is sweaty, his hair disheveled. "I have terrible news."

"¿Qué pasó?" she asks. Her hands stop moving. They're just barely lying on my belly as she waits for him to tell her what happened.

"Your husband . . ." the man says, but he falters. He tries again. "Doña Agostina, I have terrible news . . ."

The old woman reaches back for a chair at the side of the bed. Her hands are trembling, but she grabs it and lowers herself to sit. I can hear her breath becoming shallow as she braces herself for what's coming.

Maybe in other places, terrible news is unexpected. But here, it is not. Here we wait for it always. And it always comes.

That is why I grab Doña Agostina's hands—the ones that have just delivered the unwanted child, that have tried to knead away the hollow, unfillable space inside me. I hold on to those hands and

I meet Doña Agostina's tired old eyes, now alert and wide with fear and knowing, and I don't look away.

"They've killed him," the man says. "At the store. I'm sorry . . . Don Felicio está muerto."

She lets out a long, quivering wail. I hold on tight to her shaking hands. Mami and Tía Consuelo rush to her.

The baby begins to cry.

Pulga

I scramble to get the plastic garbage bag with our bloodied clothes and shoes hidden under my bed just as the front door bangs open.

Shit. We forgot to put the wooden bar up.

"Pulga! Chico!" Mamá's voice is frantic. She cries, "¿Dónde están? Dios, where are you?" She is practically screaming, desperation clawing and strangling her voice.

"¡Aquí!" I yell as Chico and I hurry to the living room. "We're in here!"

Mamá's eyes are wide and wild, her face so flushed. As soon as we're within reach, she pulls us into a fierce hug, her nails digging into the side of my arm as her grip tightens. "Ay, Diosito, gracias, gracias," she says. Mamá's heart is beating furiously, so hard and fast it feels like it could burst through to my own chest. Her body radiates heat and trembles so much, I don't think she notices how we shake, too. When she pulls away, her face is streaked with sweat, tears, and eye makeup. "I didn't know where you were . . . Why are you here? Why did you leave Tía's house? Ay, Dios . . . muchachos . . . how long have you been here?" Her questions come out in a rushed breath.

"We didn't want to hear Pequeña crying like that so we came home until after the baby came . . . Sorry we didn't tell you first. We just didn't want to bother—"

Relief floods Mamá's body, so completely, she seems to lose all strength. She sits down on the couch and stays there a moment, stunned, before covering her face and crying quietly.

"Mamá?" I say. Chico sits down next to her, reaches for her hand. More tears rush down her face.

"No llore, doña," he says, wiping Mamá's tears gently and telling her not to cry.

She shakes her head. "I didn't know where you two were," she whispers. When she looks up again, she stares at me, takes a deep breath. "Something terrible has happened . . ."

At first, I think she must know about Don Felicio. But before I can speak, a new fear grips my heart. "Is it Pequeña?" I say. What if Pequeña, or her baby, or *both,* died during childbirth?

"Is she okay? Did something—" Chico starts.

Mamá holds up her hand. "She's fine, Pequeña's fine," she says. "It's Don Felicio. He's . . . dead. Killed at his store."

I try to look like I don't know. I think of Don Felicio on that floor and I choke out some kind of response. But Mamá has leaned her head back against the couch. Her gaze has gone to the ceiling and she is saying so softly, "Ay, Dios . . . ayúdanos."

Mamá's pleas to God for help sound foreboding in that still, silent room. She takes a deep breath. "I have to go be with Doña Agostina." She stands up. "Stay here, okay? Don't go anywhere." I nod and she gives us both a weak hug and kiss before heading out again.

We watch from the patio as she slowly makes her way to the store, to Doña Agostina's side.

"You think she suspects anything?" Chico asks next to me as I watch Mamá put an arm around the old woman.

"I don't know."

We sit on the patio, staring off into the distance at neighbors who've come out to be with and comfort Doña Agostina, and at those who only observe from their doorways even though the police have not arrived. Neither has the coroner. So all I can think about is Don Felicio's body still there, splayed out on the floor. Being drenched in his own blood.

Chico scrapes his shoe against the patio floor. When I look over at him, his hair is matted down on his forehead and his face is anxious. He puts his head in his hands. "What the hell just happened?" he asks. "What happened?"

My body is still buzzing, my mind flashing with Don Felicio lying on the floor, us running, rushing to clean up. Washing off all that blood. Seeing Mamá's face frantic and crying. Trying to seem normal in front of her.

The adrenaline starts ebbing away and I feel like rubber.

Chico starts crying softly. Then harder. I want to tell him to stop, to be tough. I want to remind him this is nothing new.

But I don't trust myself to speak. I don't trust my own tears to stay away. So I say nothing and keep looking in the direction of the store.

Soon the police show up, and people trickle away to their houses.

"Come on," I tell Chico. The last thing we need is one of those uniformed men to spot us and come ask questions.

We go to my room and I watch from the window while Chico sits on the bed. Every passing moment I expect a knock at the door, a policeman saying someone saw us running from the scene, me covered in blood. But nobody saw us. Or if they did, no one said anything. Maybe they guessed the truth and were protecting us. Because everyone knows Rey's car. And everyone knows what he is capable of. And everyone knows who the police really work for anyway. So nobody comes. Nobody asks questions.

For now.

~ ~ ~

A little while later Mamá comes back and says she has to stay with Doña Agostina tonight because the woman is so grief-stricken. It means fewer questions for her to ask us. And time to get rid of our bloodied clothes.

"Will you be okay without me?" she says. "You can warm up the leftover beans in the refrigerator for dinner."

"We'll be okay," I tell her. She rushes around the house, her shoes clicking, her keys jangling, talking to herself about what needs to be done and poor Doña Agostina, asking again if we'll be okay without her and to be sure, *be sure* to put the wooden bar down as soon as she steps outside.

Then she leaves. I close the door behind her.

"Is it down?" she yells from the patio.

"Yes, Mamá," I assure her, securing the bar. When her motor scooter zooms away again, the house falls still and silent.

Like it's waiting for something. Or someone.

Chico drops onto the velvet couch and I sit down next to him. But my mind crowds with worry.

The clothes. We have to burn them. Wash the shoes because Mamá will notice if those are gone.

Nobody saw us.

Maybe somebody did.

Anybody could've seen us.

What if they did?

We sit there for I don't know how long and I can't turn off my mind; it keeps thinking and picturing the same things over and over, screaming in my head in all that silence, interrupted only by Chico's whispers, asking what happened again and again.

~ ~ ~

Night begins to fall.

"Come on," I tell him finally. We get the bag from under my bed and take out our shoes, wash them in the big, concrete sink Mamá washes clothes in. The water and lather turn pink. My stomach twists.

"Get the matches," I tell him. And when he comes back with them in hand, we go out to the backyard and build a small fire. It flickers and glows an eerie orange as it consumes the plastic bag and feeds on the clothes inside. We watch it burn.

Then, with the smell of smoke still on us, we go inside. We hide in our room.

We do not speak. We try to stop picturing Don Felicio, the way his blood spurted from his body.

I try to keep that blood from spilling into my mind.

I try.

And I try.

But my thoughts are covered in red.

Pequeña

That night, the sound of toads croaking is louder than I've ever heard before. It sounds as if the streets are filled with toads. As if they've invaded our streets, our whole barrio. I wonder if I've brought them here.

I've slept all day. Or slipped to other worlds all day. I'm not sure which is which. But now it is night, and I can't sleep. All I can do is lie here under thin sheets, feeling the blood gush from my body with each movement, each turn.

I don't know what happened to Doña Agostina. One moment she was next to me, and then she was gone. I wonder if I slipped into other worlds when I was holding her hand. I wonder if I took her with me. I wonder if I left her somewhere, a place where Don Felicio is still alive.

The house is eerily quiet.

Mami is sleeping on the couch. She's moved the baby bassinet out there, next to her, *so you will sleep better,* she says. *You need rest, Pequeña.* I think she's worried because I won't hold him. Because I don't want to hear him, or give him a name.

I'm glad she took him to another room.

The curtains on the window billow ever so slightly. Mami left the window open just a little bit, because I complained about the sour, tangy smell. *No,* I told her. *Close it.* She did as I asked, but while I was sleeping, she must have opened it again.

I can't stand it opened.

Slowly, I sit up. Each move is painful and makes me want to cry out.

No, I tell myself. *This won't break you. You can handle this.* I take a deep breath as I lower my legs over the side of the bed, as I push myself up and feel the flood of warmth between my legs. It makes me feel sick, but I force myself to get up anyway.

I take small, careful steps to the window. I push aside the curtains and a hand reaches in and grabs mine.

Pequeña.

Someone whispers my name.

Somewhere else, someone else might jump backward. Or scream. Because you don't expect the night to reach in through your window and grab you. You don't expect to hear it call your name. But I'm not somewhere else; I'm not someone else. So I stay exactly as I am.

"I'm sorry," he says, laughing quietly. "You look like you've seen a ghost. I didn't mean to scare you."

I want to tell him I'm not scared, but I am. More than if Death itself had come to take me to my grave.

I shake my head. "I'm fine."

"You seem sick," he says.

"I . . . I had the baby," I tell him. But it's seeing him here, like this, that makes me nauseated.

He looks in, takes a closer look at my stomach. "I don't believe you. You look the same," he says, but then he studies my face. I refuse to blink. "Wait, for real?"

I nod.

He smiles. "A boy, right? Tell me it's a boy . . ."

"It's a boy," I say.

"I knew it! A boy. I have a boy."

I don't want any claim to this baby, but the way he says that bothers me, too. He doesn't deserve to have *anything.*

"I mean, I knew it could've been a girl, but I also knew it would be a boy. You gave me what I wanted, Pequeña." He caresses my fingers gently and I fight the urge to pull away. "Where is he?"

"With my mother, in the other room, so I can rest."

He nods. "Well, I have to see him. And you finally have to tell your mother about us, our plans."

I stay quiet, but he laughs again. "Don't look so scared. I told you, I'm going to take care of us. You know that, right? When are you going to tell her?"

"Soon," I say.

He stares at me for a long time and then that strange look comes across his face. "Soon," he repeats. "Yeah, soon." When he looks at me like that, I can't move. There is something off in his look, something that reveals the inside of him is broken, something that lets you know he is soulless and makes you scared to turn away. "Or you know what? Maybe . . . maybe we tell her right now."

I make myself reach for his hand. I caress it as chills run through my body. I feel clammy and weak. "Let me get better, look better. Then we'll tell her. I want it to be . . . perfect."

The coldness in his eyes warms. Then he stares at my body, and I'm so relieved I am bloated and sick looking. "Yeah, maybe that's a good idea . . ." he says. "I was going to let it be a surprise, but I'm getting you a ring. It's the most expensive ring I could find, and soon you're going to be wearing it. I bet you never thought you'd be wearing the fanciest ring in this whole barrio."

I swallow the sour taste in my mouth. "No, I never imagined any of this for me."

He smiles like I've paid him the biggest compliment. "You are very lucky. That I chose you. Pequeña." He stares at my lips, licks his own.

I want to tell him that he disgusts me. Everything about him—the way he looks at me, the way he says my name, his touch, his face, of which every detail has impressed itself in my mind. His patchy facial hair, the overlap of his teeth, the glistening of his saliva, the dead look he carries, and the *smell* of him—a scent that escapes from his pores, from the dark hole of his mouth. It's the scent of the rotted heart he carries inside.

"Come here," he says, pulling my arm through the open window, forcing me closer to him. Fresh blood gushes. And then he is kissing me, grabbing my face as he forces his tongue between my lips.

"Just remember I chose *you*," he whispers. "I could have had *anyone*, Pequeña, but I want *you*. I need you. And you need me." He kisses my hand. "Take care of our baby," he says, smiling his terrible smile.

I watch as he disappears into the night.

I picture the night reaching out like a terrible claw, crushing him in its grasp. Or the earth opening under him, swallowing him, and closing up again forever. Or a stray bullet finding its way into his rotted heart or head as he walks the streets, smiling his terrible smile, the delusion of us in his mind.

The taste of him is still on my tongue, his touch, everything is all over me. Bitter vomit fills my mouth and it escapes me before I can reach for the towel near the bed. I wipe my mouth instead and toss the towel on top of the throw-up.

I know I should go to the bathroom, that I need to change my pad. I know I should clean the vomit. I know I should probably call out for my mother as sweat covers my body and I tremble.

But I just lie back in bed, grateful that the bitter taste of my own sick has washed out any taste of him.

And I try not to cry, as blood and milk and life drain from me.

Let it all drain, I think. *And let me die tonight.*

Pulga

Chico and I stay in our room for what feels like forever. But it will never be long enough to wipe away what we've seen.

"Is that how my mamita looked the day she was killed?" Chico whispers into the darkness of our mostly bare room. The stand-up fan oscillates between my bed and his thin mattress on the tiled floor.

I take a deep breath, focus on the shadows of the boxes in the corner—the ones that have held our clothes ever since Chico first moved in with us and we had to sell our wardrobe to buy him a mattress. It was supposed to be only temporary. It's been over two years.

The fan moves hot air around the stifling room.

"Pulga?" I can hear the tears welling in his voice.

"No," I answer finally. Truthfully. "Your mamita looked peaceful. Like she was sleeping." The fan whirs away from me.

That part is a lie. But it's a lie I have to tell.

"I thought . . . you told me there was a lot of blood," Chico whispers. "Around Mamita."

"Yes," I tell him. "But not like that, Chico. She didn't look like that."

I hear him take a deep breath and let it out. And in the silence, I finish the truth.

She looked worse, Chico. She looked like the kinds of monstruos that appear in your worst nightmares and haunt you for the rest of your life. If you'd seen, you would never be able to forget. And you might forget the way your mamita really looked. And how on the bus that day, just before we got to the market, she looked at you with so much love, in that last hour of her life.

I was thirteen years old and Chico was eleven and we'd been friends for a whole year the day we took the little white bus to the market together. His mamita gave us money to get horchata and we ran off to the woman selling some. The day was so hot, and I remember squinting at the orange blaze of the sun as I tipped the cup and drank the cold milky rice drink. Sweetness filled my mouth. And then we heard three loud pops.

Someone screamed and someone yelled and a motor scooter zoomed past. Chico and I stared after it, then in the direction it came from.

The market was crowded that day, and we had to shove through people. At thirteen, I was still as small as I'd been when I was ten, and could move through the crowd more easily. That's why I saw her first.

Chico's mom lay in the middle of the road, blood soaking through the white blouse she wore, embroidered with red and pink roses. A single white, papery onion had rolled out of the green mesh bag she carried and lay next to the long striped skirt that was now up around her thigh. Her small brown legs poked out, splattered with blood. Her sandals lay scattered on the other side of her, revealing bare, dusty feet.

Pulga! Chico was calling for me and I turned and ran back. I tried so hard to block him from the horrific image of his mother.

Don't look! I yelled. It was the only thing I could think to say. *Don't look don't look don't look!*

What is it? he said, trying to get around me and past people.

No! I screamed, and I was crying. But he wouldn't let up. And I couldn't let someone else tell him.

It's your mamita, Chico.

All color left his face. And then someone, I don't know who, helped me hold him back.

Chico tried to fight his way to her, he kicked me and yelled for her, his mouth so close to my ear I thought I would burst an eardrum. But we held him back. And I told him, *No, don't look.*

In the past few years, the only time Chico didn't speak to me was the whole week after that.

"You didn't let me say goodbye to my mamita." That was what he said when he finally spoke to me. "I could've whispered it in her ear. She could've heard me tell her I love her. I could've said goodbye." The words came out choked, between sobs.

"I'm sorry" is all I could say. How could I tell him his mamita would've never heard his words? That those words would have never made their way past his lips if he'd seen what I saw. That only screams would've come out of him. And *that's* what his mother would have heard. Chico. Screaming.

No. I couldn't let him see her that way. I couldn't let that image be what haunted Chico for the rest of his life—her eyes staring blankly at the sky, the whites made whiter by the blood that covered her face like a slick wet veil. Sometimes, I am jolted out of my sleep by that image and the echoes of Chico's pained voice from that day, even as he lies sleeping a few feet away.

I almost told him then—when weeks went by and the police did nothing and answers never came about who killed Chico's mamita and she became just another body—I almost told him then, *Let's go. Let's leave this place.*

I was almost ready to pull out from under my mattress all my notes, the routes and maps I'd googled and printed from computers at school. I was almost ready to tell him we should strike out together, go to the United States. But I knew we wouldn't get far. I knew I needed to gather more information. And the truth is, I was too selfish. With Chico weeping for his mamita every night, falling asleep to his sobs, I couldn't bear to leave my own. So I waited. For another day.

"Do you think they know we saw?" Chico whispers now. The fan whirs.

"We didn't see anything," I remind him.

"Right, I know . . . but do you think—"

"Nothing. We saw nothing, Chico. You got it?"

"Pulga . . ."

Silence fills the room.

"Go to sleep," I say, and stare out the closed thin curtains and into the blackness of night. I try to push away the image of Chico's dead mother, of Don Felicio's lifeless body. I force myself to picture other things—like the explosion of fireworks in the night sky when we celebrate Noche Buena. Or a crowd waiting to hear me and my band play. But I can't.

"Pulga?" Chico whispers.

"Yeah?"

"It was Rey, wasn't it?" Chico says. "Rey and Nestor."

"Cállate, man. Don't say those things aloud." I keep my eyes on the thin curtains separating us from the night. The black looks like it will absorb everything. And hear everything. And whisper our secrets into other people's ears. "Don't even think those things," I say.

"But . . ." Chico whispers.

"Go to sleep." I need him to stop talking.

I will my body to sleep, too, but my head won't let me. My mind keeps filling with more images of dead people. Of Rey and Nestor. Of so much darkness. I don't like the way tonight feels like we can't even trust this room, these walls that have always kept our secrets, our dreams—us—safe.

Dreams like how maybe I could go to the United States one day, buy a guitar and become a musician just like my father. Dreams like how Chico would go with me and manage my band. Dreams where one day we'd each find a girl to love, a girl to take a picture with in front of a cool car—one who'd look at me the way Mamá looked at my father in my favorite picture of them, so old the edges are ripped. They're standing in front of his El Camino, his arm around her shoulders, hers around his waist, and they're looking at each other as if seeing some kind of golden future.

Mamá never wanted to waste money on a guitar. She didn't like the idea of me following in my father's footsteps. But if I made it to the States, I promised myself I would. And I made a promise to Mamá too—that I would never just abandon her. So I'd bring Mamá to the States, too, and buy her a house. And someday Chico and I would accept some kind of award on a big stage, and we'd tell everyone that we were just a couple of kids from Barrios. And we'd look into those cameras and speak to all the kids from Barrios and tell them to dream—*because dreams do come true*—before we put our arms around each other and walked off the stage.

We've told each other that dream a thousand times.

But tonight it doesn't feel like dreams exist. And my body is prickly and crawling with fear.

"Pulga?"

"Yeah?"

"I'm . . . scared," Chico says.

Outside, I think I hear a rustling. And moments later, a soft whistling. I tell myself I'm being paranoid. I tell myself I'm imagining things. But I see Chico sit up and stare out the window.

"Did you hear that?" he says.

My throat and tongue feel like they're swelling. My mouth is dry.

"No," I tell him. "Go to sleep."

"Pulga," he whispers, his voice saturated with fear.

"Everything will be okay," I tell him. But all night I stare at that window.

Waiting.

Waiting.

In the morning, through thick humidity and the fog of a sleepless night, Chico and I lug a large pot to Doña Agostina's house at Mamá's request.

Several women are in the kitchen starting on the tamales that are always served at wakes. Each neighbor has brought different ingredients—masa, carne, chiles, aceitunas, ojas de banana—and together they cook and assemble, whispering quietly about what happened.

Doña Agostina sits outside. Alone.

Chico and I sit on the couch, surrounded by the lime-green walls of Doña Agostina's living room, watching television and dozing off to the sounds of the women in the kitchen, and the clattering of cooking.

The room gets hotter and hotter, pressing down on us.

And then a pickup truck arrives, with Don Felicio's coffin.

Everyone gathers around as he's carried inside, as he's situated in the middle of the room. The neighbors look, pay their respects, go back to helping.

"Come on," I tell Chico, but he shakes his head and refuses to move from the couch. So I go alone, look at a face that isn't Don Felicio's anymore. A face that's gray and ashen, bloated and serious. A body in a sharp black suit, a red tie around the stiff white collar of a shirt. It reminds me of the red blood that spilled from Don Felicio's neck yesterday. I look up, at the walls. I think of the sweet limeade Mamá makes, the green feathers of a parrot. But the walls look sickly, and I feel nauseated and each breath I take makes me feel like I am breathing in death. I go outside and sit on the ground just on the other side of the front door.

Doña Agostina hasn't moved. She's still in the chair, looking exhausted and shell-shocked. But then she turns and notices me.

"¿Cómo está, doña?" I ask her how she is before I realize the stupidity of my question. "Can I get you some water? Something to eat?"

She shakes her head. "No, gracias, hijo. Escúchame," she says. And so I do—I sit and listen.

"You know what I dreamed last night, Pulga?" she asks. Everything about Doña Agostina looks grief-stricken. Her face droops, her clothes hang, her body is slumped in the chair. And when she turns her gray eyes on me, they are dull and lifeless.

"What did you dream?" I ask.

She turns her gaze back toward the street and says, "I dreamed I saw Pequeña, riding away from here on a bloody mattress. All I could see was the back of her, but I know it was Pequeña."

I stare at Doña Agostina, confused, but she goes on.

"And then I saw you. And Chico. Both of you were running and you looked so scared."

My heart drops into my stomach; my mouth goes dry. I know she is telling me one of her visions, the visions that have earned Doña Agostina the reputation of being a bruja—and which make her words hard to ignore. There were always stories of things she knew. Some women even went to her to have their futures told.

"I knew . . ." she says slowly. "When I married him. The moment I met him, this dark shadow seemed to engulf him and I knew what it meant: I'd lose him in a terrible way. Year after year I waited. That's why we had Gallo so late. I wasn't going to have children. But he wanted one. And I agreed, to just one. As the years went on, I convinced myself I'd been mistaken. But . . . I am never wrong about these things." She takes a deep breath. "That's why you must listen."

My blood runs cold as the old woman looks back my way. "He came to me last night," she whispers. "It was . . . horrible." She takes another deep breath. "He could hardly talk, but he managed to say, 'Que corran.' *Run,* Pulga. He wants you and Chico to *run*. Pequeña, too."

My heart thumps faster in my chest. And I look in through the doorway, into the living room where Don Felicio lies in his coffin.

Terror fills my body, rushes my veins. Mamá stares out the door, at Doña Agostina and me, a strange look on her face. I try to smile at her, but my face won't comply.

I've never let myself be a believer in visions. Mamá told me once that Doña Agostina warned her about going to the United States. *And what if I hadn't gone, Pulga,* Mamá said. *I wouldn't have lived the happiest year of my life. I wouldn't have* you. *No, you can't live your life on other people's visions.*

Mostly, I thought what Mamá said made sense. But there's something else, too, something about the visions—the revelation of some kind of unchangeable truth—that scares me. So it's easier not to believe in them. To brush them away like Mamá says we should.

But what if Doña Agostina told Mamá about her vision for me? What would Mamá do? Would she believe in them then?

I don't know how to respond to the old woman's revelation.

But it doesn't matter. She turns her gaze back toward the street and lets out a loud, painful wail, as if she had been on the shores of grief for just a moment, and now the ocean has come to take her back to the deep again.

Sometimes, it feels like the ocean won't rest until it takes every last one of us.

Pequeña

He comes to the door this time, while everyone is at Don Felicio's wake.

I watch him from the window; his knock is hard, hollow, incessant. The sound of it fills the whole house and makes me feel cold and empty. I want to ignore him, but then a flash of him climbing in through the window, finding me anyway, fills my mind. So I turn the knob and open the door, just as he is saying, "I know you are home."

I forget he knows everything.

"Hi, sorry," I say, meeting the glare that expects some kind of explanation. "It . . . takes me a while to get up."

"Oh, of course." His expression changes almost immediately. "I'm sorry." He leans over and kisses my lips. I hold my breath, trying not to breathe him in, trying not to shrink back.

"I know your mami is not home," he says in a singsong voice, wagging his finger at me. He comes into the living room uninvited, looks around, taking it in. "Come here, how about a little fun . . ." He smiles and the glistening of his saliva disgusts me. My body tenses. A small amount of throw-up fills my mouth. I swallow it.

"I'm . . . bleeding," I tell him. "I've just given birth . . . I can't . . ."

He twists his lips, and studies me. "Of course. But soon." And then, as if it's an afterthought, he walks toward the bassinet and peeks in.

"Look at him. I can't believe he's really mine."

"Of course he is," I answer. But something in the way I say it makes a strange look pass over his face.

"I didn't ask," he says. "I said I can't believe it. What? You have a guilty conscience or something?" He smiles, but his eyes study me. He is always studying everything. Observing everything. He is someone who can sniff out anything you try to hide. But on this I have nothing to hide. And only more to lose.

"Of course not. I just mean . . . I can't even look at him without seeing you."

He stares into the bassinet and studies the baby there. For a long time, he stands there searching, before he suddenly smiles. "Yeah, that little fucker does look tough." He laughs. "Yeah . . . there's a resemblance. But you, too. You're a tough one, too." He turns and looks at me now. "You know, I know about the girls around here, right? I know who wouldn't give the guys the time of day. Who is impossible to conquer." He locks eyes with me. "I knew as soon as I saw you."

He comes toward me, leans in, kisses my neck. His hand reaches for my waist and he pulls me in close to him. "I knew you and I would be perfect together," he whispers. "I knew you would love me. Say you do." I look down, notice the leather strap of the knife he keeps in his waistband.

"I do," I lie.

"Say it, say you love me." I force myself to wrap my arms around him.

"I love you," I tell him. He forces his tongue into my mouth. And I fight my gag reflex. I try not to breathe. I try to fill my mind with black night, searching for a door in that darkness.

A cry fills the room.

He pulls away. Laughs. He walks over to the bassinet, reaches in, and retrieves the small bundle.

Something electric travels through my body, makes me want to grab that baby from his dirty hands. I can't explain it. I fight that urge. I fight that feeling, whatever it is.

"Be a good boy," he says. Then to me, "Come here, hold him."

I do, even though I don't want to. I don't want to feel this baby, or know him. I don't want to hate him. Or love him. I fight all the things inside me as I hold this baby I never wanted.

"I've always had dreams of better things, you know. I knew someday, I'd have better. I was going about it all wrong, though. But now . . ." He smiles, taps his temple. "Now I know better. You and I, we'll have a big house, maids, fancy cars. We'll live somewhere much better than this. And we will take what we want along the way, because *that's* how you have to do it. I'm working on all that. You'll live better than the president's wife. And you know what? It'll still be more honest than those políticos sucios. Dirty and corrupt. All of them."

I don't know what demented world he lives in.

"My mother will be home soon."

He laughs again. "Okay . . . I know. You're a good girl. Mami's girl." He walks toward the door. He pulls me along. He makes me kiss him. "I'll follow some of your rules for now. But don't forget, you're really *my* girl," he says. "And you'll have to follow mine."

I close the door behind him and lock it, even though I know locks mean nothing here.

I put the baby back in his bassinet.

And I lie down on the couch, trying to forget this reality. Trying to lose myself in other worlds, in dreams.

I slip into a half sleep. I fall into a dark cushion from reality, and there I hear a faraway cry. *El bebé,* a part of me says. But another part of me says, *No! There is no baby. It is only a rooster's cry*. And I see an image of our neighbor's rooster crying against a blue-black night. I think of Doña Agostina and Don Felicio's son, the one we called Gallo. The one I once loved.

A glowing white outline of a door becomes visible. I walk toward it, push it open.

It leads to a small room with orange-yellow walls. On my right is a dresser with a small television perched on top. In front of me, a single rectangular window sits high on a wall above a bed.

On that bed is Gallo, wrapped in a blanket. He's crying.

I haven't seen him since he left five years ago. I was twelve. I'd had such a crush on him since the age of eight. I'd go to Don Felicio's store, where Gallo worked, and make sure my hand brushed his whenever he handed me the small items I bought. He knew I only came in there to be in his presence; we both did.

One day, after watching a telenovela, I went to the store and told him I wanted to marry somebody just like him. In fact, I said, I wanted to marry *him*. He didn't laugh. He looked at me more kindly than anyone had ever looked at me before and smiled. He put his hand on mine and held it there. I thought I would die of happiness. But then, gently, he said, *I am too old for you, Pequeña. And you're better off without me. I'm not a lucky guy. Someday you'll meet a lucky guy. One lucky enough to have your love and love you back, you'll see.*

No, I don't think so, I said. I could not imagine anyone better than Gallo, who was always helping his parents at the store. Who only spoke about the way he would go to the States one day and make money so his viejos wouldn't have to work so hard and could have a better life. I didn't want to cry, but I felt tears spring up.

Don't cry, he said. But I did, and I couldn't stop. Finally he said, *Okay, okay, listen. If when you're twenty-five years old, you still love me, we will get married.*

That's a long time away, I said.

It is, but I promise. If you still love me then, we'll get married.

I'll still love you, I told him.

Okay, then, he said. He smiled and reached into one of the candy containers on the counter and handed me a ring pop. *Here's your ring.* I opened it immediately and put it on. I smiled at him and went home, eating it along the way. I marveled over the glimmering red of it, glistening like a ruby in the sun. And then when I finished it, after I'd consumed all its sweetness and was entering my house, I knew it would never be. It was the first time I'd had a clear, unshakeable vision: I saw Gallo running in darkness and knew I'd never see him again. I sat in my room, the stickiness from that promise still on my mouth, and cried so much, Mami thought I was possessed.

I was happy he made it out, but sad to see Doña Agostina and Don Felicio distraught that he couldn't return to visit them. Or say this final goodbye to his father, now.

I look at Gallo now, in that room, on that bed, alone and far from his parents.

"Gallo," I call to him.

He looks at me as if trying to remember. "Pequeña?"

I hold out my hand to him. He gets up from the bed and takes it.

Immediately, we're transported into some kind of garden. When I look down, my feet are bare, and I see trails of marigolds on the ground. When I look to my side, Gallo is gone.

Don Felicio, I whisper. And he emerges suddenly, as if from air, and stands next to me. He doesn't speak. I look around for Gallo but I don't see him. But then suddenly, in Don Felicio's arms, a small rooster appears.

Don Felicio looks down at his arms, as if noticing for the first time what he's holding. And when he does, the rooster's feathers and feet are transformed into the arms and feet of a human baby, then it becomes a boy, and then dropping from Don Felicio's arms is Gallo as I knew him.

He embraces his father, and the two men weep and hold each other. Gallo whispers into Don Felicio's ear and Don Felicio hugs him harder. After a long while, Don Felicio makes the sign of the cross on Gallo's forehead. Kisses it. And touches his son's face with trembling hands.

Gallo wipes away his tears. He looks at his father and takes a deep breath, before suddenly vanishing.

But Don Felicio and I remain. And then the old man holds his hand out to me and I take it.

We walk slowly and silently through the empty streets of el barrio, Don Felicio leading the way. I look down at my feet, covered in dust. The place feels eerie, like time has stopped. Like no one else exists. I search for our neighbors but see no one. Don Felicio turns to look at me every so often. I can tell where we are headed. But only when we get closer do I finally see people. Mourners, funneling into his and Doña Agostina's house.

The old man looks back at me, and I see the sadness in his face, and I don't want to follow him anymore. But I know I have to.

We walk among the mourners like the ghosts we are. And we make our way past them, into the living room where people are gathered around a coffin. Don Felicio's coffin. Mami and Tía Consuelo are positioning candles around it, rearranging the surrounding flowers.

Don Felicio leads me to it, and then we are staring at his face. Through the glass covering, we see his face underneath, like an ugly pressed flower being preserved. I look over at his ghost next to me and see how he begins to breathe harder.

I panic.

It's okay, I try to tell him, but my mouth won't say the words and the best I can do is think them over and over again, hoping he understands. But his breathing becomes more labored, as he keeps looking at himself under glass. He lets go of my hand, and both of his hands clasp around his neck. He breathes harder, and the sound of horrific gurgling fills the room. I look around but nobody else can hear it. People are eating the tamales the neighborhood women have prepared. The bread they've baked. They're sipping on coffee and speaking in hushed tones as Don Felicio struggles to say something. Nothing but gurgling and wheezing comes out. His face is desperate but nothing comes out, and I try again and again to calm him, but I can't.

Then comes the blood, like a faucet has been turned on. Gushing through his fingers. Blood and more blood.

I scream, or I think I scream, but nobody hears me.

I don't know what you're trying to tell me! Please stop, please! I tell him, but I can only think the words. His eyes are bulging and focused on something behind me. One of his hands lets go of his neck and he points. I turn and look in the direction of his bloodied finger. And there, in the crowd, are Pulga and Chico.

They are talking quietly to each other. Chico looks sad and scared. Pulga looks worried.

I don't understand any of it. I'm trying to piece together what I'm seeing, but none of it makes sense. For a brief moment, I think Don Felicio is accusing them, but it can't be true.

Don Felicio's gurgles fill my ears, growing louder and louder.

I don't understand!

I look back at Pulga and Chico and that's when they start shaking; their bodies start trembling. And then I watch as both of them reach for their necks, just like Don Felicio. Their eyes get wide and scared and desperate. And blood begins to rush through their fingers.

No! I scream, turning to Don Felicio, but he's holding his own neck, his eyes staring at the ceiling. *I don't want to see this. Stop it, please!*

I try to wake myself up. I try to find the door again, to escape the reality that has invaded my imaginary worlds.

But I can't breathe. And it's difficult to swallow. I reach up and feel my neck. It's wet and warm.

When I look at my fingers, they're bright red with blood.

I shake my head. *No!* I try to yell, but no one hears me. I look to Don Felicio for help. But he just stands there gurgling and wheezing, until finally he looks at me. And finally—his eyes desperate and wild—one word escapes his lips.

Just one word, but it fills my mind.

Corre.

Run.

"Pequeña." Mami's voice reaches me. I am shaking. I am crying. Saliva has collected and filled my mouth. I'm choking.

Mami whispers my name again and I open my eyes to the sound of a baby crying and Mami standing over me dressed in black. Milk trickles from my breasts.

Behind Mami are Tía Consuelo, Pulga, Chico, and Doña Agostina, back from Don Felicio's wake.

"¿Estás bien?" Mami asks. "You don't look okay. You look like you've seen a ghost."

I'm sweating and my skin feels clammy. Mami puts her hand on my forehead and makes a face.

"I think you have a fever," she says.

"I'm fine," I tell her.

She looks worried for a moment but then asks, "Did you change his diaper?" I don't answer. Mami and Tía exchange looks.

The baby cries harder. "Did you feed him?" she asks next.

I don't answer again and then all I hear is Mami's heels clicking hard and fast as she walks away.

I sit on the couch and stare at the telenovela. A man forces his kisses on a woman. I close my eyes, and when I open them again, the news is on. The newscaster tells us of more deaths. Of more bodies. Not people. People don't matter to anyone. Just the bodies.

Tía Consuelo comes over and gives me a kiss on top of my head, smooths my hair. Mami comes back with the crying, angry baby. She hands him to me, nestles him next to my breast. "There are no more of those tiny sample bottles of formula, Pequeña. And he needs to eat," she says.

I shake my head.

"I'm sorry . . . I know this is not what you want, my love." Mami's voice softens. "But we cannot starve this child."

"I won't do it."

"Pequeña!" Mami's voice is sharp and harsh. "I've tried to give you time to adjust to this. But we can't afford to buy formula each week. And if you don't start feeding him, your milk will dry up. You *have* to do this, hija. I'm sorry. I'm so sorry." I know she is. But it doesn't stop her from pulling on my shirt. The baby's mouth is searching, searching, searching.

I close my eyes, shake my head, and begin to cry.

"Muchachos, sálganse." I hear Tía Consuelo command Pulga and Chico to go outside. Mami puts the baby on my breast as she tries to explain to me how to feed him. But I can't listen. I just keep my eyes closed as that baby drains life from me. That baby who is like his father. That baby who is like this neighborhood, this land, like everything around me.

So I let myself think about dying.

I think of how when I was ten, Mami went to a bruja outside of town when she wanted to know about my father cheating. But when the woman saw me she took a chicken egg and cracked it into a glass of water. She stared in at the yolk and then looked up at Mami and said she saw me consumed by a hellish, fiery blaze.

"Look," she told me, gesturing to the glass. "I know you can see things, too. Look closely." And when I did, I saw fiery orange flames flickering in that yolk. And there I was, surrounded by all those flames. I could feel the heat in my lungs, and the fire burning, burning. So hot on my skin. I thought I was burning right there in the woman's kitchen before she took the glass away.

Maybe my destiny was to die in fire, I thought then.

Maybe it's the way Rey will kill me, I think now.

When he realizes how much I detest him, he'll throw gas on me, light a match, and watch me burn.

But the thing is, I want to *live*.

I feel the child taken from my arms, and I cross them across my chest. Tía Consuelo puts a blanket over my shoulders that I wrap around myself tight. And then Mami hands Tía the baby—that baby who never should have been, who had no right to invade my body, just as his father did.

She returns with a cup of hot chocolate.

"No," I tell Mami.

"It will help keep your milk from drying up."

"Stop!" I tell her. The thought of it makes me cringe. That milk is excreting from my body disgusts me. Like I'm some kind of animal. I get up and go to the bedroom.

"Pequeña," Mami calls. But I ignore her and close the door.

The room I share with Mami is small and crowded with the bed, the wardrobe, the dresser and mirror. It smells of mothballs, of Mami and me. It smells of the baby now, too. And of birth. I can detect it even though Mami has washed the sheets and pillows. Even though she's mopped the floor and even wiped the walls after my complaints. But the pungency of my blood, of my insides, of gushing water, lingers. Along with the sour milk that emanates from my shirt and skin. I cannot sleep in this room anymore—not since the baby. Now I sleep in the living room where there is no netting to keep the bugs away and they buzz in my ears and feed on my skin.

I sit on the bed, stare at my image in the inescapable mirror stationed in front of it. My hair, long and dirty, hangs past my shoulders. I stare at my face, unrecognizable to myself.

A knock at the door startles me out of my thoughts.

"Pequeña?" Pulga calls from the door. He opens it slightly and peeks in. "Want to play?"

He holds up a deck of cards and when I don't say anything, he and Chico slowly come in.

They sit on Mami's and my bed, cross-legged. Pulga begins shuffling and the sound fills the room. He deals and I focus on the *flick, flick, flick* of the cards as he pulls them from the deck.

"You okay, Pequeña?" Chico asks.

I pick up my cards and stare at the three of hearts in my hand. I see those little red hearts turn black. I see them oozing and shriveling up into nothing.

"Pequeña?"

"I'll be okay," I tell Chico.

I put the cards down. Those hearts are us. Pulga, Chico, and me.

They look at me.

"Something bad has happened. Something bad is going to happen."

They look at each other, and then back at me. Both of them have the same look on their faces, a look that tries to mask terror.

"We can't be here . . . we can't *stay* here," I say.

What I'm saying shouldn't make sense to them, but I can tell it does. They should be telling me I'm talking nonsense. That I'm being ridiculous. They should be laughing at me, and Pulga should be telling me he doesn't believe in my bruja thinking. But they don't do any of that.

What they do is sit there silently, waiting for me to say more.

"What are we supposed to do?" Pulga whispers.

The image of them holding their necks fills my head.

So I say the only thing I can. "We should run."

Pulga

We should run.

The words fill my mind as the priest throws holy water on Don Felicio's coffin. Neighbors slide it into its vault. Doña Agostina holds her rosary and wails.

Yesterday at his wake, she'd told me to run. Yesterday, Pequeña had told us to run, too. Today, my eyes scan the cemetery, looking for Rey or Nestor, and all I can think about is running.

The crowd disperses.

Another day.

Another death.

Another body.

When we get home, Mamá sinks into the couch, exhausted. My mind sees the red velvet cushions. Blood-red. *So much blood.*

We should run.

"You and Chico go rest," she says, pulling up her legs and lying down without bothering to change out of her black dress. "I'm going to stay here for just a little while. Close and lock the door."

Chico gets up from where he was sitting in the doorway and I do as Mamá says. He heads to our room and I follow. There is a heaviness in the air, pressing down on us. The thud of my own feet sounds terrible. But as I walk past Mamá, she reaches for my arm and grabs it.

"Pulga," she says. The force of her touch and her voice startles me. I look at her tired face and she says, "Te quiero mucho, Pulgita."

"I know, Mamá. I love you, too." But there is something else she wants to say, and doesn't. I can see it on her face. She just nods, lets go of my arm, and closes her eyes.

I stand there for just a moment, wondering if Doña Agostina told her about the dream she had. Or maybe Pequeña said something. Maybe Mamá is starting to believe in brujas and superstitions. Maybe I should, too.

Maybe Mamá will even tell me I should run, because it's the only way. That I have her blessing. That she understands broken promises.

Instead she takes a deep breath, lets it out.

And I go to my room.

Chico has the fan on the highest setting and it whirs loudly.

I close the door, even though it keeps the room hotter.

"Well?" Chico asks as I enter. He is fidgety and restless. The brown stripes on his shirt match his skin perfectly. I stare out the window.

"I don't know," I tell him. I haven't told him what Doña Agostina told me, but the strange things Pequeña said put him on edge. He hasn't been able to sit still since, and even here, he seems to be looking over his shoulder.

"She said something bad was going to happen. *To us,* Pulga. Something bad is going to happen to *us.*"

I don't say anything and try to stay calm.

"Holy shit," Chico whispers, making my heart beat faster. I look out the window, expecting to see Rey standing there with a gun pointed right at us.

There is no one there.

When I turn back to Chico, he is looking at me strangely. "You believe her . . . don't you?"

I think of the book I keep under my mattress—information I've collected over the last few years on how to get to the States. Notes.

Printouts. The train. La Bestia. I think of how my tía in the United States sends money for me every year and Mamá only gives me five or ten dollars before saving the rest for me in a hiding place. I think of how I know that hiding place. How I know that tía's phone number and address. Have memorized both. How I know where to exchange dollars to quetzales and pesos and have already done so with those bills Mamá has given me each time.

Just in case.

But I don't like the terrified look on Chico's face. The one that confirms what we are both afraid to believe.

I shake my head. My heart is racing and it feels hard to breathe, but I tell myself it's just the heat.

"You know what? This baby has Pequeña all messed up," I tell Chico. "That's all. She's not herself. All we have to do is act normal." The lies spill from my mouth. But they taste better than the truth.

He closes his eyes and tears stream down his face.

"Even if Rey thinks we saw something," I continue, "or know something, he'll keep an eye on us. And when he sees we're acting normal, that we haven't told anyone anything, he'll leave us alone."

Chico opens his eyes. They're red and watery and unconvinced. He wipes at them roughly, but tears keep streaming down his face. I sit down next to him on his mattress, put my arm over his shoulders.

"It'll be okay, Chico. I promise."

"But, Pulga . . ."

"It's all going to be okay . . ."

He stares at me for a moment, and I will myself to believe it so he will, too. Maybe I can believe it. Maybe if I believe it, it will be true.

"Come on, you trust me, don't you? I promise you it'll be okay."

After a while he says, "Okay." Guilt washes over me, but I push it away. "If you say so, Pulga, okay."

"All we have to do is act normal, okay?"

He nods again. "Okay."

"We saw nothing, Chico. Just remember that. We went there, we grabbed a soda, and we headed back home. By the time what happened happened, we were far away from there. We were never there, Chico. We saw nothing."

He takes a deep breath. "We saw nothing."

"That's right," I tell him. "We saw nothing." I grab hold of these words so they will force out thoughts of running. Maybe I can put my faith into these words instead. Maybe I can will these words to save us.

The fan whirs and catches our words.

We saw nothing.

We saw nothing.

We saw nothing.

Those words circle around us the day after Don Felicio's funeral. And the day after that. And the day after that. For over a week Chico and I go on as normal. We head to school even though all I do is watch the door, waiting, barely able to tell one day apart from another.

We saw nothing.

We take no detours. We look over our shoulders every five minutes.

We saw nothing.

We repeat those words in our heads so much that we hear them in the thud of our steps on the way home from school. We hear them as we walk past Don Felicio's store—which doesn't even exist anymore, all boarded up the way it is.

We saw nothing.

We repeat them so much that we almost believe them. And we start to think *maybe, maybe* we've escaped. Maybe we'll be okay.

But then one morning we're headed to school. And my breath catches.

I see that car.

Barreling toward us once more.

It grinds to a stop too quickly, spraying dirt and dust on Chico and me. The same car Rey and Nestor drove the other day.

"Get in," Nestor calls to us as we try to wave away the dust from our faces. It gets caught in my lashes and I can taste it. Nestor is alone, but he's positioned the car to block our way.

"No, we're okay. Thanks," I say, grabbing on to Chico's shoulder and starting to walk around the car.

"You think I'm offering you a ride? I said, *get in*." He puts his hand on a gun lying on the passenger seat.

I look at Chico and he looks back at me. His eyes are frantic and I think Chico might run. I can feel my own legs wanting to run, but there's something else in my brain holding me back, not letting me move.

Maybe it's remembering how Nestor picked on everyone as soon as he grew a few inches. Maybe it's the way he looked at Rey years ago when Rey said he should have taken care of me and Chico himself. Maybe it's knowing how eagerly Nestor is trying to prove himself.

I look back to see if anyone will see me and Chico getting in the car. People talk about how Nestor is following in his brother's footsteps, and the same is thought of anyone seen with either of them.

"Go ahead," I say quietly to Chico. I can see the fear threatening to choke him. I can feel it rising in my own throat, like bile. But we both get in.

And that's when I know this isn't going to go away. Rey and

Nestor found out somehow. They know we know it was them at Don Felicio's store. And now they've come for us.

Fate is fate. And this . . . it turns out, has always been our fate.

The thing is, I guess I've always known it would be. And still, I lied to myself.

Even if Mamá thinks I have an artist's heart, even if I try to see the world in color, even if I dare to dream—it doesn't matter when your world keeps turning black.

Pequeña

It's been nine days since that baby slipped from my body. Nine days of hearing him cry and being forced to hold and feed and take care of him while Mami's at work. Nine days of whispered lies to Rey, who forces his way into the house when she's at work and makes me prepare lunch for him. Nine days of him telling me this is what our life will be like—a family, *together, forever*—as he licks his greasy lips and smiles.

They invade everything—my thoughts, my body, my house. I hear the baby cry even when he doesn't. I feel Rey next to me even when he's not.

I stand in the shower wishing I could slip down the drain.

"Let me go to the market for you, Mami. Por favor . . . por favor . . ." I beg on her day off. I hold Mami's hand and put it on my cheek. I beg like a small, desperate child. I beg until she gets tears in her eyes.

"Fine," she says finally, caressing my hair. She stays like that a moment and I can almost hear how her heart cries for me. But in the next breath she's handing me a list of what she needs and she says, "Feed the baby first."

A thousand needles of resentment prick my heart.

"Can't you just give him a bottle, *please*?" I ask.

She lets out a breath. Exasperated. Annoyed. "Pequeña, you really want to put that on your tía?"

Fresh guilt washes over older guilt. Tía Consuelo came over with a canister of formula the day after the funeral and told Mami she would be in charge of buying it for the baby. I nearly wept with relief. But Mami, she didn't want Tía to have more worries on her shoulders. So she made me keep feeding the baby during the day and used the formula only at night, so I could sleep.

"If you just get used to it, there won't be any need for your tía to buy formula," Mami says. "And I know she means well, but what if she can't afford to help after a few months? We don't have money just lying around and then you won't have any milk and . . . it's tough already with the expense of diapers . . ."

I want to tell her I have money. That in my dresser, I have the bills Rey peels off a roll each time he visits. That even this he forces on me, even though I refused at first because it felt like I was being bought. But he insists, *because I'm not like most men, Pequeña. I'm going to support this baby.* So I accept.

But I can't give the money to Mami without explaining.

And I can't explain.

"Here." Mami hands me the baby. I take him in my arms and put him on my breast. I close my eyes as he latches on because I can't look at him. When I do, I see he needs to be loved. And I don't think I can love this baby. So he will grow up unloved—become just like Rey. And that fills me with shame. And fear.

I fill my mind instead with how I *will* get away from here—with Rey's money. People will talk when I go. What a terrible girl I am. What a terrible mother. What a terrible daughter. But I don't care. Because at night, when I pray for this to end—for my milk to dry and for the baby to somehow disappear and for Rey to die—nobody hears me. So let everyone talk. I won't hear them, either.

I'll be too far away.

The baby's lips release my breast and I pull him away, hand him to Mami.

"Don't be gone too long!" she yells as I rush out the door. "You hear me, Pequeña . . . ?" But I'm already running.

Fast. Then faster. And her words get lost in the distance and the wind.

I don't hear her.

I don't hear anyone but myself.

Run, I say, *run away from here.*

Run as fast as you can.

Pulga

Nestor drives fast and without any care, weaving in and out of traffic, cutting off motor scooters and running them off the road. We hit countless potholes in the road, feeling like our bones and teeth will crack with every violent dip. My mind flashes with white. I picture my skeleton under my flesh, my skull bleached by the sun years from now if I'm ever found.

"Where are we going?" I ask him. Nestor doesn't answer and instead turns up the music in the car.

Where we end up is a little abandoned building not very far from our school.

I can see some of our classmates in the distance in their pressed white shirts and checkered blue pants or skirts as they pass through the gated entry. Some are laughing.

Nestor gets out of the car. I'm frozen in my seat. Chico is pale.

"Come on," Nestor says, motioning toward a large wooden door, the gun casually in his hand.

Chico and I get out of the car and follow him.

The door hangs slightly off center so it doesn't close all the way. My eyes immediately fall to a lone tiny yellow flower that has bloomed in the crack of the building's wall. A weed really. But bright and unreal and for a fraction of a second, I marvel that it exists, even as my mind fills with exactly how I will die.

I have been close to death before, bodies and blood and gurgling last breaths. But this time, it feels like it is on the other side of the door, unsettlingly quiet. Waiting. Ready.

Nestor tells us to go through the door. Chico begins to cry and I smell urine. When I look at him, I see the dark, wet patch on the front of his pants. Nestor laughs.

"Let's go," he says, and bangs the door open. Chico and I enter slowly, trying to adjust to the darkness.

I wait for the round of bullets. I wonder if I will hear them before I feel them.

But we enter and there is only silence. A room black and dank, a room that smells of blood, a mixture of sweet and sour. A room that smells of the odor of humans keenly aware they are about to die.

Or maybe it's me who smells like that.

Then, suddenly, a voice. "¿Qué pasa, muchachos?" Rey asks us what's up before I see him. But then he becomes visible, sitting on a chair in the corner, his feet up on a table in front of him, smoking a cigarette. Two other guys I don't know or recognize are sitting on either side of him. One of them wears a large gold ring in his nose.

Nestor nudges us toward the table. Rey takes a long drag as we make our way over. He lets it out as we stand in front of him.

"Look at this one," one of the guys next to Rey says. "He fucking pissed himself."

Rey looks at Chico, from head to toe. Then he turns to me. "You remember me, don't you?"

I don't know whether to say yes or no. But the way he stares, the only choice seems to be to tell him the truth. He waits, unnervingly patient. And I nod.

He smiles and takes another drag. "It's been a while since that day at the school, hasn't it?"

Again I nod. He puts out his cigarette on the tabletop and then says very slowly, "But not so long since that day in the old man's store . . ." He smiles, his eyes crinkle.

I freeze. He waits.

I can't swallow. It feels like a rubber ball is blocking my throat. I try and try to swallow, but I've completely forgotten how, my body won't work. It makes it impossible to breathe. Panic sets in and I feel like I am suffocating, right there in front of Rey, as he stares at me with that terrible smile on his face.

The sound of Chico whimpering louder snaps me out of it.

"No, not so long . . ." I say finally.

"Ah, good!" he says with a bigger smile on his face now. "I didn't *think* you'd try to lie to me, but, pues, you never know." He studies my face. "What? Are you surprised I know? That I didn't go after you right away?"

I watch as his eyes light up, like he's enjoying this.

"If I'd killed the old man that day *and* the two of you, I'd get too much heat. Authorities that want to be paid off would come sniffing around. That's something a brainless thug would do. But not me. I'm careful. Thoughtful. I'm *building* something here. And I need live, young bodies for that."

He rubs his chin and then points his finger at me. "See, I *knew* I was right about you. What impresses me even more than your ability to stay quiet is that I know you and your mamá helped the old man's wife." He studies my reaction and I keep my face as expressionless as possible. "You liked him . . ." He waits. A flash of Don Felicio standing at the counter of his store, in the midday heat, looking into the distance and smiling when he saw us coming, fills my mind. I wipe it away and stiffly nod again. "And *still*, you knew to stay quiet. You'd be surprised how many guys still try to do the right thing. Like that's gotten anyone around here anywhere but the grave." Rey raises his eyebrows and shakes his head.

"Well, enough of that." He removes his feet from the table and sits up. "Why I brought you here is because you've proven you can be of use to me. What you're going to do is be my little gophers for a while."

It is at this moment that Chico does the worst thing he can do, even worse than crying and pissing himself. He vomits.

"Fuck!" the other guy next to Rey yells, as he pushes his chair back and looks at the vomit that has splattered his feet. "Este repisado, man!" He flings the insult at Chico. "What he deserves are some vergasos!" The guy's fists ball up like he's ready to deliver the pummeling he thinks Chico deserves.

Stand firm! I want to tell Chico. *Be strong!* But Chico just wipes his mouth and shrinks back. Rey fixes his eyes on him. He twists his mouth back and forth, as if weighing the pros and cons of Chico.

Then he looks at me again. "What we have here," he says aloud, "is the brains, and the muscle. You," he says, pointing to me again, "you have street smarts I could use. And you," he says, pointing to Chico, "do anything he tells you." Rey keeps sizing us up. "Would he do anything you tell him?" he asks me.

I nod. "Of course. We're brothers. He'll do whatever I tell him, anything." I know Rey needs to see the use for Chico to keep him around. I don't exactly know what not keeping him around would mean, but I can guess.

Rey's eyes light up. "Let's see. Let's have him . . . beat the shit out of you." Nestor and the other guys start laughing. "Can you do that, gordo?" Rey says, looking at Chico. "Can you prove you're the muscle and you'll do *anything* this one tells you?"

Chico won't look up. He stares at the floor and I can see snot and tears dripping from his face.

"I don't have all day," Rey says.

I turn to Chico. "Come on. Just a few punches. You know I can take it, come on." But he won't move. It's like he can't hear me.

"Chico," I say again. *"Fight me."* But he's solid as a statue and doesn't move. Out of all the times I need him to listen to me, he chooses the most important time, when both his and my lives depend on it, to do this. The panic shooting through my body, through my veins, doubles, like some kind of shot of adrenaline, as I realize if we don't perform for Rey, he *will* get rid of us. One way or another.

"Fuck, Chico, I said fight!" I yell at him. I plow into him. "Come on!" My voice cracks and the guys around Rey laugh harder, but Rey doesn't laugh. He looks at Chico and me like he's reassessing whether we can really be of any use to him.

"Damn it, Chico!" I yell. My heart is beating harder and I'm sweating as I start punching him. "Fight back! I said fight back, you fucking puerco!" I slam into him with my whole body.

When I call him a pig like that—like he's nothing more than a filthy animal, a fat boar—he looks at me with such hurt on his face. And I realize it's only these kinds of words, hurtful and terrible, that can pierce the fog of fear he's in. So I call him a fucking pig again, even though I feel something in me break when he looks back at me again, eyes full of betrayal, like he can't believe I'm saying what I'm saying. "That's right," I say, "let's go." I reach up and slap him across the face. He pushes my hand away roughly. I do it again and again.

"Stop," he says through clenched teeth.

"Come on," I say, circling him.

I know him best. I know every insecurity he has. I know how he feels about his weight. I know the sacred love he has for his slain mother. I know about her past and how she sold her body to survive and provide for her and Chico on the streets when he was little, and occasionally when he was not. And because I love him, and because I need to hurt him so he will hurt me, I use it all. All of it. I taunt him and taunt him, until I see the anger building behind the hurt in his eyes. Until finally, he lets it all out.

Chico's fists are harder than I expected. And he's stronger than I or anyone would have guessed. I don't even know what I'm saying anymore, as I yell and try to unleash as much rage inside him as I can. All I hear is his screeching, like a pig being slaughtered, as his fists rain down on me along with his tears.

And even though it hurts, I am glad for it. I am glad that he responds to each of my words with another blow, to my gut, to my chest, to my face, to my head. I'm glad for the thunderous pain, for the metallic taste in my mouth. I'm glad for the blurriness of my eyesight and the sense of falling into a deep black hole, the rest of the world getting farther and farther away, the sound of Rey and Nestor and Chico and those other two guys fading with the dim light in that room.

"That's it, Chico, just like that . . ." I whisper. "Good job." He is sitting on my chest. He is wrapping his hands around my neck. And even like this, even in his anger, I see a tenderness in Chico that makes me want to cry every single time. "Good job . . ." I say. His gaze meets mine for just a second, but that's all it takes. I smile and suddenly he stops. He gets off me. And I lie there staring at the ceiling, gasping for breath.

Laughter and clapping fills the room. "Wow!" Rey yells. A long, sharp whistle sounds and makes my head feel like it might crack in half. "That was spectacular!" More whistling. Rey comes and stands over me. "Yes, yes, you two will do just fine," he says. My vision blurs as he keeps splitting in two and merging back together. "Get up," he says, grabbing on to my arm and pulling me up. "I'll see you two tomorrow. Nestor will pick you up, same as today. Got some things lined up for you."

"We won't say anything, please . . . please . . ." I say, hoping he will understand what I don't have the nerve to say aloud. *Please don't pull us into this. Please let us go.*

Rey knows exactly what I mean. And he looks at me, shakes his head.

"I want you to know a couple of things. These two." He looks over at the guys who have been next to him this whole time. "They've watched you *sleep*. They've watched *everything* you do. That little fire where you burned your clothes, smart. The little mattress where you sleep like a fucking stray dog," he says to Chico, "I know all about it. So you boys have two choices: be my friend or be my enemy. I think you know which one will work out better for you, right?"

One of the guys smiles, then whistles a soft little tune. The same whistle we heard outside our window that night.

And I know it's useless. I know we really only have one choice.

I nod.

Rey smiles. "Good! I have big plans. I am building something special. And I need my army." His eyes are gleaming. "Welcome, my little soldiers." Then he motions to Nestor, who leads us out and takes us home, the radio blaring the whole way.

The ride doesn't feel real and each pothole splits my head more and more. But before I know it, I'm getting out of the car in front of our house. The sun blinds me. I hear Nestor driving away, the music receding with the car. I smell the dust, mixing with the musky smell of car freshener still in my nose. All of it makes me queasy.

Chico is next to me, holding me up as I sway back and forth in the heat. Mamá is supposed to be at work, waitressing at one of the restaurants of Amatique—the nearest resort. But even so I make sure the patio is empty of her motor scooter before we go inside.

I wash my face carefully, rinse my mouth, checking for any loose teeth. Chico runs to the store and gets some ice. It feels like he's gone forever. It feels like he's gone only a second; I blink and he's suddenly back, standing over me on the burning-hot couch, baggies of half-melted ice in a towel. I put it on my face, hoping the swelling and bruising won't be too bad.

Neither of us says a thing.

There are no words.

Even if there were, I don't even know if we'd need them.

We both knew this would happen one day. Living on this land is like building a future on quicksand. You know you'll go down. You know it will swallow you up. You're just not sure how or when.

Now we know for sure.

No, there are no words, only feeling. And I feel something sharp in my chest. I keep trying to breathe through it, hoping the pain there will shift and smooth out. I wonder if one of my ribs is broken and poking my heart. But I don't think that's it.

The fight with Chico, the words that came out of my mouth and cut right to the core of him slashed through the tissue and fibers of my heart as well. Everything here comes at a price.

I've tried to fight against my artist's heart, to make it steel instead. But I can't. The realization brings a new wave of panic. All I can do is let my heart tear and rip. Tear and rip. My mind flashes with the red, blue, pink—the diagram of a heart we drew in class earlier this year, the striated muscle and the tissue. And then I remember something my teacher told me about torn-up tissue. How it becomes scar tissue and how that scar tissue can affect the sense of feeling.

Maybe that's what I need—to wrap my heart, myself in scar tissue. I think of the blood coagulating, the tissue fusing together. I think of a thick scar forming over that tear. Over and over again. Over and over again. Until any pain is just a small, fleeting thing.

Maybe that way it won't shatter. Maybe that way it won't rot.

I think of Rey's heart, black and deteriorated.

I think of Mamá's heart, how it will ooze with bright red pain.

I feel myself sinking deeper into the couch, falling into the black, so I focus on pink and blue. The soft pink of heart valves, the deep pulsing blue of veins.

Something, anything to keep me from total darkness.

Pequeña

At the market, I hear it over and over again. "¡Felicidades! ¡Felicidades, Pequeña!" From the vendor, from neighbors, from Mami's friends. They all know I've had the baby, they are all asking about the baby, they are all so happy for me and the baby.

I want to laugh and never stop. I want tears to fall from my eyes like water breaking through a dam and sweep all of them away in a gushing current. I want to whisper my horrible nighttime prayers into their ears, ask them if they know girls pray such things, see what they say. Will they have the nerve to congratulate me then?

But I know if I utter one word of it, I'll never be able to stop. And I'll be whispering those prayers forever.

So instead I say gracias and continue on my way to the drugstore.

Leticia greets me as I come up to the glass counter of the pharmacy where she works. "Hey, Pequeña. What are you doing here?"

She gets up from the small stool where she was sitting, fanning herself, and adjusts her jeans. She shuffles over to me, her sandals scraping the dusty floor, and offers me a smile.

Leticia was once a beauty. She wore electric-blue eye shadow that glimmered even indoors. And she lined her eyes perfectly in thick black eyeliner. She reminded me of a telenovela actress, and when I was a little girl and came here with my mother, I always left in awe of Leticia's perfect eyes and the small black beauty mark just above her lips on the left side of her mouth. I was jealous of how her boyfriend looked at it, her lips, all of her. He was always there, leaning at the end of the counter, waiting for her to be done with a customer so he could have her all to himself again. It was like he couldn't stand not seeing her, and because he was handsomer than even Gallo, I'd once thought her the luckiest girl in the world.

"Just picking up some things," I tell her. She nods and waves the fan in front of her. Leticia still does her eyes in the same electric blue, lines them in the same black. She still has the beauty mark positioned in the exact same place.

But she is not the girl she was ten years ago.

Ten years ago, Leticia was sixteen. I know her story the way we all know each other's stories around here. Her father left for the States years ago and never came back. Her mother, like my mother, raised Leticia by herself and with the friendship and support of other women. Leticia had a baby when she was my age, too, a little girl she named California. And her handsome boyfriend left for the States, promising her the world. For years, all Leticia would talk about to anyone who would listen was how she and her baby girl would meet him there one day soon, and they would live in a pretty little house there someday, and she was going to be una americana.

Her boyfriend never came back.

California is nine years old now, still waiting to live in a pretty little house that doesn't exist for her. Her name a reminder of broken dreams, the place Leticia never reached. Sometimes I hear Leticia calling down the street, *California, come here. California, wait for me.* And it always sounds like a sad wish. And now Leticia looks like so many of the girls around here who became wives and mothers by pretty lies or ugly force. Old beyond their age. Tired. A little dead.

I stare at her, wondering how long before I look like that, too. She stares back.

"You need something for the baby? How is he? Congratulations." This is what she says, but her eyes look at me with pity.

"Leticia . . . I need your help."

"Of course, my love, what is it?"

"I need something that will . . . dry up my milk." She gives me a look, but I make myself continue. "And I need some birth control pills."

She puts the fan down, looks at the wall of pills and medicine behind her. She pulls a few packages.

"I don't have anything especially made to stop the production of milk," she says. "But these might help. Of course, it's not scientifically proven or anything." She rolls her eyes and pushes them my way. "And here is a pack of contraceptive pills." She leans on the counter, begins giving me directions. But all I can concentrate on are the people coming in.

What if Rey walks in? Or one of the guys he has who keep track of whomever Rey wants to keep track of? Or one of Mami's friends? Or what if Tía Consuelo gets off work and stops by here and sees me?

I nod at whatever Leticia says, keeping tabs on those around us. Then she looks at me again. "But you know, no guarantees with these, either."

"I know."

I can feel her gaze on me, but I don't look up. She reaches again to the wall of pills behind her, grabs another package, and sets it down on the counter in front of me. A guy walks in and seems to look straight at me. I don't recognize him as one of Rey's guys, but I don't know all of them. I look away as he heads down an aisle.

"If something should happen . . . if you think you might have gotten pregnant, you can take this pill," Leticia whispers. "But it has to be taken right away, within the first few days after having unprotected sex."

My hand shakes as I reach for it and read the information. I think of how I wish I'd known about this ten months ago. How I wish I'd known about all of this then. I think of how I wish I'd never admired beauty, and how I wish I had never wanted a guy to look at me like Leticia's boyfriend looked at her.

"Do you need anything else?" she asks gently.

I'm about to shake my head, but then I see the razors under the glass counter. "Those," I tell her. "And that." I point to the small switchblade knife next to the razors.

She gives me another look, but retrieves both from under the counter, throws the items in a little blue plastic bag.

"And I need you to do me a favor," I tell her as she adds up the price of those items on the pad in front of her.

"What is it?"

"I need you to give me all this stuff on credit. Mami will pay for it, you know she will. But, she can't know I bought these items. Not yet. I need you to charge her for it next month." I could pay with the money Rey gave me. I could. But I can't. Even if it means Mami will hate me. Because I need that money for later.

"Ay, Pequeña . . ." she says, shaking her head and looking at me with pity. "You *know* we don't do store credit."

"I know, Leticia, but I can't pay for this stuff, so maybe this once . . ."

"Dios, Pequeña . . . how much trouble are you in?" Her eyes are sympathetic, but not surprised. I shake my head. "Talk to your mami," she says. "She understands these things. She'll help you."

"No, I can't . . . I can't tell anyone," I say. "Something bad will happen."

Leticia's face flickers with fear. Emotions I've been keeping in check start to come up. But there's no room for emotion now. I won't start weeping here, in front of Leticia. I won't let the tears fall, fill up this store, be drowned in their pool. I look at her and imagine stripping away all my emotions. Like the reeds of a sugarcane. But then what does that leave except the sugary sweet of my pulsing heart?

My hand on the counter trembles.

Leticia looks at the way it shakes. It almost looks as if it has a mind of its own, like it's not even a part of my body. I try to control it but I can't. I stare at the way it flutters and flutters on that countertop, like a dark, frenzied moth.

I watch as it transforms right before my eyes.

Its ginormous wings open and close, hypnotizing me. It grows antennae and large black eyes, fixes its gaze on me. From somewhere in those eyes, from inside its delicate mottled body, I hear a strange, high-pitched sound.

Cuidado.

I look at Leticia, wondering if she, too, hears the moth's warning, telling me to be careful. If she sees what I see. If that is why she suddenly puts her hand over that omen of death, presses down on its wings, holds it very, very still and tells me to be calm.

"Tranquila," she says. "Tranquila. I'll do it. I'll tell your mami, next month." Now she is looking at me. "Is there anything else you want me to tell her on that day? Another message?"

I close my eyes and picture Mami coming into the store sometime next month. I see her, coming in with that baby. Her face a little more dead. And tired. I see her asking Leticia for a canister of baby formula. I see Leticia charging her for it, and then, gently, telling her about these things I purchased a month earlier and kept secret. I see Mami's face, asking Leticia, *What else? What else did she say? Anything? Tell me.*

"Tell her . . . I'm sorry, to please forgive me. That I love her. Very much. And that I will see her again one day."

Leticia nods. "I'll tell her, Pequeña," she says. "But mira, look at me." Her hand is still on mine, and I stare into her beautiful, tired eyes. "Que te vaya bien, amigita." And the tenderness with which she wishes me well, the way she looks at me when she does—like she's speaking to my soul—both breaks me and gives me strength. I look at her and nod. She lifts her hand in goodbye, and I see my hand is my own again.

As I grab my bag and turn to leave, I wonder how many girls before me have come to Leticia asking for the same items. I wonder if it's coincidence that the razors and switchblades are in the same area of the pharmacy as the birth control and morning-after pills.

At night, I go to sleep thinking of ways to be deadly. How to cover my body in razors. I imagine them covering my body like scales. I imagine anyone who touches me being cut and sliced and pierced.

A warning.

Nobody come near me.

Pulga

When your mamá screams, and you wake up to her face looming over you, you see flashes of yellow and orange.

"¡Mi hijo! Dios, Pulga, what happened to you?" she says. She kneels down next to me on the couch where I fell asleep. Her eyes are instantly filled with tears. And panic. "What happened? What happened?" she demands. I have to stop and think.

Rey.

The warehouse.

The fight with Chico.

"Just a fight," I say quietly. It's evening. Mamá is home from work.

"With who?!"

"Some guys at school . . ." Chico stands meekly in the doorway between the kitchen and the living room.

"¿Pero quién?" she demands. "Who did this to you?"

I shake my head. "Don't worry."

"Don't worry? You come home looking like this and you think I'm not going to worry?"

She spots Chico. "Tell me."

"Es que some guys were talking about mi mamita again," Chico says softly. "Pulga jumped in and they . . ." His voice trails off as he shakes his head and starts crying.

"Again?" Mamá asks, and I can hear the doubt in her voice. She turns to me and searches my face for the truth.

I keep my gaze steady. "Yes," I tell her.

"What are their names? I should speak to the principal."

"No, Mamá. Just leave it alone. It's done," I say. If she starts digging into our story, if she pokes the hole of the anthill and disturbs it, everything will cave in on us.

She stares at me.

"It was just a stupid fight, Mamá. Please, just let me sleep a little longer," I tell her. I smile to show her it's no big deal, but Mamá gets very quiet. She sits on the edge of the couch and puts her soft hand on my head. It makes me wince, but also feels good.

"No more fighting," she whispers.

"Okay," I tell her. "I promise."

I fall asleep again. And when I open my eyes, it is dark. The front door is closed with the wooden plank set across it. For the first time in a long time, I'm not in the same room as Chico. A fan whirs and I see Mamá has moved the fan from her room into the living room and positioned it my way. My body feels like I've been run over by a truck.

It makes me think of the time I saw a boy riding on the back of a big truck filled with watermelons. Mamá and I rode behind him on her scooter; I was only about eight years old. He was perched on top like a bird, when the truck hit a pothole and he tumbled down, falling from that great height onto the street. Mamá had been driving far enough behind to bring her motor scooter to a stop.

"Stay here," she said as she and others got off their bikes and ran to help the boy, someone having to signal to the driver to *stop! Stop!* But I didn't stay there. I was scared and wanted to be with my mother, so I followed her and I saw him.

With the blood around his head and the way his arms were splayed out and his eyes showing only the whites, it reminded me of the crucifixion of Jesus. Except one of the boy's legs was twisted in a weird way.

A few watermelons had fallen down, too, green and white rinds split open, revealing the fleshy insides. I remember red and pink and scarlet splattered all around him on that dirty street.

Anytime I sink my teeth into a slice of watermelon, I think of him. The aftertaste of iron lingers, no matter how sweet the fruit—as if I were eating the watermelon off the street laced with blood from that day. As if the sweetness that drips from my lips is his blood.

I don't remember where we were going, but I remember we never got there because I cried so much that Mamá had to take me back home. I thought about that boy all day and all night. I dreamed about him. And I asked Mamá if she thought he survived.

She said, *Yes, hijo. He survived.*

But I don't think he did. I guess sometimes lying to those we love is the only way to keep them from falling apart.

I get up, ignoring the soreness in my body. I unplug the fan and quietly take it to Mamá's room. Her door is open and I see her asleep on her bed. I plug in the fan, turn it on, and head to my room.

Before I'm even to the door, I can hear Chico whimpering, dreaming of his mamita maybe. Or Don Felicio. Or the tombs in the cemetery. Or Rey. Or our fight.

I go to Chico and try to pull him from sleep as gently as I can. Still, he jumps and whimpers.

"It's just me," I tell him. "It's Pulga."

"What's the matter? Are they here?"

"No, you were having a bad dream."

I hear him take deep breaths, try to calm himself. I creep to the window, move the curtains just slightly, searching for any figures. Searching for Rey. Nothing. But when I get back to Chico, now fully awake, I speak in barely a whisper, just in case someone is out there listening. "We have to go. Pequeña's right. Something bad is going to happen. If we don't leave, something very bad is going to happen."

I hear Chico take another deep breath. He knows it's time for the plans we've been making long before this moment. It's time for all that information we gathered outside Don Felicio's store. For the times we sat quiet in the kitchen as another mother from the barrio passed by our patio and stopped to lament to Mamá about the departure of another son they'd never see again.

We listened.

We outlined how they first took a bus to the capital, then more buses to the border of Mexico before crossing the Suchiate River. We stored that information, waiting for the day we'd need it. For the day we'd have to do the same.

"We *have* to go," I whisper.

"I know . . ." Chico says.

That's all we say. I climb into my bed. Tomorrow we will figure out when. Tonight we will just sit with the decision.

I fall back into darkness, thinking of watermelons and blood and me and Chico fighting like two dogs, Rey and his guys looking on like gamblers who've placed bets on us.

But they're not going to win.

Pequeña

A week after my visit to Leticia, Rey makes me and the baby get in the car with him.

"We are going for a ride today. As a family. I have a surprise for you," he says.

"No, Rey . . . please. We haven't told my mother yet and . . ."

But it's as if he doesn't hear me. He walks over to the bassinet and picks up the baby, carelessly holding him in one arm as he grabs me with the other. His fingers dig into my skin, and he steers me toward his car conspicuously parked in front of our house.

He shoves me in the passenger seat, slams the door after me. He gets in the driver's seat. My heart is a quivering, exploding thing in my chest.

"Rey . . ."

"Shut up," he says as he turns the key, the baby still in his grip. I stare at how his little foot dangles, the urge to reach for him, to save him from Rey, overwhelming. "Stop worrying so much about your mami. You don't belong to her anymore, don't you know that? You belong to me." He takes my hand, pulls it toward him quickly, kisses my fingers and smiles. He's about to hand me the baby when the smile is replaced by a funny look on his face. "God, Pequeña, what's happened to you?" His eyes take in my T-shirt, my bleach-stained shorts and flip-flops. "No, this isn't right. Go inside and put on a pretty dress. Fix yourself up."

My skin crawls, but I'm too afraid not to listen to him. So I nod, open the car door, and then I stop. My body won't move as I think of leaving that baby here, alone, with him. I won't reach for him. But part of me wants to. And I stay there too long.

"Go!" Rey yells. The baby cries. I worry about Rey getting angry, so I go, head toward the front door of my house.

When I turn my back on the monster, I rise into the sky and see a million possibilities.

I see myself walking, as he opens the car door, as he raises a gun and aims it right at my back.

I see him pulling the trigger and the bullet, hot and whizzing, released from the barrel.

I see it sink into my back, my body bending into an arch before I fall to the ground and that bullet explodes inside me.

I see him come up next to me, toss the baby on top of my body.

I see Mami running up to the house, finding both of us that way. I hear her screams and sobs and see how she falls on top of us both.

"Hey!" Rey yells.

And I think maybe he wants to see my face as I watch the bullet headed toward me.

"Pequeña!"

I turn slowly, hoping he doesn't see the tears in my eyes. He's halfway out of the car, that baby still dangling in one arm. No gun pointed at me. "Don't be long, okay?" he says.

I nod.

If he doesn't kill me, maybe he'll drive away with that baby. And part of my terrible prayers will have been answered, in the most terrible way. And it will be God's punishment for asking for something so terrible.

Or maybe he will drive me and the baby out to some deserted place where he will kill us both. And decide there is another girl more deserving of him.

I walk up through the front patio and into the house. I do as he says.

I choose a dress with red flowers, so if Mami finds me dead, the red flowers will disguise my blood. I put it on, smooth my hair, put on lip gloss. I shove my feet into black flats.

Because God help me, I suddenly hope he *is* in love with me. Maybe then, he won't kill me. Because I realize when death feels imminent, when it feels certain, all I want is to live. I will do anything to live.

I think of leaving Mami a note, but can't find paper or pen and don't even know what I would write. So I *hurry, hurry,* because I don't want him to get mad.

But before I open the door, I watch him for a second through the window. Holding that baby. Checking his phone.

And for a moment, I think of taking the money and running out the back door, running as far as the money will take me. I could run *right now*. I could leave them both behind right now.

But as much as I can't love that baby, I can't leave him in Rey's arms like that. And as much as I want to run right now, I know I won't get far without a plan; he'll easily find me within an hour.

So I open the door and go back outside.

He looks at me and smiles.

And I promise that if I make it out of this alive, I will find the nerve to leave. On Mami's next day off, she will stay here with the baby. I will ask to go to the market.

And I'll never come back.

Pulga

"Hey, pay attention, pendejo!" Nestor yells. He's holding his gun. "You load the magazine like this, you see?" A harsh click makes me jump. "Then you cock it like this." The sound of rippling metal grooves rings in my ears. "And then it's ready to use. You remember, right?"

My knees are weak and my hand trembles when Nestor puts an identical weapon in my hands.

"Hey, man, toughen up. No seas gallina," he says when he notices. He makes a chicken sound and laughs, but nudges me like we're friends. Just like that. We're supposed to be family now. Toro, the guy with the ring through his nose, who whistled outside our window that night, looks on and laughs, too.

For three days now, Nestor has picked up Chico and me on our way to school and brought us to the same warehouse. Yesterday, he tossed breakfast sandwiches our way and took us somewhere to shoot, where he whooped and hollered when we started getting the hang of it. Today, he arms me as we leave. Chico looks terrified.

"You're going to take this to this address." He hands Chico a backpack and shoves an address in my hand. "And you collect the money. Don't come back without it, understand?"

I'm too afraid to even look in the backpack. I don't ask what's in there. I don't want to know. And even though each morning I wake up sweating fear, today, with this gun in my pants, I feel like my body won't work. Like my skeleton has crumbled within me.

"You think these guys won't pay up?" I ask Nestor.

He twists his lips. "I mean . . . we've had small problems with them in the past. But Rey got real tough on them, so I don't *think* they'll give you trouble. But." He shrugs. "Just make sure you get the money. You want to prove yourself to Rey, right? Stay on his good side."

"Yeah . . . of course," I say as my heart races.

"Good." He tosses me the keys to one of Rey's motor scooters we use to get around now. "¡A trabajar, muchachos!" he yells.

And Chico and I listen.

We get to work.

We zoom and zip past cars. Weave in and out of traffic.

Our helmets are dark and hot, but Rey insists on helmets. Not because of safety, but for anonymity. It's the only reason I'm not terrified of someone seeing us and reporting back to Mamá. And because at the warehouse we change out of our school uniforms and into street clothes.

We ride these streets now, Chico and me, as Rey's guys. Just like that.

If we refuse, if we tell anyone, if we don't act grateful, that click and rippling sound will wake me in my room one night.

Chico won't last. I can tell already. He jumps at every sound in the house, at a motorcycle that backfires. He doesn't eat. I'll last longer, I know I can. But I don't know how long. *We have to go. We have to* go. The thought screams at me every time we get in Nestor's car. Every time I look at Mamá, waiting for the moment she demands to know why we haven't been in school for the past week. But every time I think of leaving, of getting the bus ticket out of here, of taking that first step, I can't.

I think Mamá has noticed something's off. *Act normal,* I tell

Chico. *Act normal*, I tell myself. But I don't know how much time we have before she finds out just how wrong things are.

I pass through the market. I think of the two guys on a motorcycle who killed Chico's mamita.

I think of us becoming them one day and I zoom faster, leaving the memory and the thought far behind. I look at the address again. It's a store on the other side of town, boarded up just like Don Felicio's.

I park the motor scooter, and Chico and I make our way slowly to a back door.

"Stop!" A guy we hadn't noticed steps out from the cover of lush trees behind the store. He has some kind of automatic weapon pointed at us. "Put your hands up."

We immediately do as he says.

He's tall and scrawny, the weapon practically bigger than him. His face doesn't look much older than mine. "You Rey's guys?"

I nod. "Yeah, hermano . . . sorry, yes, look." I gesture toward the backpack strapped on Chico.

The guy comes closer to us. He eyes my waistband, easily making out the outline of the gun Nestor made me take. "Don't even think about using that, *hermano*," he says. "Keep your hands up, and come on." He points to the back door and makes us walk in front of him.

Inside, some guy sits at a folding table counting money.

"Rey's guys are here," the guy with the gun tells the guy at the table.

He looks up from the bills on the table. When he lays eyes on us he laughs. "Are you serious?" Chico and I stare at each other. "You two are fucking babies." He shakes his head and laughs harder.

"Shit, Rey's really testing me . . ." he says to the guy with the gun. They stare at each other, and you can practically hear the whole conversation shared in those looks.

We could take them out. Keep this shit without paying.

I know where to get rid of the bodies.

It'd be so easy.

But Rey . . . he's getting bigger.

Yeah . . .

Better to keep him on our side.

Okay.

Get the backpack off that gordito's back.

Got it.

The guy with the gun takes the backpack off Chico and heads to a back room with it. The guy at the table stares at me until the guy opens the door again, gives him a thumbs-up, and hands him the empty backpack.

"Okay . . . looks like we're good," he says. But he doesn't move. He gives me the unzipped, empty backpack.

I can feel Chico's fear. The way every part of him wants to run. *Act normal, act normal.*

"Is that what I should tell Rey?" I ask the guy, looking at the empty backpack. I try to keep my voice steady, but I hear the way it strains, the way it quivers. "That you said we're good?" The guy sucks his teeth and chuckles. He takes the backpack from me and throws rolled-up bills in there before tossing it back at me.

"Get the hell out of here," he says. The guy with the gun comes up from behind and nudges us forward.

Chico trembles as he puts the backpack on.

I nearly crash us as I swerve the motor scooter out of there, as fast as possible.

We have to get out of here, I think as a bus honks, long and loud.

We have to get out of here, as we pass through the market again.

As we head back to the warehouse.

As Nestor claps at our arrival and Toro fills the place with an earsplitting whistle.

"Rey's gonna be impressed," Nestor says.

We have to get out of here.

As we make another run.

As we stop by the bus station.

As I take out the money I took from Mamá's secret hiding spot and hand it to the girl at the window, my hands shaking so bad I can hardly count out the bills for the tickets.

We have to get out of here.

Pequeña

He gets on the highway headed out of town, toward Honduras. And I look out those smoked windows and realize I don't have to worry about anyone seeing me with Rey. I could bang on those windows, screaming for help, and nobody would see me.

When we get to the border crossing, my heart races. And when the guy there just waves his truck through, I feel like my heart will slip out of my mouth.

"You see," he says. "The connections I've made, Pequeña? People are learning to treat me right."

"Yes, of course. You deserve to be treated right." I stare out the window, the baby now in my arms.

Rey pulls off the road sharply and I think this is it. This is where I will die.

We dip and ride through back roads and I know, I know nobody will ever find my body here.

"I want to show you a very meaningful place to me, Pequeña."

We go down a few more roads, until finally, I can see sand and water ahead.

Maybe he will drown me.

"Come on," he says, parking and getting out of the car. My legs feel weak, but I follow. "This is where I decided I wasn't going to be a nobody, Pequeña. I came out here one night, and I decided I would take things into my own hands. Be in charge of my own destiny. Take what I wanted and answer to no one. And get rid of anyone who stood in my way."

He takes my hand in his. "Dios, look at how you're shaking. I wanted it to be a surprise, but maybe you already know." He reaches into his pocket. "Close your eyes, Pequeña."

I do what he says. In my head, I recite the Lord's Prayer.

I feel him slide a ring on my left hand.

"Open them," he says.

When I do, I see a diamond so big, it has no business being on my scrawny finger. He kisses it.

"There," he says. "I want you to know, I paid for that. I didn't steal that ring. It's important you know I bought it." He studies the diamond, the glint of it. "This ring is your destiny."

I nod while on that deserted beach, where no one can hear you scream, he tells me we will be happy.

I stare at that ring, and see my future with Rey.

My lungs seize in my chest. A terrible sound comes from me as my legs give out and I fall to my knees, still holding that baby. Rey's dark figure stands over us.

I can barely make out his face.

"I knew you'd be happy," he says, his voice from somewhere far away. I feel him hoist me up roughly and lead me to the car. The baby shrieks as we pull onto the highway and I stare at the road ahead, seeing nothing but the years, *years and years*, ahead of me.

I look at the door handle as Rey presses down on the gas.

But I don't want to die.

Outside my house, he kisses me, right there in the car now with the windows down for anyone passing by to see.

"We are not a secret anymore, understand," he whispers in my ear. "I'll be back tomorrow. And by then, you better have told your mami because tomorrow night, you're coming home with me."

The day is thick with heat and humidity. But my body goes cold with shock.

"Tomorrow night?" I whisper.

He smiles. "I don't care if your mami doesn't like it." He takes my hand, lifts it. "Look at that ring," he says. But the world is fading again. My head is thick with fog. "I said, look at that ring." He grips my hand harder.

Something inside me breaks as I nod, as I look at that ring. "It's . . . beautiful . . ."

He kisses it, kisses me. His phone buzzes and he pulls away, glances down at it.

"I gotta go," he says.

I nod and quickly open the car door and get out, eager to escape. "Hey, remember though. Tomorrow night!" he yells before finally driving away.

I stand there, numb. Everything unreal. I stare at the little neighbor girl across the street, peering out at me from the front door. And I wonder if she is real. I stare at the road, waiting for water to come rushing down the streets. To carry me away.

Because this can't be real.

It can't.

The sound of a motor scooter breaks into my fog and I see it heading straight toward me, zooming up to our patio.

I know it's Pulga and Chico before they even take off their helmets, and they're saying something to me, but I have a hard time making sense of it. Pulga shakes me until his words, his voice become clearer and clearer.

"What's wrong with you?" he asks. "Why are you shivering like that?"

I stare at him, at both of them, trying to understand why they're here when they're supposed to be at school. Why they're riding on a motor scooter I don't recognize. Why their faces look so worried. Maybe I'm imagining this. All of this.

"Are you real?" I ask him.

"Listen! I don't have time to totally explain . . ." Pulga says. He keeps looking over his shoulder like he expects someone to come up at any minute. "You were right. Something bad, something really bad is happening, Pequeña."

The baby cries. My heart races. Everything becomes crisper. "What? Pulga, what's the matter? What happened?"

"Listen! We gotta get out of here, Pequeña. We have to leave *to-night.*" His voice goes high and his eyes fill with tears. "Remember what you said? Remember you said we had to *run*. You were right. We're gonna run, the three of us, okay?"

"Al norte on La Bestia. To the United States," Chico whispers.

"What . . . what are you saying?"

"I'm saying we have to *go,*" Pulga says. I watch as his hand brushes past a gun in his waistband, as he reaches into his back pocket and pulls out a bus ticket that he thrusts into my hand.

"Meet us there, okay? Okay? Tonight. It's the three a.m. bus, you got it? Be there, Pequeña."

The baby cries, but I nod and look at the ticket. "Okay," I say.

"It's not too late," Pulga says as they jump back on to the motor scooter. I watch as they race away. I stand there listening to the echoing zoom behind them, until it's gone. Until all is silent again.

The little girl is still peering at me from her front door.

Is this real? I wonder.

I look down at the ticket in my hand.

Yes. It's real.

Pulga

The room is unbearably silent except for the sound of my heart pounding loudly in my ears.

Don't, don't. Don't, don't. Don't, don't, it says.

Don't leave Mamá. It stretches and pulls under flesh and bone, it rips and tears apart and squeezes. It threatens to give out if I don't stay.

I turn to Chico. "Ready?"

"I don't know." Chico's voice is nervous and full of doubt. But we are as ready as we'll ever be. Our lives have been stuffed into backpacks. Mine holds the picture of my parents in front of my father's car, a cassette tape with his voice and favorite songs, a Walkman Mamá gave me on my tenth birthday, the money my tía sent that Mamá always meant for me but that still feels like I stole, extra clothes, a toothbrush, water, bread, candy.

"All we have to do is go through that window," I tell him. I keep my eyes on the pane of glass in the wall. I don't look away. If I do, I might listen to my heart. I might believe we can stay. I might let myself be talked into not leaving. If I look away, for even a minute, I might lose sight of our escape.

When I said goodnight to Mamá earlier, what I really wanted to say was how much I love her and what a good mamá she's been and that I'll miss her and don't worry, I'll make it. And to ask for her forgiveness—for lying and for leaving her all alone. I wanted to ask her to pray for me, to pray with me, like we did when I was little. And I wanted her to hold me, one last time, in the comfort of her arms. That's what I wanted to say instead of leaving it in the letter she'll find tomorrow.

But all I said to her was "Buenas noches."

She smiled and said, "See you in the morning, hijo. Si Dios quiere."

If God wants.

I wonder if she will remember those words when she realizes I am gone. And whether she will blame God, or me.

"Pulga?"

"That's all we have to do," I tell Chico. "Go out that window and pedal away from here to the bus station as fast as possible."

"That's not all we have to do," he says. I can hear how he's trying to hold back tears.

"Do you want to go to the warehouse tomorrow instead? Meet up with more guys holding guns to our heads? Do you want to stay here and find out what happens to us? What Rey has planned for us?"

He's quiet.

"No," he says finally. The ache in my chest and thumping in my ears subsides.

I hear him take a deep breath. I know he's afraid. But I have to push him. I have to make him. It's the only way.

You will never see this room again, my heart reminds me.

You will never see Mamá again.

Please, please, be quiet, I tell it. I don't need to be reminded of the thing I've always known but didn't want to admit.

Don't, don't. Don't, don't, my heart tells me, but my mind reminds me if I stay, I will end up dead or like Rey.

The backpacks are in my hand. All I have to do is shove them out the window.

This is our *only* chance.

So I do it. I shove the backpacks out the window. I put one leg over the sill and climb out of the only house I've known. I hear Chico's heavy breathing as we run to our bicycles and my mind immediately fills with images of someone lurking in the dark. Of someone watching Chico and me making a break for it. I think of Rey in some back room, telling one of his guys to just shoot us if we step out of line.

I wait for the bullet.

I wait for the knife.

For a quick hot slice through my neck, as we jump on our bikes and take off as fast as we can.

We race through the streets of our barrio, past a few cantinas with music blaring and people lingering outside. Every now and then, we come across a car and I worry one of Rey's guys will be inside, spot us, and come after us. Each time we approach one, I pedal faster. And then I listen—for the sound of it stopping abruptly, turning around, and the engine roaring as it comes racing behind us. But it doesn't happen.

The fluorescent lights of the green-and-white Litegua bus station appear up ahead, and we set our bikes near the side of the building. I pray that they will still be here tomorrow morning when Mamá undoubtedly comes looking for us, hoping the note we left was a lie, that we didn't go through with it.

The station isn't open so we have to wait outside, like sitting ducks, for the bus to show up that will take us out of Puerto Barrios to Guatemala City.

Chico and I are the first ones here. It is dark and I am covered in sweat from fear and from pedaling so hard and so fast.

More people arrive, everyone giving each other the once-over.

We sit on the concrete far away from the rest, in the shadows, trying to go unnoticed, trying to blend into the wall behind us. That's when I notice Chico is wearing his pale blue American Eagle shirt—the one that almost seems to glow.

"Why'd you wear that shirt?" I ask him quietly.

He looks at me like I'm stupid. "For luck. It's good luck." He smiles his stupid smile. I stare at him, wondering if he really doesn't remember he was wearing it the day Don Felicio was murdered. Wondering why he didn't burn it with the rest of our bloodstained clothes. I stare at it and wonder why Chico would ever think it's good luck. Chico, who hasn't cut a break in this life since the day he was cut from his mother's umbilical cord.

I almost tell him to change it for the spare one in his backpack, but I don't want to put anything in his head. If he needs to believe in this shirt, then I'm not going to take that away from him.

"Right," I say. "Luck."

"You think Pequeña changed her mind?" he asks suddenly.

"I don't know," I say. But I keep a lookout for her, hoping she didn't.

A pickup pulls up and three adults get out. At first I'm wary of the big guy who gets out, but then I see two elderly women get out the passenger-side door. One of them wears gold bangles on her wrist and I know she must be from the States. Even the way she sits. It's easy to spot them, the people who are from here, but are no longer from here.

More people gather right in front of the station, with suitcases and backpacks. They talk quietly, looking around, waiting for the bus to show up. I look into the darkness, searching for Pequeña, and see the figure of a guy instead.

I blink, trying to focus. I blink again, trying to see if he's built or walks like Rey or Nestor.

He's wearing a large, bulky jacket.

A baseball cap, pulled down to hide his face.

Jeans.

Old sneakers.

A backpack.

The guy glances quickly at us and starts walking faster in our direction. I look past him, half expecting to see Nestor's car turn a corner, where it will park and wait. Wait for this guy to do what he came for, run back, get in the car, and speed away while Chico and I bleed out on the street.

I picture my death. I am always picturing my death.

He closes the space between us so quickly, like time is warped, and I jump to my feet just as he approaches on Chico's side.

Chico's face fills with fear. A sound escapes him, like a whimpering dog, and his body tightens as if waiting for a bullet or a blow.

"Pulga, Pulga, relax!" the guy says. My brain tries to connect the familiarity of the voice with the strangeness of the image in front of me.

"It's me, *look*! Relax," he says.

Slowly, it clicks.

"Pequeña?"

"Yes. *Shut up*," she says, looking around. Her body is bulky with layers of clothes. Her hair is gone. I reach to touch the cropped edges sticking out from under the baseball hat hiding her face. She shoves my hand away hard, then rushes to Chico, who is still on the floor, scared and confused.

"It's me," she says. "Don't worry." He shakes his head, unable to speak.

"What the hell are you doing? Why'd you come up to us like that?" I say to her.

She stands back up, faces me. "You *knew* I was coming."

"Yeah, but . . ." Of course she looks like a boy. We all know what happens to girls on this journey. "I wasn't thinking."

A faraway rumble and the smell of diesel fill the air. A bus comes from around the back of the station and hisses to a stop in front of us.

The crowd hurries to put their luggage in the side compartment outside the bus, but not us. We climb on and sit down, look out the window. And my heart, as if in one last desperate attempt to make me stay, cramps tight, like it's just been punched, making it difficult to breathe.

You can outrun danger, it tells me. *But you can't outrun the pain.*

I take a deep breath, swallow hard as the bus slowly pulls onto the road.

PART TWO

Donde Vive La Bestia

Where the Beast Lives

Pequeña

Outside the bus window, Barrios rushes by in a blur. The restaurant Mami and I always rode to with Tía and Pulga. The church where Mami and Papi got married. The clinic Mami ran to where the doctor uttered that horrible truth I already knew.

That truth that fluttered in my stomach, that started the day I lifted my head and fixed my gaze on the horizon even though Mami had warned me so many times, so many times, not to.

You have to walk with your head down, Pequeña. Don't look around, she'd told me ever since my breasts started to develop and my hips started to fill out. *And be more aware. Of everything and everyone.*

She never explained how it was possible to be more aware of everything, take notice of everything, while keeping my gaze down.

I listened to her. I always listened to Mami. I didn't want to make things more difficult for her after Papi left, when she'd had to take the job housekeeping at the resort where Tía waitressed.

But that day, when my neck ached from being curved downward all the time, from the vision of feet and dust and rocks—that day, I looked up and I let the sun kiss my face and I dreamed of a future away from here.

It was the wrong moment for dreams.

But it was as if it were destined, as if some invisible hand would have forced my face up even if I hadn't at that precise moment thought to lift it. There he was, leaning on the counter of Don Felicio's store with a few other guys, drinking soda, laughing, smoking a cigarette. He blew out a long puff of smoke from a cigarette at the same exact moment I looked up. And his gaze caught mine through the haze.

I heard my mother's voice in that moment. *Pequeña!* and I looked down immediately. I quickened my pace, but the whoops from his friends and the sound of his feet came toward me anyway.

"Hey," he called. I walked faster. "Come on, don't make me look like an asshole in front of my friends."

I wanted to run, but I couldn't.

"Hey," he said again, and then he was right behind me. "Come on, slow down."

Then next to me. "Hey, I said slow down." He grabbed my wrist, squeezed it tight, pulled me to a stop. "I'll walk with you."

This is what happens when you're scared: Your heart takes over your whole body. It thunders in your chest, beating so rapidly that you feel it in your throat and ears and eyes and head. You hear it and feel it, on the verge of explosion.

And then it does, it *explodes*.

You see a splattering. You wonder how you can still be alive when your heart has exploded. You wonder how you can speak.

"What's your name?" he said, his voice sweet and full of danger.

"María," I lied.

He laughed. "Nah, that's not right. Your name is . . . Bonita." He nodded and looked me up and down. "Yes, Bonita," he repeated, then reached up and touched my chin, lifted my face to his.

This is what danger looks like: A smile set in a long face, revealing the slight overlapping of two front teeth. Hair that covers his eyes, but not completely. So you still see a strange kind of vacancy in them. And a smile that is easily, quickly replaced with a sneer.

"Don't get lost on me," he said, shaking a finger. "I'll be looking for you." He stopped. He laughed. And I kept on.

After that, he found me wherever I went. He didn't care that I wasn't interested. I think he actually liked it at first—the idea of *making* me do something, of *making* me love him. He bought me gifts and insisted I take them. He told me he loved me, even as he grabbed my face with his dirty hands, dug his fingers into my cheeks and forced me to look at him. He told me his name was Rey and I was his Bonita; he was a king and I was his pretty girl.

I was his. That's what he said. And one night, while Mami slept on the living room couch the way she did sometimes when she came home too exhausted from work, he made sure I understood what that meant.

"Ssshhhh," he said as he climbed in through the bedroom window. I'd just showered, I'd just put on my nightgown. He'd been out there for who knows how long, watching me. "Ssshhh," as he put his finger to my lips and laughed at the look on my face. At how I froze.

I could have screamed. My mother would have come running. Into that room, where Rey stood, staring at me with vacant eyes.

"My mother is in the other room," I said.

"It doesn't matter," he said. "Go ahead, invite her, too." He laughed and I panicked, thinking Mami would come in, not knowing what she was walking into. So when he came toward me, and held me by the back of the hair, kissing me and leading me to the bed, I didn't fight. Anything to keep him quiet. Anything to keep Mami away.

He told me not to make a sound, not to dare make a sound, or he'd kill me, and as soon as Mami made it into my room, he'd kill her, too. And just in case I doubted him, he showed me the gun he carried in his waistband.

Rey whispered in my ear, but I shut my eyes tight, silently screaming for help as he pressed himself against me, as his hands slid up my legs, under my nightgown.

I lay still. Very still. And I was so quiet, I hardly breathed. And for a little while, I died.

This is what dying is like:

You stare at the ceiling and watch it bend. Like the very air in your room can't be contained and is pressing against it. You watch cracks appear and the ceiling break open to a black, black sky and gleaming moon. And you rise. You float up to the ceiling, through the roof, and into the night.

That's when I saw her again, La Bruja. The horrible angel from the river, from my childhood, who saved me.

I'd forgotten about her, after so many years. Forgotten how she'd come to me in the water and how when I told Mami and Papi of her, they said I'd just hit my head, that I was seeing things. Now here she was again, with long silver hair and glimmering eyes, suspended there, waiting for me. I looked back toward the earth, toward my house that from there looked small and insignificant. And for a moment, I saw us all. Mami on the couch, curled up so small. Me on that bed, under Rey.

The bruja sunk down to my house, pulling me with her like a magnet. I felt my flesh scraping the rusty edges of the roof of our house. And then I sunk through the ceiling and back onto my bed. Back under Rey.

But then he rose off me, stood next to the bed as if in a trance. And there she appeared behind him. I watched as she grazed his arm. I watched as it began to tremble. She held a finger to her lips and circled him, studied him, ran her long thin fingers across his back and shoulders. She leaned toward his ear, whispered something that caused him to stumble again, and then she came around the front and leaned down to his stomach. She kissed his belly button with wrinkly lips that a moment later clasped on to him like a leech.

I watched as his knees went weak, a draining look came over his face. I watched as he stumbled out the window, telling me he'd find me again.

I got up slowly and closed it, watched him as he stumbled into the darkness.

When I turned back around, the old woman was gone. I wondered if she would chase after him in the black night. I wondered if she'd made him go away forever, if he'd be dead by morning.

I hoped I would never see him again.

But he kept finding me.

Pequeña? I hear someone call my name, but I don't want to be Pequeña anymore.

Pequeña?

My eyes flutter open to the dimness of early morning light. I'm on the bus. Pulga is next to me, whispering my name.

"What's wrong?" I ask him.

"They know by now," he says, looking out the window as if he can see our mothers there, desperate and heartbroken, angry and scared.

"They have each other," I whisper. "And they're strong. They can take care of themselves." I swallow emotions threatening to overcome me as I think of Mami. Of her waking, the baby in her arms as she goes to the couch to wake me. As she stares in horror at the things I've left for her there.

The gold earrings I've worn since I was a little girl. The long ponytail of hair I left for her to sell. And the note with the last words Pequeña will ever write, explaining that I'm gone.

I will shed the girl I was, the girl who lived there, until I am someone new.

Pulga sighs. "Do you think . . ."

"Don't," I say. "We can't do this. We made the decision and now we just have to keep going."

"They'd forgive us," Chico says, a hopeful look on his face when he sees Pulga second-guessing. "We can still go back."

A conflicted look crosses Pulga's face.

I shake my head. "No," I say. "We *can't* go back. Not ever."

Pulga looks at me and nods. His dark brown eyes are scared but trusting, and for a moment, I remember us small. When we used to play together while Mami and Tía Consuelo had coffee and whispered and laughed together on the patio and watched us chase lizards and iguanas in the middle of the day.

"Don't worry," I say.

He gives me a weak smile and we fall silent. There's nothing more to say. So I close my eyes as the bus rocks back and forth, dips and swerves. I close my eyes and open them again, never sure if I've fallen asleep. Over and over this happens as I picture us getting farther and farther away from Barrios, from Rey, from the pieces of me in my mother's arms and on the couch that I leave behind.

From the future that would have been if we didn't leave.

Pulga

Six hours after leaving Barrios, the bus hisses and brakes into Guatemala City Litegua station.

I breathe a quick prayer of thanks, and hope God hasn't forgotten me.

Chico, Pequeña, and I stumble out of the bus, groggy from the ride, and into the bright midmorning of Guatemala City.

"Where do we go now?" Pequeña asks.

"Another bus, to Tecún Umán. The station for that one is a couple blocks from here." I show her the map I printed from school, hoping it's still accurate.

"I thought Guatemala City had palace-sized buildings," Chico says, looking at graffiti and run-down storefronts as we head to the other station.

"It does. I remember from when I used to come with Mamá to try to get visas to visit my father's family in the United States," I tell him. "Just must not be this part." Most of it looks like Barrios.

The station is up ahead and when we go in, we're immediately greeted and tempted by the smell of food. My stomach lets out a groan. But we focus first on finding the schedule and heading out on the next bus to Tecún Umán.

"It leaves in an hour. That'll get us there around six," I tell them. "Then we cross the Suchiate River and make it to Mexico by six or seven. And there will still be sunlight."

"But not for long," Pequeña says. "What do we do after that? Where do we stay tonight?"

"I think we should be able to catch a taxi or minibus right on the other side, to take us to a shelter in Tapachula. We'll sleep there tonight." I try to sound confident but now that we're here, now that this is actually happening, I'm not too sure of anything.

Chico glances between the two of us, a nervous look on his face. "I know we have to do this, but I just don't know . . . if I can."

"You can," I say, grabbing him by the shoulders, trying to convince him, trying to convince both of us.

"Listen to me, Chiquito," Pequeña says, turning him toward her. "We can *never* go back. Our mothers know. Everyone knows. Rey knows," she says.

At the mention of Rey's name, I look at Pequeña, wondering if Chico's blabbed about the things Rey made us do. But the look on his face lets me know he didn't.

"How'd you know we're running from him?" Chico asks her. He looks between the two of us.

Pequeña looks at us and shakes her head. "Never mind. All I'm saying is we can't go back. I won't."

She's right, of course. He'll *kill* us if we go back. But Pequeña's words hang ominously in the air, mixing with the smell of food from just moments ago. Now those words and the food and the smell of exhaust and diesel makes my stomach turn.

But we need to eat because who knows when our next meal will come.

"Let's grab some food," I say, breaking the silence between us and trying to forget about the danger we leave behind, the danger that lies ahead. I point to a stand where a woman stands fanning herself and waiting for customers.

We buy warm tortillas from her, and some chicharrones that look so good and crispy, a few bags of chips, three grape sodas, and two bags of candy Chico picks out. Soon enough, it's time to get on the bus and we settle in for the six-hour trip. The bus pulls away and I unpack the food for us to share.

I bite down on a warm, salty piece of pork, wrapped in a piece of soft tortilla. It tastes so good that for a moment, everything feels okay. I look at Chico, who smiles at me with greasy lips and takes a gulp of his soda. Pequeña crunches on some plantain chips and for a moment, it almost feels like an adventure. For a moment, my stomach flutters with anticipation, I think. But maybe it's just fear.

For a moment, I think of it happening. Of us making it. And it seems so possible. The tires whir. We bounce over the occasional pothole. And with our stomachs full, we are lulled into a quiet tranquility.

Chico falls asleep. Pequeña stares out the window. I look at her, so different with her hair cut short like that. At a glance, she looks like a stranger. But then she's Pequeña again, the Pequeña I've always known, the same outline of her face. The same slope of her nose and short eyelashes; the same look in her eyes that reminds me of that day on the patio when she told me we had to leave.

The same as they looked in the clinic the day she fell off the bus.

The same as they looked when Chico and I got to her house with bus tickets.

Something wants to break through in my thoughts, but she turns to me suddenly and her dark brown eyes search mine.

"We'll make it, won't we, Pulga?"

The grease from the chicharrones is thick on my tongue.

"Of course," I tell her, searching for something I know is right there, but she looks away. I open my grape soda and take a long sip.

It fills my mouth and I remember being in the back room of Don Felicio's store with Chico, of holding grape sodas in my hand as he was killed.

I swallow the food that's bubbled up in my throat and force myself to finish the rest of the soda because we can't afford to waste it. And I fall asleep, the artificial taste of grapes, of animal and death, in my mouth.

I wake to the same taste, now stale, as the bus pulls into the station and we get off. A sense of déjà vu comes over me as we walk into the thick heat of the day and into the streets of Tecún Umán, where people rush back and forth all around us.

"We need to head to el Río Suchiate," I tell Chico and Pequeña.

An old man, frail and leathery, sits on a half wall made of rocks in a small park near the town square. He startles as we come closer to him, and stares at me carefully as I ask him for directions to the river. He points in the direction everyone seems to be going and coming and nods. "Sí, sí. El río," he says as people walk and bike and zoom past us. Women with large baskets and people on bicycle rickshaws rush past, too. I look up at the sky, at the way the sun has dimmed in just a few minutes.

"Come on," I urge Chico and Pequeña. "We want to cross the river and find a way to the shelter on the other side before dark."

We head in the direction the old man pointed and I keep looking up at the sky, wondering how much time we have.

"What do you think they're doing right now?" Chico says.

"Who?" I ask, walking faster. We need at least one hour. But I'm still not sure we'll be able to cross the river as easily as everyone makes it seem. What if it takes longer?

"Our mothers," Pequeña whispers.

I have to focus, but with Chico's question, my mind is thrown back to Puerto Barrios—to Mamá on our red velvet couch, Tía next to her crying and holding Pequeña's baby. Mamá is probably thinking of the promises I made her, all those promises, and wondering how I could break them.

Maybe Doña Agostina and the neighborhood women are there, too, comforting them. Maybe Doña Agostina is telling them about her vision. Or is she staying quiet, keeping our secret? A bicycle honks loudly at me and we move out of its way.

"You think they'll come looking for us?" Chico asks, looking back in the direction of the bus station. As if Mamá and Tía might come running out of there, break through the crowd, and find us right at this very moment.

I shake my head. "I don't know, Chico. We can't think about that now. Let's just focus on getting to the shelter, okay?"

"I just feel . . . terrible," he says. "Your mamá will never forgive me." He grabs on to the straps of his backpack, staring down at the ground. I don't answer him. I just want him to be quiet, to stop reminding me of Mamá.

We follow the crowd toward an embankment farther up the way, where the rafts I'd heard so much about from the men at Don Felicio's store come into view. Wooden planks attached to huge black tires, carrying people and packages back and forth across the water, guided by men, or boys.

We hurry to one of the guides, a guy who looks no older or bigger than me, and we ask him to take the three of us across. He tells us to climb on, and then begins to push away from the rocky shore with a long pole.

"You're lucky," the boy says as he slowly pushes us along past some empty rafts. "It's not as busy now as this afternoon. Usually, I have at least twenty people on this thing. You guys aren't visiting for the day . . ." he says, glancing up at the sky, then at our backpacks.

"Nah," Chico answers. "We're heading to La Bestia." He says this loudly, too loudly. And then takes a deep breath, like he has to steady himself. Or like saying it aloud is the only way he can go through with it. Pequeña glances over at me and I make a quick note to tell Chico not to go around blurting our plans to anyone.

"¿La Bestia? Really? Wow . . ." he says as he pushes the long rod into the water. "My cousin tried getting to the States that way." He shakes his head. "Pero le fue muy mal. If I tell you how bad it went for him, you'd turn around right now." He laughs but a brick forms in the pit of my stomach.

"You see?" Chico says, his voice full of worry again. "We should turn around."

"Don't tell us, then," I say to the guy. "Because we're going to make it." I turn my eyes away from the shore on the other side for a moment and look at Chico. "We're going to make it," I tell him. He nods as a hot breeze blows. Mexico. We're almost one step closer. All I have to do is stay focused on what's ahead. Get from one moment to the next.

"Of course, of course, you are," the guy says, pushing the pole into the water.

"Is he alive? Your cousin?" Chico asks.

The boy is quiet for a moment as he raises the long pole and gives another steady push. "Oh yeah, he's alive," he says. "He's alive."

I keep my eyes on the shore. I won't look at him to see if he's lying. Even if he is, it doesn't matter.

"Listen," he says. "They say when you're running to get on, you need to put your leg closest to the train up first. That way you don't get pulled under it. Because that thing is powerful, you know? If it doesn't eat you alive, it takes your soul. That's what I've heard anyway . . ."

The words of the guys outside Don Feli's store echo in my memory. *Man, it's hellish. Like el diablo himself is sucking at your feet, trying to pull you down into that infierno.* I look at Chico, so anxious I wish the guy would stop talking already.

As we approach the banks of Mexico, the quiet of the river is replaced with the loud sounds of commerce. "Here we are," he says, and slowly guides us in.

"Thanks, man," Chico says, and the guy holds out his hand and they slap each other five like old friends. "Hey, you seem to know enough about it. Why don't you come with us? You can drive cars in the United States instead of rafts here."

I know he's joking, but I know a part of him isn't.

The guy laughs. And for a moment, his eyes light up. He looks back at the river and shakes his head. "Nah, brother. Those dreams are not for me. But good luck. To all of you. Que Dios los guarde," he says. We pay him and he salutes us like we're soldiers as we get off.

A few people board his raft and we watch as he pushes away, floats back to the other side. Chico looks like he might be sick as he watches him go.

"Where are the taxis and minibuses?" Pequeña asks me.

"Probably down by the road," I tell her, heading toward the streets of Ciudad Hidalgo. But as we walk down the dirt path, out onto the main road, I don't see anything but a few people on motor scooters. "Let's keep walking," I tell them. "I'm sure we'll come across one soon."

"Are you sure they drive by here?" Chico asks.

The uncertainty I felt before intensifies. I gathered as much information as I could, but now that those places that were once just dots on a map are real it's hard to make sense of it all. I push down my worry, swallow the panic rising in my throat.

"Yeah, of course . . ." I say as I keep walking into the unknown.

A woman rides by on a bike and I call out to her, but she goes around and past me without a second glance.

"I'm pretty sure . . ." I tell him. I try not to think of how we must look wandering around, of who might already be targeting us.

"Are we going the right way?" Chico asks.

"I don't know," I say. "We just need to find a taxi."

"It's getting late . . ." Chico says.

"It's okay," I tell him, but even I can hear the panic in my own voice. The sky is darkening and night is falling faster than I expected. An eerie silence begins to set in, just like it does back in Barrios, as everyone heads home. As doors are shut closed and wooden bars are set in place. We continue down a mostly empty road looking around for a bus, a taxi, someone who doesn't rush past us when we call out to them. But there are no vehicles, and less and less people.

"This doesn't feel right," Chico whispers, crowding closer to me and Pequeña.

"Chico's right. This isn't safe, Pulga," she whispers. "We can't just walk around like this."

"I know, I know," I tell her. "I just . . . let's just keep going this way."

"But do you know where we're going? Where we're headed to?" Pequeña asks, an edge to her voice that heightens my fear and irritation.

"Just keep walking," I tell them both, trying to wish a bus or taxi into existence. There are parts of this trip you can't figure out. There are stretches of it you can't plan for.

There are parts of it that you travel only on hope.

But how can we be at that point *already*? How can we be so lost *already*?

Soon it's really dark, and the night feels dangerous. And Pequeña and Chico are looking to me for answers.

But I don't know.

I don't know where to go.

I don't know what to do.

I don't why I thought I could do this.

I don't know.

Pequeña

Sometimes night feels like a faceless terrible thing with claws, a wild thing with a black, palpitating heart.

It rides on our backs, our fear growing with each step.

"I'm scared," Chico says under his breath.

"Relax," Pulga tells him. But I don't think Chico was talking to Pulga. Or to me. I think he was telling the night he's scared, so maybe she will take pity. Maybe she will leave us alone instead of reaching out, grabbing us, swallowing us whole.

We move farther away from the street, scared now of any car that might go by. We can't trust anyone. But especially not now, not at night when all kinds of darkness awaken.

"Pulga . . ." I say finally, when it's apparent there are no taxis, or houses or people or buildings nearby. "It's okay . . . if you don't know where we're going. Let's just figure out what to do, okay? Let's find a place to hide, camp out, until the sun comes up."

"Out here?" Chico says, his voice immediately filling with panic.

"I thought . . . I mean . . . I don't know what I thought," Pulga says, looking around. His voice is strangled and I know if I could see his eyes, they would be filling with tears. But he clears his throat. "Yeah, we'll hide out somewhere," he says, the softness gone now, the street-smart tone back.

"No way," Chico says.

My stomach clenches like a fist at the thought of spending the night out here, too. "We'll figure things out in the morning. For now, let's just look for somewhere—"

"But I thought you had this figured out, Pulga," Chico says. "I thought you *knew*—"

"Shut up," Pulga says. "Tell me what you've done to get us this far. Tell me where we have to go next. Do *you* know?"

Chico's face is hurt and angry and I try to reach for his hand, but he suddenly says, "Wait! Look, is that a house? Do you see? Over there?"

I try to make out where he's pointing in the distance.

"It is!" he says again, and I think he's right. There *is* a small house, with fencing all around it. "Let's knock, ask them to let us stay just the night," Chico says.

"Are you crazy? For all we know that house belongs to someone we want nothing to do with . . ." Pulga says. "Who knows who lives there . . ."

"Or it might be abandoned," I say.

"If it is, it won't be for long. Someone might come there in the middle of the night and I don't want to be there if they do."

"No, look, I think I see some toys out in the yard. That's gotta belong to a family. Come on."

"No, Chico, stop," Pulga says, but Chico is running toward it now, and we are hurrying behind him, Pulga whispering for him to stop, to wait. But he doesn't. And as we get closer, I notice a dim light coming from the back of the house.

"Wait . . ." Pulga warns again as Chico runs up to the tall chain-link fence, barbed wired along the top.

But Chico's already yelling, "¡Bueno! Is someone home? Please . . ."

Pulga pulls Chico away from the fence, and I think I see the curtain move slightly at the front window, but it's so dark it's hard to tell. "¡Bueno!" Chico calls again, and suddenly, a bright white floodlight is flipped on, so bright it practically blinds us, and I put my arm up, shielding my eyes. I hear a door open, and the harsh voice of a man yelling out to us.

"Who's there? Who's out there? What do you want?"

"I'm sorry," Chico calls. "We're just . . . we crossed the river . . . and can't find a way to town. Please, señor, can you help us? We have nowhere to stay."

The man takes a few steps out, and I see his dark figure against the bright lights. I see the shotgun he carries in his hands, aimed right at us.

"He has a gun," I whisper to Pulga and Chico.

But already Pulga has his hands up. "Please, señor!" he yells. "We're just three kids. Don't shoot, please. We'll leave. We're sorry."

"Please, don't shoot!" Chico cries, "Please, we need help!"

"Come on," Pulga says, grabbing on to Chico. "Let's go."

"Keep your hands up! Walk away from here with your hands up."

"Señor, please . . ." Chico begs.

"I'm sorry, but I'm not a shelter. And I don't care who you say you are. You need to leave. Right now."

"Pero, señor, por favor . . ." Chico cries. "You don't have to let us inside your house. We'll sleep out here, on your patio . . . please."

"Get out of here. I can't help you. There's a cemetery up the road where migrants sleep. Go there."

"Pero, señor. . . ." Chico begs, his voice full of desperation.

The old man cocks the gun. "I'm warning you, kid."

"Come on," Pulga urges. "Chico, come on! You're gonna get us killed!" Pulga takes a step back, pulling Chico back with one hand while he keeps the other one in the air. Chico holds on to the fence like a life raft and Pulga yells at him again. "I'm serious, Chico!" he says, pulling him so hard.

"Stop!" Chico yells, clutching on to the fence tighter. "I don't want to sleep in a cemetery! Please!"

Chico is bigger, stronger than Pulga. Nothing Pulga does or says makes him let go.

"I said go!" the man yells.

"Come on, Chiquito," I whisper. "Come on, we'll be together, okay? I promise, you'll be okay. I'll take care of you," I tell him gently. "Please? Okay?" He starts crying, but finally, he nods. Finally, he lets go of the fence.

"The cemetery is about ten minutes that way," the old man says, pointing his gun. "You'll see the tombs. That's all I can help you with. And don't come back here again."

We walk away backward, away from the house. After a few minutes, the bright floodlight goes out and we are enveloped in the night once again.

Chico's crying fills the silence as we walk. "It's all right," Pulga whispers, his voice tinged with irritation, but mostly compassion.

I pull him close to me, hold him tighter so he won't be so afraid. But I can feel how his body shakes.

"I want to go home," he says. "We can't do this. *I* can't do this."

"Yes, you can," Pulga says. "Look, look right there. I think that's the cemetery."

"You think that's comforting? I'm scared of muertos," Chico says.

"There are good spirits, Chiquito. Ones that help us," I tell him, making out shadows up ahead, tombs rising out of the darkness.

"There's bad ones, too," he says, and I think of the stories Mami has told me about spirits. How they can be angry about leaving this life and do bad things to the living. How they roam the streets and the cemetery, at night, waiting.

"We don't have a choice," Pulga says.

Chico sucks his teeth, but he knows Pulga's right. Turning back now is impossible.

We walk slowly to the cemetery, crickets chirping loudly as we approach the tombs cautiously. I try to open my eyes wider, trying to take in everything, to detect any movement. We try not to make any noise as we come up on the tombs.

We walk in, but not too far. I feel like we're being watched. I strain my eyes, looking for others, and I think I see figures on the ground. I think I hear whispers rising in the stagnant night air. But I can't be sure. And I don't know who they are.

Are they like us? Or are we who they like to hunt?

"Here," I whisper to Pulga and Chico, ducking down behind a tomb. "Let's just stay here."

"Okay," Pulga says quickly. Chico is breathing so hard, but he doesn't cry. He holds on to me tighter; even as we settle in, he grabs on to me and tucks his body against mine.

I get a flash of that baby and it takes my breath away. An electric pulse runs through my breasts and I feel for wetness on the bandage I've wrapped tight around my chest. Just a small amount of milk.

But I swear I hear a heartbeat, and I don't know if it's mine, or Chico's, or that baby's. A sick feeling washes over me, and tears spring to my eyes but I wipe them away quickly. I won't cry for something I never wanted and can't love.

We lie back against the concrete slab and I look up at the sky. I wonder if my bruja angel will come if I call for her. If she'll whisk us away from here and deliver us to the border if I wish it hard enough.

I stare at the sky, looking for her in the stars. It seems impossible that a sky can be so full of them. It seems impossible that anything beautiful can exist.

I hear Chico take small quivering breaths, trying not to cry.

"Look at the stars, Chiquito," I whisper. "Look at the stars and listen to the crickets and don't let anything else fill your mind. I'll stay awake, you can rest," I tell him. I reach for his hand and hold it. He squeezes my hand and looks up.

I hear a rustling in the grass, and I tell myself it is just insects and rodents. And I try not to think of Rey—a cockroach who scurries through cracks and defies doors and locks and windows.

I imagine his cockroach legs scurrying through the streets of Barrios, climbing on to the bus that led us here, onto the raft that crossed us into Mexico. I imagine him biding his time, waiting to climb up my leg as I lie here, to scurry across my torso, my breasts, my neck. To whisper in my ear, *I'm here. I found you. You can't run away from me.*

I wait. For him. For ghosts. For the cries of the dead. For La Bruja.

The crickets chirp louder. *Cuidado, cuidado, cuidado,* they say.

Chico is balled up as small as possible, tucked next to me on one side, Pulga on the other. And together, we outwait night. I feel some blood leaking from between my legs and hope it is not enough to soak through the pads I layered there.

"Day will come," I whisper. And it will. Because the world doesn't care how much pain you are in, or what terrible thing has happened to you. It continues. Morning comes, whether you want it to or not.

Bugs crawl on me as we wait, mosquitoes and ants bite me. I don't smack them away; any movement might wake up Chico and Pulga. Instead, when I feel the sting, I think of Rey and let it remind me why I'm running.

I close my eyes and dream of bugs, entering my ears, my nose. Of them crawling down my throat. I wake to the sound of a fly in my ear, and my eyes snap open to bright white and a voice too close.

Pequeña.

I reach for the knife in my pocket, and with a quick press of a button and swift click, the blade shoots out, within inches of Chico's face. He shrinks back, suddenly wide awake, and he and Pulga both stare at me, at the blade.

"Sorry," I tell Chico, my hand still clutched tightly around the handle as others in the cemetery—men, women, children—emerge from behind tombs, begin walking toward the road.

"Let's go," Pulga says, staring at me, at the knife. I put it away and we hurry, following the people staggering out of the cemetery.

The warmth of the sun gets hotter with each step; the humidity grows thicker. My skin slicks with sweat as we pass a few little houses. We pass fruit vendors. And then small stores. And a run-down restaurant.

And slowly, the world seems to bustle around us as we enter town. As more cars and motor scooters and people with commerce zip past.

"Look," Pulga says, gesturing to a driver leaning against his car, smoking a cigarette. "I think that's a taxi. Let's see if he'll take us to the shelter."

The tall, lanky man stares at us as we approach.

"Perdón, señor. Can you take us to the Belen shelter in Tapachula?" Pulga says to him.

The man looks us over, takes in our clothes, our backpacks. "You have to pay in advance."

Pulga digs into his backpack and takes out an envelope full of money in dollars, quetzales, and pesos. The guy stares at him, then laughs and shakes his head as he takes another drag. I look around, wondering if anyone saw.

"You're lucky I don't steal from kids. Here's some advice: Don't pull all that money out in front of anyone. Especially those dollars. You're not going to get far making mistakes like that."

Pulga nods, looking embarrassed. And like a little kid. I take a deep breath and push away the fear and worry I've kept at bay. I think instead about where I would have slept last night if I hadn't run away.

The man gestures for us to get in the car, where it is even hotter than outside and smells of heat and sweat and baby powder. We pull away from the curb and as we drive through the streets, more people seem to appear out of nowhere.

People on foot, clutching on to their backpacks.

People who look lost and dazed.

People who woke from the dead.

People who look like us.

Pulga

We pull up to the shelter, a low building painted bright orange. A flash of Chico's face, glowing by the fire the night we burned my clothes, flickers in my mind.

There are people sitting outside the shelter. A woman in a bright pink shirt near the doorway, staring out at the street and standing on one foot, who immediately reminds me of a flamingo. A man in a blue-and-white-striped shirt sitting on an overturned paint bucket. His eyes take us in as we get out of the taxi, but then his gaze goes back to the street when we walk up to the entrance.

A priest in a long white robe spots us as we peer inside, nervous and unsure of where to go, what to do. He gestures for us to come in.

"Bienvenidos, hijos," the priest says. "Bienvenidos a Belen."

The thing in my chest, my heart, stirs at the way he welcomes us, at how he calls us hijos. I stare at the blue walls that make me feel peace. I exhale a breath I think I've been holding since we left. Relief washes over me.

I did it. I got us here.

I blink away the tears in my eyes and tell myself not to get emotional. I look at Chico, who smiles his stupid smile and says, "We made it." I shake my head at him. But I can't help smiling back, as my heart flutters in my chest like it's grown wings. We didn't make it yet. Not yet. We have so far to go. But we made it *here*. And that seems like something.

The shelter smells like home—like coffee and warm tortillas and sugar and green chiles and onions and simmering beans.

It smells like someone cares.

"I'm going to use the bathroom," Pequeña whispers to me, looking around. I nod and watch as she asks someone and then disappears.

One of the women smiles at me, a flash of silver glinting from between two of her teeth. I watch as a boy younger than me, younger than Chico, holds his plate out to her.

"¿Sabes que?" she asks him, speaking to him gently. "When I make this food, I sing. And I pray to Papá Dios. So it will nourish your soul as well as your body."

He smiles and she spoons eggs and beans onto his plate. She places two tortillas on top and hands him a wrapped chocolate cupcake.

My heart fills with a kind of emotion I've warned myself not to feel. It's dangerous to feel too much, whether it is hope or despair. I wish I could reach into my chest, wrap my hand around that pulsing thing, and calm it.

"Sit down," the priest says, gesturing to the long table in the center of the room. "I'll be with you in just a moment." He goes back to talking to a man who has the look of a beaten dog to him. We sit down near the boy, who is by himself eating his food, and I stare at the man, at others who walk past us with that same expression.

They don't look like people who have dreams. They look like people too tired, too scared, to dream. I wonder how long before I look like that, too.

Maybe I already do.

In a far corner, there is a small television but it is off. My eyes scan the wall where maps outlining different routes to the border hang alongside children's drawings—stick figures of families. Some of the figures have happy faces and others, sad ones. Some of them have rainbows and some of them show stick figures fallen on the ground, their eyes tiny black x's. A calendar marks the days.

"Hola." A voice is suddenly next to us. "My name is Padre Gilberto." When I open my eyes, the priest is there. A woman with glasses stands next to him with a clipboard in her hand, her gray hair pulled back in a frizzy ponytail. "This is Marlena, the co-director who works at this shelter," the priest says, gesturing to the woman. "Where are you coming from?"

Chico looks at me and I answer. "Guatemala," I say quietly.

The priest nods. "You're headed to the United States?"

I nod.

"Well, Marlena will take you to answer some questions and get you settled in. Don't worry, hijos. You are safe for now." He reaches for my hand and holds it for a moment, before letting go and doing the same with Chico. I hope God's grace will transfer to me in that touch, keep me safe for more than just now.

"Come with me," Marlena says.

"Wait, there's one more . . ." I tell her, looking around for Pequeña, who just then is heading back to us.

Marlena looks at Pequeña and nods, leads us to a room with a small desk and two chairs. Everywhere there are boxes—some stuffed with papers, others with random things like cereal and blankets and socks.

She closes the door behind us, even though the room is stuffy and hot.

She asks us our full names. When it's Pequeña's turn to answer, she hesitates before giving her real name. Marlena looks over her glasses and nods when she realizes Pequeña is not a boy.

"Don't worry," she says. "I understand."

Marlena asks again where we are from. And exactly why we're leaving. Chico and I tell her about Rey and she listens intently, quietly.

"So it was you two who witnessed the murder."

"Not exactly, but yes."

"And then he pressured you to work for him, to be part of his gang?"

Chico and I nod and she turns to Pequeña. "You too?"

Pequeña hesitates. "Why are you asking us this? You're not going to stop us from going on, right?"

"No. It's a dangerous trip. It's an almost impossible trip. I won't stop you, because I know you're running from worse. But I do have to make sure this shelter is as safe as possible. That crooks and criminals aren't coming here *pretending* to be migrants who then turn around and prey on real migrants. Some people do that, you know. They'll say, 'Oh, come with me, I know of someone who can help you.' Or 'I know a way you can make some money.' And then . . ." Marlena shakes her head. "Who knows with who or where you'll end up? Bueno, I know it sounds heartless, but I have to make sure you're really in need."

Pequeña's eyes fill with tears and she wipes them away roughly before they can even flow down her cheeks.

"Our stories are real," she says, glaring at Marlena. Pequeña's face turns dark red as she tries to hold back tears, hold back her anger.

"I'm sorry . . ." Marlena says, looking at Pequeña carefully. "I didn't mean . . ."

"I'm running . . . from the same guy, too," she spits out. "Do you need me to tell you more than that?"

If Pequeña's words were visible, they'd be black, tinged with red and orange like burning coals.

When Pequeña looks at Marlena, something passes between them that makes Marlena shake her head, "No, that's enough," she says, before going on to the next question.

It hits me then, so suddenly, it feels like I've been struck. The truth is silver and white and flashes, like lightning. It comes from somewhere above, cracks into your brain, shoots down to your heart. Zaps you.

Rey.

Pequeña is running from Rey.

Because that baby, that baby she didn't want, that she couldn't look at and could hardly stand to hold, that baby is Rey's.

I look at her, but she won't meet my eyes. She is looking at her feet, wiping at tears I can't see but I know are there.

"Pequeña," I whisper, but she shakes her head.

Marlena directs more questions at me and I answer. She explains the rules of staying at the shelter; a stay here is limited to no more than three days; backpack searches are mandatory to ensure we are not carrying any weapons (I glance at Pequeña, who puts her hand in her pocket); men and women sleep in separate quarters unless there are no bunk beds left and then it's the floor in a common room; two meals are served a day—breakfast and dinner—and only at specific times; we're allowed one shower during our stay, and we must stand in line and wait our turn; showers must be done one at a time except for mothers helping their children; no belligerent behavior; no threatening or harassing other migrants; no alcohol; no drugs. Breaking any of these rules will get you kicked out and back on the streets.

When Marlena is done, she looks at us and asks if we understand.

"Yes," we say in unison.

"Good," she says as she searches each of our backpacks. Then she walks us out to the dining area, where she adds them to the shelf piled high with other backpacks, and past a volunteer who looks over them and makes sure that nobody takes anyone else's bag. And then, finally, she tells us that even though breakfast is over, we can still get some food if there's any left.

The women who scrape the last of the breakfast food onto our plates look at us warmly. Speak to us. Look us in the eyes. Tell us to eat.

Chico sneaks glances at Pequeña as we sit down at the table, now empty except for us. We don't ask Pequeña anything more about Rey.

We eat our food in minutes. Around us, people play cards or talk quietly. Every now and then, there is laughter and the sound of it is odd and out of place. The television is on now and plays loudly in the corner; a gossip show Mamá used to watch even though she said it was garbage flashes on the screen. Television people in bright, crisp, expensive clothes.

A woman sits inches from the television, staring at the faces of the made-up women, listening intently to stories of celebrities.

We watch from the table, one show to another to another.

We go outside and watch a few guys kicking a soccer ball.

We watch people wash clothes by a cement sink outside.

The hours pass.

Marlena finds us before she leaves for the night and tells us we can shower tomorrow. That there are no more beds available, but there is another large room around back where we can sleep on the floor.

"We have no mats and the floors are concrete, but here are some blankets," she says. She hands them to us and shows us where the room is.

"They turn the lights off in an hour," she says.

I think about asking Marlena for my backpack. For the Walkman I carry there, with the tapes Mamá gave me a few years ago. Things that belonged to my father that his sister had sent us.

But I remember the promise I made to myself. That I would only listen once I got on the train.

"Gracias," I tell Marlena, who is all business and efficiency, who gives us a small smile and nods. But her eyes flicker with compassion.

"Nos vemos mañana," she says. "Buenas noches."

And then she is gone, and there is only us, and the woman in the corner playing some kind of game with a teen girl and a toddler girl. Another two women near her. An old man with a girl about Chico's age. And us.

Chico, Pequeña, and I settle down in the far corner of the room, opposite a wall with a huge mural of la Virgen.

We watch as one of the women gets on her knees, inches over to la Virgen bit by bit—her knees scraping against the concrete floor.

I've heard of people traveling miles this way, over dirt road and pebbles and gravel, on their knees to appeal to the altar of a saint or holy figure. It is a way of showing sacrifice, suffering, and respect. A way of making one worthy of their prayers being answered.

As if her actions are a cue, one by one, the other migrants do the same. Even the old man, who topples over and has to steady himself with his hands every few inches but does not give up until he is right in front of that mural.

Chico looks at us and is the first of us three to follow. Then Pequeña. Then me.

My jeans protect my skin, but the boniness of my knees makes them ache.

I look over at Chico and Pequeña, at how they close their eyes. Chico's face is scrunched up and I can almost hear the pleading I imagine repeating in his head. *Please, please, keep us safe.* Pequeña's face is stoic, almost expressionless, but her lips move ever so slightly.

I try to pray, but all I can do is wonder why we have to hurt to be worthy of God's grace. And then I worry it's blasphemy. And then I worry I'll be damned.

So I concentrate on the mural. How the colors seem to glow even in this space partly lit by a weak night-light plugged into the room's only outlet. Red like blood. Turquoise like the water in Río Dulce. Blue like the sky I'd look at on the back of Mamá's motor scooter. Green like the walls of Don Felicio's house. Yellow like that flower outside the warehouse.

I think of Mamá.

I don't want to think of her. Until now, I've pushed her out of my mind each time she's come in.

But there is no more landscape to watch and there is no sound of wind or tires or hissing of the bus. No television or people to distract me.

There is only Mamá.

My eyes fill with tears that flow no matter how much I don't want them to. I don't want to think of her, back home, staring at the ceiling, thinking of me. Wondering how I could leave her. How I could lie and tell her everything was okay. How I could hide so much from her. I don't want her wondering what kind of trouble I was in and how she could've protected me.

I don't want her wondering if I'm okay now.

Or where I'm sleeping tonight.

I hear a cracking sound and I wonder if it's my heart breaking.

Maybe it's not made of muscle and chambers. Ventricles and arteries.

Maybe it's made of glass. Maybe those sharp pains in my chest are shards slicing me from the inside out.

And maybe it can never be put back together again.

I look up at la Virgen.

I squeeze my eyes shut.

Even if I'm not sure God will hear me, I pray. I pray like Chico.

Please, please keep us safe.

~ ~ ~

The next morning, we sit outside for breakfast. The shelter is off a side street that's off a side street from the main road, so I can hear the muffled sound of traffic, of horns blaring and vendors selling, just through the surrounding trees and just under the louder noise of the shelter. Of pots and pans in the kitchen, of people waking and conversing, of water running and the television blaring with morning cartoons and small kids giggling.

A couple of guys approach us, sit nearby. "Where you guys headed?" one of them asks.

My heart races at the question. I remember Marlena's comments from yesterday about people at shelters who pretend to be migrants.

But Chico, with his mouth full of eggs and beans, quickly answers. "Arriaga," he says just as I say, "Al norte." I realize I forgot to tell him to stop answering questions when strangers ask.

"Arriaga," one of the guys says, "to catch La Bestia, right? Us too! Are you leaving today? We can travel together. I've made the trip before. I know the way."

"Oh, wow!" Chico exclaims. "That would be—" His voice stops and I can see that Pequeña has turned to him and blocked him from the guys' view.

"Really," the guy goes on, "last time I got caught crossing el Rio Bravo. But, I mean, that was probably a good thing because honestly, I almost drowned." He shakes his head and looks at me.

He looks honest enough, but I can't tell if he's being truthful. Can't tell if he was convincing enough for Marlena but is really someone trying to lure us out of here. Lead us to who knows where. Maybe he's another wolf—just like Rey.

I can't take the chance.

"Nah, man. We just got here," I tell them. "We'll be here for a couple of days."

Pequeña is talking to Chico in a low voice and when she moves out of the way again, I see he avoids looking at me.

"We'll probably stick around that long, too," the guys says. "Maybe we'll see each other on the other side one day." But I don't respond and he gives me a funny look. I nod and turn, stare at my plate so he won't keep talking to us.

The thing is, he could be perfectly harmless. I might have messed up bad because maybe he could've helped us out.

But there's no way to know for sure.

I try to imagine how the three of us look to others.

Targets.

I keep eating, but the beans get stuck in my throat. It's hard to swallow past the fear that we've run into guys like Rey here already. The three of us stay quiet and eventually the two guys finish their food and walk away.

I turn to Chico. "*Don't* tell anyone else what our plans are. Now we have to keep our eyes on those guys and make sure they aren't keeping their eyes on *us*."

"Sorry," he says, staring down at his feet.

I shake my head, feeling bad because I made him feel bad, on top of all the worry of the trip.

"It's okay, Chico," Pequeña says gently. "But Pulga's right. We can only trust each other."

"It's fine," I mutter to Chico. "Just . . . por fa, be more careful, okay?"

He nods.

Pequeña looks at me. "When do you want to leave?"

"Tonight. We'll catch one of those white minivans from here all the way to Arriaga. The trip is only a few hours, but it will take us a lot longer than that because there are checkpoints. We'll have to get off before checkpoints and walk through the fields, then make our way back to the highway, past the checkpoint, and catch another minivan."

Chico looks worried. "At night?"

I shrug. "From what I've heard, the checkpoints are less active at night and there are less of them. So we'll cover more distance faster."

Pequeña nods.

"If we leave at seven tonight, we'll have twelve hours of darkness to make the trip. After sunrise, there are more officials out," I continue. I look down at the food on my plate. My stomach is in knots, but I also know I need energy to make the trip.

I think of what lies ahead of us. I think of the women who made us this food. And even though it falls like a heavy brick in my stomach, I eat it all. Chico and Pequeña do the same.

Father Gilberto suddenly comes out and begins talking to those of us who have gathered there. Marlena is handing out leaflets with information about other migrant shelters along the way, numbers migrants can call for help, organizations that aid migrants, and in the same breath, reminds us to always be on guard and not be too trusting. Warnings about the dangers along the way and then a whole section on the dangers of riding La Bestia.

We listen intently, and a sobering quiet comes over us when the father pleads for us to be vigilant and careful. I glance at Chico. He looks like he's going to throw up. I glance at Pequeña. Her face is almost expressionless, but there is a kind of stoic anger building in her eyes. Padre Gilberto tells us that we are standing next to those who will die along the way. People turn ever so slightly, looking at one another. And those of us who are lucky enough to survive will carry injuries and trauma that will last a lifetime. He lets that sink in for a long time, before reminding us to trust in God. Nothing is impossible for God.

I think of all the people who have passed through here, just like us, only to die hours or days later.

The brick in my stomach grows heavier.

Father Gilberto prays over us, and then the crowd disperses, quiet at the father's words of sobering reality.

We understand danger. We grew up with danger. But this danger feels different.

This danger feels more crushing, but maybe because it's so close to where hope lives.

Father Gilberto is right. But the problem is if we think about all that can go wrong, we won't go on. And if we *don't* think about it, we'll probably die.

I try to push it out of my mind. For now.

"We'll shower before we leave," I tell Chico and Pequeña. "It'll probably be a while before we get another chance. And the fresher we look, the less attention we'll draw."

When we go to Marlena to get our backpacks, she hands them over and shows us to the long line of others waiting. "There is only one shower, so it'll be a while. There is no hot water and you have five minutes. But it's something."

I nod. "Thank you."

We sit on the floor as we wait, moving up every few minutes as someone goes into the shower and then emerges back out into the hallway. If someone is taking too long, the next person bangs on the door. We move up, and up, and up; we are near the kitchen, where I can see another line of people. That line is for those who can afford to buy a calling card. One by one they are handed a cell phone to borrow.

I watch as a guy dials. He waits, and then I hear him say hello to whoever is on the other end of the line. Then he is telling them he made it to Mexico, that he's in a shelter, that he's okay, but each word comes out more choked than the one before. Then he is staring at the ceiling, tears streaming down his face. He stays like this a few minutes, trying to compose himself. He nods at whatever is being said to him, but he can't seem to get any more words out.

I look at Pequeña.

"Let's call them," I tell her. "Let them know we're okay."

She looks at me. "We should. But . . ." She stares in the direction of the guy. He's hunched over now. "Do you really want to?" she asks.

I know what she means. I know she thinks I will dissolve in a pool of my own tears if I hear Mamá's voice.

And she's right. I think about it. I think of her voice. Of the strangle in it as soon as she hears mine. Of the way she will want to crawl right through the phone, to hold me, to pull me back to her. Of the way I will have to hang up. Not knowing if I'll ever hear her voice again.

"If we call, we won't go on. We won't be able to. And they'll convince us not to," Pequeña says. "Before you know it we'll be back in Puerto Barrios, back to the things that sent us running."

I look down, hoping she doesn't see the tears in my eyes just at the thought.

Another person is on the phone now. More tears streaming down another face. Another person choking on his words. Swallowing his pain. I hear my mother's voice in my mind again. And some part of me inside crumbles.

"We'll call when we're closer," she says.

I nod. *When. Not if. Because we'll make it,* I tell myself.

I look over at Chico playing cards with the little kids who were watching cartoons. They're laughing as he acts like a clown and makes silly faces at them. And even though somebody might get irritated because I'm saving his place in line, it's worth it. Just to see him being himself. Even if only for a little while.

That night, as seven o'clock approaches, my heart starts drumming faster. The beat picks up with each second that passes.

I get my bag and make sure the Walkman is still there. Soon enough I'll be on that train and able to listen to my father's tapes. I focus on that. That moment. My father.

And I wonder if he'll be with me on that train. If his spirit is walking next to me, even now.

I look at the clock—five more minutes. I look at Pequeña and Chico, who are both looking at that clock, too.

"Está bien, Abuelo?" I hear a girl say. It's the one old man who hobbled to the mural of la Virgen last night.

He nods and smiles at her, trying to reassure her.

They both have their bags and are headed to the front door. They must be going to catch one of the minibuses or vans also. A part of me wants to ask but then, I don't really want to know. I feel bad for the old man. Already, I'm worrying about him, about his granddaughter. And I don't have room for any more worry or ache in my heart than I already have.

I see their silhouettes in the doorway, the evening light behind them. The old man is wearing a cowboy hat and a pair of sneakers I saw Marlena giving him earlier. He starts coughing, so violently, he has to stop walking.

And then he is grabbing his chest. And then the young girl is screaming.

Just like that.

People rush to him. Father Gilberto is on the ground next to him, yelling for someone to call an ambulance.

The girl is screaming.

She is screaming. And screaming. And screaming.

She is begging him not to leave her. She is begging God not to let him die. She is begging everyone around her.

And we are all standing there, unable to move, unable to do anything. And I think, to her, we must look like we can't hear her. A woman goes to her knees trying to hug the girl, trying to pull her away as the priest says the old man needs room. But she is holding on to her grandfather's hand so tight. And she is screaming.

"We've come so far, Abuelito! Please! Please! Stay with me!"

I turn away from it. But before I do, I see her looking at me. And I see the flash of desperation.

"Don't leave!" she yells, her voice so shrill, so high, I don't know how God wouldn't be able to hear her.

I know she means her grandfather. I know that's who she means.

But the way she says it, the way she looks, I can hardly move.

"I'm sorry," I whisper, though it's impossible for her to hear me. And we go, into that dusk, far away from her.

Far away from the dying.

Pequeña

Outside, we don't say a word. We hear the wail of an ambulance.

Pulga looks around, his eyes intense and glistening as he tries to figure out where we are and where we need to go. I know a part of him wants to cry. I know his heart is aching for that girl and her grandfather. Mine is, too.

We've come so far!

Her scream was so primal. So scared.

Even with the rush of voices of all those who hurried to help, voices yelling for someone to start CPR, yelling for someone to call an ambulance, for everyone else to stand back—even with all those noises, it's her scream, and the way it reverberated through that shelter, that I'll always remember.

I feel that scream inside me, too.

"I think it's this way," Pulga says. The words bring me out from inside my head. He's reading his notes, looking down at the notepad I saw him scribbling in earlier, as he stared at the maps on the wall in the shelter. Up ahead there are more people who have left the shelter and are headed in the same direction, and more still who appear on the street. All of us looking lost.

We walk faster and a tangy sour smell fills the air, mixed with the smell of roasting meat. The ambulance wails louder, its lights flashing in the early dusk, until it wails past us like some creature in pain. Like the girl screaming back at the shelter.

Maybe it's still her I hear.

I grip the straps of my backpack tighter.

We turn down a street.

"Muchachos . . ." A woman with a small child heading down the same road as us gestures, trying to get our attention.

"Is this the way to the highway?" she asks. She has a backpack. Her little girl has one, too, with a unicorn stuffed animal peeking its head out of the zipper.

Pulga glances in the woman's direction and gives just a quick nod. Chico looks at the little girl and gives her a smile and a little wave. She waves back shyly.

"I think so," I tell her.

"Oh, good," she says, sighing in relief. "I wasn't sure but I saw a lot of people with backpacks walking this way so . . ." She struggles to walk fast and talk, to keep pace with us. But Pulga has sped up and is walking so fast now, it's hard for me and Chico to keep up. Within minutes, there's a good amount of distance between us and the woman. I look back and see a look of defeat on her face as she pulls her little girl along with her.

Chico looks at me and then at Pulga.

"Why'd you do that?" Chico mumbles.

"Do what?" Pulga says, scratching his head and looking irritated.

"Leave them behind like that? She was just asking . . ."

"And I answered," he says.

"Yeah, but . . ."

"But what?" Pulga says, moving even faster now, keeping his gaze ahead. He doesn't bother to look back at even me or Chico as we struggle to keep up. We have to jog to match his pace.

"You want them to ride the buses with us, too? You want to know what happens to that little girl, Chico? To her mother? You want to be around when one of them drops dead like the old man back there? Or worse?"

We don't say anything. And we pretend not to notice when Pulga wipes his eyes quickly. Pulga's words hit me like little knives.

"He's right," I tell Chico.

Chico looks at me, then shakes his head. "We shouldn't be like that, though."

"I know," I tell Chico. He's right, too.

The streets smell like urine. The stickiness of the night and the blood still draining from my body make me feel like I haven't showered in days. My jacket is bulky and hot, but I keep it on.

I think of the old man back at the shelter. He'd been behind me in line for the shower, so I overheard when Marlena gave him a pair of sneakers to replace the ones that had fallen apart on his journey from Honduras.

We've come so far!

He smiled and thanked her and showed me his shoes proudly. "These will take me all the way to los Estados Unidos," he said, looking at the sneakers like they were magical. He and his granddaughter were headed out tonight, just like us. He'd showered and gotten ready for death.

I look down at my own sneakers, dirty and old. I wonder if they will take me all the way to the States, or if I'll end up like the old man. Dead before he even set foot out the door.

And his granddaughter. What will happen to her? Will she be sent back home—back to whatever it was that she was so desperate to escape?

I force myself to stop running all the scenarios in my head, to leave the thought of them behind no matter how terrible it makes me feel.

Just keep walking.

Soon the crunching of gravel underfoot gives way to a louder rushing sound. We're near a highway, I think; cars are passing us by, some beeping and some people shouting out to us every now and then.

"Why are they yelling at us like that?" I ask Pulga. His eyes are looking everywhere.

"Some don't want us here," Pulga says, shrugging. "We are to Mexico what Mexico is to the States."

We walk along that stretch of road for a while, before finally one of the minibuses pulls up right ahead. Pulga starts running and we follow.

He has the money ready for the three of us, separated from the rest of his money this time. He takes a seat right behind the driver, and we squeeze in next to him. More people get in.

"¡Rápido!" urges the driver. The line of people moves faster, paying the fare and trying to settle down quickly. The van takes off before everyone has even found a seat.

We stare out at the road, cars passing us by, minibuses and vans, people still on the side of the road walking trying to catch a ride.

"Perdón, how long before the first checkpoint?" Pulga asks.

"Depends," the driver says. "They move around. Sometimes you only ride ten minutes and suddenly a checkpoint has popped up." The driver keeps his eyes on the road. Has a phone on his dashboard.

"Let us know, man. As soon as you see a checkpoint."

"Relax, relax," the driver tells Pulga. "It's not good for you if you get caught and busted. But it's not good for me, either. I need to make a living. Don't worry. I'll let you know." He turns on norteña music and plays it loudly.

But Pulga sits upright in his seat, looking out the front window like an eagle. I keep my eyes on the side of the road, dark and thick with trees. A flash of the girl with that unicorn in her backpack punches into my mind and I imagine her walking tonight, in all that thick darkness.

A lump forms in my throat. A heaviness in my chest. She looked tired. And her eyes seemed sad even as her mouth smiled.

I'm glad Pulga wouldn't let us wait up. I'm glad she's not in this minibus. I don't want to know her fate.

Up ahead there are red taillights as traffic slows down. My body tenses up. The loud music feels strange, the horns and accordion blasting in the minibus as we sit here like springs ready to burst. I look at the time lit up on the dashboard as minutes tick by.

Too much time passes while we're stuck, unmoving.

Suddenly, the driver's phone flashes. He looks down and immediately makes his way to the far right lane of the highway. A car horn blares.

"This is it, get out. ¡Que Dios los guarde!" the driver yells as he turns down the music. "Get out, get out!"

The door opens and there's a rush as everyone gathers their things, calls to one another to hurry, and we spill onto the side of the highway. I catch a quick glimpse of a woman running with a rosary in her hands before she gets lost in the trees and heavy brush.

"Chico, Pequeña!" Pulga calls. I grab Chico's hand and pull him along, trying not to lose sight of Pulga as he makes his way into that forest. He turns, searching for us, but keeps running toward the field.

"We're here." I catch up and grab on to his shirt.

We run, grass crunching under our feet, stumbling over tree roots, not stopping even as branches smack our faces and bushes and leaves brush against our clothes. My abdomen is clenching, my heart pounding. My backpack swings from side to side with the heaviness of the water bottles we took from the shelter. Chico clutches my sweaty hand harder as it begins to slip from his grip.

"Don't worry, Chiquito," I manage to say. "I won't leave you."

But these little sounds escape him, terrible sounds like those of a hurt or scared animal, and it puts me even more on edge. I hold his hand tighter. "Don't worry!" I say as we dodge through trees.

Pulga is ahead of us and he runs so fast, like a mountain goat, over the uneven terrain. It's impossible to keep up with him as he yells, "Hurry, hurry!" But we run faster, under that darkness, *into* that darkness. Into someone who will want to rob us, or authorities who are already waiting out here, knowing that drivers drop migrants off before checkpoints. Or worse—narcos who will kidnap and hold us until they get money from our families.

My insides feel like they will fall out of me at any moment with each hard thump of my feet on the ground. For a terrible moment, I think, *I can't. My body can't do this right now.*

But then I remember what my body has already done, what it has been through. What it will go through if I don't run.

Fear and adrenaline rush through me.

So I run. I keep going, until finally, Pulga slows down. We ease up the pace, until we are jogging.

"Stop," Chico says. "Stop . . . just . . . for . . . a . . . minute."

We slow down to a stop, finally, and Chico falls to the ground.

"We . . . gotta . . . keep moving," Pulga manages. But he's bent over now, trying to catch his breath. I fall next to Chico. And we all stay quiet for a minute.

Chico starts coughing, trying to catch his breath. And then his coughing turns to crying.

My body is buzzing, buzzing. My scalp is itching. I feel like I'm made up of a million buzzing bees. And tears are stinging my eyes.

"It's okay," Pulga whispers. "It's just because it's the first jump, that's all. It'll get easier." But his voice is high, it's unnatural. It's scared.

"Yeah," Chico whimpers.

"We'll be okay," I say, putting my arm around Chico.

And when we are finally able to catch our breath, and swallow our fears, we stand up again. My legs tremble, I don't know if from fear or adrenaline.

"Okay, okay," Pulga says, taking deep breaths. "Listen, we're going to walk out here for about two hours. We walk out and up, northeast; imagine an arc in your mind that will take us around the checkpoint. That's what we're doing. There are a lot of trees and cover here, but we'll walk that long, just to be safe. I think that will be enough."

Our feet crunch through the brush and my eyes try to adjust to that infinite darkness. The moon seems nonexistent, though I catch the faintest sliver of it through the trees every few minutes.

"Out and up for an hour then back toward the highway for another," Pulga says as we walk. I hold out my hand and grab on to his backpack because I can hardly see him. I take Chico's hand and have him hold on to my backpack. "We have to be quiet, though," Pulga whispers again. "Then we'll catch another minibus. See how far it takes us."

"Before we have to run out like this again?" Chico says.

"Yeah," Pulga answers.

"How many times?" I ask. I can't tell if the slickness between my legs is blood, or sweat, or my insides. I tell myself I layered enough pads; everything will be okay. My body can do this.

I hope I'm right.

"I don't know . . ." Pulga says. "However many checkpoints there are." His voice is so quiet. And then we all walk in silence, holding on to one another.

The night is quiet, too, disturbed only by the sound of our rustling, and every now and then, the rustle of something farther away. Maybe just an animal, or maybe others who were in the van. Or maybe those who were already out here before we came.

We don't see anyone else, but we feel the fear, palpable in the air, as if the trees and bushes themselves have absorbed the weight of this journey from everyone who has ever roamed through.

And with each step it feels like we're deeper and deeper into some kind of dark maze, some labyrinth or trap, that we might never find our way out of.

Pulga

We walk on in silence, listening for danger. I lead, keeping the image of the path we need to take—a white glowing arc—in my head.

My mind wanders, all the way back to Don Felicio's store, the time a guy named Felix from our barrio had just returned from his attempt to reach El Norte. He talked about the routes through Mexico on La Bestia. His stories are the reason I googled articles and maps and information from the computers at school. They're the reason I kept a book with notes under my mattress for the moment I would have to run. For this moment, when I would have to walk through brush and trees and fields.

Felix had talked about walking like this. I can almost hear his voice. *They call us animals, Don Feli. Rodents and beasts. But let them call us what they want.* He took a long swig from one of the coldest Coca-Colas in Puerto Barrios. *I'll run through brush and fields, cross borders, go where I'm detested and eat scraps if I have to. Whatever it takes to survive.*

Felix was killed five months later. Chico and I were walking to school when we saw the police cars and morgue truck that came to collect his body. Thrown on a gurney. Whatever was left of him, scraped up. And the first thought that came to me was how he looked like a butchered animal, lying there in the street. So much carnage, so much blood. Like an animal in the slaughterhouse.

That was before Chico's mamita. And right before Gallo left and never came back.

I hear Pequeña's breathing behind me and I remember the huge crush she'd had on Gallo. How he would walk by and wave to her when we were outside playing and he was on his way to work in his parents' store. Pequeña would whisper to me, *We're going to get married someday*. I'd laugh at her and tell her she was crazy. Gallo was older and besides, I'd already seen him pressed up against Leticia's best friend, kissing her one afternoon around the side of Don Felicio's store. But I never told Pequeña.

She was heartbroken when his parents finally told some of us he'd gone to the States, days after he'd left quietly in the middle of the night.

But he made it.

I imagine Gallo, walking like us, never looking back.

I imagine Felix, walking like us, only to be sent back on a plane and travel in a few hours what took him weeks to trek across. Only to return and be killed.

I imagine I am an animal. Skulking through the darkness.

Keen.

Instinctive.

Alert.

Alive.

Some don't make it. But some *do*.

Why not me?

Why not us?

I hold on to this thought as we walk.

Why not me? my feet say with each pound to the ground.

Why not us?

There is nothing but silence and the sound of our feet and breathing.

Chico's voice cuts into my thoughts. "I'm thirsty," he says. "And itchy, like bugs are all over me." He runs his hands on his arms, scratches his head. I feel itchy, too, and as soon as he mentions it, I can't help but start scratching.

"We'll have water as soon as we get back near the highway, when we catch another minibus."

"It won't be that easy," Pequeña says.

"They're up and down that highway all the time . . ." I tell her, hoping it's true.

When we head toward the highway, I think of sitting in the minibus again sipping water. For now, that keeps me going. When I hear the sound of cars again, I think of water. As we inch farther out of the brush, toward the highway again, I look for a white minibus or van. And think of water.

Suddenly—lights.

"Wait here." I run out and wave my hands at the headlights, blinding after so much darkness, and close my eyes as the van approaches.

It roars past me.

Flashes of bright dots fill my vision. I blink, trying to see, as I hear the beep of a horn, and see more headlights. Then Chico and Pequeña running to a van that has stopped for us, that we board, and pay this driver just like the last one, and continue on, before we have to do it all again.

Each time feels like maybe we never made it out of those trees and fields. Each time I wonder if we really did. The same silence. The same crunching. The same darkness.

The same blindness as we make it back to the road.

Another white van. Another driver.

The same exchange of money.

The same sips of water.

On and on and on.

But by the third time, my feet feel like they're on fire. And my head bobs back and forth in exhaustion, just like Pequeña's and Chico's do, as the van's tires whir us to sleep.

I'm not sure how much time passes before I fall sleep. But even in my dream, I am traveling. I'm in the back seat of my father's El Camino and there he is, driving with Mamá next to him in the passenger seat. I can't see his face, only the back of his head, but I know it's him. We ride—top down, wind blowing, bass booming. The air smells of ocean and sand, seaweed and salt. My father stares straight ahead. I keep wishing he would turn around. There are so many things I want to ask him. So many things I want to say. But I say nothing. And he keeps driving, face forward.

Mamá nestles up next to him and he puts his arm around her. She looks back at me, smiles, and opens her mouth to tell me something.

A loud screech fills my ears.

Then someone yelling.

Others screaming.

A man cursing.

"¡Hijo de su pinche madre!"

"¡Cuidado! ¡Cuidado!"

"¡Dios!"

I open my eyes just in time to see something blurry in the headlights, I think.

I'm thrown violently against Chico, who is half out of his seat. Pequeña is on the floor. The driver jerks the wheel and we are thrown in the opposite direction. Chico holds on to me, Pequeña holds on to the seat. The sound of screeching tires. I wait for the impact, for something to come slamming into us, but only the sound of it comes. The boom of metal hitting metal.

The driver glances anxiously in the rearview mirror as he gains control.

"What happened?!" Chico yells.

"Did we hit him?" a man in the row behind us calls out. There are four other people in the van. A man, a woman, and two teenage girls. I don't know if they're together or not. The two girls hold on to each other. The woman is sitting, shaky hands covering her face.

"He ran out, out of nowhere," the driver says, still in shock, though the van is steady and in his control again now. We look back and see cars positioned haphazardly across the highway. People out of their cars, shouting, pointing at something on the ground.

"Oh my god," Pequeña whispers. Chico's eyes go wide.

Was someone trying to flag down the van? Like we were?

I look toward the driver, who is wiping his face with one hand as if trying to bring himself back from the shock.

My body itches from nerves. I take a deep breath.

Pequeña is looking at me, her face exhausted and scared.

"Is any of this real?" she says.

"We'll be okay," I tell her. I sit back, try not to think about what's behind us.

The van continues on.

I turn and ask the man behind us, "What time is it?" He looks at his watch.

"Four thirty."

Four thirty? More time has passed than I thought. I turn back to the driver. "How far are we from Arriaga?" I ask him.

"We're *in* Arriaga," he says.

"Really?"

He nods. "Really, joven. You got lucky, sometimes those bastards are too lazy to set up checkpoints at night."

"Yeah, real lucky," the man behind me mutters to the woman. "He almost got us killed."

But Chico, Pequeña, and I look at each other. *We're here, in Arriaga. Where La Bestia lives. Where she waits for us.*

"Some make it. Why not us?" I whisper to them. Chico smiles his stupid smile, Pequeña sighs with relief, and I feel my heart swell. *Not too much,* I tell it. *Don't feel too much.*

Moments later, the driver is pulling into some run-down area lined with shops and vendors. The man, woman, and two teenage girls rush off together as soon as the van comes to a stop. But I have no idea where we are.

"Will you take us to the tracks, to where La Bestia starts?" I ask the driver.

He shrugs. "It'll cost you more, but yeah . . . I can take you there."

I watch the world outside, people in other cars, headed who knows where.

While we head to the beast. The beast who will deliver our dreams.

Pequeña

We ride in the van and I think of the fields where we ran, where I buried bloodied pads in a small hole while Chico and Pulga gave me privacy and kept watch. Where I layered myself with more.

It's less now than before, and I will my body to stop bleeding. To stop draining. To reserve my energy as much as possible as I run away from Rey. As I run toward safety and maybe . . . *dreams*?

But lately, I've forgotten to dream. No, that's not right. I made myself stop dreaming.

The day after Papi left, when Mami came back from going with Tía to get the housekeeping job at the resort, she'd looked at me with a smile on her face that wasn't really a smile.

"Pues, mírame, una sirvienta," she said, the maid's uniform in her hand. "Ay, Pequeña, I tried. I endured things from your papi because I thought it would mean better for us, for you, if we were together. But now you get to see me go and change the sheets of the rich and los americanos. Clean the shit they leave behind."

Mami is beautiful. She could have probably married any man she wanted. But she'd loved Papi, whose love ran out, and who then ran far away from us.

"It's an honest job," Tía Consuelo told Mami. "You'll get tips. Sometimes."

Mami's eyes filled with tears and mine did, too. The way Mami shrank into herself, like she was so ashamed, hurt me more than even when Papi left. Tía hugged her. "I'm sorry, Lucia. I'll help you learn some basic English and maybe then you can waitress," she told Mami. Tía Consuelo had learned enough conversational English the year she lived in the States.

"I know, Consuelo . . . and I'm grateful, like I'm supposed to be. How else could I support us? It's just not something I *dreamed* of doing."

"Los sueños y los hombres son para las pendejas," Tía Consuelo said, squeezing Mami closer to her. Mami let out a half sob, half laugh, agreeing that yes, only dumbasses believed in dreams or men. And then they told me and Pulga we were going to celebrate Mami's new job, a new future. So we got on Tía's scooter and rode to the Miramar, where Pulga and I ate and Mami and Tía drank beer and said, laughing, "Sueños y hombres son para las pendejas!"

I decided then they were right. And I told myself dreaming up a future wasn't worth the pain that would come when eventually, inevitably, it would get crushed.

"Look, there it is!" Chico yells, and he's right. "Oh my god, that's it!" Already we can see the train. Dusty steel that looks like it's traveled through hell. I hear Pulga gasp next to me as we near the tracks, and my heart races as something like a dream feels like it's being born inside me.

"Listen," the driver says. He turns around to look at the three of us directly. "You see that?" He gestures toward a warped chain-link fence. "You can climb the fence or find an opening. There are openings all along there to get into the Ferromex train yard."

Outside the smudged, dirty window of the van, the yard looks mostly deserted. But there sits La Bestia. Waiting for us. My stomach flutters with anticipation.

Pulga looks excited, too. "Okay . . ." he says, digging into his pocket for the money we owe the guy.

"Listen," the driver says again. "How old are you boys?"

A sense of dread comes over me as I glance at the man's face.

I'm relieved he thinks I'm a boy, but why does he want to know our ages? Why, even, hasn't he collected his money and thrown us out of the van already and driven away?

Pulga clears his throat. "Seventeen." His voice is harsher as he spits out the lie, and I can tell he wants to seem older, tougher. I can tell the driver doesn't believe him. There's a hesitation around the edges of Pulga's voice that reminds me he is just as much a little kid as Chico.

The driver looks at each of us. "I have three boys—a couple years apart but about your ages. Listen . . . be careful."

Pulga nods. "How much extra do we owe you? For the drive to here?"

The driver shakes his head. "Forget it." But his voice is tinged with regret, as though he'd like nothing more than to collect more money from us and be on his way. As though he'd like nothing more than to dump us wherever and forget about us. But something won't let him. "Just be careful, you understand? The three of you have no business making a trip like this. Do you know how dangerous this is?"

"Yes," Pulga says. "But . . ."

But if he only knew what awaits us back home, maybe he'd take us all the way to the border. All the way to the States.

The driver nods. "I know. I know." He hesitates a moment, and out of nowhere says, "That guy who ran out onto the road last night . . . he couldn't have been too much older than you boys." He lets out a deep sigh, and I wonder if bringing us here, not charging us a single peso, wasn't some kind of penance. "Bueno," he says finally as he takes off his cowboy hat and runs his hand over his hair before putting the hat back on. "Que Dios vaya con ustedes."

Pulga nods, and we climb out of the van—one after another—

into the hot, dusty day and head toward the fence. We walk along it until we come across an opening, just like the driver said.

"You think he's for real?" Pulga asks, as we look back and notice he's still there, looking in our direction. "For all I know, he is calling someone to let them know he got three suckers here." Pulga looks around. But no one comes.

"Who knows," I tell him, and I think of how we can't trust anyone, but how the only way to do this trip is by sometimes putting your life in a stranger's hands.

A minute later, the white van drives off and we are walking along the tracks alone, except for a man in a neon worker's vest walking next to the train on the tracks.

"Come on," Pulga says. We avoid him and hurry toward some trees a bit in the distance, where we can sit on the ground and try to go unnoticed.

I look at the train cars; some are graffiti covered, some are plain gray steel and rust. Closer now, I can see the Ferromex name in faded paint on the side. I notice a few people in the distance, emerging from a building, approaching the worker. Relief pours over me when I see their backpacks. Here are others just like us.

"Those guys are gonna get on the train, too," Pulga says, eyeing them. "They're asking that worker when it'll take off, I bet."

"When will it?" Chico asks.

"I don't know," Pulga says. "I mean, sometimes it takes a day or two, maybe more. People just camp out and wait."

"For days?" Chico asks.

"Sometimes. But the train is already here, so I don't think we'll be here for days. And the worker is inspecting it so I'm betting it will leave soon," Pulga says, his eyes still taking in the worker, the yard, the train.

I look at the run-down buildings along the track. All of them look abandoned, with broken and dusty windows. But then I see some figures moving behind the windows. For a moment, I wonder if La Bruja is here, watching over me. I stare, trying to conjure her up, trying to make her fly out of one of those windows. She'd swoop down toward me and take me away, let me hold on to her hair as she flies me through the sky and takes me somewhere safe. Somewhere I won't be afraid to dream.

She will take Pulga and Chico, too.

And go back home and get Mami and Tía, and bring them along.

Even that small baby.

Some kind of pain shoots through my chest and for a moment, I feel that baby's mouth, sucking at my breast. Still demanding of me even as I get farther and farther away.

I wrap my arms across my front and the feeling stops. I stare back up at the windows. Nothing is there. No one comes.

It's only my mind, playing tricks.

"I'm so hungry," Chico says. We ate yesterday, but my stomach is rumbling, too.

"Here," I tell him, pulling some cookies from my bag that I've brought all the way from home—the cookies Mami and I would eat for breakfast in the morning. They're broken and practically crumbs, but I pour them into each of our hands.

"You know what I could go for right now?" Chico sucks up his crumbs. "The tamales, frijoles voltiados, ponche, and hot chocolate we have on Noche Buena."

My mouth waters at the thought of the food Mami and Tía prepare for Christmas Eve—especially tamales with that rich, earthy recado made of toasted pumpkin seeds, a strip of red or green chile, an olive, a few garbanzo beans, a little nugget of pork, all nestled in perfectly seasoned masa, wrapped in a slick banana leaf, waiting to be opened like a gift.

I swallow the saliva that has gathered in my mouth.

"And some of your mamá's chirmol," he says to Pulga. "With a fried tortilla, that salt on top like she does when it comes right out of the oil. Man . . . or oh, Pequeña! Your mami's rice," he says to me. Both my stomach and my heart are hit with fresh pangs of pain. "Or the sopa mein from El Miramar," he whispers. "That place has the best sopa mein."

"It *does,*" Pulga says.

"I know . . ." I say, closing my eyes and getting lost in the smell of the food cooking at El Miramar, that smell that hits you while you're still on the street, before you even enter the small restaurant. The one where Tía and Mami celebrated her new housekeeping job, and where we started going every Thursday and the owner would fill our bowls of sopa mein with extra noodles because he was in love with Mami. We'd sit and slurp them, having contests on who could suck them up fastest while Mami and Tía drank their cervezas and talked about life.

La vida this and *la vida that,* our mothers would say. And look exhausted by *la vida,* before looking at us and smiling.

"Stop," Pulga tells Chico as he rattles off more food.

"I could eat a mountain of chuchitos. God, I could eat a thousand of them. One right after the other. I'd sit in a corner with a pile of chuchitos and just peel each one and shove them into my mouth. All that masa melting on my tongue . . ."

"Man, stop it! Don't talk about food anymore," Pulga says, but he's laughing and I can tell he doesn't mean it. Even as our stomachs moan and echo with emptiness, the memories feed our souls.

"Close your eyes," I tell Pulga.

"I want to keep watch . . ."

"Just for a second, close your eyes. Both of you."

I tell them to imagine they're in my kitchen, and I explain how my mother makes her rice. The hundreds of times I've watched her wash and season it. I tell them to picture Pulga's mamá in the kitchen, too. Cooking that chicken she prepares en crema. And Chico's mamita is there, too, making tortillas from freshly ground corn.

"Can you see them, cooking for us? Can you see us, sitting with them, sharing food?"

The tears are streaming down my face before I realize it, and I am wiping at them, reeling back from the table to the bright, dusty yard.

I look at Pulga and he is sitting up, his eyes are watching the yard, trying to look tough, refusing to cry.

"Don't be a macho, Pulga," I tell him.

He gives me a dirty look. "I'm not. We just . . . we can't get emotional, or lost in the past, you know?"

But he's wrong. "Maybe thinking about the past is exactly what will make us keep going . . ." I tell him. I need to make it for myself, but also for Mami. So she won't see what would've happened to me if I'd stayed.

He shakes his head. "No. That's what will keep us back."

I stare at him, not sure whether the fierceness I see in his eyes is a good or bad thing. It seems different than the little-kid toughness he's always used to cover up his sensitivity. This is harder. Colder.

It worries me.

The sound of clanking and rumbling fills the yard, and instantly, Pulga is on his feet, looking toward the tracks. One of the cars is moving, then another. The workman in the vest is walking along beside them, inspecting. But the train only moves a few feet before it stops and sits idle again.

"It's gonna leave soon," Pulga whispers. "But if we get on now, we're gonna bake under that sun."

"I definitely don't want to get on till we have to," Chico says. "I heard the steel is burning hot."

"Won't that worker guy kick us off if we get on?" I ask.

Pulga shakes his head. "Nah, they can't keep up with everyone. The most they'll do is ask for some pisto." Pulga rubs his fingers together and I nod. Everyone can be bought.

"Still, we should be ready," Pulga says.

In the distance, I see people come out of the nearby buildings and the overgrown brush. They climb on the train, some with bags of supplies, with blankets and pillows. Others with just a backpack. Some wear boots, others sneakers, others flip-flops. I notice the small platforms between the boxcars already have people tucked away in them.

Pulga follows my gaze. "Those areas are easier to ride than the top. But those people have probably been here for hours, maybe since yesterday. And sometimes, when the train stops or slows down abruptly, there are these parts between the cars that hit together. Crush whatever is between there." Pulga smacks his hands together. "People lose their feet like that all the time."

I suck in my breath, impressed and a little surprised by how much Pulga knows, despite how much he doesn't.

We watch as women reach down for their children, as men lift toddlers and babies into waiting arms. There are pairs and trios of young people traveling together, and men who look much older than us, walking up and down the train figuring out where might be the best place to sit.

Those on board sit on the beast's back under the grueling sun. They cover their faces, the backs of their heads and necks from the sun. Others use cardboard pieces as sunshields. We watch them sweating and melting, and as time ticks on, some climb back down and seek shade closest to the tracks.

We wait, all of us, for the beast to wake up again. We watch as it sleeps, unbothered, unhurried. It doesn't care that my heart is racing. That my mind feels dizzy from the heat and hunger. That my body is prickly with sweat and readiness. It doesn't care that we're dying, literally *dying*, to get as far away as possible from the places we love but that have turned on us.

It doesn't care how desperate we are to go on.

We wait. Until La Bestia is ready.

Finally, it hisses awake again. It clanks and rattles. It rumbles. For a moment, no one moves. We wait to see if this is really it. And then we hear the call—"¡Vámanos! ¡Vámanos!"—and see people gesturing to each other to *come on! hurry up!* as the wheels begin to move. People run from every direction.

"Let's go," Pulga says, "I think it's really leaving this time."

We grab our backpacks and run toward the train, crowded by others running, too.

It's gathering speed and soon more people are running alongside the tracks, looking for the perfect place to grab on, pushing others out of their way. Already, it's crowded with people on top who withstood the heat for hours, looking down at those of us running. Others are clinging to its side, urging and instructing those running below.

You suffer either way.

La Bestia. This is it. A moment ago just fragments of cars, now an enormous steel centipede groaning and hissing to life, its power vibrating through the ground.

"Hurry! Hurry!" Pulga yells. "Before it starts moving too fast!" He runs ahead of Chico and me.

We race to the tracks and run along the gravel, just like everyone else. Brown faces and arms, reaching.

I run faster, pumping my legs, my heart in my throat. My feet are a flurry and I feel like I am both in and out of my body.

I hear Pulga's voice faintly, yelling something up ahead, but I don't even know what he is saying anymore, the world feels like it's whirling faster as I run, as others run past me and next to me and behind me. As that beast rumbles and roars in my ears.

I watch as Pulga grabs on to one of the metal bars, the side of a ladder that leads to the top of the train. A few more steps and then he is pulling himself up and climbing the ladder, to the top of the train already crowded with so many people. I see his panicked face as he looks down, tells Chico to run faster. I watch Chico reach for the same bar—watch him miss it once. Twice.

My abdomen tightens and tightens, pulsing with pain. The sun gleams behind Pulga like a golden corona around his head and in that instant, he reminds me of Jesus. Jesus's fate was sealed.

But ours is not—not yet.

I run faster, and I have a chance to get on. Then I see Chico's face, the terror as he runs, as he realizes he's falling behind.

I won't leave him. I can't. I'm already leaving so many things behind. If he doesn't get on, then I won't, either. And we will watch Pulga go on without us.

I fall back, point to where he needs to grab, and watch as Chico runs faster.

I stay right behind him, those steel wheels speeding up next to us.

I can feel the train breathing, like it wants to suck me in, under its body, under its wheels. I can feel it practically slicing through my ankles, detaching my feet from my body.

I stumble.

"Come on, come on!" Pulga screams. At last, Chico grabs on, and he is being dragged, his feet coming so close, so close, to those wheels. Pulga is shouting at him, but I can't hear anything except the roaring and heavy breath of that beast.

Chico finally manages to get one foot on the lowest bar, and he pulls himself up, climbs to the top like Pulga.

The train gathers speed. My backpack swings back and forth, making me lose my balance. They are both looking down at me now, their faces in and out of focus, their mouths wide as they yell and scream to me. I run faster as the train sucks at my feet.

I reach up, the bar just out of reach.

I run faster, faster, reach for the metal bar again. This time I grab on, and the full power of La Bestia is suddenly traveling through my body, shaking me violently.

I struggle to get one foot up, feeling like as soon as I do, La Bestia will gnaw at the other, and then pull my whole body under.

Please, please, God, please, God, please, please . . .

I close my eyes and lift the other foot onto the lowest bar, pull my weight up with all my strength. Then I am climbing, one, two, three, four bars, wedging myself between people as I pull myself on top of the train.

Chico and Pulga are yelling and hollering with relief and joy, grabbing on to each other and then me, too. I laugh and their faces shine even more with happiness. Chico's cheeks so round, highlighted by the sunlight. Pulga's more serious face and downcast eyes now gleaming with achievement.

The train gains speed and the ground becomes a blur. One by one, people in the distance stop running as the train and all hope leave, come to a defeated stop when they realize they will no longer catch it.

But *we* did.

"We did it!" Pulga yells over the clacking of the tracks. Chico throws his arm around Pulga's shoulders, turns his head to the sky and lets out a long wolf's howl. Pulga cracks up and begins howling, too.

I know I will always remember this exact image. I can't remember when I last saw them looking so happy, so free. I can't remember the last time I felt that way, too.

Everyone around us laughs and lifts their arms in the air. Together, we howl and holler and yell in victory. And with so many voices, so many of us clustered together, not even the train can mute our celebration.

We did it.

We are not those in the distance who have stopped running and have to wait for the next train. We are not those back in our neighborhoods, waking up to another day and another and another of whatever threat has climbed in through our windows, whispered our horrible fate into our ears.

We are luchadores. We are fighters. We are those who dare to try against impossible odds.

We determine our own fate.

The train speeds up even more and the hot wind is whipping at our faces. The sun beats down on us, so bright it hardly seems real. We settle in, weaving our fingers into the small holes of the grates on top of the train, and holding on, so tight.

And even though we are afraid, even though the fear is right there beneath the surface, it's a different kind of fear.

It's fear with hope.

And hope matters, as we ride into an unknown future.

PART THREE

El Viaje

The Journey

Pulga

Hours have passed. I think. It feels like we left Barrios years ago, but it's only been three days. I think. Already time feels like it's shifting beneath my feet, something that bends and cracks like the ground during an earthquake.

The thrill that everyone felt when the train first pulled out of the Arriaga station has slowly diminished as we ride, tree branches whipping at us from either side, the sun burning our skin.

I look at Chico, leaning on Pequeña, their arms interlocked. She looks over at me, her eyes tired, but attempts a smile.

The incessant heat and swaying of the train make me tired, too, but I don't want to let myself sleep. My body rocks back and forth, to the sound of steel and tracks, to La Bestia's rhythm. And I suddenly remember the promise I made to myself if I got to the train. I quickly reach around for my backpack, clutch it tight as I unzip it and feel for the Walkman. The headphones.

I put the headphones on. I turn up the volume all the way. The train sways and I hold on tighter; the deep green of trees, the yellow glow of the world under the intense sun rush past me. I press play—set it all to music.

The sound of a harsh click rings in my ears. A door slamming shut. And a creaky mattress as someone sits down.

Then, my father's voice.

Okay, so listen, this next song right here, Consuelo, I've loved it forever, right? But now when I hear it, I think of you and I see us dancing. But, like, I see us dancing in my mom's backyard with a lot of people around us at our wedding. Ah, I can't believe I just said that! You got me thinking corny shit, you know that? Haha, I can see you smiling. I can see exactly how you're smiling right now. You'd marry me, though, right? That's the future I see. Because I love you so much. Ah, I feel so corny saying this shit. You're laughing now. Anyway, that backyard wedding, my mom will invite the whole family, and the band. The guys will be playing this song right here, and you and I, we're gonna be dancing, Consuelo.

Good times are coming for us.

Lots of good times.

And your pain, you can leave all of it behind you now.

Okay, so this here es para ti.

I hit rewind. And listen to his message again. My lips silently mouth each word Juan Eduardo Rivera García recorded so long ago. I've listened to this tape hundreds of times. I know my father's words. I know the lyrics to each song. I know the name of every band. I can recite it all.

I've listened to it more times than I count—since the moment Mamá gave me the tape and told me that even though thinking of my father made her sad, that I deserved to have something of his. But she worried the tape would make me sad, too.

"I always want to protect you, Pulga," she explained. "But I *do* want you to know him. Even if it's just in this small way."

I can still see her face as she got up from where she'd been sitting on my bed and left my room, closing the door behind her, already knowing it was the most I would cry in my whole life.

But also knowing the pain would be worth the joy it brought me.

I hit rewind again as heat, thick and humid, smacks at my face and La Bestia screeches loudly at a slight bend in the track. I wonder if that's what it sounded like, the car that smashed my father's body and Mamá's heart and my future.

Don't get emotional, I tell myself. There is a reason I didn't listen before—I needed to stay focused on getting us to the train. But now I allow these words to fuel my dreams, dreams of becoming a musician in California, like him. Of someday bringing Mamá there again, too. *Don't get emotional,* I tell my heart that is swelling with every feeling right now. It's just a small reward.

I know I shouldn't keep listening. I've gotten us this far by thinking with my head, not my heart. I have to stay focused to get us through the rest of the trip.

But I let my father's words fill my ears once more, and even though I know they are for Mamá, that there was no way my father knew about me or what the future held, I feel like his words have always been meant for me, too.

I see us dancing.

And I see us, jumping around to the bass of these songs. You, all cool and young, your tattooed arms reaching for me in a living room that would have existed—if only you had known not to go out that night. If only you had lived long enough to know Mamá was pregnant.

Haha, I can see you smiling.

I can see him smiling, too. I've even studied that picture of him and Mamá. I've memorized his smile. I've tried to match my smile to his. Sometimes, I think I do. Mamá gets this look, and she gets lost for a moment, before her smile erases and she looks away.

That's the future I see.

What future did he see, really? A lifetime of Mamá and him cruising in his car, along the Pacific Ocean? The sun glinting off the water? Did he see me, even then, sitting in the back? Did he see me, the son he would have someday? Did he know that I would miss him, a father I never got the chance to meet? The one who could've saved me, Mamá, from *all* of this. If only he hadn't died. Why did he have to die?

I love you so much.

Could he love me even though he never knew me? The way I love him.

Your pain, you can leave all of it behind you now.

I'm heading there, to the future, to the place where he grew up. But now there's a different pain. Because I'm not leaving just pain behind. I'm leaving behind everything I loved, too.

I let the rest of the tape play. My father sounds like a gringo, like the tourists and missionaries who sometimes come to Barrios. His mouth stumbles over Spanish words, like his tongue doesn't want to cooperate when he says them. The first time I heard it, I ran into Mamá's room, and asked her how she never told me that. She laughed and said it never occurred to her. *Your father* was *Mexican, but he was born and raised in California,* she said. *So he understood Spanish but hardly spoke it. It was cute to me, his accent. I used to tease him about it.*

Tal vez no te recuerdas, but this song, esta canción estaba en el radio cuando te vi la primera vez. He laughs. *Maybe it wasn't a big moment for you,* he mumbles in English. *Pero era un momento muy*—another laugh—*muy bonito para mi. Es una de mis favoritas. And you, tú eres mi favorita.* He laughs again. *Shit, girl, I can't believe you got me making mixtapes.*

The sound of a guitar fills my ears and mind.

After I heard this tape for the first time, I went to school the next day and stayed after, googling lyrics and asking my English language teacher to help me get enough of the lyrics to google the songs and titles and groups. It took a while, but it felt like I was finding bits of my father. And each song helped me know some part of him better.

And now, as I ride through this land, I feel like he's here, too. Somehow, I know this land is in his blood. And mine.

I listen to the songs, so many of them with a twangy, beachy guitar sound, like you could just be relaxing by the ocean, enjoying the sun instead of being killed by it. That guitar, that is how California is, I imagine. Where the sun has mercy on los americanos, where it kisses their skin and turns it the right shade of brown.

Not like here. Not like ours.

When you're from here, the world thinks less of you. The world thinks we are ants. Fleas.

The world thinks they are gods.

My father was a god.

Someday I'll be a god, too.

My arms and legs ache from sitting and gripping the roof of the train. Someone sits up and I have just enough room to lie down on the other side of Pequeña. Just for a little while.

"Don't let me fall asleep," I whisper. She looks at me, her eyes sleepy, but nods.

I stare at that sky, all that sky. And I turn the volume up as high as possible.

An image of my mother alone in her room floats around in my head. *I'm sorry,* I say to her. My heart trembles, loosens the emotions I've been trying to keep tight.

Don't get emotional.

I put my hand to my chest, press down hard. Keep pressing, until the image fades away to black.

I open my eyes to streaks of pink and purple and orange and roaring that becomes louder and louder.

I sit up with a jolt, realizing I must have fallen asleep. In my chest, panic and fear—this is how people die. By falling asleep without realizing it. By forgetting where they are.

I look over at Pequeña. Her eyes are closed. Next to her, Chico is asleep, too, still holding on to her arm and curled toward her.

I notice a man with his arm over a woman's shoulder. He stares back at me, hard. The look, a message to not even think about messing with him or his girlfriend. The guy could chew me up and spit me out.

I open the cassette player and flip the tape over.

Esta aquí es muy buena, Consuelo. Cool as hell, baby.

I look at the sky again, the colors burning and intensifying with every passing second, so beautiful, it seems almost impossible to think we won't make it to the States.

I focus on the intense red as we ride to Ixtepec, a red that, up in the sky like that, doesn't remind me of blood. And I watch as the sky darkens, going from purple to a deep indigo.

I watch as the bright colors get swallowed up and night finds its way in.

Pequeña

The black velvet sky is scattered with estrellitas.

We're huddled together, hunched over, quiet, letting the wind sweep over us.

There are so many of us that each turn, each jerk of the train makes those on the very edges push toward the center for fear of falling, tightening everyone in between. We press on each other every few minutes and I feel the squeeze of the group, the desperate pulse of us.

Chico traces the stars in the sky with his fingertip, randomly connecting one to another to another. He does this over and over again as we rumble on.

The train is going so fast—my fingers ache from holding on, my body feels pricked with needles. My head is itchy and my eyes sting from the rushing wind, from dirt and dust.

La Bestia shifts slightly, winding through the night, and it screeches and howls like some kind of banshee as Chico holds on to me tightly. It straightens and lulls us again with its rocking back and forth, with the rhythmic sound of the tracks. Chico loosens his grip.

"You okay?"

He nods, but he looks so scared. He takes a deep breath, and looks again to the sky. Begins tracing the stars again. I think he is making wishes on all of them.

I look to the scattering of dust, not to the brightest or biggest. I look to the stars nobody cares about, that don't hold anyone's gaze and nobody bothers to wish on.

If they could grant wishes, what would I wish for? Where would I start?

When I was born? On this dirt instead of that? As a girl instead of a boy? As poor instead of rich? When Papi left and didn't come back? When Rey was born? When I lifted my head to the sun? When he saw me? When he climbed into my window? When the child was that bundle of stars inside me? When I threw myself from the bus, hoping it would take a life, not caring if it was mine or that baby's.

It had been so hot. I don't even know if I was in my right mind. I hadn't thought to go to Leticia. I didn't even think of doing what I did until I saw the bus drive past, so full of people, their arms poking out from the windows and the door that had long been taken off so people could more quickly and easily enter and exit.

For six months I'd carried that secret. For six months, Rey kept finding me. That morning, too, as I walked among tomatoes and green peppers and eggplant at the market.

He smiled his terrible smile and was at my house before me, waiting. I couldn't stand his smell anymore. He filled the air, my room, with the smell of sulfur, rot and evil—a smell that had been stuck in my nose since that very first time.

When he left, I walked through our barrio from end to end, climbing hills and rocks. I walked and walked, willing my body to give up.

And then the bus, with those arms, bright and reaching in the sun. And the driver, who stopped when I raised mine and let me on. It was so full, so clustered, so thick with people. The day was broiling. And the smell of *him* followed me everywhere.

Can you smell it, I wanted to ask them. But their faces, apathetic, brown and tired. Greasy with sweat.

Maybe I died and went to hell. Maybe this is hell, that's what I remember thinking. And then I panicked, that hell should be the barrio where I grew up, with my people, on a white van to the market.

I had to get out. I had to escape. I leaned out the door and let go.

But now, on this train, packed with all these people, I hold on.

I ride and hope and stare at the night sky forever, for hours, until the stars above me blur and spin like a kaleidoscope. Until I feel like I am out of my body and realize some part of me is.

I am looking down at the train, at Pulga and Chico and me on it. I see the tracks, as if they are glowing, and the trail of things the train leaves behind as it travels into the night.

The track is littered with bloodied limbs; with sliced-off feet and legs and hands and arms. With tearstained faces. With crushed photographs and fluttering flowers. With bloodstained dollar bills, with whole and broken bones.

A sense of dread comes over me and I feel myself falling, but in the distance, a faint glow catches my eye and when I focus on it, the glow becomes bigger, brighter. Until I see it is my house, illuminated by the sun.

On the patio, I see my mother. And I feel a sharp pain in my chest, a pain that travels down to my abdomen. A pain that grinds and crushes and breaks my body apart. The pain of life coming out of me. I call for my mother and back there, in that land, I see her hold out her hands. And I watch that child fly to her, the long cord still attaching us.

She holds his small bloodied body, and looks into the distance, into the darkness, searching for me.

I feel myself crash back into my body, to the top of the train again, to its jagged metal and violent rumbling.

My eyes snap open to someone grabbing my shoulder, jerking back harshly. A strange man's face is inches from mine. "Stay awake!" he yells at me.

The person who was close to the edge has moved, and little by little, I've shifted closer to the edge. My feet are nearly hanging over it.

I pull them up and away. Pulga and Chico jolt awake as La Bestia screeches and howls. The brakes are being applied and it screams into the night. The guy who told me to stay awake suddenly looks toward the front of the train as we hear more and more voices, shouting back to one another.

Cars suddenly appear, racing alongside the train up ahead.

The night is cut with the flash of headlights.

With screams and yells.

With desperation and fear.

Pulga

N*arcos! Kidnappers! La migra!* People shout over one another.

"We need to jump off now!" a guy yells—it's the man I noticed earlier with his girlfriend. He hurries over to her and I can see him shouting, telling her not to be scared but that they have to jump.

"What's going on?" Chico yells.

"I don't know," I tell him and Pequeña. The sound of La Bestia's brakes being applied cuts through all our voices as cars come up along the right side of the train.

The headlights and taillights. Cars. Of either narcos or officials, racing next to the train. There is nothing in sight, not a building or lights of a town. Nothing but seemingly endless field. So, whoever it is, whatever they want, it can't be good.

The woman climbs down the ladder, and the guy keeps telling her to *jump, now, jump now!*

The train is still moving fast enough that just the thought is terrifying.

"Come on," I tell Chico and Pequeña. We have to do the same or whoever is in those cars is going to do something to those on this train, as soon as it comes to a stop. "We have to jump!"

Ahead, I can see other migrants jumping, like bodies from a burning building, and running into the fields.

Then the woman lets go. We watch from above as she stumbles and falls to the ground, as the guy jumps right after her, staying on his feet and running to her. Even though the train has slowed, it is still going fast. But they are okay.

We will be okay.

"Go!" I tell Chico, because the way he's clasping on to the top of the train, watching in terror as more bodies fall to the ground below, I know he won't jump unless I make him.

"No way! I can't!"

"You have to!"

He shakes his head. "No!"

The train and the cars are slowing now, the screeching more piercing as it fills the night. If we wait too long, those cars, whoever they are, will stop and collect all the people jumping off.

We have to go now.

"Fucking jump, Chico! Fucking jump now or you're gonna get us killed!" I feel like I'm choking on panic. I feel like my chest is going to explode with it.

"I can't! I won't make it!" He's at the bottom of the ladder. All he has to do is jump. Just a small jump. A terrible part of me, the part that is trying to survive, thinks of stepping on his fingers, of crushing them so he will let go.

"Please!" I beg. "Please, Chico, please!"

"Chico, you can do this! Come on, Chiquito!" Pequeña yells over me.

"Oh, God," he says, and I can hear his cries, blending in with those of La Bestia.

"Now!" I yell. "Fucking *now*!"

And then I see his hand let go.

I hear a terrible bang and I look to see Chico's body flopping around and then rolling, rolling, rolling in the darkness.

There's another terrifying screech and my legs feel like they're about to buckle underneath me. They feel like rubber, from being scrunched up on top of the train, from being in the same position for so many hours.

My heart is a furious drum as I throw myself and jump.

For one millisecond, there is nothing. No rattling, no sense of feeling anything other than stillness, before I come crashing down on the gravel, just like Chico, rolling and seeing blurry snippets of train and tracks, and steel and wheels and sky and rock. There is grass, and dirt, but I can't tell what I'm moving toward and what I'm moving away from. I brace myself for the feel of cutting, for the wheels, sharp as blades, to slice through me.

Somehow, finally, my body comes to a stop, and I rush to my feet, just as Pequeña rolls like a tumbleweed, away from the train. But it's Chico I can't find.

"Chico!" I run to where he jumped. I don't see him anywhere in the darkness and there's no answer when I call his name.

But then I see him, there, on the ground, far enough from the track—unmoving. I run faster and fall next to him.

"Chico, Chico! Are you okay?" I check to see if a part of him was ground up and spit out.

He is perfectly still, his eyes glistening and staring upward. He is gasping for breath and I'm afraid to turn him over, to see some horrific slice through his back, or blood seeping out from under him.

"Man, please, please!" I beg. "Be okay, Chico." He looks at me and seems stunned. "Say something," I tell him.

He gasps for breath, like the time we were running to school and he fell over a concrete block and flipped in the air, like a fucking ninja landing on his back, the wind knocked out of him.

"Chiquito." Pequeña is on the other side of him, her mouth gushing with blood, and she's holding her hand up to her mouth, spitting into her hand. But checking on Chico, patting him and looking over his body.

He gasps and finally, finally speaks. "Am I alive?"

I start laughing and crying, because I'm so glad to hear his stupid voice. "Yes, pendejo. You're alive!"

"Are you alive . . . ?" he asks, looking at Pequeña.

She nods. "I . . . I think I broke a couple of teeth, Chiquito." She looks stunned but her words are calm as she wipes her hand on the inside of her jacket pocket. "Come on." Pequeña rushes to her feet, starts pulling him up. "Come on, Chiquito, we have to hide," Pequeña says. "Can you walk? Are you okay?"

"Yeah, yeah," he says, stumbling to his feet.

The faint lights of the train and cars are far off in the distance but still visible. We hear yelling and crying. We see lights flashing and dashing back and forth on the train's top where just moments ago we rode.

I feel sorry for those who didn't jump, who *couldn't* jump. For the women with babies in their arms, or people who were too scared. I don't want to know what their fate will be.

We rush into the darkness, Chico stumbling as we grab him on either side and hurry him along into the overgrown grass. There aren't many trees here, and that makes the walk easier and faster to navigate, but also makes it harder to hide.

"Slow down," Chico says. "My head, it feels like it's splitting open."

It's hard to see in the darkness. But I picture what we must look like. Walking through that field.

Chico's arms outstretched, his head dripping blood.

"Stop, stop," Chico says. "I feel dizzy." He is leaning on us more and more, stumbling loudly as he walks.

"Just a little more," I whisper to him. But he is becoming dead weight in our hands.

"I'm trying," he says. "But—"

"Shhhh," I say. I hear the crunching of grass, someone coming up behind us. I pull him down, but too hard, and he falls between Pequeña and me, letting out a moan.

The walking stops.

My body wants to run and also seems frozen in place. My brain is trying to stay calm even as it hollers a warning and a command. Someone, something, is out there.

We stay in place and the crunching starts again, comes closer.

Something tells me to scream. Something tells me not to make a sound. The sound is nearly next to us, and then it is here.

It is the guy from the train, the one whose girlfriend jumped first. He has a gun in his hand, pointing it into the dark, in our direction.

I can just barely see him thanks to the small bit of moonlight as it shines on his face.

"Please, don't shoot," I whisper. "Please."

"Who's there?" he says. Chico moans and Pequeña whispers to him.

"We were with you on the train," I hurry to explain. "We jumped after you." He takes a step closer, looks at us, shakes his head.

"You're lucky I didn't blow your head off," he says. He lets out a soft whistle and the girlfriend who was with him emerges from the darkness. She looks a couple years older than Pequeña.

"Just those three kids from the train," he tells her.

"Oh . . ." she says. "You okay?" she whispers to us. But the guy starts talking over her, telling her they can keep walking now.

"Come on," he says, taking her hand and pulling her away.

"Wait," she says. "What happened to him?" she points at Chico, who is still lying on the ground. "And you," she says when she sees Pequeña.

"He hit his head hard when he jumped. He's dizzy, having trouble walking. I think he needs to rest," I tell her.

"I hit my mouth on some rocks when I jumped," Pequeña says.

The guy is pulling at his girlfriend's arm, but she pulls away from him.

"Get him up," she urges, coming over to us. "He needs to keep going. Come on," she says, helping Pequeña and me get Chico back up on his feet. "If you don't get back on the train, you're going to be stuck out here for who knows how long."

She calls over to the guy. "Come help," she says. "Let him lean on you."

"No," he says, "we don't have time to babysit these three. I told you. Before we left, didn't I? We can't get attached to anyone. I already woke them on the train when you asked me to."

"Help me," she says, ignoring him. "Or you can go on without me."

He sucks his teeth and sighs, but comes over and pushes me out of the way, then puts Chico's arm around his neck. The woman goes on the other side.

"Gracias," I whisper to her as we walk into the darkness.

She doesn't say anything at first, and then suddenly, several minutes later she says, "You three reminded me of my little brothers. Are you brothers?"

"Yes," I say. It's only half a lie.

"I could tell. I left my brothers in El Salvador." Her voice is heavy with longing and guilt suddenly.

"I left my mamá," I tell her. "In Guatemala."

"I left my mamá and papá, too," she says. "I didn't tell them I was leaving . . ."

"Me neither. Just left mine a letter." My heart pulses with regret and shame. Mamá deserved more than just a letter. I press down on my chest, push away those feelings.

Her eyes catch the little bit of moonlight there is and I can see in them exactly how I feel.

"Stop talking," the guy whispers. "We don't know who's out here. All I know is we can't go too far from the train," he continues. "We have to catch it when it starts up again."

He doesn't need to say what could happen if we don't.

We quiet down, keep walking, dragging Chico through the night until the guy tells us to lie down in the grass and stay quiet.

We follow his instructions because he seems to know what he's doing. Every few minutes, I look over at Chico and he's closed his eyes. I don't know if it's exhaustion or his head, but I know he can't sleep now.

"Wake up, Chico." I give him a nudge. His eyelids flutter.

"I'm awake," he whispers back. And then I look toward the train, trying to make out what's happening in the darkness, catching only glimpses of people when they are in the headlights of the cars. Three cars.

From here it looks like some of the people on top are being ordered down to the ground. They are being lined up. My heart quickens as I think of the stories I've heard outside Don Feli's store—of people being executed.

I look over at Chico. His eyes are closed again. Pequeña nudges him and I say, "Chico, wake up."

"I'm awake!" he says loudly, scratching at his head.

"Be quiet," the guy snaps.

The lights on top of the train hop down to the ground again. I think whoever stopped the train got their payoff from those on top. After a while, I see those who were lined up being forced into the cars on the road. Then the cars are turning around, driving back down the length of the train. The headlights get brighter and brighter as they come in our direction, as their engines roar in that quiet night, and finally pass us.

I watch as the red rear lights get smaller and dimmer, disappearing into the night, and am relieved the sound of bullets didn't break the silence.

Even so, my nerves won't quit jangling, and I feel like I'm going to throw up. But there's no time.

"We have to get closer now," the guy says. "It might start up and leave at any minute."

Chico moans as we move him. "I'm awake," he says.

"I know, but you have to walk," I tell him. "Come on, Chico. Keep walking."

He tries but he still needs help. If this guy weren't here, I don't know what we'd do.

His girlfriend and I are on one side of Chico and the guy is on the other. Pequeña follows behind us, rubbing her jaw.

My clothes are sticking to me and the smell coming off Chico's armpits keeps wafting up. I feel sweat trickling along my scalp, down my face, falling into and burning my eyes as I hold him by his waist. I wipe my face on his shirt.

The train clanks and comes back to life.

"Hurry!" the guy yells. "It's getting ready to leave." He picks up the pace and I run to keep up, but Chico's legs are like rubber. If we were to let go, he'd fall. We drag him.

"I'm awake," he says, his eyes half-closed.

"Just a little more," I tell him. The guy moves faster and we are running then, jostling Chico every which way as he cries and moans.

The train hisses and shakes. People are emerging from every direction, running past us as the guy curses and tells his girl to leave us behind. But she won't let go of Chico. People are yelling, climbing on to the train, urging one another to hurry. When we're only a few yards away, it whistles and shakes and the wheels start to move.

The guy curses and runs faster. Pequeña is running ahead,

to one of the cars, its door slightly opened, barely visible in the darkness.

"Here!" she yells, trying to slide the door open more. "Here!"

The train is waking up, slowly moving.

"Grab him!" the guy yells at her, and Pequeña holds Chico as the guy climbs on. Within seconds he's pushed the door open farther and climbed on board. He reaches for Chico and pulls him on as we push him up and in.

Then he pulls his girlfriend on board. Then Pequeña. And finally me.

The train is rolling faster now, but more people see the open cargo door and jump inside with us. More and more, until the car is filled. Some try to climb down from the roof, but are forced to go back up by two guys at the opening who take it upon themselves not to let it get too crowded because we won't be able to breathe with too many bodies in the car.

I watch as a woman on the ground passes her child to someone in the car above before she can climb up. A hand reaches down to grab the baby, gripping him by his arm. The child dangles in midair, screaming, before he's pulled up all the way.

One wrong move. One jerk of the train. One arm too weakened to hold him, and the boy would fall to the tracks.

A part of me, the part that lives inside my chest and is aching all the time, tells me to climb out. To find the woman and the baby and have them take my place in the car where it is safer.

But my mind reminds me if I get out of this car, another body will fill it up before I can even get to that woman.

My mind reminds me that the best way to survive this trip is to forget about that part of me deep inside my chest.

The car is stuffy. It smells of sweat and body odor. The itching on my head that I've been feeling for days becomes more intense, and I scratch so hard I draw blood beneath my nails. Chico moans off and on, mutters that he's awake. The guy who helped us gives us a dirty look as he holds his girlfriend.

When I close my eyes, I see that child dangling.

Dangling in midair like that, then falling.

I jolt awake, search for him and his mother, before my eyes close again.

Pequeña

The odor of urine and feces and sweat fills the small boxcar. Even with the door open, the air is thick and stagnant. My stomach turns as the heat of our bodies makes the smell even more pungent. I hear some someone retching, then the sour smell of vomit.

I want to close my eyes, sleep, but when I do, the faces of others on this train with me flash through my mind; I see their lives and what they're running from. I see fruitless farms and families with nothing to eat. I see people held at knifepoint. I see money exchanging hands. I see blood and smell fear. I hear threats and feel intense desperation.

So I keep my eyes open, focused on the door of the boxcar.

When you watch the dark for hours, it's not hard to focus on the noises you hear. Mostly you hear your own voice. Telling you all kinds of things. Like maybe you were meant to die. That maybe your fate is your fate and there is no way to escape your fate. That maybe your body is too tired, too weak.

You hear the voice of giving in. Of giving up.

But there's another voice, too, that comes from the pit of your stomach.

And it's the voice that says, *You deserve to live.*

Look what you will do, what you will put yourself through, just for *a chance.*

You hold on to that voice, and you make it louder and louder, until it fills up your head. You listen to it as long as you can because you know how it goes silent as you ride, you know how it gets drowned by other voices and the sound of the train. And then you have to find it all over again.

Over and over, you find that voice.

Over and over, you lose it again.

For miles and hours you play this game, until you watch the darkness fade and the sun come up and the sky somehow, like a miracle, ablaze again.

I look at the guy and his girlfriend. She's sleeping. He's not.

He's watching the day rise outside, too. And his face is lit up in a way that, for a minute, I see his hopes and dreams. For a minute, I hear his voice, his thoughts, how he wants to get her there safe. How they will get married. How they will have children. He just has to get them there safely.

He turns his gaze on me and I look away.

The train screeches. Chico's eyes flutter. I hold his head in my lap, trying to minimize the jostling he feels as the train trembles and screams.

Trees and ramshackle buildings blur by past the opening. More people on the train wake up, and now in the daylight, I see there are even more of us than I realized. Maybe more than a hundred. And that's not counting the small children swallowed up by the crowd, who I don't see but can hear crying and asking for food. Someone close to the opening yells that we must be in Ixtepec, and after a while, he yells that we're near the train yard. And industrial warehouses, ugly and solitary, come into view as we rumble in and come to a gasping, lurching stop.

Everyone from the boxcar begins climbing off the train. As they walk into the sunlight, I see them covered in the remnants of the dust and powder of whatever this train car carries. They look ashen. They look like corpses.

I look down at my clothes, my hands, and know I look just like them, too.

Pulga and I lift Chico up as the guy helps his girl off the train.

"Let's follow them," Pulga whispers to me, nodding toward the guy and girl. "That guy knows what he's doing."

I nod and we hurry to the exit, helping Chico, who is awake but looks stunned and keeps holding his head and leaning on us.

The sun is bright and blinding and Chico shields his eyes. People are stumbling across the field, looking around, and that's when Pulga spots the couple.

"No way, hermanos," the guy says as soon as he notices us following them. "My girl may have a soft spot for you, but you can't be following us. I'm not a pollero or any shit like that. And I don't want to be responsible for the three of you."

I look at his girlfriend. She reminds me of Leticia years ago, pretty even in all this dirt and dust and heat. She looks at us like she would like to help, but this is as much as she can do.

"Come on," Pulga begs him. "We won't bother you. I promise. We'll stay out of your way. Please."

Chico drops suddenly, like his legs have given out, and he sits down in the dirt. "Chico," I say, bending down next to him. "Get up, Chico. Come on."

"Shhh," the guy says, putting his finger to his lips. "I don't want to know his name. Or yours. Or yours," he says to each of us in turn.

"Please," Pulga begs, looking between the guy and his girlfriend.

The guy takes a deep breath. "I'm going to say this once, and that's it. So listen to me, okay?" He puts his hand on Pulga's shoulder. "Your brother can't go on this way, right now."

"But we have to—" Pulga says. But I know the guy is right. Chico can't go on like this.

"I said, listen," he says. "He needs to rest for a few days. He cannot be running to catch this thing, or riding it, being thrown around for hours."

Chico's skin is a grayish pale and even though he's sitting there, listening to us, his eyes, when he opens them, have a kind of vacant look.

"You're okay, right, Chico?" Pulga says. "You can go on, right? Tell him you're fine," he says, gesturing to the guy.

Chico nods. "Yeah, yeah . . . it's just the sun, it's so bright." He holds on to his head. "My head is pounding."

"Pulga," I say, realizing there is no way this guy is going to let us tag along with him any farther. Realizing that Chico needs help.

"He can go on," Pulga insists to the guy. He sounds like he used to when we were little and he was begging his mamá for something. "He'll rest right here while we wait for the train to take off again." Pulga gestures back to the train on the track. "We take it to . . . hold on . . ." He jerks his backpack around, rummaging for his notebook.

The guy stares at Pulga, then points to the tracks next to the ones we just came from. "You go on the next train on *that* track," he says. "*That* one heads to *Matias Romero*. *That's* the one you want to be on." The guy sighs. "Just follow the others until you get to Lecheria, okay? Then you have to decide which route—man, forget it. I can't be explaining all this to you three. You should've figured this stuff out."

"I did," Pulga spits out, holding up his notebook. "I studied the maps, listened to stories."

The guy laughs. "Stop. This is exactly why I can't be helping you. You know you're not going to make it, right? Not this time around. Not even with your little notes. This trip takes more than one try. There's shit you won't know, mistakes you can't avoid, until you're actually doing it. Then you try again. Fuck, man, this is like my fourth time. I've almost died on these trips. I didn't come all this way to help *you*. I have to focus on me and my girl. Do you understand? On getting *us* there. I can't be looking out for no one else except me and her." He looks at his girlfriend.

Her eyes are full of tears.

"Now look, you're getting my girl all emotional." He shakes his head, looks at us again. Then turns away from Pulga and to me. Sighs. "Look, down that way is a shelter. Most people don't know about it or go there, because you have to backtrack; only those who can't go on right away go." He looks at us. "You guys need to stay put. Follow the tracks. But keep your eyes open for a small blue house, about a quarter of a mile from the tracks. You'll get help there. Stay there for a few days. Catch the next train that leaves here. Got it? That's it. That's all I can do for you."

"Please, man. Please . . ." Pulga says.

I stare at his pleading face and I swear I can feel the fear in his heart. Last night scared him. Maybe he's afraid if we don't keep going, we'll die.

Maybe he's right.

"*Listen* to me, hermano. Just trust me. It's the best thing you can do. Get your little hermanito checked out, okay?"

He turns his back on us and grabs his girlfriend by the hand, leading her to the other side of the other train on the other track.

She looks back once, but the guy, he doesn't look back at all.

"I'm sorry," Chico whispers as he squeezes his eyes shut. "It's my fault. I'm sorry."

Pulga shakes his head. "Forget it," he says, but his voice is tight. Angry.

Chico starts crying and I see how Pulga presses his lips tighter, like he's fighting back saying something terrible.

"Let's go," I say, reaching for Chico's arm gently. "Let's get you where you can rest and feel better, okay?" I lead him back down the track in the opposite direction as everyone else. Away from where we need to go.

We are the only ones going backward. Pulga turns back every few steps, like he's hoping the guy might have changed his mind. Shaking his head like we're making some kind of terrible mistake.

Finally, he gets on Chico's other side and helps me hold him up as we walk. It's scary to see how dead he already looks. His eyes look empty, and I think of how people say that those on the train turn to mummies on this trip.

"You okay?" I ask him.

He nods, then wobbles and holds his head tighter.

"We'll be there soon, Chiquito," I say. But he suddenly doubles over and starts dry heaving. I rub his back as he keeps heaving, his body shaking.

"Hey . . . hey, Chico. It's okay. You'll be okay," Pulga says, rushing over to Chico.

I try to keep panic from taking over. I tell myself he is just dehydrated. Or it's just the brightness of the sun distorting things and making him feel sick.

"You'll be okay," Pulga repeats as we help him up and head to the shelter.

"Don't worry, Chico," I say, but the words run dry in my mouth.

The shelter is not that far, but with Chico getting weaker with each passing second, it takes us forever to walk through the thick dry grass, the draining heat. And we spot it only because the guy told us about it. Its blue paint is faded to practically white and it's not very visible sitting in the overgrown grass. More panic sets in as I wonder if anyone is even here.

The place looks like it's falling apart, but as we get closer, I see there are a few people sitting outside. And then there is a woman rushing outside to us as soon as she spots us.

"What happened?" she says, looking Chico up and down.

"He fell pretty hard off the train," I say.

She scans his body as if making sure it's complete. "Come on. He needs to sit down." She moves me and Pulga out of the way, and grabs Chico with impressive strength and helps him the rest of the way into the shelter.

Inside, she sits him down, gives us all water, tells Chico to drink it slowly. She asks him simple questions—his age, his name, where he is from, but he just stares back at her, fixated on her face.

"He's got a bad concussion," she says finally. "You all will need to stay here, give him time to recover."

"How long?" Pulga asks immediately.

She sighs. "Concussions can take weeks to get better. The stay here is limited to three days, but we'll overlook that since we haven't been crowded lately." She looks around at the almost empty room.

"We can't wait even three days," Pulga says to me. "We *have* to keep going."

"If you don't wait, he's going to shake that brain around more," the woman says. "And you risk more swelling."

"We don't have a choice," I tell Pulga. "He can't go on like this."

"I'm so tired," Chico whispers.

"I want you to sit here, talk to me for a while," the woman tells Chico. "Then I'll let you sleep. Okay, niño?"

Chico nods.

The woman looks at Pulga and me. Her face is shiny, and her cheeks are round and high. She smells like Ponds, and for a moment, I'm taken back to the bedroom I shared with Mami after Papi left. How she would rub that lotion on her face each night before bed and she'd stare into the mirror, looking at my image in bed reflected there.

We'll be okay, Mami would say to me those nights when he first left, when we were both scared and lonely. And then she'd crawl into bed, the smell of her filling my nose as we fell asleep.

The woman looks at us and says, "You two, get something to eat. Over there in the kitchen. Bring him something, too. Wash your hands first."

I hear her talking to Chico, making sure he answers her. When she is satisfied, she leads him to a room so he can sleep. Pulga and I eat bread, drink glasses of Gatorade, but she warms up some beans and plops them on our plates, too.

She watches us as we eat, as we scratch our heads.

"Come here," she tells us. She grabs a thin wooden stick from a drawer, and runs it through my hair, parting it and examining.

"I know," I tell her before she says anything. I've suspected I have lice for days.

She checks Pulga's head, too, and then sighs. "It's better if you shave your hair off. Then use some shampoo to kill what remains. I have some." She smiles.

She grabs some shears and points us to a chair in the living room, telling Pulga to sit first. She starts to sing softly as his hair falls down in small clumps. Sitting there with his eyes closed, he looks so little. When he's done, she points to me.

"Your turn," she says. One of the people who was sitting outside comes in and laughs.

He's a short man, wearing only a pair of too-big shorts and a thin white T-shirt. "This is a record, Soledad. They're hardly here more than fifteen minutes and already you're shearing their hair off. Esta Soledad," he says, shaking his head. "She'll use those shears while you're sleeping if she has to." He laughs and she laughs, and the sound fills the room.

"It's just, I can't bear the thought of you all having to go on like that." Her laughter dies down. "You're not animals, after all," she says. "Come on, help me. Sweep this hair up," she tells the man, and he nods, grabbing a broom and dustpan.

"That's your name?" I ask her. "Soledad?"

She nods as she runs the shears through my hair. "Can you believe that?"

"You don't like it?"

"No!" she says immediately. "How could I ever like a name like Soledad? It's so sad, to be named loneliness. When I was little, I hated it because it sounded like a name for a grown-up. And now I hate it because it sealed my fate."

I know she must mean she is lonely. But I don't want to pry, so I keep my thoughts to myself.

"Even here, I am alone," she says, looking around the shelter. "This little shelter is falling apart, only the most desperate come here. Most times, migrants keep going because they feel strong enough to make it to the next one. But I like being here. I'm here for those who are the most desperate. Who need help the most. And people, generous people with giving hearts, help us stay open. Help us survive."

Pulga stares at her and then looks away.

Something about the way she talks makes me feel close to her. She stares at me suddenly, studying my face closely. "So, what's your name?" she asks.

I know she knows, so I don't lie. "Pequeña."

"Pequeña." She shakes her head. "That's not good. It will keep you small. What's your *real* name?"

My real name. Already I feel like I don't have one. Already I feel like the person who walked the streets of my neighborhood, who lived in that house and slept in that bed, already I feel like that person doesn't exist. And I don't know if she was left behind, or if she's disappeared, like water evaporating, over buses and fields and trains.

Who had I been when my mother looked at my face the day I was born? "Flor," I tell Soledad.

Her shiny face breaks into a smile. "Ah, Flor," she repeats. "Now, *that's* much better."

I smile but it fades when I suddenly remember the boy I refused to name. Who's a part of me, but whose name, if Mami gave him one, I do not know.

Soledad rises from the chair and unplugs the shaving shears. Wipes them with alcohol and puts them away in a drawer. She reaches into a cabinet, retrieves an old ragged towel and hands it to me. "Go on, shower and wash your hair with that shampoo, Flor."

I watch as she walks away, only now noticing the way she walks with the slightest limp, favoring her right side.

"How long have you been here?" I ask.

"Five years," she says, taking a deep breath. She turns and stares at me again and I can't help but wonder if she's looking for someone in my face. But what she says is "You must always remember your name. Say it to yourself. You cannot forget who you are. La Bestia, the wind, a lot of people on the other side, they will try to make you forget. They will try to erase you. But you must always remember. Eres Flor."

I nod. That's who I was. That's who I can be again, even if I'm no longer Pequeña.

I walk to the bathroom, lock the door behind me. I check to see how much I'm bleeding—hardly at all.

Maybe my body is magic.

Maybe my body knows what it needs to do now.

Maybe I'm not who I was.

I look at the warped image in the plastic mirror in the bathroom, my shaved head. I look nothing like Pequeña anymore. I reach into my pocket, gather the bits of my teeth that rolled around my mouth like sharp gritty dirt, and I wash them down the sink.

Here I leave more of my hair.

Here I leave bits of my teeth.

Here I leave more of who I used to be.

And there, somewhere in the face reflected in the mirror, is who I'll become once I cross the border.

Somewhere inside me, Flor waits to be born.

Each night we are there, Soledad sits on a couch by the window. That's where she sleeps, like some kind of lookout for those who might come stumbling in the middle of the night.

For seven days, we watch her nurse Chico back to health, making him special meals. Shearing his hair carefully and washing his scalp in the sink. For seven days, he sleeps and sleeps, and Soledad tells us it's the best way for his brain to rest. A train comes, and goes. Then another, the whistle shrieking as it passes us.

"We have to get back on it soon," Pulga says anxiously as we sit outside. As we watch those on top of the train heading north and we stay in place. "We can't stay here forever. We *have* to go."

"I know," I tell him, anxious to leave, too.

When the man who delivers food to the shelter tells Soledad the train headed to Matias Romero is supposed to leave the following day, Pulga and I tell her we'll be leaving.

"But why?" Chico says. The color has returned to his cheeks. His eyes have lost that vacant stare and he leans into Soledad as he looks at us. She smiles and puts her arm around him. "We can stay a few more days, can't we?"

Pulga shakes his head. "We have to go, Chico. Or we'll never get there."

Chico shrugs. "So . . . ? I'll just stay here, with Soledad," he says, looking over at Soledad, her shiny cheeks smiling. A look crosses Pulga's face and I know this is exactly why he wants to leave.

Soledad looks at Chico. "You *can* stay here. But . . . this is my life. Just this, day in and day out. There's no future here."

"Besides," Pulga says suddenly. "You're not from here. You don't have papers. Mexico doesn't want us any more than the United States does. You'd be an immigrant here, Chico. If you try to work here, live here, whatever, Mexico will deport you right back, too. To Rey."

The sound of his name again, tossed around so casually, reminds me of the reach of *him*. Would he guess what we've done? Would he send someone to find me? Would he come himself?

"We have to go," I tell Chico.

His face falls. "I know . . . I just . . ." he says.

There is a silence in the room, broken only as Soledad takes a deep breath and says, "You know what? I'm going to make you all a feast before you go, okay? How does that sound?" She looks at Chico and he smiles back at her.

And right then and there, she hurries to the kitchen and starts cooking.

She boils chicken and somehow from very little makes a hundred flautas.

She uses the broth to make fideos.

She makes a red salsa, and the smell of jalapeños and tomatoes fills the air.

She makes a green salsa; the tang of the tomatillos and cilantro is on my tongue before I even taste it.

She makes beans, adding extra cheese.

She whips fresh cream.

I watch her the whole time and I swear, I see a glow. Like she is outlined by light. And I begin to wonder if we are dead and Soledad is a ghost. I begin to wonder if she's my bruja incarnate. Or if I'm dreaming. If any of this is real, as we eat food too good to be made by human hands. As we sleep a sleep so deep, it seems like a spell.

But the next day crashes in, and in the early morning we are heading back to the tracks where we'll wait. Soledad walks us to the edge of the shelter.

"I'd walk you there, but I have to stay here in case anyone arrives," she says to us.

She won't leave this place, not for a moment.

So we say our goodbyes right there. And it takes all I have not to sob as she holds my face so gently, like a mother would her child, and says, "Cuídate, m'ija. And when you make it, send me word. I'll be here. But I'll be waiting to hear from you. Don't let me down. You hear me?"

I nod, and when we hold each other in a tight embrace, just for a moment, I let myself pretend we are mother and daughter. And just for a moment, we are.

She hugs Pulga.

And Chico.

La Bestia calls to us.

And we turn to leave in answer.

Pulga

The train doesn't come until almost night—almost twelve hours after we left Soledad. It slows as it approaches, slows some more as it enters the yard, but it doesn't seem like it's going to stop, so we have to hurry.

People appear, running toward it and taking their place by the tracks as the train comes into view.

"Look for the bars on the side!" a man yells to those with him. "That's where you can pull yourself up!" His voice is barely audible over the train's long, blaring whistle.

The first car goes by with a clattering that makes my ears ring.

Then the second, third, fourth . . .

I'm running, staying with Chico as he runs along beside me, slower than usual. I'm watching the guy who I think is a pollero, one who guides a group, as he points to one of the train cars and the three people he is with attempt to board that one. They do, and he gets on behind them.

I hear voices, calling, yelling, telling one another to *grab on! grab on! hold on tight!*

We run, that train sucking at our feet, the sound of its wheels like that of knives being sharpened. The same terror as before grips me, but I ignore it. We keep running, reaching, hoping, lunging for a bar to hold on to.

I'm afraid of being pushed onto the track by someone else who wants to get on just as badly as I do. Or that I'll trip and die. Or be left here, far from home, limbless. In pieces.

I ignore the pain in my legs, the burning sensation in my thighs, the fear in my heart.

And then Pequeña is grabbing the bar, pulling herself up, looking down at us from the top of the train, telling us to *run, run.*

When I look up, it's as if the world slows down. Her mouth open, her face desperate, her voice silent, the dusky blue sky around her.

I look down again and the world is a blur and a cacophony of sound.

"Faster!" I yell at Chico, as another car passes us by and Pequeña gets farther away. The distance between us grows and I see her looking back at us desperately.

She looks at the passing landscape and I think she's considering jumping back off if we don't get on soon.

But I won't get on until Chico does.

"Get on!" I tell him. "Come on, get on!"

I glance back for a moment, and there are only a few cars left. Soon, the train will pass us.

It's only a moment, but I hear a scream from behind. And I see him, a man, being sliced by the train's wheels.

My insides drop and instinctively, I shut my eyes for a millisecond as my brain screams, *Keep going! Keep going!*

Chico turns and I yell, "Don't look back!" Because if he does, he will see that man's legs, how they were cut away from his body, how his arms were still moving around wildly as half of him was spat away from the train.

Chico runs faster, and I pump my legs.

The last car passes us, and we see the back of the train.

Chico reaches for the back bars of the train, grabs them. I hurry next to him and grab them, too. And we pull ourselves up, the train sucking at our feet like a hole in the earth.

My arms and legs are trembling and I tighten my grip, afraid my body will give out on me.

"Climb up to the top!" I yell to Chico. The train has a kind of ladder on the back that leads to the top of the train. Chico listens and we scramble up like spiders.

On top of the car, I search the passing landscape for Pequeña, making sure she didn't jump off.

I look up ahead at the other cars and see the outline of a person who I think is her, waving a hat. I wave back, relieved, before sitting back down, next to Chico.

"You okay?" I ask him as we settle in. He nods. I look back and can still see the crowd gathered around the man spat out by the train.

Even now, I can see him clearly, his denim shirt, his dark face, his arms flailing wildly as he was sliced in half.

My heart slides up my throat, lodges itself there.

I look at those around us, who were already on the train as we ran to get on. Either they didn't see or realize what happened, or they did, but it barely registered. Another horrid image, on top of a train that covers your eyelashes in dust, that burns your body until you feel nothing. The train that turns you into a zombie, unfeeling, unaffected. Half-dead.

Maybe we *have to* become zombies to survive any of this. Maybe part of us has to die to endure this.

"Did you hear that scream? Did you see what happened?" Chico asks.

I shake my head, and lie.

He shakes his head. "I think . . . Pulga, I think that guy . . ." His voice gets choked up.

"No," I tell him. "Nothing happened back there. Don't think it. Don't let yourself feel anything," I tell him.

Chico nods, but I see how his face contorts, trying to hold back tears, trying not to think about it.

We ride into the black night. My heart wants to cry out, but I put my hand over it, apply pressure, keep it quiet. Even as the truth plays over and over in my head.

We ride for hours, the incessant clack of the track drilling into our minds.

We jump off this train, and onto another.

Then another.

Each switch weakens my body but strengthens my determination. We are doing it. We are getting closer, and closer, with each train. And even when the trains and sunrises and nights blend into one another, I don't want to stop. I want to keep going. Each time Chico and Pequeña want to stop, find a shelter, I remind them, one more train, one more leg of the trip. Just one more. I know we can keep going, if we just push through. We have to get closer. We have to get closer and closer.

"We should stop and rest," Pequeña tells me, after we've jumped on the third . . . no, fourth train since we left Soledad's. "I don't think we can keep going like this, Pulga."

"We have to make up time," I tell her. "We have to keep going."

When we ride, I try to look only at the line where sky and earth meet, because when I look to the side, the world blurs by so fast I feel like my head is going to burst. It feels funny, and my eyes can't focus and then I get such a headache, it's like a dull machete has been embedded in my scalp.

One day, we ride along tracks that run past the back of some run-down houses, and as we ride, I see women hanging laundry. One of them waves, then holds her fist up in the air like she is urging us on, giving us strength. The small child next to her starts running with the train. He looks at us in wonder, and the mother stares at him as he slows down, his path obstructed by trees.

I wonder what we must look like to him—I wonder what his little-kid mind imagines about us. I know his mother must have had to explain to him who the people on the train are who go past his house. And I know he must see the train full of people over and over and over again, leaving.

And I know, even at that age, that he's already thinking about leaving, too. That he's already imagining himself on that train.

And I wonder if he'll ever be on it. In search of someone who left long ago.

Or if he will be killed when he's four by bullets meant for someone else.

Or at eight because an older brother refuses to join a gang.

Or at twelve because he refuses to join a gang himself.

Or under the wheels of this train, because he ran for his life.

Before he's completely out of view, I wave at him. I don't know why. Like my hand has a mind of its own. Like it's gone soft—like my heart. And I look away, but not before I see him wave back.

I feel some stirring in my heart and some tears spring to my eyes before I can stop them.

Feeling too much will kill me, I tell my heart.

Not feeling anything will, too, it says.

I look in the direction we are traveling, letting the wind dry unshed tears and letting the clack, clack, clack of the train lull me back to numbness. Hours and hours of numbness. Miles and miles of numbness.

An eternity of numbness.

I look over at Chico and he looks like hell.

Why are we doing this?

I stare at his dusty, cracked face. His lips are chapped and bleeding. He licks them, and they dry out again, and crack more. I feel my own face, the leathery feel of my cheeks chapped by the wind.

Why?

I remind myself of Rey. My mind rushes red with Don Felicio's blood.

I try to ignore the hunger in my stomach, but it won't go away. It's so empty in there. So hollow. My gut is its own enemy—turning on itself, over and over again. I press on my belly, trying to squelch the tiny beast that keeps groaning and punching and wrestling inside—reminding me of hunger.

Relentless hunger.

I can't think of anything else except food. It's almost enough to distract me from the pain in my back, my legs. My hands are permanently cramped; they are clenched in a pain that makes them stick, that makes it impossible to unclench, and I have to concentrate to straighten them out again. I try to move each part of me, just a little bit, to prevent my joints from getting stuck, but even that hurts.

The tiny beast in my stomach erupts and erupts and erupts. I try to let the saliva in my mouth gather, so I can pretend it's a gulp of water and swallow it. But I don't even have enough saliva.

My eyes close. *Open,* I tell them. *Open.* They listen only for a moment before they start closing again.

There are so many hours. So many miles. Through Medias Aguas. And Tierra Blanca.

Danger behind us.

Danger ahead of us.

Danger all around us.

It's hard to make sense of it all. And when I think too hard, my mind gets fuzzy again. Or gelatinous. And then it quivers as my head pounds.

The mountains look fake. I feel like I'm not real and this is not real and the mountains are not real.

Like this life is not real.

And that's when I panic—slap myself and shake my head. Because that feeling is dangerous.

That feeling of unrealness makes you think you can do all sorts of things. Like lie down. Like sleep. Like close your eyes and not worry.

It makes you forget you have a body that can fall and break and be crushed.

Pequeña

The girl sits between her mother and father. She can't be more than seven years old. Even on this trip where we are forced to the barest, most primal state of who we are—rotting teeth, sweating, smelling bodies—her mother has fixed her hair in two long braids on either side of her head, each tied at the end with a small, dirty red ribbon.

The mother is staring at me and when I look at her, I know she's figured out I am a girl. Because she doesn't give me a dirty look. She doesn't shield me from staring at her daughter, who reminds me of me, of who I was a long time ago—a small girl loved by a mother and father.

A kind of understanding comes into her eyes, and I blink back tears. She gives me a soft reassuring smile just as the train screeches and jerks and loses speed.

I watch as her brow furrows, as she holds tight to the girl, speaks to her husband.

There's a man next to us, who Pulga is certain must be a pollero, the way he directs the three kids with him and is constantly on alert. He stands up, looks toward the front of the train, where small bits of light dot the night, and then signals and says something to his charges, who begin inching over to the closest ladder.

¿Qué es? ¿Qué pasa? people ask one another, as the train screeches and slows down more, until it almost stops.

"Come on," Pulga says, keeping an eye on the pollero, carefully making his way behind the three kids in the man's care. People crowd behind us as we reach the ladder, pushing us forward so we almost fall; we scramble down as quick as we can. Others skip the ladder altogether and jump down to the ground, falling and rolling before getting back up again and running. I hear someone scream and look around to see a man who has fallen being practically trampled as people run past him, over him.

Children begin crying.

The sound of gunshots fired in rapid succession breaks through the night, and then panicked, urgent yelling, the sound of feet pounding the ground, running in every direction.

My eyes search the crowd for Pulga and Chico.

When I find them, I reach across bodies and backpacks and grab on to Pulga's shoulder just as he turns, searching for me. We race in the same direction as the pollero, into the darkness of the fields, running with our heads down as more shots are fired and bullets race past, our shoulders tense as we wait for them to explode into us at any moment.

Desperation and roaring engines and doors slamming and commands and threats being yelled fill the air. *¡Por favor! ¡No! ¡Mamá! ¡Papá!*

The words reverberate in my mind as we keep up with the pollero, running, running, running farther out into the brush under faint moonlight.

The pollero and the kids lie down in the overgrown grass and we do the same.

Screams and begging pleas pierce the night, over and over again, over the sound of my heart beating in my ears, drumming through my body, pounding pounding pounding.

I am trying to catch my breath. I think I've forgotten how to breathe. I try to pull oxygen into my lungs, but it gets stuck somewhere in my neck. I try again and again, trying to keep my panic from taking over.

Pulga and Chico are breathing so hard, too, I worry they might die, and the ground feels like it's shaking and I think I can feel their hearts vibrating through the dirt.

Pulga is looking in the direction we came from, his eyes wide and blinking rapidly, as he searches for anything coming our way. Chico is curled in a ball, his hands over his ears, his eyes shut tight.

The adrenaline that ran through our bodies slowly begins to drain and I watch as Pulga's trembling arms give out and he lies down completely, falling face-first into the dirt.

And then I hear rustling and hollering coming closer, and I know, I *know* we will be found. Sweat and the scent of fear escape every pore in my body and the rustling comes closer, closer.

"We will find you," a man calls out in a teasing, singsong voice. "This is no time for hide-and-seek," another says.

A bullet splits the silence and they laugh. And somewhere out here, a child screams. And they run toward that scream.

Then comes the sound of a man pleading, and a woman crying, and that child screaming. Louder.

And I know, I *know* it is them.

The girl's braids flash in my mind, her mother's soft smile when she looked at me, the man with his arm around them both, on top of that train just moments ago.

Something in me jolts, dislodges, and I feel a part of me travel through the night, to look down at that field. I try to pull myself back, I don't want to see. I don't want to know. I want to turn away.

But I can't.

And then I see—

I see the father down there on his knees, a gun to his head. And the mother being touched and grabbed by the other. And the girl, her eyes closed so tight, her mouth opened so wide in a scream that does not come, as her mother tells her, "Cierra los ojos, hija."

The father lunges forward and is knocked across the head with the gun. The woman doesn't scream. She doesn't cry. She just stares up at the sky. At me, as if I am her angel. I hold her gaze, and I hear the thought that loops through her mind.

Help me.

But I don't know how.

Help me.

But I can't move.

Help me.

I can't even look away.

I open my mouth, but no words come out. Only silence, and something like air, a breeze that moves the grass in the field below.

The grass rustles and when I look, I think I see something faint. Ghosts. Forgotten spirits looking for a way out. I feel how tired they are from roaming.

Help me.

My gaze returns to the woman, and as her eyes lock with mine, something surges through my body. Something that breaks me into a million little pieces that fall away and drop to the ground below.

Then I see it, an army of spiders emerging from that field. I watch as they climb up the men, under their pant legs, up their backs, and onto their faces, into their hair. Hundreds and hundreds of spiders. Clusters and clusters of spiders.

I hear the men calling out to one another. I hear them asking each other what is going on, if they feel that, as they swat at their skin, as they swat at nothing, at the spiders they can only feel biting them with their pinchers, scurrying all over their bodies.

More and more come. Marching around the girl, around her mother, around her father. Converging on the two men, who run stumbling from that field, run back toward the track where they get in a car and speed away, the spiders following, following.

And then I am back, next to Pulga and Chico.

We don't move. We don't make a sound. Hot tears burn my eyes.

The pollero's gun shines in the moonlight, and I see a spider on the revolver. A few scattered around Pulga and Chico. But no one moves, they don't say a word, they don't see or feel them.

I feel as one crawls into my ear, whispers, *Stay still, Pequeña.*

I stare up at the moonlit sky as the sound of clicking and spinning fills my ear. Then *tap, tap, tap* as the spider walks along my cheek, my nose, to my other ear, where she spins a web that covers that one, too.

The spider *tap-tap-taps* on one of my eyes—spins a web over it, then the other. Until all I see is gauzy webbed white.

For a moment, the world is silent and there is no more darkness.

For a moment, I feel some kind of peace.

Pulga

Silence. We let it wash over us.

My heart cowers in my chest as we follow the pollero back to the train. As we look for an open boxcar and find them all locked. We climb on top, and stare into the night while La Bestia sits idle on the tracks. As we hear the conversations of those around us.

There are less of us now.

"Those weren't cops just looking for money," someone says.

"Kidnappers," says someone else.

"Pobres," says someone, referring to the people who were taken. Who knows where they are now? Those men and women and children who just wanted better—who are just like us—whose lives will depend on whether their families can come up with money for their release.

"We barely escaped," Chico whispers to me. "They were so close to us."

The train wakes up and the vibration of it rumbles beneath us. We hold on, wait to once again continue on. Then the train jerks forward, pulls away once more.

"Pulga . . ." Chico whispers. "I'm scared. I just want to rest."

I hear him, I do. But I can't shake the feeling of what almost happened. How close we were to being taken. Maybe, probably, killed. Like we cheated something. And I know it will catch up with us; I know we are pressing our luck if we don't keep going.

But when Chico looks at me, his eyes are empty, like his soul has been scooped out. And he looks so tired. "Okay," I whisper. "Next shelter, all right? I promise."

Chico leans against me. "Okay," he says. He smiles, white saliva crusted in the corners of his mouth.

He closes his eyes.

I can feel the first rays of morning sun shining over us. It's the colors that wake me. The glowing colors of it behind closed lids.

In those colors are memories. Of Puerto Barrios and Mamá. Of familiar places and a longing that I know is longing because it comes from my heart, but it feels like hunger. Like a deep, unending hunger.

I grasp on to the grates on top of the train, holding on tighter as we're swayed, back and forth. I'm awake but not, I'm aware but not. Because the rocking motion feels like being on the hammock on our patio and if I stay in these colors and in this motion, if I block out the noise, I can almost believe I am back home. I can almost see my mother through the woven mesh of the hammock, standing in the doorway, looking out at the street and then at me. The splotches of pink and yellow and red get brighter. They turn black and forest green and then to neon orange. They turn white.

I want to stay in this moment.

I don't want to open my eyes to the reality of the train, to the dust and dirt and the tired faces of everyone on this journey. I don't want to see the hopelessness, or the desperation. The hunger in their stomachs and hearts that shows through their eyes.

"Pulga." I hear Chico's voice call to me, so faintly through my sleep.

"Pulga," he says again. The train rocks and rocks. As I open my eyes ever so slightly, the sun so bright in the sky, I am blinded. If my body worked, if it didn't feel like I was made out of lead, I could sit up. But I feel like I can hardly move.

The train screeches into that fiery morning, like some giant centipede being hacked to pieces.

I can feel Chico struggling to get up next to me. I use all the strength I have to sit up, squinting against the sun as I try to adjust to the blinding light. I can hear Pequeña mumbling something about how we need water.

"Easy," I tell Chico as he bobs forward like his head weighs a thousand pounds. His face is so coated with dust, but he nods.

More screeching and braking and I hope wherever we are stopping, a shelter is close by.

"Hang on, Chico," I say.

He sits, eyes closed.

I see his mouth open as he says something, and he turns to look at me, his eyes bloodshot and tired. But the train lets out a horrendous screech and I can't hear anything he said, and Chico's words are lost in the wind as the weight of his entire body pulls him forward. And I watch as he topples, topples, topples over. I watch as my hand, too slow, reaches to grab his shirt and catches nothing. I watch him disappear.

Over the side of the train.

What happens is your brain refuses to believe what it has just seen. What happens is that it tells you you are hallucinating and your ears recall what Pequeña just said about needing water. Even with the scream stuck in your throat. Even as you try to yell and your screams are cut off by those of La Bestia, who won't be outdone.

So the screams form in you like a thousand bubbles, multiplying, squeezing one on top of the other, filling your chest and your throat. Where they stay there and choke you.

And you realize you're choking on screams.

And you can't breathe.

And you can't hear because even the screeching sounds far away.

And your head, your head doesn't work. Because it refuses to realize what's happened.

Even though there's this part of you, the deepest part, that knows exactly what happened.

And you see Pequeña, lying on top of the train, her arms outstretched over the edge, screaming. And you're sure she is screaming even though you can't hear anything.

And you know.

You know.

You know.

As the train slows and screeches and cries and whines and howls and roars and *screams* a scream so piercing, you feel your whole self shatter.

And that's when you jump off, you jump off before it comes to a stop and you're on the ground, the world a blur as you roll and scratch at the dirt and try to get up.

And you run.

You fucking run.

You run even though you can't breathe.

You run as your mind flashes with horrific images.

You run even though it's miles, right? Miles? Or days? Was it days ago?

Or did you already pass him.

You stop, because maybe you fucking passed him already.

And you fall to your knees and you feel around as the snot and tears drip from your fucking nose because my god, a moment ago, your ears and your head didn't work so maybe your eyes don't work and maybe you already passed him.

And you're screaming, screaming, screaming his name under that white-hot sky.

You start running again, even though your body barely works

and you have to keep telling it to go. Keep going. And you do, you keep running, you keep running, you keep running, until suddenly there's a car coming up next to you and you wonder how did this car get here? and there's someone yelling to you to get in and you see Pequeña's already in there, too, and you get in and the car races ahead to wherever it is you were running.

And you keep your eyes on the window full of smashed bugs, trying to see.

And then you do.

You see the lump on the ground.

And you think, it *can't* be him, it *won't* be him.

But it is.

His shirt. It's the one he switched into in the last place we stayed, the blue one that was his favorite.

I get out of the car and run to him, his crumpled fucking body—his leg mangled like it's been eaten by a pack of wolves, flesh and veins exposed, and so much blood. An impossible amount of blood.

Like Don Felicio.

"You're okay, you're okay! You'll be fine, Chico. I promise!" But I can hardly get the words out because I'm crying so fucking much.

And he's looking at me and he smiles. He fucking smiles even though his eyes are closing and he's turning gray and clammy *right in my hands, right in my arms, oh god, no!* as I tell him to *please, please hold on.*

The train whistle blows and drowns out my words, but I hold him closer to me and I whisper right in his ear and I tell him, *Don't worry, okay? Don't worry.*

He stares at the sky, the endless sky above us, and his eyes roll back in their sockets.

"No, no, no, look at me!" I yell at him. "Chico! Chico!"

"Pulga . . . don't worry . . ." he says. "I'm okay . . . don't cry . . . okay."

Except he isn't. I'm watching the life drain out of him, just like I watched it drain out of Don Felicio, and I don't know how to make it stop. I don't know how to make any of this stop. All this life, always draining. And nobody cares.

"I'm okay . . . I . . . we made it. I see it . . ." He looks past me, back at that sky.

"No! Stay with me, Chico! Please . . . *please* . . ."

But he doesn't. Right there, on the ground, in my arms, he stops breathing. His eyes go vacant, their gaze set on something far away.

His body goes limp.

And right there, Chico dies.

My brother, my best friend.

And I hold him to my chest and I tell him that I love him and I tell him that I was supposed to protect him and I tell him he's the best person I've ever known and please, please don't go and leave me here all alone.

I tell him please come back,

Don't fucking leave,

I'm sorry,

I'm so sorry,

I'm sorry,

Chico.

Pequeña

There are a man and woman, next to Chico. They are talking fast, they are moving fast, they are tying something around what remains of his leg. I want to get out of the car and run to them, but I can't. I can't even stand. I open the door and fall onto the ground, crawl. My body wants to vomit but I have nothing more to give.

The man and woman are pushing Pulga out of the way.

Pulga—punching, kicking, screaming at the ground. I crawl over to him—reach out and hold on to him.

The man is giving Chico, *Chiquito*, CPR. The woman is running to the truck, she is coming back with a red box with a heart on it. And then they are tearing open that shirt he loved so much and putting paddles on Chico's chest and they are shocking him—again, and again, and again—trying to bring him back to life.

Each shock makes his body flop like a fish out of water. Each shock makes my brain flash. Each shock is a knife viciously cutting up and slicing and slivering my heart into pieces.

Then they are stopping.

Try again! Try again! Pulga shouts.

"Ya se fue," the man says. Pulga pulls away from me and scrambles over to hold Chico again. I wrap my arms around my body because I feel myself coming apart. I am sobbing and I am trying to say, *No, no, no,* because I can't believe it. It can't be real.

But the words won't come out.

Only my insides slide up my throat, out of my mouth. And I sit there, spitting out my heart, my stomach, my spleen. I choke on broken pieces of ribs, on piece after piece of myself. Next to Chico. Next to all that spilled blood and *pieces of him.*

The man and woman are saying something.

"Come, don't look anymore. Come," she says as she helps me up and takes me to the truck.

The man tries to help Pulga, but Pulga won't move. He won't leave Chico there alone.

The man crouches next to him, talks to him for what seems forever. But Pulga just shakes his head. He says something I can't hear, something that makes the man take a deep breath and nod.

Then they are both picking up Chico, what's left of him, and bringing him to the truck. They are putting him in the back and I'm worried about Chico's head being banged around, that's what I'm worried about, and I tell the woman, *His head, please, watch his head,* but when I look, Pulga is back there with him, holding his head in his lap.

The man gets in the driver's seat.

I watch the world outside race by in a blur until we are at a shelter and the man and woman are telling us they will help.

There are so many people standing outside the shelter; I think they were the ones on the train with us. They stand there looking.

A few men come from inside to help the man who brought us here. They call him Padre. He's a priest.

The woman who was at the scene goes into the shelter and comes out, holding sheets that she gives to the priest. They lay them on the ground. A few men come out of the shelter and remove Chico from the truck, lay him down on those sheets.

The woman wraps him, like a child. Wraps his whole body, but leaves his face visible. Then she tells a few of the men who are standing around to take him inside and they do.

I watch, Chico's blood already blooming through the sheet.

And I feel myself *falling,*

falling,

falling.

Through darkness, through imaginary worlds with water and spiders and stars—where witches who are also angels watch over you.

Her dazzling eyes and long silver hair come into my mind's eye. *Come and tell me this is all a nightmare,* I tell her. *Come, wake me. Please.*

Maybe she will come to me on top of the train, maybe she will whisper in my ear that none of this is true.

But before the image of her slowly fades away, I know she's not coming.

And I know all of this is real—achingly, terribly real.

Pulga

Time does not make sense.

The sky was just orange and then blue and now it is black. In seconds it changed. How can Chico be alive this morning and then dead this morning? How can I have lived a lifetime in just hours, and how can hours feel like seconds, and how can seconds feel like eternity? And how can today not really feel like a day, so maybe today never happened. Chico is not dead.

Except, I'm stuck in today. There is only today. Which means it happened.

He really is dead.

He is.

Because I'm looking at him, there on the table where they've laid him. On the back patio. I stare at his body, wrapped in sheets. Like a mummy. I think of how I've heard that La Bestia, this journey, turns you into a mummy.

He was so hungry. He was so tired.

I pushed him too hard. I pushed him until I broke him. My mind fills with his smile. With his voice. With the nightmares that made him cry in his sleep.

My mind reels back to the day Pequeña's baby was born. That stupid shirt he wore, the shirt he's still wearing now, dead.

Shut the hell up, man. It's my favorite one, okay?

It's wild, you know? Pequeña having a baby.

I think of how he ran that day, in the sun, running to meet

Pequeña's baby that took so long to come. Was it this same body? Is this really him?

Maybe that's why the woman left his face visible. So I can keep looking at it and remind myself, yes, it's really him. It's really him.

But even his face is not his face. This face is gray and dirty. This face doesn't smile or look at me.

I close my eyes because I can't look anymore. My mind goes back to Barrios, to our streets. How we ran that day, how dust swirled around like it was trying to hide us. I see Chico and me, headed to the store. Chico with that stupid grin on his face, the one not even the death of his mother could completely erase. And me, throwing rocks by his side. I watch as we walk up to the counter. I watch, like some kind of sad god, the last moments we were kids.

When I open my eyes again, there is the glow of candles all around the patio. And there are people behind me, filling this place with prayers as soft as that light.

And there is a woman, there, gently washing his face.

And it is Chico.

It *is* Chico.

My chest cracks open with pain too big for my heart to contain. Tears burn my eyes and my cheeks and I weep for him. For the person he never got the chance to be. I weep for myself, too. For all of us.

The candles burn down.

The sun goes down.

And I close my eyes to this day.

When I open them again, it is morning and Pequeña is sitting next to me, holding my hand, staring at Chico.

I look around to the empty patio; the only other person here is the priest, Father Jiménez, who tried to save Chico. He walks over to us after a few moments.

"I know this is difficult," he says. "But I need to talk to you about . . ." He gestures toward Chico. "Your friend?"

"My brother," I tell him. "Chico."

"Chico," he whispers. "I'm sorry to have to talk to you about this now. But I need to know what you would like us to do with Chico. Sending him back will be difficult. It'll take a long time." The father speaks slowly, letting his words sink in. Letting my brain have time to process them.

"Authorities will come and get him if I call, but . . ." He chooses his words carefully. "Then he will be in the morgue for who knows how long. It is difficult, right now, to keep track of . . . people. I've heard of some not making it back to their loved ones for proper burial."

I imagine Chico's body crossing borders back to where we ran from, all of this, our whole journey, in vain. Ending up exactly where we started.

I can't stand the thought of sending him back. And I can't stand the thought of him in a morgue like someone forgotten and left behind.

I look over at Pequeña. "I don't want to send him back," I tell her.

She nods and Father Jiménez continues. "We have buried people here . . ." he says, pointing to a field in the distance. "There is a cemetery out there, for those just like Chico, who met their fate on this journey."

I look at the crosses in the distance. I think of Chico, here, for eternity. In a cemetery far from home, so far away from where he dreamed of being. I think of him forever caught in between.

"I don't know . . ." I say.

"We will do it properly. And I will take care of him once you leave here. I visit the cemetery every day and pray for all of them. He won't be alone." Father Jiménez looks out at the field behind the shelter to where the others who have fallen lay, those whose dreams and hearts stopped here, broken and crushed on the rails of La Bestia.

Just like their bodies.

Just like Chico.

Pequeña stares out in the distance. "It seems like the best thing to do," she says quietly.

But suddenly the idea of leaving him behind is unbearable. I can't imagine leaving him here. I can't imagine going on without him.

I shake my head. "No, no, we . . . we have to go back," I tell her. "We have to take him home."

"We can't go back . . ." she says.

"Then I will," I tell her. "I'll take him home, to Barrios, and bury him next to his mamita. It's what he would want. I have to . . . I can't leave him here, alone."

Pequeña stares at me, her eyes filling with tears. "He's not here anymore, Pulga," she whispers. "He's gone."

"He's right here," I tell her. "And I'm going to take him home."

"Listen to me," she says, gently grabbing me by the shoulders. I push her away, but she holds tighter. "Do you think he'd want you to go back? Do you think he'd want you to set foot back in Barrios now? Would you want *him* to go back if it were you on that table?"

"Let go of me," I say, but she doesn't. She won't.

"You *have* to keep going," she says.

I close my eyes and shake my head. No. What I *have* to do is grab Chico. I have to lift his broken body onto my back, and carry him home—past borders, through fields with narcos and policemen and screeching trains. Back to that place we loved and hated, that loved and hated us.

"You're going to keep going," she says to me. "We're going to keep going. And we're going to make it, for Chico, okay?"

I shake my head again, but then I'm crying because I hear myself promising Chico the same thing, just days before: *We're going to make it.*

What did you know? I say to myself, staring at his body, and then I am hugging his body, even though it smells like death, and even though his face is not his and I am telling him, *I'm sorry, I'm so sorry.* And Pequeña is pulling me away and then she is hugging me. And she is telling me, *He's not there anymore, Pulga.*

"He's here," she says, putting her hand over my heart. "He will always be here."

But I don't have a heart anymore. It is destroyed.

Pequeña doesn't understand. She could never understand. She didn't love Chico the way I loved him. And she is not the reason he is dead.

I am.

Some men from the shelter begin to build a coffin. Father Jiménez stays with me and Pequeña.

We sit outside like that for the rest of the day. Pequeña is still and stoic; I keep forgetting she's there until I cry and I feel the slight touch of her hand on my arm or shoulder as she reaches out for me.

I think of the flash of Chico's last smile.

Somewhere in the distance—somewhere far away from where Pequeña and I are—women come in and out of the shelter, putting cups of water, cups of coffee, pieces of bread in our hands.

The sun moves across the sky and Father Jiménez is suddenly standing up, speaking. His voice fills the patio as I stare at Chico.

I don't even remember going inside.

He tells everyone, all those strangers who aren't strangers because they've been here mourning Chico, too, that we on earth mourn the dead, but that they are in a better place. He talks about the glory of God and how Chico is now reunited with his maker.

But I think of how he is reunited with his mother. I imagine him running into his mamita's arms.

Father Jiménez talks about how Chico will now want for nothing, and will feel no pain, no hunger, no thirst.

How he is safe now—secure in the hands of God.

I know these are the things Father Jiménez has to say. These are the things all holy people have to say. And even though there's a part of me that doesn't want to hear it, there's a part of me that lets the father's words wash over me like water, holding on to the hope they offer.

But I don't know what I believe anymore. I don't know if I believe in God. Because if God exists, and if he sees everything, why doesn't he see us?

Why?

And why do we have to die to finally, *finally* be safe?

And how can the world hate us for trying to survive?

And how are we only reunited with our mothers in death?

But these are questions no one ever wants to answer. Or maybe there are no answers. Not really.

When Padre Jiménez is done, all that's left is the humming of prayers and the flickering of candles in that patio.

And Chico.

Then they lift him and put him in a box.

A box.

They raise him up onto their shoulders.

And we walk to the field.

And he is lowered into a hole someone has dug.

And the father says more words, but all I can think of is Chico's stupid grin. Then I am throwing dirt in a hole in the ground, and each particle of soil that falls is a heavy weight in my heart.

How can I leave him here?

But I do, we do. I throw more and more dirt on him. We pile it on and on and on.

All that dirt.

Until he is deep in the earth, like he never existed.

But he did. He did.

Even if the world didn't care.

PART FOUR

Despedidas

Goodbyes

Pequeña

I can feel someone's gaze on me as I wash my spare clothes in the sink outside behind the shelter. When I look up, I'm not sure she's real at first. But it's her, the woman from the field. The one whose eyes locked on mine as I floated over her in the sky, whose thoughts—pleas for help—I could hear.

She's standing by the door, her head tilted. Her look intense as she holds on to her little girl's shoulders.

"Cómo está, your brother?" she asks, meaning Pulga. "Will he be okay?"

When I first noticed them here, the little girl, the mother, the father, I'd thought they were ghosts. I didn't know they'd made it back to the train that night. I didn't know they'd stopped here, too. But then there she was, one of the women who washed Chico's face. There he was, the father, one of the men who helped build and carry his coffin.

I look up from scrubbing my jeans. "I don't know . . ." I tell her.

She nods. And I don't know how you can feel connected to a stranger, feel that you have known each other in some other life, but that's how I feel with her.

"There's a train that leaves tomorrow," she says. She stares at me with that intense look, like she's trying to place me. "You should make sure you're on it. You need to make him keep going."

I know she's right. Pulga hasn't said a word since the funeral three days ago. I worry that if I don't get him to leave soon, he will go further and further into his grief and it will anchor him here forever. But I'm worried he won't go, that he won't be able to leave Chico.

From here, I can see the graveyard. And when I think of leaving him, pangs of guilt hit me and tears fill my eyes and spill down my cheeks.

The woman comes over to me, gently takes the soap from my hand, and begins scrubbing at my clothes.

"I know it may seem impossible, to go on after something so terrible has happened. But . . . it's the only way," she says, reaching for my hand, squeezing it tight. And when she does, I know I have known her before. I know our connection is one that doesn't die— one woven through centuries, through the past and the future. She has loved me and I have loved her and our paths have crossed before this life.

She smiles. "You remind me of someone," she says.

"Who?"

She shrugs, keeps scrubbing at my clothes, the smell of lemon soap filling the air. "I don't know," she says, sighing. "But you do."

I look at her and wonder if she was my mother in another life, or my sister, or my aunt, or a cousin, or best friend.

She hands me one side of my pants and she holds the other and we wring the water from them like we've done it a million times before. She takes them from me and grabs wooden pins and hangs them on the drying line strung across the backyard of the shelter.

And then she helps me with the rest of my clothes. And Pulga's. And we do the same with each piece, in a rhythm.

The little girl tugs at her, tells her she's hungry.

"Bueno, we're going to be on that train tomorrow. Make sure you and he are on it, too," she tells me again.

I nod. "I will."

She goes inside with her little girl, and I stand there, willing myself to remember that other life when I must have known her, but I can't.

So I sit on a bucket and stare out at the graveyard.

I think of Chico.

And my mother.

Dreaming of when I'll see them both again.

And I cry, shedding the tears I need to shed in order to go on.

That night, I lie on my side on the floor and look at Pulga as he stares at the ceiling.

"There's a train tomorrow," I begin. He doesn't turn to look at me, but I know he's listening. "We need to be on it, Pulga."

I watch as his breath quickens, as his chest rises and falls faster. As his throat swallows, holding back sobs. But he stays quiet.

"I know you don't want to. I know it's terrible to leave him behind, but . . . we can't stay here forever."

Tears fall out of his eyes and slide down to his hairline. I look away as my own tears start again. "We have to," I tell him. "It's what he would have wanted. It's how we have to honor him. It's why we have to keep going."

We lie in silence for a while, until Pulga finally speaks.

"I know," he whispers. "I know. Even if it kills us."

Pulga

We wait, but the train sits idle on the tracks. I can feel Pequeña's gaze on me every few minutes.

"Here," she whispers, offering me some food. I turn away from her. I don't want any food. I don't want anything. "You should eat something," she insists, but I ignore her. I don't want to hear her voice, or eat the bread, or wait for that beast that doesn't want to leave.

She offers me the bread again, and I push her hand away. "Stop."

"Don't be mad at me, Pulga."

I stare at the tracks. I want to tell her I'm not mad. But I can't. I don't know what I am.

I want to tell her I don't want to be mad. And I don't want to be sad. And that what I'm trying to do is feel nothing, to tune out the words my heart keeps shouting, the words I hear Chico whispering back there, under all that dirt, from the darkness of his coffin.

Why are you leaving? How can you leave?

I could run back to the shelter now, let her get on the train by herself, stay with Chico's grave. Except I don't have the energy to go back. And I know he wouldn't want me to. So I sit here and wait with Pequeña, who is eating bread and staring at that train like the world has not just ended.

"Do you even care? That he's dead?" The words come out before I even realize I've thought them. And my hand grabs the bread out of hers, throws it on the ground.

I tell my heart, *Stop!* But it's too late. It's spilled anger and sadness all over the place and I expect Pequeña to shout back, to be hurt, to insult or yell at me.

But she just picks up the bread, continues eating it, dirt and all. She looks at me for a long time, until I turn away from her face that holds too much compassion, too much understanding, and makes my heart want to weep.

"No matter how long we stay here, no matter how long we wait, he's not coming back here," she says.

Tears flood my eyes and I watch as they drop, seeping into and darkening the concrete.

Stop! Stop! Stop!

But they don't.

All afternoon, we sit and stare at that train, waiting for it to come to life. Waiting for the fourteen-hour ride ahead that will take us out of Lecheria to Guadalajara. But only when night falls does that beast wake up, rumbling and clanking.

We grab our backpacks and hurry toward it, before it begins moving, before it pulls away. There are only a few of us that I recognize from the shelter, and only a few others who were already here waiting when we arrived.

Maybe by this point people just need to rest longer at the shelters. Or maybe they've changed their minds. Or given up. Or died.

Like Chico.

The train pulls away, gaining speed, and Pequeña looks over at me, her face sad and worried. I think she's sorry she's making me go on. I think she knows that if she didn't, I'd just stay here.

I put my head down as we leave, because I am tired of the view from the top of this train. Tired of holding on for dear life. I'm tired of so much dirt and earth all around us, under our feet and on top of our loved ones. I put my head down because I can't look, I can't bear to look at this land where my best friend died. Where the earth will eat his flesh, turn his bones to dust.

I don't want to remember this moment of leaving him behind.

I close my eyes, but I don't sleep. And suddenly I hear my father's voice in my ears. *We're gonna make it.*

I stare at my backpack. I don't know if I want to hear the tape, but I'm tired of the sound of wind in my ears, of the clanking of the tracks. So I reach in, pull out my Walkman. I put on the headphones and press play. I wait for a song to finish, to hear his voice.

Someday, Consuelo, the band's gonna make it, baby. I swear, we're gonna make it. And I'm going to give you everything you want. Everything you've ever wanted. There's only you. You and me. Now check this one out, right here. Listen to that bass.

I listen to his words again.

And again.

But my mind begins to wander, and thoughts about the stupid dreams my father had, and the dreams Mamá had, and the ones I latched on to roll in before I can push them back out. And I wonder if my father had lived, if he *really* would have made it as a big-time musician. I used to think, man, how the world missed out on him. On his music. How death robbed him of more than just his life. But now it makes no sense. Why did I ever believe that? Because not many people make it big. Hardly *anyone* makes it. And probably, my papá *never* would have made it. And maybe that would have made him angry, and maybe he would have blamed Mamá and me, and maybe he would have broken Mamá's heart just like Pequeña's papi broke Tía's. And maybe all the dreams I ever thought could've been real were always, *always* destined to be crushed.

I rewind and listen to his voice again.

All I hear are lies.

Like the lies I told Don Felicio about Gallo coming to see him soon. Like the lies I told Chico as he lay bleeding. And the ones I told Mamá when I insisted everything was okay.

Like the lies I've told myself, about the future *I* would have.

Maybe my dreams were always meant to be crushed, too. Maybe I wasn't meant to dream.

I'll play bass for a kick-ass band, man, I told Chico. *Cruising up the West Coast, in a car just like my papá had, headed to gigs at night with the guys.*

What guys?

The other guys in my band.

Oh, right, Chico said with that stupid smile.

They're out there right now, walking around somewhere in the States, not even knowing how great we're gonna be. How I'm that missing piece of the puzzle. But wait, you just wait. Someday.

Me too. Right?

Hell yeah, Chico. You too. You're gonna be right there with me.

I never even asked him to be part of my stupid imaginary band. He was my best fucking friend, and I never even asked him what instrument he'd play. And those dreams were *my* stupid dreams, stupid dreams that I fed him, that I dreamed for him and made him believe. I don't know what dreams he had for himself. Because I never bothered to ask him.

I'm sorry, I tell him. I close my eyes tighter, shame and selfishness flooding through me. I hold on to the train tighter as it begins to rain.

It comes down slowly at first, a few plops. But then it comes stronger, sharper, whipping at our bodies. It stings my arms and saturates my clothes. I watch as people turn their faces upward, open their mouths.

Soon the rain changes directions with the wind and comes at us sideways, then whips around and comes at us from the other side, attacking us from wherever it can. Spraying us with needles. Pequeña inches closer to me, both of us holding on as tight as possible to the top of the train, trying not to slip as the sky fills with lightning.

I don't know, but I think I'm crying. I can't tell because of the rain. I can't tell because I've cried so much for Chico that maybe I haven't stopped, maybe I will be crying forever. Maybe even when there are no more tears for my body to shed, I will still be crying.

We slip with the rocking of the train, this way and that. Thunder cracks the night, like it wants to split the world in half, and La Bestia cries over it, reminding us of her strength, reminding us of the steel blades underneath, ready to slice us if we fall. Pequeña and I hold on.

It feels like the end of the world.

Maybe it is. I almost wish it were.

My hands feel like they won't work from holding on so hard, and my body goes numb from the rain and cold. And I wonder if it's Chico in all that fury, in that rain and wind and electricity, so angry that we left him behind.

Don't be angry at me, I want to tell him.

But he has every reason to be mad. Me, who made him believe, who told him we would be okay, who made him save me from a schoolyard fight and then brought him to his death.

The beast squeals, like scared little pigs being led to the slaughter.

I killed him. I killed Chico.

It's my fault.

I'm sorry.

I keep my eyes closed.

Finally, I give in to sleep.

I give in to darkness.

The storm rages on. La Bestia does, too.

Pequeña

The mother and father sit with their little girl between them again, all of us atop the same boxcar. I can see their silhouette against the glow of the sky, and every now and then their faces, as lightning flashes.

And then, in one of those flashes, I think I see God.

He is a brown hand cupped to a child's chin, where rainwater is gathering so she can drink from it.

He is riding through the desert on a journey known as the hell route.

Hot tears burn my eyes. White light fills the sky, so bright, I'm almost blinded. And then my tears are mixing with the cold rain that falls on us, and I am turning my head upward, drinking from glowing skies.

It's not that I didn't believe in Him before this moment. It's just hard to see Him in the world I've known—a world where madrecitas tell their children to walk fast and keep their gaze on the ground. Where viejos and viejas walk with crooked backs and survive only because other poor people take pity on them. Where the young die younger and younger each day.

No. It's not that I didn't believe in Him.

It's just that anytime people have asked God to be with us, to go with us, to shelter us, I never believed He was listening.

I turn to look at Pulga; he rides with his eyes shut tight, those headphones on his ears. I shake his shoulder, try to get him to look at me, to drink the rain, but he ignores me. I take out my empty water bottles, and his, and fill them with rain.

All night we ride, wet and freezing cold. The rain falls like small ice picks on my back and the wind grows colder and colder each hour. I huddle next to Pulga, force myself to think of warmth, to picture the blazing sun. I think of it in the sky, its heat on my skin.

I think of the sun.

Only the sun.

It becomes an orange portal that swallows me up, that surrounds me with warmth and fire. I feel my body relax as I travel through the heat of it. Then, suddenly, I am falling from the sun, I am drifting down to a street lined with houses.

My bare feet land on the black pavement. And I walk right down the middle, looking at the sidewalks on either side, at small trees with branches weighed down by heavy pink and white blooms. Sunlight reflecting off parked cars.

I walk slowly, taking in the houses one by one. A white house, a gray house, a small blue house with red rosebushes.

Then I come to a pale yellow house. Three stairs lead to a porch where an old woman sits on a wooden chair, staring at me, walking down the street.

Her hair is long, peppered with gray strands that seem to glow. Her eyes are dark but they glimmer. She wears a white dress. She is watching me.

As I come closer, she stands, comes to the very edge of the porch but does not take another step. She gestures for me to come to her, but my feet are unmovable stones.

The door to the house is closed, but from a slightly opened window come voices and laughter. Voices and laughter I recognize but can't place. I know I love them, whomever they belong to, even if I don't know who they are.

The old woman is trying to say something, yell something to

me. Her lips move, and her face is full of love and pity, and the desperate want to tell me something, but no voice comes out.

I want to run up those stairs and look at her up close; I need to know what she is trying to say.

I want to open the door and see those inside.

I want to hear her voice.

But instead the world grows brighter, and when I look at the sky, the sun is growing larger and larger. It grows so large it is filling up the whole sky, and I can feel everything I just saw disappearing below. But even as I rise, I *feel* myself back on that porch.

Someone's phantom hand in mine.

I think it's the hand of someone I love. Or someone I might love. Someone who doesn't exist but might. Someday.

And I wonder if that house is full of ghosts.

The sun swallows me up and delivers me back onto the train where I can still feel the echo of someone's hand in mine. I open my eyes and see Pulga next to me, staring out at the land blurring by. The sun's morning rays are warm; they dry what the wind has not of my wet clothes from the night's storm.

But then the sun intensifies, growing hotter and hotter by the minute. It burns our backs, our necks, our heads, until we are made of fire.

For hours, after so much rain and cold, we ride engulfed by light.

"I'm tired," Pulga says. His head is turned toward me, his eyes barely opened against the heat and brightness. He looks tired. He looks more than tired.

He looks like he is giving up. Like he's becoming the kind of mummy everyone says you become on this trip. One whose soul is dying, bit by bit, whose heart is losing faith.

"I know," I tell him.

I hand him the water I collected, and he takes a sip, winces at how hot it is. "It's starting to not make sense, all of this," he says, the hot wind blowing on our faces, howling in our ears so I can barely hear him.

I see the way he looks out at the world, at the mother and father hovering over their daughter, whose face, even in sleep, looks worn-out and in pain.

He's right. It's doesn't make sense.

"It never made sense," I tell him. Staring at the little girl who, even in this heat, is shivering.

He looks at me for a second, like he understands, but then his eyes go dull and he looks away.

I stare at the little girl, shivering more violently with each passing hour, her mother holding her so tight now to make the shivering stop. And I worry about her.

I worry about Pulga.

I worry that even if we make it, nothing will be left of him.

Pulga

We wait for another train in a small town near the tracks that looks made up of lost souls—of people on the streets sleeping with arms over their faces. People in fetal positions, their backs against dirty, graffitied concrete walls. People who stare endlessly at the darkness of the world from a town that doesn't seem to have a name.

This is the hell route, I remind myself. My notes flash in my mind.

And this must be purgatory.

I suddenly wonder if we have died, too. Pequeña and I.

"Are we alive?" I ask her, sitting next to me on the dirty ground. Her eyes are wide as she stares out at all those lost souls.

"Yes," she tells me. "We're alive. We're going to make it."

The family that was at the shelter, that was with us on the train, is nowhere to be seen. I don't know where they disappeared to, but they're gone and when I ask Pequeña if they were real, she says yes.

"They're taking the little girl to a hospital," she says. And I remember now, that we watched them walk away when we got off the train, our bodies numb and our minds thick. They headed to the hospital and we stumbled here, where we wait for another train.

"You think she'll be okay?" I ask Pequeña, but she just closes her eyes and shrugs.

"Your notes kind of stop here," she tells me, taking out my notebook from her jacket.

I look at my notes in her hand and shrug. I reach for them and glance through the pages. I look at the little stick figures I drew in the margins, Chico and me, on top of a train. I remember thinking those notes would be enough. I remember sitting by my bed, studying those notes the night before we left with a flashlight under the covers as Chico kept watch, and believing in them like the bible.

The name Lecheria stares back at me. It's circled in black ink, as if the future was already marked even back then. If I had a pen, I'd draw a stick figure on the ground. Black x's for eyes. I'd write, *This is where my best friend died.*

I give the small notepad back to Pequeña.

"We'll get on this next train, and then there should be another one that leads us to Altar. That's where the little girl's father said they were headed before they had to get off. I guess migrants can rest there and get supplies for crossing the desert. Does that sound right?" she asks.

Altar.

I shrug. I don't remember. I don't care.

I stare out at the darkness.

I retreat back into my own.

Pequeña

We wait for the train.

Suddenly a faraway whine breaks through the eerie silence of the night.

"¡Aquí viene!" someone yells, then a chorus of people yelling that the train is here, the train is here. People run to the train tracks, staring at the barely visible headlight that shines small from far away.

People tighten their backpacks. They double-check shoelaces. They untie shirts and sweaters wrapped around waists and shove them into backpacks so they won't get caught in the wheels of the train. So they won't be dragged under.

The light gets brighter as the train hurtles toward us. My stomach flip-flops, my legs quiver with fear and adrenaline, and it shrieks and screams and cries as I grab on to Pulga and pull him toward the tracks.

"We have to run soon, Pulga. Corre, okay? When it gets closer, run as fast as you can! Grab on to something as soon as you can!" I yell. But he stands there, looking at the train coming toward us, and doesn't move an inch.

"Okay, Pulga?"

He doesn't answer and then my words are cut off by the rumbling of the train, the clanking and roar.

"It's not slowing down at all!" a voice shouts, barely audible as the first cars race by. I grab Pulga by his thin arm, so skinny and fragile that I worry if I grab it too hard, it will break. But I pull him with me as I start running, and he has no choice but to keep up. And then we're running, trying not to bump into anyone else, praying not to trip on anything in the darkness, as the wind created by the train's speed whips hot and strong around us.

I'm pulling Pulga beside me, but the train is going so fast, like it wants to kill us. Like it wants to remind us that it is a beast, a demon, a thing that passes through hell.

I see others running ahead of us, running as fast as they can, barely able to reach out for the train. It is a black blur. Going past us so fast, it is gone before we realize it, leaving us with nothing but fumes and dust.

And then we are just shadows, catching our breath, looking out in the direction it went, doubled over, falling on the ground.

"It still goes through here too fast," an old man says, shaking his head. A younger man is with him. They both make me nervous, but the old man looks at the younger man and says, "Come on, hijo, we gotta keep going. About an hour up ahead, there's a bend. It slows down there. We'll go there and wait for the next one that comes through."

They begin walking, and those who have overheard the old man begin walking in the same direction.

"What do you think?" I ask Pulga.

But he's sitting down, not even looking at me. Not even listening.

"Pulga?"

"Did you see how fast it was coming?" he whispers. He has his eyes shut tight, like he's trying to unsee something. Maybe he's trying to forget how Chico looked on the ground after the train left him to die—like I am.

"I know, I know," I tell him, but he is shaking his head, hitting it with his hands like he can knock the images out. I reach for his hands, stop the blows he's delivering to himself. "Don't do that, Pulga. Please, please . . . stop . . ."

He does, and then he sits, dull and lifeless, as the old man and the son and the group we were running with get farther away.

I pull Pulga up. "We have to walk," I tell him. "You have to get up and you have to walk and we have to get on the next train, do you understand? Please, okay?" My heart is racing and my body is sweating. I reach for his face, force him to look me in the eye.

That's when I see how much of him is gone.

So I talk to the piece of him left.

"Stay with me, Pulga. Stay and fight, okay?"

Something in him snaps awake and he looks at me then, really looks at me, and nods.

I smile at him, at the Pulga I have always known, at the part of Pulga who is still there.

"Okay," he says, reaching for his backpack.

"Okay," I repeat. And relief floods through me, for a moment, as we hurry into the darkness, down the tracks, follow the beast.

Pulga

Hours later we are in a field near tracks that veer off to the right sharply. We wait here with the old man and his son and a small scattering of others, all of whom are just as tired as we are, all of whom look too tired to do us harm if ever that was their intent.

We watch the sun eventually come up. We sit there all day. Waiting. I don't even know what I'm doing anymore—or if I care if La Bestia ever comes again.

"Look," Pequeña says as the sun sets. I look at the way she stares at it dipping down. Like she sees something there.

"You think it's stupid? To imagine a future?" she asks.

I shrug.

"What are your dreams, Pulga?"

Something like a pang hits my heart. I want to tell her my dreams are dead, that all that is left of them is a kind of dull phantom pain. That that's what dead dreams feel like. I want to tell her I don't dream anymore, like she means, because my head is filled with nightmares. But instead I shake my head.

We watch the sun rise again.

"What do you dream?" I whisper to her between hours of silence, hours of watching and waiting. She turns her head toward the sky and shrugs.

"All kinds of things, I guess. I could go to school? Maybe? Learn how to help people—women—somehow. Maybe a . . . counselor, or therapist, or something."

I imagine that future for Pequeña as we wait. I try to see into my future as well, but I can't.

So maybe that's why when the train finally comes again, rolling down the tracks and screeching that horrible screeching that has crawled beneath my skin and zaps every nerve and makes me want to give up, I don't.

I run.

I run for Chico, and for Pequeña. Because for two sunrises and two sunsets she's filled her head with dreams. I run because this field is dark and because it feels like the dark is consuming me.

I run for all those things.

And maybe some small part of me runs because *not* running feels like death.

We run and we reach and we climb on the beast, tamed by a bend in the road. Pequeña smiles at me, like it means something, that we got on quickly, easily. But I know that whatever good luck we get, we will pay for in some way eventually.

We ride for hours and hours. We ride until our bodies are numb from sitting and lying down and holding on. I try to remember how many trains since the last shelter. How many days since the guy and his girlfriend who wouldn't let us go on with them. How many days since Chico died. How many days since we left Barrios, since I last saw Mamá.

Has it been three weeks? Maybe more.

I don't know, not really. It's one never-ending day.

And now again. Still we are here. Riding through so much countryside, and parts that feel like a strange dream. A dream where we're floating over trees and mountains, over trees *bursting* from mountains.

Until I see all that green, I'd forgotten color like that existed. Then we ride through tunnels, so long the world turns black, and I'm surprised when we're spit out again among so much green.

Pequeña marvels at it, tells me to *look*. And I do. But I don't think I see what she sees, what makes her face look so at peace.

When I don't react, Pequeña leans closer to me, her face dusty and dirty. She studies my face, like she is searching for something. I'm not sure for what. Then she scoots very close to me and places her hand on my chest.

"I have to tell you a story," she says. "One that Mami told me about a woman in Guatemala City, a cousin of one of the women she worked with."

"I don't want to hear a story," I tell her, pushing her hand away. But she places it there again, goes on.

"Close your eyes," she whispers in my ear, her hand steady over my heart. I refuse, but the wind around us gets stronger, forcing me to close them against so much dust and warmth.

And suddenly, I feel something electric go through me and an image of a small boy riding a tricycle flashes in my mind. He is riding on the dirt in front of his house, faded pink, guarded behind a peeling white fence.

He wears a white shirt and blue shorts and rides in circles. Then come popping sounds and his shirt blooms with red.

I want to open my eyes. I want to erase the image, but it feels like I'm stuck in a dream I can't wake up from.

I see his mother running out from the house, scooping him up in her arms.

Pequeña's voice fills my ears. *Her cousin said that all night at the vigil, and at the gravesite, the woman didn't stop wailing. All through the night, her wailing filled our streets, like a howling coyote. Like an animal with a missing limb.*

I hear the wailing, so loud, so clear, that I think it is the train screeching to a stop. Or someone crying next to me.

She couldn't stop wailing, not for a single second. At his funeral . . .

I see a small coffin, his mother next to him, her mouth open, issuing that terrible sound.

. . . just as the priest was committing her child's body to the earth, she stopped her wailing. And when the priest said her son would live forever in the kingdom of God, she threw herself into that hole.

I see the woman's black dress flutter around her as she disappears into the ground. I hear the thud of her body as she lands, and then the commotion as men jump in after her, grabbing her, pulling her out forcefully, as she scratches their faces and begs to be buried with her son.

They took her home. But the next day they found her lifeless body on top of her child's grave. So they opened the earth again. They opened the coffin again. They took the child out and placed him in his mother's arms. They placed them in a larger coffin. And returned them to the earth. Together.

When I try to open my eyes this time, they snap open, my sight blurred. They sting and burn and I realize I am crying. I shove Pequeña's hand away from my heart, and when I do, I feel a kind of jolt.

She tries to put her arm around me but I won't let her.

"Don't touch me," I tell her. "Why? Why did you tell me that?"

I look at her face, angry that she's filled my ears and my mind and my heart with these images. She stares back.

"Because if you don't run toward something, Pulga, at least remember what you're running from," she says.

I shake my head, trying to forget.

But I can't. And the tears won't stop.

And my heart keeps beating, beating, beating in my chest.

When the lush landscapes disappear, I feel a spiteful kind of satisfaction. As we ride through land that is ugly and drying and without any color, I look over at Pequeña and want to say, *Yes, dreams are stupid.* But I don't. Because even as we ride into a rail yard that is nothing but dust, even as we get off again, Pequeña looks like she believes in them.

And so we board another train. One with even less people. Pequeña talks to one of those on board and leans over and whispers to me, "I think this is the one that will bring us into Altar." She waits for a reaction, studies my face as we ride into the desert, into a sand-blasted landscape and fiery orange sky. Into the inferno of the hell route.

"This is the last one," she says again. I stare at the desert, waiting to feel *something*. Excitement. Relief. Joy. But nothing comes. So I nod.

We sit through hours, hours and hours that make no sense. That drag on and race forward. That ripple like heat waves. Hours of hot wind lashing at my face, cracking my skin, making my cheeks bleed. Hours that make me imagine I'm in the middle of some kind of battle between God and the devil.

But even if I am, I will never understand why He did what He did. I know it should have been me. *I* should have been the one who fell from the train, whose blood spilled. I should have been the one God took, so Chico and Pequeña could go on. Maybe then I would understand sacrifice. Maybe then I wouldn't be so confused and angry at God.

Maybe then I could still believe in Him.

But it was Chico. It was his blood that spilled, and for what? What would he think if he knew—

That I don't want to go on.

That I don't want to run.

That I just want to stop. I want everything to stop.

And then finally, *finally,* it does.

Pequeña

The train pulls into the yard.

We are dirty, dusty. We look like insects that burrow deep in the earth for years, before finally emerging.

We look like corpses, things of the underworld, that have scratched their way to the surface of the earth.

We look exactly like the mummies this beast makes of everyone, as we stumble off the train, walk away unsteady and limping, in a desert haze and stupor.

That is what we look like.

But inside I am swelling with relief and hope. Inside I don't feel dead.

I feel *alive*.

I look back at La Bestia, that beast, that monster, the devil's shuttle. I stare at that terrible thing that took away Chico's life but delivered Pulga and me here. And something fills my chest and I want both to whisper *thank you* and hurl rocks at the unfeeling murderous thing. I'm afraid to open my mouth, afraid of the sounds that might escape me, the emotions that might erupt and flow over me like scathing lava.

But Pulga is lifeless.

"We don't have to ride it anymore," I tell him, choking back sobs.

But it's like he doesn't realize. Because Pulga, with hunched shoulders and dust-coated lashes, keeps his gaze straight ahead and refuses to look back. And not a tear, or a word, or a flicker of emotion passes over his face.

~ ~ ~

We follow others from the train into the town of Altar, where as we walk, something in the air gets heavier. First I think it is because of the dust we've breathed, that has made it into our throats and noses and lungs. But the longer we go, the more I realize it is not dust. It is a *feeling*. A sense of danger that penetrates this town with a holy name.

Altar. Where we get on our knees. And pray.

It is small and eerie. It is quiet. There aren't any people on the streets except for the occasional car that passes us by, slowing down, the faces inside taking a good look at us. I know what we must look like to them.

Every gaze that falls on us does so with suspicion. Every gaze takes in our appearance.

"There's something terrible here," I tell Pulga. He looks at me, but his eyes are dull. "Do you feel it?"

He doesn't.

I look around at the others we're walking with, those who have made this journey same as us, and I see they look lost, dazed. They look like Pulga.

But something feels wrong. Something that makes me want to run even though I don't know what I'm running from here. That makes me want to hide. Like when animals sense the coming of a storm.

"Let's find somewhere, so we're not out in the open," I tell him.

There are just a few other people from the train, all of them scattering in different directions.

Ahead, there's a stand selling backpacks, canteens, first aid kits. The guy at the stand wears a cowboy hat and looks at us suspiciously. "Do you know of a shelter nearby?" I ask him.

"Are you buying anything? Look here, you will need these shoes. You see how they're lined with carpet at the soles? So you won't leave footprints. Those you have on will fall apart once you start walking." The guy looks at us, shakes his head. "Camouflage shirts . . . hats . . . canteens. I have everything you need right here. If you have money."

"No . . ." I say. The idea of all that we need, of how unprepared we are, overwhelms me with panic.

He scowls and gives me a dirty look.

"I mean, gracias, but not now. We're just looking for a shelter."

"Ah, a shelter. For free, I guess, right?"

I nod. "Yes, señor."

The guy twists his lips. "Well, nothing is free. You think you can just get everything for free, eh?" The man goes back to counting his merchandise.

I give Pulga a look.

"Thank you, señor," I say, stepping away.

"If you need a place to stay, you have to pay."

I don't answer. The man looks at us as we hurry on. And then he is on a cell phone when I look back, his gaze still on us as he speaks.

"Hey! ¡Muchachos!" he calls out after us, but I pull Pulga away.

"Don't turn around," I tell Pulga, speeding up. He is lagging behind but then I see a small, dirty white sign advertising shelter for forty pesos a night outside a run-down building.

There aren't any other signs, or anyone to ask. A truck passes us by and the driver slows down, looks at us before driving on a bit, slower than before.

"Come on, let's check this place out." I look up and down the street, wondering who has their eyes on us and why. "Get your money out, carefully."

Pulga digs into one of his socks and puts some money into my hand. I separate forty pesos so I won't have to pull out money in front of anyone, and then we walk up the pathway to a small shack of a house with more run-down houses behind it.

When we enter the small patio in front, the smell of dog feces is immediate. A big black dog on a chain stands up instantly and growls at us. The place seems empty, except for a loud television on a desk just inside the doorway of the house.

A person stands up from a seat hidden behind the television.

"Bueno," he calls. He takes one look at us and then gets down to business. "Eighty pesos a night."

"There's a sign back there that says forty," I tell him.

"The sign is wrong. It's eighty," the guy repeats. "Each. That includes a blanket, a cot, and safety." The dog lunges in our direction and barks loudly, echoing off the walls.

Pulga stares at the dog as if hypnotized. "We only have forty . . ." I tell the guy. He looks at Pulga, up and down like he is assessing how weak he looks. How tired. How easy a target he might be.

"Really, carnal? You just happen to have *exactly* forty pinche pesos?" The guy laughs. "You must think I was born yesterday. I haven't lived here to not know better. But bueno, good luck to you."

"We just want somewhere to rest . . ." I say.

He looks at me now, closely. Studying my face even though I look down, pull down the brim of my hat. "I know you have more," he says, his voice taking on a teasing tone. "The price increases the more you waste my time. It's a hundred pesos now. And . . . I know you really *need* somewhere to stay, right? A pretty . . . boy, like you, can't be out on the streets at night."

I look up at him slowly, and when my eyes meet his, a flicker of satisfaction flashes in them. Then he nods, smiling, confirming what he thought. "Yes, trust me. *You* don't want to be out there tonight."

The fear crawling on my body intensifies, and I suddenly know this was a bad idea. That no matter what we give this guy, it won't be enough to keep us safe. I look back out across the patio, on to the street. "Okay," I say, "we'll be right back. I'm just gonna get my brother a drink first."

The guy looks at me suspiciously. "No need, man. I have water right here for you."

"I think a Gatorade might be better for him right now."

"Got that too. Best price in town."

"We'll be back," I repeat, inching away, pulling Pulga with me.

"Like I said, no need . . ."

"Really, be right back!" I yell, turning and walking across the patio as fast as possible.

But the guy is yelling at us now, following after us.

"Hurry, Pulga, please . . ." I tell him, and something in my voice, the fear in it, snaps him out of his trance and he speeds up. But so does the guy. So we start running, and then he starts running behind us, too.

"Hey, hey," he calls out. "Come on, carnal . . . don't be that way."

We run faster, and when I turn back, I see he's stopped in the distance. He watches us for a beat longer and then he is turning and heading back to the motel.

"He's gone," I tell Pulga, who looks at me now, his eyes wild with fear that has awakened him. We duck near a small restaurant, where those inside look out the window at us. I feel like some kind of stray dog. Some kind of worthless thing that will be shooed away. But from here I see a church, and relief shoots through me. I'm about to tell Pulga we'll head there, when I see the guy again, this time with the dog, looking up and down the streets.

Pulga grabs my arm just as the dog looks over at us and begins barking. The guy turns, sees us, just as we start running. My legs are weak even though I will them to run faster. But I am in slow motion, and the faster I try to run, the slower the world passes me by. My breath is coming in shorter breaths and I'm dizzy. I feel like I am splitting in two, like my soul is separating from my body, and I float up a little, and my body gets heavy and my legs don't want to work. And then I am back in my body, and I run faster, but I keep floating up, like a helium balloon.

But there is the church, right there is the church, and I point to it because I can't speak. Because speaking might cost me the breath I need to run just a little faster from that dog whose barks are so loud, so harsh, they scrape my eardrums and echo in my head. I turn and see Pulga, the guy and dog behind him as he stumbles up one, two, three stairs, and that barking, that barking as the dog pounces on Pulga and sinks his teeth into Pulga's shoulder.

And then Pulga is yelling, and screaming.

I pull at Pulga, hollering at that dog to *stop!* He pounces on Pulga's back and keeps his teeth in Pulga's shoulder even as I kick and scream at him. The guy is there now, too, grabbing the dog by the collar. But the dog won't let go.

The church door swings opens and a nun comes out yelling, a gun in her hand.

"Get that dog out of here, now!" she yells. The guy yanks on the dog's collar, yelling at him, giving him a command that compels him to release Pulga. "And stop having him attack people. *Desgraciado,*" she says to the guy, who sucks his teeth at her, but grabs his dog and drags him away.

The nun hurries to Pulga, who moans, blood seeping from his shirt.

"Come on, niño," she says. "Here, hold this," and she shoves the gun in my hand. "It's not real," she says to me as she helps me pull Pulga to his feet and into the sanctuary. He is up on his feet but groaning in pain as we walk through the church. I hold on to him as we walk toward the front. A bronze crucifix glows bright and saints look down on us as we make our way.

The nun leads us through a back room, down some stairs, and to a hidden maze of rooms underneath the church. We pass a priest sitting in an office, who looks up as we walk by.

The nun rushes us into a room stocked with first-aid supplies. She makes Pulga lie down on the table and gathers her supplies. Pulga looks like he's going to pass out.

"Don't faint on me, niño," she says as she cuts his shirt open and looks at the bite. Pulga's eyes roll back and she breaks something in her hand, wafts it under his nose, and suddenly Pulga's eyes open wide.

The priest comes in. "¿Qué pasó?" he says.

"That dog again," the nun says. "That owner sics him on these poor people so he can steal their money."

Pulga's flesh is torn red and pink and the puncture wounds where the dog's teeth sunk into Pulga's shoulder are deep. The nun places a towel under his shoulder and pours alcohol on Pulga's wounds. He cries out in pain.

"Perdón, criatura, but we have to make sure this is cleaned immediately or you'll get an infection."

That is when I notice how thin Pulga is. The outline of his ribs shows through his skin—his skin that is mottled with bruises. And it makes tears come to my eyes.

"He'll need to be sewn up a bit," the nun says, and the priest gathers the supplies she'll need for that. I stand nearby, telling Pulga he'll be okay. His eyes are shut in pain as the nun applies something on the wound before she begins stitching him up. Pulga sucks his teeth each time the needle goes into his flesh, cries out in agony. The whole area is raw and red and terrible looking.

I watch as the needle pierces Pulga's flesh, in and out and in and out again, the fresh pinpricks of red and the blue gloved hands of the nun. The act of being sewn back together.

I tell myself these are holy hands, healing Pulga, mending him. Putting him back together. And maybe that means he will be okay. Maybe he will not be as broken as he looks. Maybe all of him can come together again.

I watch as the nun finishes up. As she rolls off those blue gloves and throws them in the trash.

"I will take them to the shelter," the priest says. "After they have a little bread and juice." They leave the room and say they'll be right back.

"Are you okay?" I ask Pulga. He nods, but his eyes tell me he's not. Now that the needle has stopped, he is lying there dull and numb again in that room that smells like disinfectant.

The nun comes back, with a clean shirt for Pulga, a plate of crackers, two paper cups, and a bottle of juice. The sight of it makes me want to cry—watching her hands as she pours the juice for us and hands us the small paper cups. The way she whispers over us, her eyes shut, asking of God on our behalf.

"Despacio," she says gently as we drink, as we eat. I close my eyes and try to eat slowly as the sweetness of the apple juice fills my mouth and I swear I can see the apples it came from and I can taste the sweat of the laborer who picked it. It makes me weep and I can hear the weeping and I know it is me, I know it is me crying like that, but the sound of it, my voice, doesn't sound like my own. I wonder if—like Pulga—I've become someone else, too.

And then the nun's hands are on my shoulders and she is whispering, but I can't stop eating and drinking and crying. Even as a metallic taste fills my mouth, and even as the crackers taste of dust and crunch too loudly, too sharply, in my mind I see blood and bones.

"Creatura, creatura," she whispers, like a prayer. A prayer I get lost in for a moment, before I open my eyes and see Pulga's gaze on me. Then the priest is in the room and is telling us he will take us to the shelter he runs.

Pulga gets up from the table, his wounds bandaged, a clean shirt on.

The nun makes the sign of the cross in front of me, then in front of Pulga. And we follow the priest out, back through the maze of underground offices, back up the stairs, into the sanctuary, where Pulga stares at the altar with a few flickering candles as we pass by. I stop and light one for Chico.

I put some money in Pulga's hand so that he can do the same.

But he does not.

Pulga

The ride to the shelter is short. It's hot and bumpy. We ride with the windows open and the hot wind whipping at our faces. I bury my face in Pequeña's shoulder because each bump jangles us and each creak makes me feel like I'm back on the train.

We don't have to ride that screeching beast anymore. That's what Pequeña says. But she's wrong.

The priest who has introduced himself as Father Gonzalez is talking but I don't know what he's saying and after a while, he is quiet and we ride in silence, except for the wind, the creaks, the jostling of the keys on a key ring with each bump.

What I'm thinking of is the glow of the candle at the altar. And how I used to go with Chico to light one for his mother at the church near my house. He was always so quiet when we left but then, not too long ago—or maybe it was a hundred years ago—as we walked by some patojos kicking a soccer ball in the field next to the church where they once found a body, Chico whispered real low, *I wish I could see her again.*

He blinked like crazy, trying to hold back tears, trying to be tough like I told him to be. *Chico, you have to be tough, or el mundo te va a comer, man.*

Why was I always telling him the world was going to eat him up? I think of his chewed-up body on the side of the tracks, the way the beast tore into him.

I sealed his fate in so many ways.

My shoulder throbs; maybe this is my punishment. Maybe I shouldn't have fought. Maybe I should have let that dog tear me to shreds.

But I wanted to *live*. And I'm ashamed that even though I tell myself I have no right to live, after this trip cost Chico his life, even then, I still want to live.

That day, Chico walked wiping the tears from his face in the late afternoon sun of Barrios, when the sun isn't so bright. When the sky is so pretty it can make you sad, especially when your friend is crying for his mother. It was the saddest I'd felt in a long time, and I didn't know what the hell to say to him so I said nothing and we just kept walking.

That's the kind of friend I was.

The kind who broke him. Who pushed him. Who he would never tell he was too tired to go on, because he knew I'd just say, *Be tough*. So he kept going. And going. Until he fell off the train, just as if my hand had pushed him.

I close my eyes. The candle at the church glows in my mind.

"Is the pain real bad?" Pequeña whispers next to me. I open my eyes, feel tears on my cheeks that I don't remember crying.

"I don't know," I tell her, because even throbbing pain feels like nothing now. How can it be both? And then I remember what I'd heard about people who fall off the train and live to tell about it, the ones who are sliced by its wheels but don't feel it even as they stare at their dismembered bodies. At first, they feel nothing.

The pain comes later.

Maybe Chico didn't feel it. I hope he didn't feel it. I hope the pain of it never came.

Pequeña takes a deep breath, a worried look on her face, just as the truck slows and we roll up to the small shelter.

~ ~ ~

We get out of the car slowly, the sand-colored building blending in with dirt and landscape. Father Gonzalez urges us to follow him into the shelter, where he introduces us to a woman named Carlita. She has full cheeks and smiles a lot.

"Bienvenidos, m'ijos," she says.

She listens intently as Father Gonzalez tells her what happened and how we'll need to stay here awhile. Carlita's shirt is blue.

It's American Eagle.

American Eagle blue. If I had a box of crayons, it would carry crayons like Chico's blood-red. Rey's warehouse yellow. Hell-route orange.

"You need some food. A shower. Some rest," Carlita says as Father Gonzalez goes and says hello to other people in the shelter. "You need to feel human again."

I don't want to feel human again. I want to feel human again. I want to live. I want to die. I want Chico back. I want a million contradicting impossible things, I want to tell them. *How are any of them possible?* But I stay quiet and follow her as she shows us where the restrooms are. And where we'll rest, bunk beds lined up in rows in two back rooms—the left room for women, the right for men. She shows us to the men's quarters and points to an empty bunk. Then digs in some boxes in the corner of the room, pulling out T-shirts and jeans we can wear.

"I'll be right back," she says as she leaves, and returns moments later with a small, thin towel for each of us. "Shower now and I'll get you some food. Usually dinnertime is at five, but I will warm some food for you both now and you can come to the kitchen when you're ready." She smiles and her smile, her kindness, almost don't make sense. How can there be good when there is so much bad?

As soon as she's gone again, everything goes silent. A couple of guys at the other end of the room are playing cards and glance at us. Something in their look immediately makes me think they've been on La Bestia, too. Something in their eyes. They give a short nod in my direction, like they recognize something in me, too, but I just lie down on the top bunk and stare at the ceiling.

"You want to shower first?" Pequeña asks, standing next to me.

I shake my head. She says something else but I don't answer and then she's suddenly gone.

"El viaje es muy feo," I hear one of the guys say from the other side of the room. "But you'll be okay, paisano. You'll be okay." That's all he says, and I hear the shuffle of the cards as they go back to their game.

I close my eyes and shut out the world.

I told him we would make it.

I told him to trust me.

I told him if we didn't run, we'd die.

I open my eyes to the smell of soap and warm earth, and it's Pequeña standing next to me. "Your turn," she says.

In the shower, the water is cold. I keep the dog bite from getting wet, but I stare at the stiches and wonder if when the dog bit me, he stole whatever was left of my soul. Because I feel nothing, except for the cold.

When I'm done, I go to the kitchen, following the smell of food that I don't want but my body does. Pequeña is there, talking to Carlita. I sit across from them, where there is a plate—beans, tortillas, and eggs. I mutter a thank-you before eating.

It tastes like nothing. I look at Pequeña as she finishes the last bites. As she accepts a second helping from Carlita, her eyes closed, and I wonder if it tastes good to her. I stare at her and she looks guilty.

"We'll be okay, Pulga," she says.

"Claro que sí," Carlita says. "With the help of Diosito, you will both be okay."

But I don't say anything. I don't tell them how I was just thinking about what a lie that is and how I'm not sure if God exists, even as I look at the wall behind them and see the words *DIOS ESTÁ AQUÍ* painted big and white. Lines that look like beams of golden light surround it, and on either side, red roses.

Where? Where is He?

I put another forkful of food in my mouth and chew.

That night, I dream of La Bestia. She's angry I refused to say goodbye. She rides into my dreams, roaring just like I knew she would.

And then I am being shoved all over the place on a night ride, pain shooting through my shoulder, and I see that I've tumbled from the top and the wheels have sliced through my arm. And I am crying and screaming in the pitch-black of night but no one knows I fell. And I am left alone on the side of the tracks.

Light replaces dark in a flash and Pequeña is suddenly next to me, yelling at me to *wake up, wake up!* And I am back in the room at the shelter, Pequeña telling me I'm okay, *it's okay,* as the two guys sit up and stare at me from their bunks on the other side of the room.

"I'm fine," I tell her, pulling the thin sheet over me, turning away from her and the glaring overhead light in the room.

"Are you sure?"

When I don't answer, I feel her slip away, switch off the lights in the room again.

I stare at the darkness, trying not to fall asleep. Fighting to stay awake so I won't have bad dreams. But fighting sleep reminds me of being on the train.

Everything reminds me of La Bestia.

I wonder if I will ever truly escape it.

In the morning, my eyes snap open at the sound of clanking.

I take in the cracks and patches of brown on the water-stained ceiling, the voices of others, the bittersweet scent of coffee, the sound of running water and more clanking. My heart races, and I have to clutch at my chest to calm it down.

"Breakfast." Pequeña stands at the door, a new cap on her head, but her dirty jacket still on her back.

I'm sweating and Chico's face flashes in my mind. I hear the echo of his voice; I think I was dreaming of him.

I want to go back to the dream.

"You need to get up," Pequeña says, her voice snipping through the thin thread of my dream, my faint connection with Chico.

I sit up quickly, too quickly, and blood rushes to my head, making the whole room spin. But I get up and follow Pequeña to the kitchen anyway.

Seated at the table are the two guys from yesterday and Carlita. There's also a woman, a man, and a little boy. The woman is holding food up to the boy's mouth, feeding him.

"This is my brother, Pulga," Pequeña says, and they all nod and greet me with a chorus of *buenos días* and *mucho gusto*.

"These two are brothers also," Carlita says. She gestures to the two boys with whom we shared the room. "José and Tonio."

The two guys nod at me.

"I'm Nilsa," the woman feeding the child says. "This is my

husband, Alvaro. And this is our little one; we call him Nene," she says, smiling down at the small boy. He looks at me and gives me a little wave. I look away.

Carlita puts a plate of food in front of me—some shredded chicken and mostly potatoes stewed in a tomato sauce. I thank her quietly and her hand touches my good shoulder and I can't help but shrug it off. Everyone continues talking as my hands pick up the spoon and bring the food to my mouth. My jaw chews it and my tongue pushes it down my throat. But I don't taste it. All I can do is stare at it and remember how hungry we were on the whole trip.

I could eat a mountain of chuchitos.

I don't want it but I won't waste any of it.

"How's your arm?" Carlita asks me. Her voice reaches me from somewhere far away and when I look at her, I shrug.

"I'll change your bandage today," she says.

"And you," she says to Alvaro. I hadn't noticed at first but now, as I take him in more, I notice the bruises on his face. "Are you feeling stronger?" Carlita asks him.

He nods. "Yeah, yeah, I feel stronger." He smiles as if to try to prove it, but his wife looks worried. "You know, sometimes you have bad luck on this trip, that's all. You can't expect to come out of it unscathed. But you have to keep going."

"Así es," Carlita says, sighing and looking down at the table.

"What happened?" Pequeña asks Alvaro.

"We got mugged along the way," Nilsa answers instead. "They took our money and beat Alvaro."

"But God was with us," Alvaro says, looking at Nilsa. "They just took our money and beat me up. They didn't hurt you or Nene." She nods and lets out a sigh.

Alvaro's words—that God was with them—repeat themselves in

my ears. I think of God there next to Alvaro as he was being beaten. As Nilsa and Nene watched in horror.

I wonder where He was when Chico was dying. On the train? Watching?

"Anyway," Alvaro says. "Now we are close." His eyes brighten a bit. "We were able to scrounge up enough money from a cousin I have in the US and Nilsa's family. And now we have enough for el coyote to lead us the rest of the way. And then we're there."

"Oh, sí . . . just like that," Nilsa says, shaking her head and taking another deep breath. She and Alvaro exchange a look that makes me think this trip was more Alvaro's idea. "How many die, Alvaro? How many die in the desert?" she asks.

Alvaro stares at her intently. "How many die back home, in Honduras?"

Nilsa doesn't answer and instead goes back to feeding Nene.

"What about you two?" Alvaro asks me and Pequeña. "How are you crossing?"

I look down at my plate. With the last of my tortilla, I wipe the plate as clean as possible and shove the food in my mouth.

"Well," Pequeña says, "things went bad for us, too . . ."

Don't say it, don't speak it, don't . . .

But she begins, and I hear Chico's name, and the way the air is sucked out of the room as she tells them, and the gentle horror of their responses.

Don't.

And I see how Carlita and Nilsa wipe their faces, how Alvaro and the brothers look down at the table.

Don't.

As Pequeña's voice gets choked up and she tells them how we really only thought of how we would get this far and don't know what our next step will be. Maybe find a coyote.

Don't, don't. Don't, don't.

Don't tell anyone what our plans are, I remember telling him. Back when I thought I had it all figured out.

I press down on my heart, trying to stop it from remembering.

I guess this is where we are now, so desperate it doesn't matter. So desperate we can't be so guarded with plans that have dissolved into nothing anyway.

Alvaro takes a deep breath. "You can have the trip planned, but it never goes that way," he says softly, shaking his head. "And I know it's hard to trust anyone, but if you can gather the money, call your family and ask them, I'll ask the coyote we're crossing with if he will lead you, too. He's very good, so I've heard anyway." Alvaro shrugs, like he doesn't want to make any promises.

The two brothers at the table nod. "Us too. My friend crossed with him a few months ago and he's living in El Paso now. Working, sending home money to his mother."

Pequeña looks at Alvaro, wiping tears from her eyes, but I see it. Some kind of spark that has reignited there. "Really? You would? Do you think he'll really help us?"

"If you have money, he will."

She nods. "We'll get the money . . . sí, please, ask him."

He nods. "I'll ask him. We're supposed to leave here in three days."

"Three days," she whispers, with a strange look on her face.

I don't know where Pequeña thinks we will get money. I don't even ask her.

"Go without me," I whisper. Because I don't think I care about making it anymore. Because I don't feel like a person anymore. Maybe I'm not.

"No," she says. "I won't, Pulga, so please . . ."

I put my hand over my heart, wondering if it's still there, if it's still pumping blood.

"Okay?" Pequeña asks. I think I nod. I think she reaches for my hand.

I don't know.

I don't feel real anymore.

Maybe I'm just a ghost. A ghost who has lost his best friend, his home, faith. Everything.

PART 5

Al Borde de Tantas Cosas

At the Border of So Many Things

Pequeña

Three days.

I take out the ring from my jacket. It could have been shaken loose by the constant rumbling of La Bestia, fallen to the tracks and been lost forever. It could've fallen into a hand slipped into my pocket those times I slept like the dead because I almost was. It could've lain hidden in the pocket of my jacket in a bag filled with the clothes and belongings of other migrants if we'd been robbed and stripped along the way.

But it wasn't. We weren't.

Rey's face fills my mind once more, his hot breath in my ear whispering the only truth he ever uttered.

This ring is your destiny.

I stare at the diamond—bright, sharp, indestructible—that will carry me the rest of the way. That will give Pulga and me a chance.

I almost laugh at how it sparkles in the bit of sunlight coming into the room, like the script silver letters on Rey's car. White prisms dance on the floor as I move it to and fro, and I see myself, walking over white light, to that place of dreams.

Alvaro appears in the doorway and I clutch the ring in my hand, hiding it from view. "I spoke with el coyote," he says. He puts his hands in his pockets, shakes his head as he delivers the news. "He wants five thousand US dollars for the both of you."

"Five thousand dollars . . ." I whisper, clutching the ring tighter, until it is digging into the palm of my hand.

He takes a deep breath and nods. "Do you have gente in the States who can get a collection going?"

I shake my head.

His face fills with pity. "Lo siento," he says, and I think he does. I think he feels every bit of the impossibility of five thousand available dollars.

"But tell him yes," I say.

Alvaro looks at me strangely. "Yes? Are you sure you can pay? These are not men you can lie to . . ."

"I know, but . . . I'll have it for him," I say, careful not to let him know it is in the palm of my hand. Letting him think that maybe our family back home can come up with the money somehow. "I can get it," I assure him.

His dark eyes are doubtful, but he nods. "Bueno . . . all right, I'll let him know. But if I say yes, you better be sure you can get it."

"I'm sure," I say. I know the ring is worth at least that, or more. Maybe even double. I'm sure it is. I can feel it. Because it is my destiny. This ring was always my future.

"Gracias," I tell Alvaro, and he nods and backs away, heading to the other room, where I can hear Nilsa telling Nene a bedtime story.

That night I sleep with the ring in my sock, up near my toes, and both my shoes on.

For the next couple days, we pitch in around the shelter helping Carlita. Helping each other. The brothers clean the bathrooms and the floors. I play ball with Nene while Nilsa washes clothes. I drag Pulga to play with us, and he does for a little while, barely kicking the ball before he disappears and I find him later staring at the ceiling. Alvaro prays. Day and night, he prays at a little altar in the corner of the kitchen.

When we go inside, I can't help but look at him and wonder about praying and God and things that are holy. I wonder what Alvaro would think of a witch who's an angel, too.

When he opens his eyes and catches me staring, I look away.

He calls everyone to the room, and when we are gathered there, I know why he was praying so hard.

"The guy who runs this small coyote ring will be here tonight," he tells his family, the two brothers, Pulga, and me. "He will just be taking the seven of us on this crossing. He will collect the money when he arrives and then drive us to Nogales, where we will walk at night across the desert, to the other side."

Nilsa's eyes get big and she holds Nene tighter. "Tonight? Dios, Alvaro . . . tonight." She begins smoothing back her hair, her face full of worry.

Alvaro nods. "Tonight. So let's all make sure we have everything ready," he says, looking at all of us. "It's a new moon, so the desert will be pitch-dark, easier to go unnoticed."

We stare at each other, letting the news set in.

Tonight, when the sky is at is darkest, we'll set out. My stomach flutters with fear, with anticipation and hesitation. Pulga and I made it on La Bestia, but we lost Chico. And Pulga is hardly whole. What more will we lose?

As soon as the thought crosses my mind, I wish I hadn't thought it. I wish I hadn't tempted fate. Because despite everything we've been through already, everything we've lost up until now, there is still so much more.

So much more to bear and so much more to lose.

But also, the possibility of something new.

We slowly disperse and begin preparing. Carlita gives us cans of tuna and energy bars, empty bottles to fill with water. Alvaro prays again. And Nilsa prepares their backpacks.

Back in the room, Pulga and I pack the clothes Nilsa washed and hung to dry for us.

"Are you scared?" I ask.

He shrugs and puts his hand over his heart. For a moment, I think he's praying like Alvaro. But Pulga's eyes are open and his lips don't move and he makes no promises.

"I'm scared," I tell him, hoping he will say something more, but he nods and zips up his backpack without a word.

Pulga, as he used to be, back in Barrios, flashes in my mind. How he and Chico used to run around, joking, laughing. How they always had some stupid made-up song to share with me. How beautiful they were.

Pulga is not that boy anymore.

I look away before I remember anything else. Before the hope that has begun to burn inside me is completely extinguished.

Carlita calls us all to the dining area. And we sit for our last meal together.

And it feels like a last meal, even with Carlita talking and joking, trying to lighten the mood.

She ladles soup into bowls for each of us. Frijoles charros, she calls them. Beans and sliced-up hot dogs and onion in a rich tomato broth. Each bowl she tops with toasted pork rinds and some chopped-up onion, cilantro, jalapeño, and fresh tomatoes. On the side, a bit of yellow rice with vegetables and some sliced avocado.

It is the kind of meal that makes you want to cry as you eat it. Maybe because it is that delicious. Maybe because we know Carlita has been working on it ever since Alvaro said he'd gotten word. Maybe because we know she made it carefully, thoughtfully, with the kind of love and humanity you can forget exists when you're running for your life.

Maybe because it might be our last meal ever.

I don't make eye contact with anyone as I eat. As I imagine each spoonful filling my body with nourishment and strength and something spiritual. And then there is only an empty bowl, and a silence around us.

Carlita gets up and brings over a bowl full of canned fruit. She pours condensed milk over it, asks Nene to help her top it with whipped cream, which he does with the biggest smile I've seen since I don't remember when.

"This is all I can do for you," Carlita says, suddenly melancholy as the light in the room shifts, and late afternoon sets in. "I hope it will carry you the rest of your trip." She wipes tears from her eyes.

"We may come from different countries," Alvaro says, "but we are all brothers and sisters. And we thank you, hermana," he says to Carlita.

Just before dusk, a white van rolls up to the shelter and we know it's time. Carlita and Padre Gonzalez walk us outside.

The driver asks for his payment from each of us, and when he gets to me and Pulga, I place the ring in his hand.

I feel how everyone's eyes fall on me, how they look between me and the man's hand and his face. Pulga's eyes flicker with questions when he looks at me, but he doesn't say a word.

"What the hell is this?" he asks me. He is short and corpulent and his voice sounds strained, like it gets stuck in his fleshy neck.

"It's worth more than five thousand dollars. I swear you will—"

He shakes his head. "No, no, no, muchacho," he laughs. "You're fucking loco to be trying this shit with me." He looks over at Alvaro, his eyebrows raised like he's expecting some kind of explanation, but Alvaro shrugs helplessly as Nilsa clutches on to his arm.

"This is not the way I do business . . ." he says, but the ring catches the last of the sunrays and glints impressively, and his eyes narrow as he studies it for a moment.

"A narco back home was in love with my sister; he gave her that ring. It's worth a fortune. If you take it, you can sell it for *more* than five thousand US dollars. I could get more for it, but I don't have time."

Everyone is silent as he stares at that ring.

The guy rubs his chin, and finally drops it in his shirt pocket and nods. My body goes weak with relief. I feel Pulga's hand on my shoulder, the slightest squeeze, I think, of appreciation. It makes me want to cry.

We did this together, I want to tell him. But there is no chance. And even if there were, I don't trust myself to speak. A quick glance between us is all we share.

Somehow, it's enough.

Padre Gonzalez says a prayer over us. He blesses us, making the sign of the cross on each of our foreheads, and Carlita hugs each of us as we climb into the van.

"Vayan con Dios," she says as we pull away from the shelter. And I watch her and Padre get smaller, waving at us, as we head to Nogales, where we will cross through the desert.

It's one long ride, down a single highway, out of Altar. The van's windows are open, and the wind whips and rumbles. No one says a word except for Nene and his mother. His sweet voice, just barely audible over the sound of the wind, asks his mother questions every so often.

When will we get there?

Will Tío be waiting for us in the desert?

Will he have candy for me?

Will he teach me English?

Will I live in a big house?

Nilsa begs him to sleep and rest because soon he won't be able to.

I know how he feels. I'm too scared, too anxious, for sleep also. So instead I watch Pulga, who has tucked himself beside me, not looking out the window once. I watch how he seems to sleep soundly, but his body twitches and his breathing quickens as if he's fighting something in his dreams.

The driver slows down. "This is a checkpoint, but don't panic," he says.

When we come to a stop, my chest tightens as some men holding guns peer in at us, count the seven of us inside. The driver gives one of them money and the other guy gives the driver some kind of receipt. Each second I expect us to be ordered out by those armed men. Each second I expect to be our last. But we are allowed to continue on and I breathe a sigh of relief.

There's another checkpoint maybe twenty minutes later, up ahead where another man with a gun gathers the receipt given at the last checkpoint. Again, another count. Again, another receipt. Again, a sigh of relief.

We drive like this the whole way, through various points where the driver pays and we are counted and confirmed as the red sun dips below the horizon.

And then after what seems like a couple hours the driver is pulling off the road and comes to a stop between tufts of dry desert brush.

"Okay," he says. "Here we are." We all get out of the van and grab our backpacks. Pulga winces as he pulls his on. His dog bite. It must be painful with the weight of the bag, the rub of the strap.

"¿Estás bien?" I ask him. He nods, but repositions the bag on his good shoulder instead.

Outside the van is an impossibly thin man wearing a cowboy hat and plaid shirt. "This is Gancho; he is the one who will actually lead you through the desert. This is as far as I go, amigos," the driver says proudly. "Que les vaya bien." He waves at us lazily before getting back in the van and pulling out onto the main road.

Gancho begins his instructions. When he opens his mouth to speak I notice one of his front teeth is crooked and another is missing.

"This trip will take us three nights. Each night, from sundown to sunrise, we walk. During the day, I will take you where there is shade and you will rest so you can continue walking at night. You must follow and listen to me, or you'll die. You have to keep up, or you'll die. I will not wait for anyone. It's that simple. Understand?" he says.

Something about the way he says it strikes new fear in my heart—and the way he looks at Pulga, then at Nilsa, who is holding on to Nene's hand.

Nene looks up at his mother, his eyes wide. "Are we going to die, Mamá?" he asks.

Nilsa shakes her head. "No, Nene, of course not, hijo. Don't worry," she says without looking at him. But I hear the concern in her voice.

And as I look at Pulga, with that faraway look on his face and his body looking like it will buckle under his backpack, I worry, too.

"Bueno," Gancho says, barely glancing at us. "Vámonos. Time is money and the sooner I get back, the sooner I get the rest of my cut." He adjusts his own backpack and begins leading us into the desert as night falls.

We walk, following each other, in a kind of silence that feels intimate, in a place that feels holy. Where we can almost hear each other's thoughts and dreams and fears and prayers. Where we are a very small part of something bigger, something so big it can consume us. This vast land we must cross.

I look over at Pulga, who barely looks up from his feet. "We are so small," I whisper. But he doesn't hear me.

After a while, our soft footsteps become louder in my ears. Our hearts beat like drums and echo in that empty desert as the night turns cold.

And we walk.

We walk.

We walk.

Pulga

The cold of the desert night numbs my fingers and feet. It numbs the hot throb in my shoulder. I take deep, huffing breaths to numb everything—my lungs, my insides, my heart.

But the cold has not reached my brain yet, that place where memory still lives. So Chico breaks through. And Mamá. And my father who I never knew but I made a god.

Maybe Chico is next to him, and they are both looking down at me. I wish this felt comforting, but instead I worry about what they see, who they see, when they look down at me.

I hear Nilsa say something about all the stars in the sky. "So many estrellas, Nene. Mira todas las estrellas."

I hear how he gasps, how he tells his mother they're so beautiful. I wonder how they can talk about stars. Already, it feels like we have been walking for hours. My legs burn and my feet hurt. And I think of how Gancho looked at me as we set out.

But I keep my head down. I stare at my stupid feet taking step after step, but what I want to do is reach over and cover Nene's eyes with my hand. I want to tell him, *Don't look. There is nothing beautiful here. The world is ugly and terrible. And one day you will have a best friend, someone too good and too pure for the world, so the world will get rid of him. And then you will know.*

But I don't say that.

So I walk, even though I could lie down right here and not care.

I walk because Pequeña won't let me stop—not yet.

I walk, waiting for my body to give out.

I walk because I'm not afraid of dying anymore.

I walk, my backpack getting heavier with each step, weighted down with all the things we carry.

I walk because I am already dead.

Pequeña

We walk, each step deepening the cramps in my sides, the aches in my legs.

We walk, taking small sips to ration our water, trying not to drink more, until the temptation is so great that I take a huge gulp, feel it go down my throat and slosh into the emptiness of my stomach.

We walk, blisters forming and burning with each step.

We walk, and walk, and walk, until our tongues are wagging, our brains telling us just *one more step.*

Now one more.

And one more.

We cover miles, we cover hours, we cover night by lying, tricking, manipulating ourselves.

One more step.

Now one more.

And one more.

One more and one more and one more and one more.

Until the sky begins to lighten.

Gancho leads the way with the two brothers, José and Tonio, behind him. Then Nilsa, who has Nene on her back, using a scarf to tie him in place. He's so tired he can't even hold on to her. His arms flop on his sides and his head on her back. Alvaro follows behind them, carrying their bags. And Pulga and me behind Alvaro.

~ ~ ~

It seems impossible when I see the night begin to lighten. I look over at Pulga and say, "We did it."

He stares at me and shakes his head.

"¿Qué te pasa?" I ask.

"Nothing," he mumbles, turning away from me. I want to tell him, *We are this close. This close.* Why is he giving up the closer we get? But I can't talk to him with the others around. While Gancho leads us closer to the mountains, there is too much silence. We can hear each other's breaths. We can hear each other's steps and gasps as the sky gets brighter and we see the first bits of sun shining over the horizon. We climb over rock, and then more rock, until finally we are in a little hollow on the side of a mountain. A little hiding place for the day.

"We'll rest here until the sun begins to set again," Gancho tells us. "Then we'll continue. I advise you all to eat, drink water, and get plenty of sleep. We have another long night of walking ahead of us and you have to keep up."

I look over at Nilsa, who looks exhausted and like she might vomit. Her lips are turning pale and her eyes are half-closed. Alvaro is whispering to her, putting a protein bar up to her mouth, until she takes a bite and chews it slowly, mindlessly. Nene, who has been sleeping on his mother's back, is now wide awake and wanting to play.

"Let Mamá rest," Alvaro tells Nene, and then even though he looks exhausted, he pulls a small rubber ball from his backpack. Nene smiles as his father plays catch with him. I get lost in the back and forth of the ball, and almost fall asleep before I remember to eat first.

José and Tonio are in a corner, finishing up a can of tuna each. They position their backpacks as pillows and settle in. Gancho puts his hat over his face, crosses his legs at the ankles, and tries to sleep.

I pop open a can of tuna and take out a protein bar, then look over at Pulga, who hasn't moved since we got here. "Are you okay?"

He doesn't answer.

"What? You're not talking to me all of a sudden?" He stares out at the opening of the smallish cave, at the sun getting brighter and brighter out there. I can feel it warming up the earth, the rock, which lets off the heat and reaches us even in here. But Pulga looks out there like he's thinking of something.

"Say something, Pulga. What is it?"

"I just . . . I don't care anymore, Pequeña."

Out of the corner of my eyes, I see Gancho lift his hat, and stare in Pulga's direction for a moment before putting it back over his face and again settling into sleep.

I move closer to Pulga. "Don't say that," I whisper. "We're almost there. We're so close. How can you not care?"

He shrugs. "I'm so tired," he says.

I'm too exhausted to give him a pep talk now, my mind a little too thick to think clearly. So I just take out another can of tuna, pop it open, and hand it to him. "Here, eat this and rest," I tell him. "You'll feel better."

He takes the can and I begin to eat. The warm, fishy taste in my mouth makes me want to throw up, but I know it'll give me energy. So I keep eating it, and then the protein bar, too. I look at Pulga; he is still just staring.

"Eat," I tell him. But he puts down the can and curls up.

"Later," he tells me.

I think about taking that food, about shoving it in his mouth and forcing him to eat it. But instead, I let him rest.

And I give in to sleep too.

Pulga

Everyone sleeps except me. And Nene. He sits between his parents' exhausted bodies, their hands clasped together like a protective barrier so they will sense if he gets up, walks away.

I stare at him as he looks around the cave. As he studies José and Tonio on the far side. Gancho next to them. Then he looks at his parents, puts his face right up to his father's to see if he's really sleeping. He switches to his mother, pats her head.

Then he looks at me and waves, but I don't wave back. He waves again, but I don't wave back. He reaches behind him and retrieves a small rubber ball. He points to it, then to me. "¿Quieres jugar?" he whispers. When I don't answer he stares at me like he's trying to decide something.

Maybe he wonders if I'm dead.

He puts the ball down on the ground in front of him and rolls it to me.

I watch as the dirty pink ball, the color of a tongue, slowly rolls in my direction. I watch as it stops right in front of me. Nene looks at me expectantly, waiting for me to reach for it and roll it back. But I don't.

He smiles at me, points at the ball like maybe I haven't seen it. When I still don't move, he whispers, "Come on, it's right there." When I still do nothing, he starts to stand to retrieve it, but even in sleep his mother's arm presses down on him and prevents him from getting up.

He scowls at me. And I think, *Good, he should know there are mean people in this world.*

But then, the more I stare at him, the more I picture Chico and my father looking down at me. And tears well up in my eyes. Was that who I was? Was that who I'd always been? Or was that who I was becoming?

I don't know.

I don't remember who I was. Or who I am now. The trip has erased so much from my mind and all that's left in there is La Bestia and exhaustion and ghost voices and Chico's death.

I stare at Nene, at the way he stares at the ball. And I watch as my dirty hand reaches out, clasps it, and rolls it back.

His face transforms. And he looks so happy, my heart aches.

My heart, that thumping thing in there that feels too much, that artist's heart that is a curse; and before the ball has even reached Nene, I shift, turn my back to him, and stare at the dull gray of the cave.

"Gracias," he says. And I try to unhear his gentle voice. I try to will my ears, all of me, to stop functioning.

The gray gets darker and darker, until all the yellow of the sun has disappeared and night begins to fall.

"Let's go," Gancho tells everyone. "Hurry up, get up, we have to walk all night."

Pequeña's eyes look at me. "Two more nights, Pulga. That's it. Just two more nights."

Until what? I want to ask her. What impossible future is on the other side of two nights? But instead I just nod, strap on my backpack, and follow everyone outside the cave, kicking the can of tuna aside with whatever bit of strength I have left.

Pequeña

The temperature drops and the desert gets cold. As we walk, I can hear Nene complaining of how he's tired now, and Nilsa telling him to keep walking as she struggles to keep up with Gancho's pace. Is it just me or is he walking faster tonight than last night? Alvaro picks up Nene and carries him, sets him down, carries him again, his breath coming harder and faster.

I hear Nilsa tell Alvaro not to strain his heart, that the walking is already too much strain. And then I watch Nene climb on her back again, and Nilsa securing the scarf around him. My mind flashes with the memory of the baby that lived inside me.

I can almost feel the weight of him in my arms.

Gancho slows down only a little as she does this and then they have to hurry to catch up again. And even with all this, Nilsa, Alvaro, and Nene are ahead of us.

"You have to walk faster," I urge Pulga. We are at the back of the group. Again. "Please, Pulga," I beg as he takes slow steps, barely looking up, not noticing the gap that is growing between them and us. "They won't wait up."

"Échenle ganas," Alvaro calls back to us, trying to motivate us to walk faster. But Pulga doesn't seem to hear anyone or anything.

We walk, and I keep my sights on Nilsa and Alvaro, urging Pulga to walk faster over and over again.

My skin scrapes against the inside of my shoe, full of dirt, forming more blisters. My back aches from the water in my backpack. My head aches from straining to see the figures of Nilsa and Alvaro and Nene in the dark. They get farther ahead, and I pull Pulga along until we catch up.

Over and over again.

For ten hours, then eight, four, one more hour. Until the sky begins to lighten. Until another night feels like another miracle, and fatigue and irritation are once again replaced with hope.

Gancho looks at me and Pulga as we slide into the small man-made shelter we barely fit in, built of brush and rocks, tucked into a dip in the earth. "You're walking too slow," he says. Then he looks at Pulga. "Your hermanito there doesn't look too good," he whispers.

None of us looks too good. Alvaro's face is red and abnormally glossy, even with the dirt on it, and it looks it's going to pop. Nilsa looks half-dead. And the two boys, the strongest ones of us, look exhausted also.

"He'll be okay," I tell Gancho, as he wets a T-shirt with some water and puts it on his own head.

Pulga's eyes are only half-open, and he looks ashy and gray. Almost as gray as Chico did in his coffin. The thought startles me so fiercely that I quickly get a protein bar out of my backpack. "Here," I tell him, breaking the bar up in little pieces and feeding it to him even though he barely opens his mouth. The smell of tuna and powdery iron and metal fills the small area and makes me nauseated. But I eat a protein bar, too, and force myself to eat a can of tuna.

I scoop some tuna on my fingers and put it in Pulga's mouth. He gags, and then vomits the protein bar and the bit of water he's had. Gancho stares at us, tells me to scoop up the vomit and take it out of the small structure.

I reach for the warm vomit, scoop it up, trying not to look at it, and fling it outside. I wipe my hands on the dirt, and then on my dirt-encrusted pants, but still the smell lingers. In the air. On Pulga. And on me.

This space is too small to hold all of us. We can smell each other, and our hot breath makes it even harder to breathe as the air gets hotter and hotter with the sun rising overhead. Nene whines about the smell, but even he has no strength to do more. Flopped like a little brown rag doll between his parents.

I feed Pulga another protein bar, even as he shakes his head. I keep putting small bits in his mouth, piece after piece, until it is all gone.

"One more night," I whisper to Pulga. "Hold on. Just one more night."

The stuffiness in the shelter becomes unbearable as the day wears on. We sleep. And I don't think any of us would be surprised if one of us didn't wake. It feels like being in an oven, and with each minute that passes even just breathing takes such strength.

"Get rest," Gancho says. "Tonight is more walking."

I close my eyes and try to sleep, but every few minutes I wake to the sound of Pulga's breathing. He's taking these deep, spastic breaths that sound terrible and ominous and loud in this small space.

It sounds like death.

I fall in and out of sleep, to those sounds. When they stop, I open my eyes and make sure he's alive. When they start up again, I worry they are Pulga's last breaths. Until finally, the heat subsides, and night begins to fall.

Gancho, looks out of the shelter, "Get ready," he says, pulling on his backpack.

"Okay, Pulga. Let's go." But he won't open his eyes. I touch him and his skin feels clammy. "Don't do this," I whisper as everyone begins to slide out of the shelter. "Come on, come on." I shake him and his eyes open, and I breathe. "It's time," I tell him, grabbing his backpack. But Pulga doesn't move.

"I said, let's go," Gancho says, looking over at us. The whole group is looking over at us. Nilsa looks better, the brothers look better, even Alvaro looks less waxy and shiny.

"We're coming!" I yell back. "Pulga, let's go." I try to keep my voice steady, try to sound firm. He stares at me, and then ever so slightly, I see him shake his head.

No.

"We have to go. Now." I grab my water and pour some into his mouth. He lets it dribble out.

"Please, Pulga, don't do this . . ."

Gancho shakes his head, comes to the small opening again. Half of my body is out and the other half is grabbing on to Pulga, trying to pull him along. But I can feel the way he pulls back, actually resisting me. I stare back at him. "Why are you doing this?" I whisper, but even as he looks right into my eyes, it's like he's not there.

Pulga is gone.

Gancho leans down, looks at Pulga. "Well? What's up? ¿Te vas a venir, o qué?"

Again, Pulga shakes his head ever so slightly. No, he's not coming.

"Okay, muchacho, that's your choice," Gancho says, shrugging. He looks at me. "And yours, amigo. Because we're not waiting, and you either go with us or stay."

Alvaro leans down and tries to persuade Pulga, then Nilsa next to him. But nothing registers with Pulga, no word, no plea. He just stares.

"I just have to give him some water, that's all," I say, grabbing another bottle.

Gancho takes off his hat, wipes his forehead, and shakes his head again. "No, amigo. That's not just dehydration you see there," Gancho says. "That's him giving up."

"What are you saying?" I ask, sitting outside the shelter now, looking at Gancho, at the whole of the group. The two brothers look at me with pity but don't say anything. Nilsa holds Nene close. Alvaro looks in at Pulga, still speaking to him softly.

Gancho shakes his head. "I'm saying your brother is not gonna make it. And you have a tough choice to make."

I shake my head and the world feels like it's spinning, like my head is going to burst.

"No," I say. "We can . . . we can carry him." I look at the two brothers, at Alvaro. "Between all of us, we can do it, please . . ."

"Whoever carries him will lose time," Gancho cuts in. "And strength, and they will dehydrate quicker. Mira, lo siento, but those are the facts," he says, looking at the brothers, at Alvaro. "It's everyone for themselves out here. That's just the way it is."

"But I can't leave him out here! Please . . . I'm begging you, please, don't leave us!" I say, looking at each of them, trying to catch their gaze. But they all look down or away. My heart feels like it's in free fall. A new kind of fear and desperation grips me as I realize they are going to leave us here. "Please . . ."

Nilsa's eyes fill with tears. The brothers both look away. Alvaro wipes his eyes.

"Please, please . . . I can't leave him. Don't leave us." I'm sobbing.

The coyote looks remorseful, but still, the next words that come out of his mouth break me. "Vámonos," he tells the group. And begins walking.

"Ay, Dios . . ." Nilsa says, staring at me, trying not to cry. "Forgive me, please. Look . . . look at my son." I look at Nene through tears.

He's staring back at me with sad, tired eyes.

"I *have* to keep going," Nilsa says. "For *him*. You understand? Perdóname . . . perdóname," she says, and turns to Alvaro. "Vámonos," she says. Alvaro takes a deep breath and nods. He closes his eyes and says a prayer before making the sign of the cross on my forehead.

"Que Dios los guarde," he says.

"Please," I say as they begin walking away one by one. *"Please . . ."*

The brothers look at me. "Here," one of them says, opening his backpack and grabbing a few more protein bars and his bottle of water. "You take this . . . We'll pray for you."

He puts his hand on my shoulder. "Perdón, hermano," he says. His brother says nothing, but looks sorry as they both hurry to catch up with Gancho.

Pulga is sitting in the little structure.

I grab on to him, pull with all my strength, but he won't budge.

The group gets farther and farther away, smaller and smaller as night falls. And with each step they take, I am filled with more and more fear.

This can't be happening. This isn't how it was supposed to go. Please, please . . .

One of the brothers looks back, I think. I can hardly see them now. And then suddenly, they disappear and I can't see any of their silhouettes anymore.

"Please," I whisper to Pulga, my tears coming faster, my nose running. "We have to make it!" I yell at him. Even as I realize no, we don't.

No, we won't.

And this is it.

This is it.

This is how we're going to die.

Pulga

I hear a desperate kind of crying. Pequeña. Her voice is somewhere far away, and she keeps pleading with me.

But there is so much darkness, I don't know if my eyes are open or closed.

We have to make it, I hear her say. And suddenly I remember home. I remember my room. I can almost hear the fan. And I can see Chico, how he looked when we first met.

It was just after he beat Nestor with that one punch, and Rey came and slapped us, and Chico's mamita was still alive, and we were just beginning to learn each other's secrets.

I'd brought him to my room, and lifted my mattress and showed him all my stupid notes on how to get to the United States. All the notes I'd been keeping and hoarding and no one knew about. And I told him about my father and California. And how I was going to go there someday.

Up until then, it'd been a dream that never had voice. A dream I hadn't admitted even to myself.

That day, I said it aloud. It felt like destiny. Even though I lied to Mamá every day after by promising never to leave.

But here is what happens when you utter dreams—

They haunt you. Even if you discard them, they refuse to let you go.

They whisper in your ear as you walk through the streets, as you take in your surroundings, as your barrio splatters red with blood and black with death.

And it doesn't matter if you never say your dreams again, because they're inside you.

And they embedded themselves in your heart and grew.

And you believed.

Even if it was an impossible dream.

I'll go with you! Chico had said, that stupid smile on his face.

Because your words planted that seed in *his* heart, too.

And you thought, *We're going to make it!*

But you didn't know then, that dreams weren't enough.

And even though a part of you feels sorry for Pequeña because she still believes in it all, you don't feel enough to help her out. You don't feel enough to prolong the pain. Even as she drags you out of some hole in the earth and pulls you to your feet. Even if she throws your arm around her shoulders and makes you walk.

You don't help. You don't try.

"We're going to make it," she whispers. But we won't.

Because now I know—those dreams were never meant for us.

Pequeña

They walked toward that other range of mountains. I'll keep walking in that direction. I'll drag him the whole way if I have to. Because I can't crawl into a hole and wait for death. I can't go into my grave alive. We can't have come all this way for nothing.

I keep my gaze in the direction of the mountains. I drag Pulga's dead weight next to me, stumbling and falling.

"Stop this," I tell him through clenched teeth. "Why are you doing this? Stop it. Fucking stop!" I yell at him as his body gets heavier, as my body gets exhausted so quickly, so easily. I listen to the sounds of the desert, coyotes and rustling and the sense that we are so alone and also not alone. That something is out there.

I hear a kind of hushing wind sound then. And that sound gets louder, and suddenly I can make out *words*, like the desert if full of people whispering. For a moment, I think maybe someone is out there who can help. But when I look, there is only darkness, even as the voices get louder. Even as I hear people praying, calling on every saint, people talking to one another, people crying out for help.

Then I see them—walking in front of us, beside us, all around us. Ghosts.

"Pulga?" I look over at him, wondering if he sees them. But he's just looking at his feet.

They don't see us, they don't notice us. They walk, slow and slouching. And I watch as they fall. I hear the squawk of vultures, and when I look up, I see birds like glowing white shadows, circling the sky. I hear as they cry and plunge down to the bodies that have fallen. I watch as they peck and eat the ghostly flesh. I smell death and rotting.

And then the figures flicker back to life. Bodies get up. Begin again. They have no rest.

That's going to be us.

If we die out here, this is where we will always be.

"Please," I tell Pulga. "Please walk."

And he does. For a while he does. Until he doesn't and I have to pull him along.

Little by little we cover some ground, as the ghosts die and revive around us, as the desert reminds me over and over again of all the death out here.

We walk. And we stumble. And we fall and I get so tired.

So very tired of it all.

When I open my eyes, the sun is staring down at me like the eye of an angry god. I look and see Pulga just behind me. And I realize we dropped, we passed out sometime during the night.

I hurry to Pulga. *Please don't be dead, please, not you, too. Please be alive.*

I reach him and he looks dead.

"Wake up," I tell him. "Wake up, Pulga, please . . ." I say over and over again. I smack his face gently and his eyes flutter and I call his name louder until he opens them.

"Get up!" I tell him. "Get up." He slowly staggers to his feet and we start to walk. But the sun, it already feels like fire and is so bright. I look toward the mountains in the direction we are trying to go and they look still so impossibly far away as the sun gets hotter and hotter with every passing second.

Images of me being cooked to death, of my skin smoking and toasting like animal meat, fill my head as we walk.

With each passing second, our bodies feel like they are shriveling up, like the sun is sucking every bit of water out of us. My lips are split and dry and sharp every time I run my tongue against them.

If I were sweating, I would wipe my sweat; I would lick the wet saltiness from my hands and drink it. But we don't even sweat anymore. The sun rages, heating up our insides, our organs and muscles and blood.

I'm so thirsty. A strange image of piercing my skin and drinking my own blood runs through my head. And I know the sun is getting to my brain.

Bright white flashes in my mind and makes my head throb with more pain. Thoughts flit in and out quicker than I can catch them, and I keep walking.

I feel like I am in slow motion; sometimes I think I'm just walking in place. Every desert shrub looks the same, wild and dry and ugly. Like us.

"Chico," I hear Pulga whisper. His voice is unreal. His voice is dust.

"No," I tell him. I don't want him to see Chico, I don't want him to walk toward him. *Tell him to turn back,* I say to Chico. And I want to cry, but I can't. And I want to tell my mind to *shut up* because what it keeps telling me is *We're dying, we are actually dying out here.*

I think I hear some kind of squawk and I look up at the sky. I see black dots, or maybe they're vultures. Maybe they already have their sights set on us, ready to feast on our bodies.

No.

"We're okay," I whisper to myself. And then I see it. I see *water.*

Water.

Beautiful, shimmering water.

"Water," I say to Pulga, raising my hand to show him, even though he can't see. *Look! Look! There it is!* Water to jump into, to shock our whole body awake.

"Hey!" someone shouts from far away, from where the water sparkles in the distance. "Hey, come here!" And I look and it is *me*. It is *me*, all the way over there, on a bloodied mattress, using it as a raft in all that *water*. It is me, with the long black hair I used to have, that I used to love, that Mami used to comb into two long braids when I was little. It is me, waving her arms as she stands on the mattress, looking at me and Pulga.

None of this is real, I tell myself. *You're hallucinating*.

I feel the way my nose tingles, and the way my breathing quickens, and the warmth behind my eyes preparing for tears.

But the tears don't come.

It is only the *feel* of crying. It is the way you cry when you have no more tears. I blink over and over as I see myself, and then Pulga is on the mattress, too. And Chico.

Chico.

And we are all smiling, and jumping, and waving. I'm watching a movie of all three of us, as we once were. We are not real—*were we ever like that?*—but I don't care. I love us.

I laugh and I wave back. I see the white of Chico's teeth as he smiles, and the orange glow of his cheeks as he throws an arm around Pulga. And Pulga, laughing, clapping his hands together as if he is so proud we made it this far, and there I am, in a white dress, so clean and pretty and glowing, standing next to them and looking at them like they are two halves of my heart.

Look at how we glow, with life.

Pulga moans but I don't want to take my eyes off the three of us.

"Look," I tell him, "Look at us."

I walk faster, slipping Pulga's weight off me. I walk toward all that water.

"Pulga!" I shout. But then I look back; I see he has fallen to his knees. I stumble to him. *Come on, come on*, I tell him, *don't die*. But he doesn't hear me. *I* don't hear me. My voice is less than a whisper, it doesn't exist.

I lift his body again, pull him along beside me again.

Come on . . . please . . . come on. Please. Please.

I hold him and I beg God, please, please, please. I look over at the three of us on the mattress, at the way we've stopped laughing. At the way we are staring at me and Pulga here in the desert. But then over there, Chico begins to convulse, and blood comes out of his mouth as he falls. Pulga falls to his knees. And I stare down at my dress, watching as it goes from white to blood-red.

We're dying, my mind tells me.

We're dying.

The image fades.

"We're okay," I tell Pulga, to keep him here, in *this* world. But my words are barely a whisper. I don't even know if I say them out loud. Or if hears them.

Up ahead, I see dirt being lifted up toward the sky. And then a white truck, barreling toward us. And I don't know whether it is real or not, even as it gets closer.

Closer. Closer.

So close, so impossibly fast, until it is braking just inches in front of us, a cloud of dust surrounding us.

Then the slam of a car door. A man in green coming toward us. Border Patrol.

We're on the other side. We made it.

My body pulses with renewed energy at the realization. I start crying as I try to tell Pulga, *We did it, we made it to the other side!* but the agent shouts at us before I can say anything.

"Vengan aquí," he says in Spanish even though he looks like a gringo. He pushes us toward the truck. Pulga sways back and forth as the man pats him down. Then he pushes me against the truck, pats my shoulders, my torso, and then my breasts—where he stops. Where his hands linger and I know he knows.

"Oh . . . okay," he says, laughing as he squeezes my breasts. I jump back and he pushes me harder against the car, presses his weight against me as he says something in English that I don't understand.

The car's surface is burning hot, but my blood goes cold. Even when he's done, I can still feel his hands on me, his mouth next to my ear as he felt my breasts. He's saying more things in English I don't understand and a few words in Spanish. "No muevan. No muevan," he says, telling us not to move, to stay put as he walks around to the back of the truck. When he walks past, he stares at me. His face is red and leathery. His eyes are cold and judgmental. And he looks at me like he can do anything he wants to me—to my body.

And he can.

I hear a loud thud as Pulga falls suddenly, as his arms and head bang on the metal of the car on the way down. And then I hear the Border Patrol agent yelling something as he comes to see what happened, a water jug in his hand that he begins pouring right on Pulga.

And that's when something in me tells me to *run!*

I look toward Pulga. I have only seconds, no, less than seconds, to decide.

He's safe. He'll be taken in. He'll be okay, I tell myself.

¡Corre! ¡Corre! ¡Corre! my mind screams. *Now!*

So I do.

I run for my life.

Or toward my death. I don't know.

But in that moment, it's all I can do.

I run.

Pulga

I hear yelling, shouts and commands, but I don't know to who. I see tires, a truck. And then water splashing over my face.

The shock of it cuts through my darkness like a scream, letting in the sun overhead that bursts into sight achingly bright. I bring an arm up to my face, shielding my eyes from it, but still it flashes in my head.

Somebody is asking me something; the voice is warped and thick. My ears go mute at first and then are at full volume again as the blurry figure talks its warbled talk. Then I am drinking water and he is pulling me up to my feet even though I can hardly stand. He shoves me into the back seat of the truck, where it is cool and dark as the static of a radio breaks the silence. And even through all this, the relief of how good the air-conditioned car feels, and to finally be out of that blazing desert, is immediate.

He's blurry and his figure comes in and out of focus. And I look for Pequeña and see her nowhere. I remember her standing next to me as the guy patted me down.

And then she was gone.

She's out there. And we are driving away. And he is saying something about muerte. Muerte.

I stare out at the desert, reach for the door latch, but there's none. I put my hand up to the glass, searching for her.

My eyes fill with tears, my vision is blurred, and my heart, whatever is left of it, shudders in my chest.

Pequeña

You'll die!

There's nothing, nothing out there!

There's no one to help you!

You'll be lost!

Forever!

Stop running!

Turn back!

Turn back!

My mind flashes with warnings, with the promise of death. But my legs push me forward. When I look over my shoulder, I think I'll see his terrible face, his terrible mouth, his breath heavy in my ear. *Oh . . . what do we have here?*

But there is nothing, no one. Still, I run. I run faster—over brush and squat dry bushes, over boulders and rocks. Past rocks stacked high. My feet run, trip, stumble, pick me back up. I've spent days, weeks running. I don't think I can stop.

I don't.

I think of running until I die, until my body gives out.

But I want to live.

So I slow, because my chest is burning and wants to explode. Because my feet are on fire and my body feels like rubber. My blood and heart pump so furiously, it is all I can hear.

I scan every direction for that truck, waiting for it to come over the horizon, toward me. There is nothing but a thin white line. A glowing white line, a border, one between land and sky.

Between heaven and earth.

Panic shoots through me, through my mind as I realize what I've done. As I realize I'm going to die.

I feel the sobs in my throat. *How? After everything, how can this be the way it ends?* I search for the truck that was there, that came and took Pulga away. It was just moments ago that I left Pulga there on the ground.

How could I just leave him alone like that? I have to go back to him. I have to find that truck again. I turn in the vast emptiness, for any flicker, any movement, anything.

There is nothing.

Nothing.

My head gets full and the world tilts one way, then another. I can no longer tell where I came from, or where I was going. The world becomes blurry. The sky and ground are one. And my body won't go on.

I waste energy sobbing tearless sobs, and I crawl under a tree that smells of burning. The thorns of little hidden nopales slash at my face and neck, tiny little cuts that sting and burn as my mind keeps telling me the horrible truth.

You're going to die out here.

Pulga

Black metal gates close behind us, and we're in some kind of parking lot, near a building the color of sand. I am shivering now. My clothes cold from the car's blast of air-conditioning.

"Vamos," the agent says, opening his door, then mine.

I try to get out, but my legs won't work and I stumble and crash to the ground, my face skidding across the concrete. All I want is to stay there. But the agent grabs me and pulls me to my feet, back out to the heat.

"Camina," he tells me, the word sounding ugly in his mouth. Walk. All I've been doing is walking. He mutters more in English, some words I only sort of understand. "Don't pull that shit with me. I know you can walk." But my legs feel like paper as he pushes me along.

The building's doors open and close behind us, blasting coolness again. He pushes me down a hall to some kind of office where I sit on a chair, hard and rigid as the ground, and he asks me things I don't understand as my body begins shivering again. I don't answer him.

He looks through my backpack and gives it to another agent.

He smiles and nods. "Okay," he says, grabbing some kind of folded-up foil and walking me back down the hall to another room. When he opens the door, a colder air rushes out and I see a room full of people huddled and covered in foil blankets.

"Here you go, amigo," he says, shoving the blanket in my arms and pushing me in. "Have fun."

He closes the door and several boys who look about my age, plus a few older men, sit on concrete benches along concrete walls. They look over at me for a minute before huddling back under their aluminum sheets again.

The room is freezing, exactly like walking into a cooler. Cold air blasts from an air duct in an empty corner of the room, over a dirty-looking toilet only slightly hidden by a half wall. The room is gray and fluorescent white and silver—no warmth at all.

I wrap the crinkly blanket around me, sit down on the concrete floor where the cold penetrates my body, my wet clothes, instantly. It seeps into my bones and makes me ache with cold. But I'm too tired and weak to get up.

Everyone here looks dead—either lost in sleep or half-consciousness. I wrap the thin silver covering around myself tighter, silver like ice and steel and blades.

I can feel my blood slowing, my heart barely pumping. I can feel my body slowing down, shutting down. I can feel myself freezing.

Maybe this is what dying is like.

Maybe my body has finally decided to give up.

The thought is almost comforting. And for the first time in a while, I let myself think of Mamá and Barrios. I push away the fear, and the blood, and the shouts and the bullets, and my head fills with colors. Tones of marigold and tangerine and burnt sienna. Memories of warmth on my skin as we walked in that sun. I think of the pinkish red of Mamá's lipstick, the flush of her cheeks, and the vanilla scent of her perfume.

And then other thoughts creep in. Pequeña. Out there, alone. Burning in the desert. I wonder if she is alive.

The door opens and somebody hands us some crackers, that my hand reaches for and puts in my mouth no matter how much I tell it not to. I don't want to eat. I don't want to keep going. But my body has fought to survive too long to listen to my mind. This happens again, and then again, until I'm wondering if I'm imagining things:

The door opens and somebody else is pushed into the cold room.

How long have you been here? he whispers. I look at him. I try to speak. But nothing comes out. He just stares at me and pokes my arm.

"Hey, you okay?" he says, but then I don't hear any more as I wrap myself tighter in the foil, frozen like meat kept in a freezer. I stare at the fluorescent light. There is no day or night here. Only that light.

My blood doesn't feel like it's pumping to my brain anymore. All I can think about is the cold and how my heart has become a frozen lump with razor-sharp edges.

That's all I can feel, the sharp sting of icy needles every time I take a breath.

I really think we're gonna make it, Chico's voice rings loud and clear in my head. I look up, and there he is, draped in a silver blanket over his head, like la Virgen María. His face and lips, blue. His eyes, staring at me.

He's both terrifying and beautiful.

Don't give up now, Pulga, he says. When I blink, his ghost is gone. But I heard him. I know I did.

"How long will they keep us here?" somebody says, interrupting my thoughts. When I look, it's the guy who asked me if I was okay, his face tired, his lips chapped and split.

I look at the light bulb overhead. I think of Chico. And through shivering whispers I tell the guy the words that have been running through my head, "There is no day or night here."

I don't know how long it takes me to get the words out.

But I do, I get them out.

And I picture Chico's stupid grin.

~ ~ ~

A bright light shines in my eyes, making them pulse and throb. I can't see anything but I can hear somebody yelling to keep moving. And somebody else laughing. And the smells of air and dust and diesel fill my nose. A sudden warmth penetrates my skin.

First, I think I'm back in Guatemala City with Pequeña and Chico.

Then I remember them. I remember that I lost them.

Then I think maybe I'm in the desert again, my backpack in hand.

But when I can finally open my eyes enough against the blinding sun, I see I'm outside and there is a bus in front of me. An agent is holding a bag of apples and telling me and the other guys my age, as well as girls who seem to have come from nowhere, to grab one as we get on the bus.

It's bruised and half of it is mushy and brown and I don't want it. I'm about to toss it onto the floor of the bus, when Chico's voice reaches me.

Eat the apple, Pulga, he says.

I look for him, but only see tired faces. My stomach groans with more hunger the harder I try to resist.

I don't want to, but my teeth bite into it. I keep eating it, even as my stomach aches with each bite of apple I consume. It makes me feel sick, but I eat every part of it, even the seeds and the core. And when only the stem of it is left, I twirl it in my dirt-encrusted hands, hoping Chico sees.

The bus is hot and it feels like there is not enough oxygen for everyone. The sun burns through the window. We ride and my eyes feel heavy. If I close them, I might never open them again.

Little by little, the world falls away.

And I along with it.

~ ~ ~

We pull up to another building, also sand-colored, with rounded edges that look eroded by wind. Desert brush and big rocks and chain-link fence surround it on four sides. I can't see any other buildings at all, only dirt and faraway mountains. We are in the middle of nowhere.

We drive through a metal gate that slowly closes behind us.

One of the agents gets up and yells at us to get off the bus, and we are separated into two different lines as we file out. Girls to the left. Boys to the right.

I wonder if we're being brought here to die.

I look at the girls walking away and I suddenly remember Pequeña. And I wish I could see the girls' faces, see if she is here, if somehow I missed her.

But then I remember that Pequeña's hair is short, and she's become someone else, and I left her in the desert. And then I think of how she's probably dead and something in my chest aches and wants to rise in my throat.

So I shut off my mind and instead, I follow the boy in front of me as an agent tells us to keep moving.

We are led past the main building, to a large metal warehouse behind it.

A guard opens the door to the warehouse and we go inside.

Inside is a large room with metal cages. We are lined up against the wall and instructed to remove our shoelaces and put them in our backpacks. A guard takes our backpacks, tags them, and throws them in a pile before handing us a number.

I look down at my piece of paper. 8640.

Another guard opens the door to one of three metal cages, all three filled with more boys, and closes it behind us.

My legs feel weak and a clamminess over my whole body dampens my clothes.

Some of the boys talk to one another, but my lips won't form words even if I try.

So I sit on the ground, my back against the metal cage.

And I try to forget how I got here.

I wake up to a guard hitting my shoulder with a burrito wrapped in a napkin.

"Here, eat this." I take it from his hand and look at the pale lump of food. I can hear some boys complaining.

"Eat it and be quiet!" the guard yells.

My stomach growls and I take a bite—the tortilla is sort of warm, but the inside is cold. And the more bites I take, the colder and harder it becomes. I chew the tiny frozen bits and swallow. Another guard hands us cups of water. And then they take the trash from us and lock the cage door again.

I turn away.

I pull my knees up.

And fall back into a black so deep, so wide, I don't think I'll ever come out of it.

Pequeña

I stare into the night until everything goes dark, until all I can do is listen to my breathing. Each breath is raspy, but it calms me, listening to the inhale. The exhale. Even as I wonder which breath will be my last.

I stare at the white pinpricks of light that appear through the black night sky and feel my body going cold. I look over, searching for Pulga, but he's not there.

I remember the truck. The agent. The feel of his hands on me. Running.

And then I leave my body.

I float upward, from under that mesquite, into the cool night breeze of the desert, and higher still into the sky. I hover high above and all the pain, all the thirst, all the heartache I felt goes away. I don't even care that I must be dead. I don't even mourn that my life has ended, and somewhere down there, the vultures will eat my body.

I stare at the stars and I reach for them, and instantly, I can feel their heat, and when I reach out to touch them, electrical currents zap through my formless body. I feel like a thin delicate piece of cloth as the night breeze passes through me, as I stare at that whole desert down below. And I can see and hear *everything*.

I can see people walking down there, under cover of darkness. I can see the Border Patrol pickup trucks, cruising slowly, big white searchlights mounted on their trucks shining through the darkness. I can hear the crunch of feet walking, the soft whispers of mothers telling children to be quiet. I can hear the radio in the pickup truck. And the laughter of border agents. I can see a highway in the distance.

I can hear someone trying not to cry.

And someone crying. And someone dying.

Is it me?

And then I see her, La Bruja, with her dazzling eyes and long hair.

"Pequeña," she whispers, and she is suddenly next to me. She smiles with lips that shimmer. Her silver hair ripples like waves. Her eyes sparkle and hypnotize. She reaches for my hand and suddenly, my body is light.

I think she's come for me, finally. To take me.

I hear the voices of women, singing, laughing, over music I know cannot exist. They beckon me and I feel myself following them. I feel the coolness of La Bruja, that cold that ripples off her like a breeze.

I don't know who she is, except . . . I do.

And then I become her.

And I am all the women who are leading me through the land of the dead. I feel all of their spirits inside me. I hear their voices, from inside my head. I see their faces flickering in my mind, all their faces.

I feel their spirits entering my body. Filling me with some kind of strength, with some kind of will.

I stare at the blue-white glow coming from my body, lighting up the desert, the night. And I wait for death.

In death, the sun rises. And mountains move overnight. In death, you find yourself close to a highway that appeared out of nowhere. In death, you crawl out from a tree too large to be in the desert.

~ ~ ~

When I open my eyes, my body is quivering and flickering, like I'm on fire.

I walk and walk, the fire in my feet and body burning, but refusing to be extinguished. It is a burn that moves my legs so that I am stumbling, running to the side of the road. It is a burn that fills my lungs and unleashes a reverberating scream from my body into that desert.

My head feels like it might burst from the sound of my own scream—that noise, thunder, roar, wail—that escapes me. It is so long, so all consuming, I can't believe I could carry it. It fills the sky and as it does, I know it has been building inside me since the day of my birth.

I am not the only one to hear my scream.

A car slows, passes me.

The rear lights flash red.

The rear lights flash red.

The rear lights flash red.

The passenger's and driver's doors open.

Two women emerge and call out to me. They begin walking toward me as I feel my knees give way. I am a flower sprouting from ashes. I am *life* in the desert, and they pluck me and carry me to their car.

In the car, I lean my head on the window as they continue talking and calling on Diosito Santo. My eyes are barely open, but my sense of smell is strong.

The scent of burning lingers in the air.

The person I used to be dies.

But in my heart lingers some kind of hope about who I will still become.

Pulga

At first I think I am seeing things, but when I blink he's still there. I blink again, and still, he's there.

In the corner, looking out at the room. His eyes are glazed over, but he looks scared. I walk up to him quietly.

"Nene?" I whisper. Four-year-old Nene from the shelter before we crossed. Nene, being carried on his mother's back through the desert. Unless maybe it's not him. Maybe it's another four-year-old boy that only reminds me of him.

He stares back at me and I'm almost sure my mind is messing with me again when he says, "I know you."

I nod.

His eyes fill up with tears. "I don't know anyone here. They took me away from Mamá." His voice is high, and even though he tries not to cry, his tears spill and he puts his head down and begins to sob.

"Hey!" someone calls out to me. "Stop making that kid cry."

I look over at a uniformed man in the room. But already, he's distracted and occupied with another child who has started screaming and kicking his feet on the floor. Stomping and raging. Getting up and throwing himself back onto the ground.

The guard grabs the little kid, who only screams louder. The man picks up the boy harshly, by the arm, dragging him out the doors, where his screams get louder and sharper even as he's being taken away.

Nene swallows back his sobs, even as more tears stream down his face.

"I want my mamá," he whispers to me. His breath is sour, and his face is filthy. He's still wearing the clothes I saw him in last, now dirtier. Little bits of crud get stuck in his eyelashes from his hands as he wipes away tears that won't stop coming. "Do you know where she is?"

I shake my head.

I sit down next to him and I listen to him cry for his mamá, for his papá. And I want to walk away from him, but I can't. "I was with Mamá, together, in a cage," he tells me. "And then they asked me if I wanted some cookies to eat and I said yes, and they took me away and never gave me anything to eat and never brought me back to her." His tears come faster, his words harder to get out. "They brought me here instead. It's my fault."

I know I should walk away, but I can't. "No," I tell him. "They tricked you to get you away from your mamá and papá."

He shakes his head. "Papá . . . fell asleep in the desert. He had to stay there . . ." he tells me, his voice breaking. "Mamá said he was just resting, that he will meet us in the United States, but . . . I don't think she was telling me the truth." He puts his head down and cries harder; his small body shakes with sobs that he tries to swallow down again. And I watch him, wishing that I could reach into his small chest and detach his heart from the rest of him so he won't feel anything anymore.

We are so small, Pulga.

Pequeña's voice from a lifetime ago reaches me now. And I remember her. And her baby. And Chico. And how she was right. We are so small.

We are specks that don't matter to this world. Our lives, our dreams, our families don't matter to this world. Our hearts, our souls, our bodies don't matter to this world. All it wants to do is crush us.

It crushed Chico.

It crushed Pequeña.

It's crushing Nene.

And it will crush me, too.

I pull my legs up and wrap my arms around them. I inch closer to Nene and he inches closer to me. And we sit like that, small, together.

Hoping maybe the guards will forget us.

Hoping maybe we can become small enough to disappear, but not so small we are forgotten.

"Just try not to think about it," I whisper to him. "Try to erase it all from your memory."

He nods, closes his eyes. His face looks pained, like he is trying to wipe away every image. But when more tears escape, I know he can't.

That night, I dream of Chico.

I am reaching for him, and this time, I grab hold of his arm. I pull it so tight, just before he falls. But it detaches from his body, like a prosthetic limb, and it becomes light in my hand as the rest of him, the weight of him, falls to the ground. And I hear him screaming as he is chewed up by the train, as I hold that disembodied arm in my hands.

His screams wake me. But they are my screams. And the night fills with the sound of little kids crying. They call out for their parents, for their hermana or hermano, for their tías and abuelas.

They cry out because their stomachs hurt.

Nene calls out for his mamá, his papá.

I squeeze his hand, tell him it will be okay. My chest cramps up at the sound of him whimpering like that.

When he falls back to sleep, I pound on my chest, hard. Harder. Hoping I can finish breaking whatever is left inside.

Pequeña

I see Pulga's face. And Chico's. I see the faces of people on La Bestia who I thought I'd never see again, but here they are, in my dreams. In my nightmares. Floating in the dark when I open my eyes. The face of a woman I don't know comes in and out of focus often.

I have to remind myself it is Marta, the woman who saved my life.

I am clean, but I only have memories of water. I am dressed, but I don't know how. I am not hungry, but I don't remember eating.

"Estás bien?" Marta asks. She sets a cup of coffee in front of me and I nod. Marta seems like a nervous woman. I can't believe she picked me up.

"How long have I been here?" I ask her.

She stares at me. "Just one night, m'ija. I picked you up yesterday morning."

"Why did you . . ."

She raises her eyebrows, tilts her head. "Pues, because . . ." she says, shaking her head, "how could I not?" She stares at me like how could I doubt it was her only option.

"A lot of people wouldn't," I tell her.

She nods. "I know. But . . ." She shakes her head again. "The truth is, I have selfish reasons, I guess." She flutters around her kitchen, big and full of light, grabbing cookies and setting them down in front of me. Then warming tortillas on the comal. Scrambling eggs in a pan.

"I have a sister, she lives in Mexico. Her daughter, my niece, died trying to get to the States. This was years ago. It nearly destroyed my sister. She was her only daughter."

Marta gets lost in the memories for a moment. "I thought my sister was going to die of grief. But then she calls me. Tells me she's in Mexico, working at a shelter near the train tracks. I tell her she's crazy. She tells me she wants to care for people, the way she wishes someone would've cared for her daughter. She's alone out there, but well . . . I think it's her destiny."

An image of Soledad immediately fills my head.

"Soledad . . ." I whisper.

Marta stops what she's doing, stares at me. "What did you say?"

"Soledad."

"That's her name!" Marta's eyes go wide. "How did you know?"

"We stayed at that shelter for a week. She shaved my head." We look at each other, and even after that trip, seeing and hearing and bearing witness to the things I've seen, I'm amazed.

Marta shakes her head, starts laughing. "Dios mío, yes, she shaves everyone's head. It's impossible, but . . ." She stares at me, her eyes shining.

It *is* impossible—to travel so many miles, on the border of dreams and reality, of life and death, and come across the kindness, and love, and humanity of two sisters. It's impossible.

And yet.

Marta puts the plate of food down in front of me, asks me questions about Soledad, and we laugh over the impossibility, the triumph of odds.

I laugh.

Impossible.

And yet.

I laugh.

~ ~ ~

Marta and I talk into the evening. She makes me atole to eat, and some tea to drink, and then another tea that she soaks rags in and puts on my chapped and scratched skin. The tea will help me heal, she says.

We sit on the couch, and she keeps me company, as if she knows I'm afraid of going to sleep, of facing the darkness that sleep and night bring.

"So, por qué te viniste?" she asks me.

"The same reason everyone comes," I tell her.

"Did you make the trip by yourself?"

I shake my head. And I stare out her window, at the thick dark. I think of Pulga and Chico. And all the people still out there, *now*, tonight. My eyes fill with tears, spill over before I can stop them.

"I came with two others." I tell her about Chico. And Pulga. I tell her I know where Chico is, where he will be forever. But I don't know what happened to Pulga after the Border Patrol picked him up.

"If he has family here, you have to get in touch with them! So they can try to get him out of there. The centers . . ." She shakes her head. "Están muy malas, m'ija."

"I would have to call home to find out. I would have to speak to my mother and I haven't . . . spoken to her since we left."

Marta's eyes go wide. She gets up quickly, suddenly filled with urgency, searching for her cell phone. "Dios, m'ija. Your gente don't know you're alive? Call them. Call them now."

She hands me her phone, and I stare at it, paralyzed.

I'm not ready to hear Mami. I'm not ready to know if she will or won't answer the phone. If she's okay, or if Rey took his rage out on her. Things I didn't let myself think about when I ran, but now, now they are the things that fill my head.

Marta asks me for the number, her fingers tapping each digit as I utter them slowly, one by one, putting it on speaker so we both hear the first long, beeping ring. Then another. And another.

My chest fills with a strange heavy pain, and Marta looks at me with worry as I try to catch my breath. Each beeping ring places another brick on my lungs.

"¿Bueno?"

My hand shakes as I reach for the phone.

"¿Bueno?"

There is a long silence before my voice works, before I'm able to say anything. She sounds so far away. Like a dream, like a sketch, or a memory.

"Mami?"

"Pequeña?" Now her voice is frantic. It is the sound of someone clambering up wooden walls, splinters piercing the skin under bleeding fingernails. It is the sound of someone escaping danger below, to a bright light above. It is the sound of excruciating pain and relief. It is the sound of grief and happiness.

"Hija . . . hija . . . hija . . ." Mami cries.

"Estoy bien, Mami," I tell her, through sobs. Through emotions that feel sharper than La Bestia's steel wheels, that slice through my body and heart and voice box so all that comes out are broken words and tears.

Marta speaks into the phone, explaining to Mami who she is and where I am and how I got here.

Mami asks if Pulga and Chico are with me and I look at Marta, afraid of that phone, afraid of making things more real. Afraid of Mami's voice.

I bury my face in my hands as Marta speaks the words I can't. When I hear Mami cry for Chico, I put my hands over my ears and shut my eyes tight.

I keep my eyes on the ground, on the flowers on Marta's rug. And I hear Soledad's voice telling me I'm a flower.

Marta gently pulls my hands away from my ears and tells me Mami wants to speak to me again.

"Pequeña? Hija? Háblame, hija," Mami says, over and over, begging me to speak. She sounds as if she thinks I might have died in the time she spoke to Marta.

"I'm here," I tell her.

"I'm going to call your tía, hija. To let her know Pulga is alive. I'm going to call you right back, hija, okay? I have Marta's number. I . . . Don't worry, hija."

"Okay, Mami."

"I'll call you *right* back. In a few moments. Te quiero, hija. Te quiero tanto."

"Yo te quiero también, Mami," I tell her.

And then there is silence. Only Marta and me and this couch and Mami's phantom voice in my ear and words that linger in the air.

"It will be okay," Marta tells me. "We'll find your cousin and get him out and he'll be okay, you'll see."

I nod, even though I don't know if it's true.

"And you can stay here as long as you need to," she says, resting her hand on mine. She looks in my eyes, and I don't know what she sees there, but she suddenly says to me, "I'll help you. I know you have seen so much bad. But there is good in the world, Pequeña."

"Flor," I whisper. Her brow furrows in confusion. "My name is Flor," I tell her. "Not Pequeña. I don't want to be called Pequeña ever again."

She nods. "Flor."

And I feel a small bit of relief in my chest, like a long-held breath finally being released. And I see inside my chest, dark and empty, but I see a glow come from a small space within that grows brighter and brighter. It's a flower bud and I watch as it opens up, as luminous petals unfurl. More and more petals, growing larger, taking up more space, filling my whole chest.

With life.

With hope.

Pulga

I keep count of the days by the meals they give us. Oats and tepid water for breakfast. Soups from packets for lunch. Sandwiches with a slice of cheese for dinner. Sometimes a piece of old fruit. But then I lose track of the meals that repeat every day until I don't know how long I've been here.

Some of the boys try to steal food from others. I give Nene some of my food.

"Do you know how long you've been here?" I ask him one day. I know he's been here longer than I have, but he shakes his head as his scalp begins to crawl with a familiar itch.

We stay in our filthy clothes, we sleep on filthy floors, we breathe rotting air.

But we are the ones rotting. We are like forgotten overripe fruit, left to soften and mold and leak. Left to crust over and turn to nothing. If they could, I think they would just throw us out in plastic bags.

At night, the sound of the whimpering and crying, the clanking of doors, the screaming from nightmares, fills the air. But my ears are muted, like I've turned the volume down low. And all I really hear, all I concentrate on, is the *thud, thud, thud* of my fist hitting my chest. Beating my own heart to death. *Stop,* I tell it, *stop already.*

I will my brain not to think, and finally it no longer does. I don't think. There's something like a switch that has been hit inside me, and I move and do whatever I'm told.

"Come here," a guard tells me one day. And I do. He leads me past the room where days ago they asked me questions I barely remember answering. And he delivers me to a back room where days ago a woman with a kind face said she was my lawyer and explained that she found me because of Pequeña. Pequeña, who somehow survived—who contacted Mamá, who contacted my tía in the States, who contacted her.

"Here," the guard says, handing me some soap. Handing me a set of clean clothes. "Clean yourself up; they're letting you out today."

I look at him, but his face is serious as he points to a door that leads to a room with two shower stalls.

I take the soap and clean clothes and do what I'm told.

The water hits my bare skin, and I can't remember the last time I've seen my body. My feet don't look like my own. My legs are so skinny and bruised I can't believe they're mine. A part of me wonders whether I'm still made of flesh and bone, or whether parts of my body would detach if I pulled hard enough

When I look down at my chest, I see the deep black, blue, purple skin over my heart, across my chest. I press on it, soft and tender to the touch, and I know it must be the rot of my heart spreading beneath, coming through my flesh.

I close my eyes, block it all out.

I lather slowly, the soap turning brown in my hands as I wash off so much dirt. That small bar smells so good, I want to eat it. I press my tongue to it and it tastes like lotion and roses and beautiful things I forgot existed.

I rub it over my head. I fill my ears with bubbles and rub them up and down my arms, across my chest, over my whole body, over and over and over.

And still I feel like I will never be clean again. Like there is not enough soap to wash away all of this pain, this rot. I think of how things, once rotted, can never be fixed.

"Hurry up" comes a call from the other side of the door, and I do what I'm told. I hurry. I rinse and dry and get dressed.

The clothes are too big on me, but at least they don't smell. I exit the bathroom, my filthy clothes in my hand, and feel strange, too exposed without the layers of dust and dirt. As we walk through the maze of halls, the guard points to a trash bin and tells me I can throw my clothes out if I want. I hold on to them tighter.

He takes me to another room, where someone yells, "¡Número!" and points to a backpack. I shake my head, not knowing where the paper went, trying to explain. He gives me a dirty look, but hands me a paper to write down the number.

8640.

He looks at it and then disappears to another room. When he comes back, my backpack is in his gloved hand. It looks like an old relic. An unearthed artifact, taken from another life.

"Here you go," the man says, pushing it all toward me. "Your whole life, right?" A semi-amused look passes across his face. "What a life."

I stare at my backpack. If I unzip it, will Rey emerge, gun raised in my direction?

Will Mamá? Maybe my father. Maybe Chico and Pequeña.

Maybe the sun in Guatemala and the hammock on our patio.

Maybe Don Feli, hands to his neck, as he lay dying.

Every good thing. And every bad.

I nod and grab my backpack—my whole life.

Yes.

~ ~ ~

The guard leads me to another part of this building, to a place I've never been before. And here, in a room, the lawyer waits. And another woman.

"Hello, Pulga," the lawyer says.

The other woman looks nervous. But maybe, also, familiar. She stares at me, her eyes filling with tears.

"Do you remember?" she says.

It takes me a moment to place the face of so many years ago. To look at it in real life instead of in a photo album.

But it's her, my father's sister. My tía. Tears stream down her face, but my mind and heart are numb. Even as I notice the features of her face that resemble those of my father I've only seen in pictures.

I nod and she rushes over to me, hugs me tightly. But still I don't feel anything except the pain of her pressed against the rot on my chest. A part of me worries it will spread on to her and I pull away.

"You're going to stay with me while we wait for the courts to hear your case. You don't have to be here anymore, okay?"

I nod as she thanks the lawyer over and over again, who nods and promises me she will do all she can, but their words sound empty in my head.

We walk out, and I suddenly remember Nene. I think of him waiting for me to come back from the shower. Waiting for me tonight. Waiting for me tomorrow. Going hungry because I won't be there to give him any of my food.

My heart gives a weak quiver, and then we walk outside, where my eyes throb from the brightness. When we get in the car, my father's sister asks me if I'm okay and I nod. "Yes, thank you." My voice is not my voice. It is robotic and cold and doesn't care.

I stare out the car window at that building that crushes those it contains, that grinds what little humanity is left in any of us into nothing.

Then she is on the phone, in that parking lot where I can still see the fence and chains around where I was for I don't know how many days. And I hear her say my mother's name and my heart quivers slightly again. And I hear her say, *Yes, I'm with him. I am looking at him, Consuelo. He is right here! He's okay. I promise you. He's right here. He's alive.*

She holds the phone to my ear, because I can't reach for it. And for the first time in forever, I hear Mamá's voice.

"Pulga, Pulga, hijo . . . It's okay. I understand. I'm not mad. Te quiero . . . Do you hear me? Te quiero. Dios mío, you're okay! And Pequeña, too! Ay, gracias a Dios." She is sobbing. And her voice is so far away. Like she's outside the universe, even. I feel so far away from her. More than ever.

"Say something, hijo. Por favor, hijito . . ."

I clutch the phone, not knowing what to say. Not knowing what I'm supposed to do.

I sit there, listening to her voice, listening to her cry, listening to her say my name over and over again. Like she's trying to remind me who I am. But I don't know what to say, what to feel. I look at my father's sister, whose eyes are wide, scared. And I have to turn away.

I turn back to the window and my father's sister takes the phone. I hear her assure Mamá I am here. That I'm just in some kind of shock. That we will call back soon.

She puts the phone to my ear once more and my mother tells me she loves me, over and over again, before my father's sister takes it away.

I try to remember feeling loved. Feeling real.

The car is on, the vents are blowing cold air. We are backing out of the parking space. And then we are driving away.

That's when it hits me. Everything—all those days of desperation and holding tight, of fighting and never stopping, all the nights of crying and fearing and starving and not caring, all the sacrificing and dying. It really happened. All of it. To me. To us. To all of those in cages.

It happened.

And it's finally over. I can finally leave it behind.

That's when I feel it—my heart.

It explodes.

That thing I've been beating to death, that I don't know if I've been trying to kill or revive, shatters. It breaks into a million pieces, the noise so loud, I hear a great crashing in my ears, like glass, so much glass breaking. And I cannot breathe.

But then I fill my lungs. And I hear it—my heart. I feel it, thumping furiously in my chest—a raw, bleeding, living thing that pumped so hard, it shattered and broke free of whatever it had cocooned itself in, steel or metal or glass or scar tissue.

From my chest comes a shriek louder than La Bestia, so long, so loud, it scares my tía and she pulls the car over and reaches for me and holds me and tells me it will be okay. *I* will be okay.

"I promise you, Pulga. Vas a estar bien, I promise."

That scream travels from my heart and out of the car and, I hope, back to Nene. I hope his heart hears mine. I hope all of them trapped in there hear me, and that they will all scream a scream that will break their hearts free, too. A scream that will wake our ancestors and send their spirits running through that desert to save us. A scream that will reach our parents, across borders and past locks and gates and through cages. A scream loud enough to shatter the walls of that detention center and break everyone free.

One never-ending scream.

My heart thunders in my chest; it shakes and trembles and gasps for air.

It reminds me I am alive.

It reminds me who I am.

It reminds me I want to live.

And that maybe, I *will* make it.

Author's Note

I began writing this book in 2015, as news spread of children fleeing their countries and arriving unaccompanied to the United States, many of them making the journey aboard La Bestia—a train so dangerous it is known as the beast, as the death train.

As a mother, and a daughter of immigrants, I could not stop thinking of the children on that train. Of how luck, circumstance, the dirt on which I gave birth were the only difference between them and my children. I could not stop thinking of the danger that had made a journey like this their only option. I could not stop thinking of their fear, or desperation, or the parents who were left behind, sometimes not knowing their children had left. Of the lives and families fractured, before, during, and after the journey.

That is when I saw Pulga, riding on that train. And Pequeña. And Chico. And I started to put their stories to paper.

But this book is an imagining of an unimaginable journey, one that could never portray the brutal reality of it. I strived for accuracy, but this is a trip impossible to truly know, unless one has taken it personally. Until it is over. Each migrant's story is vastly different. And each migrant's story is also the same.

The truth is, a trip like this breaks people, even as it delivers them to a new life. It is a journey of incredible trauma—one taken with few things other than faith and hope.

Which makes it even more tragic that migrant children who do make it, who do survive such a treacherous journey, are met with cruelty by the United States government. In response to their pleas for mercy or help, they are held in United States detention camps where they are treated inhumanely and abused, and many even die. That they are likely treated this way because they are poor and brown and desperate, because their parents are poor, brown, and desperate, and our government sees little to no value in their lives is horrifying.

This is the hardest book I have ever written. It is a story I was afraid to write and sometimes that fear was paralyzing. I doubted myself, and asked myself, *Why did you think you could do this? Why are you doing this?*

And I saw Pulga and Pequeña and Chico standing on that train, yelling at me over its roar. I saw them waving their arms at me. *For us,* they told me. *Write it for us.*

So I did. I wrote it for them because they asked me and I could not fail them. And this is *their* story. But I also wrote it for children like Pulga, Pequeña, and Chico. Whose faces flash for a few seconds on the television, or flicker through a social media timeline. Who have similar stories, stories they may not live to tell or may not want to relive or that the world might turn their backs on.

I've tried my best to give their stories a place in this book.

Their stories will not be forgotten.

Research and Select Sources

Open Veins of Latin America by Eduardo Galeano

The Land of Open Graves by Jason De León

Tell Me How It Ends by Valeria Luiselli

The Beast by Óscar Martínez

A History of Violence by Óscar Martínez

For more information about migrants and to support migrants' rights, please visit:

The Refugee and Immigrant Center for Education and Legal Services (RAICES): raicestexas.org

Young Center for Immigrant Children's Rights: theyoungcenter.org

Kids in Need of Defense (KIND): supportkind.org

International Rescue Committee (IRC): rescue.org

Asylum Seeker Advocacy Project (ASAP): asylumadvocacy.org

Immigrant Families Together: immigrantfamiliestogether.com

Acknowledgments

Mil gracias to those who have been with me on this journey, especially:

Kerry Sparks for your continued support and belief. For knowing how important it was for me to tell this story and for helping make it happen. Liza Kaplan Montanino for your steadfast belief in my writing and in me. For your patience and understanding as I searched and found and put all the pieces of the heart of this book together.

All the journalists who refuse to let truth die in the dark. Who risk their lives in seeking and reporting what the world must know. Without your work, this book would not have been possible. And all the activists and organizations who do the work—who fight for and support migrants, who sound the alarm. You are an inspiration.

Toda mi familia. Para mí, son todo. Y sin ellos nada es posible. Mami, Papi, ustedes saben el dolor de dejar sus tierras, sus familias, y el miedo de empezar de nuevo—sin dinero, sin saber el idioma, solitos. Sus sacrificios son mi motivo siempre. Ava, Mateo, Francesca, my bright, beautiful beings who remind me the world is not all dark. You pushed me on and gave big hugs and said, *You can do it, Mom.* I'm so lucky. I love you guys so much. And, Nando, I am forever grateful for you. For your love, your patience, your support always. Te amo.

Y todos los migrantes e inmigrantes, los que han llegado, los que están de viaje, los que vienen mañana, y los que nunca lograron llegar. Que Dios los guarde siempre, y los ponga en las alas de los angelitos y los traiga con bien.

Discussion Questions

1. Growing up in Puerto Barrios, the three main characters in this book encountered violence throughout their childhood. How does the experience of seeing extreme violence early in life change you? If you don't know because you have never had this experience, research the term "ACE" (Adverse Childhood Experience) and how it may psychologically and physically change the body. How can we prevent such experiences? In the case of Chico, Pulga, and Pequeña, can they be prevented?

2. While all three main characters struggled with harsh conditions growing up in Puerto Barrios, as a girl, Pequeña has faced a particular set of challenges, and those challenges continue for her on the journey north as well. What has she had to deal with that the boys have not, and how does that affect her?

3. In what way does Pulga serve as a protector for Chico? How does this role force him to mature or grow up sooner than a child should have to?

4. Toward the end of Part One, Pulga says, "I guess sometimes lying to those we love is the only way to keep them from falling apart." What do you think he means by that? Are there any experiences in your own life that you might connect to that sentiment?

5. What dreams does Pulga have about life in the US? How do those dreams evolve over time?

6. Pequeña's character has many instances where she connects with her spirituality, and often, these moments involve a supernatural element. Why do you think that the author chose to depict her spirituality in that way? What message do you take from that part of Pequeña's narrative?

7. Chico doesn't feature as a narrator in this story, but his presence is very much felt throughout the book. What is it about Chico's personality that allows for that to be the case? How do his relationships with Pulga and Pequeña help both of them on their journey?

8. The main characters are Guatemalan and they have a complicated relationship with surrounding countries. At one point in the story, Pulga notes: "We are to Mexico what Mexico is to the States." What do you think he means by this statement? What is your understanding of the relationship between Mexico and the US? Why don't some people want Mexicans to enter the US?

9. At times, La Bestia is personified. Why do you think the author made that choice? How does the train represent both safety and danger for the teens? What is their psychological relationship to it?

10. What is Pulga's relationship with his father? How does music connect them, and how do his memories of his father connect to his desire to risk everything to travel to the US?

11. How do the people riding La Bestia care for and support one another? What does Pulga notice about the things all the

travelers have in common and what sets him and his friends apart? What do you notice about the relationship between compassion and competition for survival happening within Pulga's character?

12. How does the reality of the characters' journey compare to their expectations for it ahead of time? What do you think accounts for those differences?

This discussion guide is based on questions created by Julia E. Torres, a veteran language arts teacher librarian in Denver, Colorado.